# MADE IN BRITAIN

## A Very British Horror Affair!

## Compiled by Kevin J. Kennedy

A HellBound Books Publishing LLC Book
Houston TX

**2nd EDITION 2023**
**A HellBound Books LLC**
**Publication**

### *Foreword*

Well, a very warm *how do you do*, dear reader!

We would like to wish you a very proper and incredibly British welcome to our exceptionally special selection of horror tales from the Sceptered Isle.

When we approached our good friend and much-admired author, Kevin J. Kennedy to compile this volume, he agreed on one proviso – that the cover reflect that most quintessential of all things British, the *Carry On* films!

Naturally, being from the great tea-drinking nation myself, and having been brought up chuckling along to the ribald antics of the *Carry On* gang – *Carry On Screaming* was always a firm favorite in our household ("Frying tonight!") – how could I possibly say no? We do hope you love our cover art as much as we do, created by the ever-patient Kevin Enhart, as a loving homage to those gloriously un-PC films of yesteryear.

Of course, if you are reading this in the UK, you will not be alarmed to see the likes of colour, aluminium, and caramel (I'm merrily ignoring the little red squiggly lines Word is *insisting* beneath those words!) nestling amongst the boots, bonnets, pavements, and lorries. For our international friends – brace yourselves, for the British are coming!

There is really something quite extraordinary about this fine collection of tales of terror, each and every one crafted in the dead of the night by twisted, fevered minds, who have brought crawling and slithering to life the darkest denizens of the blackest shadows to terrify those of you who are brave enough to read on.

For your delectation, dear reader, we have pulled together between these illustrious covers an array of the finest British authors writing today, including my own personal hero, one Guy N. Smith – who is genuinely one of the main reasons I write horror today; it is an honor for me to be included in the same title!

So, do read on – we dare you – and enjoy all of the dark stories we have on offer. We would recommend that you read *Made in Britain* with all of the lights on, and stay within safe shouting distance of help. But, like any other fervent horror aficionado, you wouldn't listen.

Would you?


TTFN


James H Longmore
HellBound Books Publishing, December 2018



Addendum, July 2023


Well, so much water has flowed beneath the British bridge since this wonderful tome hit bookshelves on both sides of the Atlantic!

Firstly, not long at all after *Made in Britain* was published, my literary hero, Guy N Smith passed away – a sad day indeed for horror fans the world over.

Secondly, HellBound Books grew from a fledgling indie publisher amongst many to a mature, soon-to-be-8-year-old publisher publishing some of the greats and rubbing shoulders with the big boys.

From my new home in the USA, I've watched (amongst so many changes) as Brexit kind of happened (then didn't, then did again), Prime Ministers came and went (can't help but wonder how Liz Truss feels about being remembered in history as the shortest-serving premier in UK history – at least she'll get a mention in Trivial Pursuit, I guess), Jeremy Clarkson was sacked from the BBC, and our dear Queen Elizabeth left us.

And yet, as the man said, the show must go on…

So, HellBound Books proudly presents our second edition of this phenomenal anthology – all polished up, sporting a new take on its iconic cover, and two brand-new tales of terror (one from yours truly, the other from Trevor Kennedy)

We hope you enjoy…


James H. Longmore

MADE IN BRITAIN

# Contents

# Britain's Best Clown
## Ross Baxter

Samantha Kirk looked up from her table in annoyance at the overly-loud knocking. The thin aluminium door of the caravan amplified the noise, completely swamping the small living space inside. As she stood up, the door burst open and Klunn stepped inside still dressed in his clown outfit despite the show having ended two hours previously.

"Oh, please come in!" said Sam sarcastically.

"I am in," Klunn muttered, ignoring the circus-owner's sarcasm. "What do you want?"

Sam sat back down, motioning for Klunn to take a seat opposite her at the small table. She closed the lid of her laptop and straightened the papers on the scratched table top, not looking forward to the conversation.

"I've been going through the finances again, and things are getting worse," she sighed. "Chello Circus is still making a big loss, and that means, unfortunately, that I can't afford to renew your contract at the end of the season."

"I've been waiting for this!" Klunn hissed, his face burned red under the layers of white makeup. "This isn't about finances; it's about us. You've been wanting to kick me out of the circus ever since we split up!"

"No. We split up over a year ago, and I've moved on," Sam replied calmly, trying hard not to rise to the bait.

"Yeah," scoffed Klunn, "you've moved on by trawling the dating sites in every town we stop in!"

Sam sighed, already tired. "This is just about business. Chello Circus is haemorrhaging cash, and if I don't do something quick this season will be the last season. People just don't take to clowns anymore; your act no longer brings them in. In fact, clowns probably scare many away; I'm doing you a favour by keeping you on 'til the end of the season."

"And who else are you letting go?" demanded Klunn.

"Petra is leaving at the end of next week; she's just too expensive for us," Sam replied, brushing a strand of auburn hair back from her face.

"So, getting rid of performers is your way of saving the circus?"

"Performing animals and clowns aren't what people want now. The demand is for Cirque du Soleil or Circus of Horrors-type of acts, and to survive that's what Chello Circus needs. There's a double-jointed woman and a guy with over a thousand piercings who I'm interviewing on Friday when we move on to Bristol."

Klunn banged his tattooed hand on the flimsy table. "I'll get the crowds flocking in. By the end of the season you'll be begging me to stay!"

"And how are you going to accomplice that?"

"Have you heard of The Great Karpescu?" said

Klunn, leaning forward and regarding her closely with bloodshot eyes.

Sam shook her head.

"The Great Karpescu was one of the greatest clowns in Europe in the 1930's; a legend amongst clowns. When the Nazis moved into Romania in the winter of 1940, he was rounded up with all the other Romani Gypsies and taken to the Pechora extermination camp. But instead of ending up in a gas chamber, the Nazis decided to keep him alive to entertain the guards at the camp. He became so popular that between 1941 and 1942 he toured many of the eastern-European concentration camps, entertaining guards and SS units. He even performed in front of Heinrich Himmler in Dachau."

"What has this got to do with us?" challenged Sam, wrinkling her nose in distaste.

"In the summer of 1943, the Reich Ministry of Propaganda commissioned a film to be made about Karpescu's act, detailing how he performed some of his best stunts. A Nazi film unit toured with him for three months in the concentration camps, compiling this detailed documentary. They finished filming in November 1943, and Karpescu and the film unit set off for Berlin by train to present it to the Reich Minister. On-route the train was attacked and destroyed by partisans in the Carpathian Mountains, killing all on board. But neither the film nor Karpescu's body were found, and the film has become one of the lost legends on clowning."

"Again," asked Sam, "what has this got to do with Chello Circus?"

"I may be able to obtain a copy of the film!" Klunn whispered excitedly.

Sam looked at him blankly. "We're a circus, not a nutcase cinema."

"If I can learn how he did his stunts, and emulate him,

every performance will be sold out!" Klunn enthused.

"And you really think what worked for the Nazis will work here in post-BREXIT Britain almost a century later?" she sighed, trying not to show her annoyance. "Modern audiences want modern acts; that's what we need to save the circus. We need to look to the future, not the bloody past!"

"Believe me, this film is incredible. It's everything the clown historians imagined it to be, and so much more. It has the power to make me the best clown this century," he said, eyes burning with excitement.

"Well, I hope so, Klunn," said Sam sadly. "Whatever you think, I do still have feelings for you, but I can't let the circus my family has built up over generations fold. I'll need to let you go at the end of this tour."

Klunn stared at her in shock. "But I can obtain a copy of Karpescu's lost film!"

"Good for you, but it won't help."

"Yeah, right," said Klunn bitterly, standing and stalking towards the door. "The only act that can save your ass is me!"

"You've got six weeks; Nottingham is your last show with us," Sam shouted after him.

***

The next night the tent was less than half-full again. Sam tried to give a rousing performance as Ring Master but she felt as beat as most of the other performers. Only her glittery top hat sparkled, not her false smile. As Petra finished her act and rode the horse out of the tent she was not even certain Klunn would show, but went straight into the announcement anyway.

"Ladies and gentlemen, hang onto your seats and welcome the one, the only, Klunn the Clown!"

A smatter of tired applause rippled round the tent and most eyes looked towards the entrance. A few seconds ticked by, and some of the audience started to mutter. Sam sighed inwardly, hoping the next act would be ready to go on early, but just as she was about to make a fresh announcement Klunn bounded onto the stage, his long colourful coattails flapping. The clown reached the centre of the Big Top before tripping theatrically over his huge clown-shoes and doing four fast forward-rolls to the far side of the ring. A few muted laughs sounded, mainly from the small children.

Klunn picked himself up and exaggeratedly dusted himself off. He then pulled a small loudhailer from the pocket of his over-large jacket.

"Ladies and gentlemen of Swindon. I know many of you come night after night just to see my act; and to those people I must make an apology. For tonight, I will not be doing the normal act. Tonight will be mind-blowingly different!"

Klunn paused for a reaction, but received nothing but silence.

"In that case I will go straight into it; prepare yourself to be astonished!"

Just a few claps answered him. Undeterred, he ran to the side of the ring and produced a large sword, a stool, and a big watermelon. He placed the watermelon on top of the stool in the centre of the ring, and then performed a dozen hammy sweeps of the sword whilst dancing around the stool.

"This is a real sword—actually used by Lord Cardigan at the Charge of the Light Brigade. It didn't do much for him then, but watch how sharp it is!" Klunn shouted, lunging at the watermelon. The sword sliced cleanly through it. He then swung the sword at the melon and neatly chopped it in half. "I will now dive from the top of the big top directly down onto the sword!"

In the ensuing silence of the big top he quickly taped the sword to the stool with gaffer-tape, the sharp shining tip pointing upwards, before moving to a rope ladder hanging from one of the supporting poles of the tent. After taking off his massive shoes he began to climb, slowly but steadily, reaching the top where a narrow rope walkway joined the pole to the pole on the opposite side. In a dozen careful steps he reached the centre point of the walkway, where he gingerly slipped a coiled rope around his waist. Having tied it securely he reached again into his flapping pocket for his loud hailer.

"Those with a nervous disposition should look away now!" Klunn yelled.

The crowd looked up expectantly as he pocketed the loud hailer and assumed the position of a diver on a diving board. He then launched himself off the walkway, falling prone over forty feet before the rope caught and snapped bone-jarringly tight, stopping him suddenly just a few inches above the sword.

The crowd paused a moment, unsure of what they had witnessed, before bursting into a rapturous applause and cheering loudly. Sam rushed forward in a panic, completely caught off guard by the stunt that she had never seen before, and which she had no clue that Klunn was going to perform.

"Klunn, are you all right?" she yelled in shock.

"Just move the sword away," Klunn replied evenly.

Sam kicked the stool and sword away before moving to support the clown. "I'll call for an ambulance, you'll be alright," she blathered.

"I am alright," said Klunn, removing a small knife from his pocket and sawing through the rope. The rope parted and he dropped into Sam's arms.

"Just like old times," the clown remarked bitterly.

"How can you be alright?" shouted Sam over the continuing applause. "A drop of forty feet stopped by a just a normal rope is enough to kill. What the hell were you thinking?"

"Just listen to the applause," Klunn countered.

"You've probably got internal bleeding," Sam said, hooking Klunn's arm over her shoulders.

"Stop!" Klunn demanded, pushing her away. "I'm fine, I've got to finish my act."

Klunn ran off to retrieve his huge shoes from the side of the ring and made a show of trying to get them on. He then took out his loud hailer from his pocket and moved to the centre stage.

"Thank you, Ladies and Gentlemen!" he shouted. "Don't worry, I'm f..."

Klunn fell over backwards and lay flat on his back, as if dead. As the audience gasped he sprang back upright and did a little jig, bringing a cheer.

"Fine! Thank you, and see you next time!" Klunn shouted, bounding off the stage.

Sam moved back into the ring to introduce the next act, her face in white contrast to the bright red of her Ringmaster's jacket.

The audience was bigger the next evening, and Klunn repeated his dive to huge applause. Reviews of the circus in the local newspapers were all positive, and all mentioned Klunn's act as the highlight of the show. Sam tried to talk to Klunn but the clown pointedly ignored her every time. By the end of the week Sam had had enough and stormed over to Klunn's battered caravan, knocking hard on the thin door before marching in.

"Please come in," said Klunn sarcastically, pausing the picture on the small television on the small table.

"I am in," Sam muttered, ignoring his sarcasm. "We

need to talk."

Klunn put the remote control down, and motioned for Sam to take a seat. "About what?"

"That dive is the most dangerous stunt I've ever seen a clown pull. I don't know how you do it but you're going to get very hurt, and we'll get a visit from the Health and Safety Inspectorate!"

Klunn shook his head bitterly. "There you go again. Everything is always about money with you. Instead of coming here to congratulate me on a crowd-pleasing act that gets good reviews and is starting to fill seats, you just want to lecture me on health and safety."

"No, I don't want to lecture you," breathed Sam. "But, although we're no longer together, I do still care for you. I just don't want you to get hurt. I want you to stop doing the stupid dive."

"Well, I've got news for you; next week when we open in Bristol, I'll be doing the dive and something else I've been working on, something even more dangerous," said Klunn, defiance written all over his painted face. "I did get a copy of Karpescu's lost film, and each week I'll add something new into my act. By the time we get to Nottingham there won't be an empty seat in the house."

"So, the dive is from that Nazi film?" she demanded, staring at the indistinct grainy black and white image frozen on the TV screen.

"It's not a Nazi film; it's a clowning masterpiece!" Klunn shot back.

"Whatever it is, it's going to get you into hospital. Or worse! Stop this dangerous stuff."

Klunn shook his head. "You have to understand that the film is what every clown wants; it takes your aspirations and makes them real. The film simply enables me to take my profession to the next level."

"I don't care. Forget the film and just concentrate on what you do best."

"I won't," Klunn said flatly.

"I own Chello Circus, and I say what the acts do," Sam countered.

"The contract says that my act is my own," Klunn growled, "and you said it lasts until Nottingham. Now get out!"

***

Sam was nervous as she started the show the first night in Bristol. She had no idea what Klunn would do, and did not like surprises. As Petra finished her act and rode the horse out of the tent, her mouth was dry and she had a tight knot in the pit of her stomach.

"Ladies and gentlemen, hang onto your seats and welcome the one, the only, Klunn the Clown!"

The applause seemed louder that it had been for the other acts, and Klunn let it run before bounding eagerly onto the stage, going straight into his dive routine over Lord Carigan's sword. Sam watched uneasily from the wings whilst Klunn did the dive and cut himself free. Klunn and two stagehands then dragged a large water-filled glass tank on wheels from outside into the centre of the ring. Sam had not seen the tank before, and had no idea where Klunn could have kept it hidden. After carefully positioning the tank Klunn dashed off stage to retrieve a huge stopwatch, which he placed by at the end of the ring where most could see it. Then he got out his loud hailer.

"Ladies and Gentlemen! Does anyone know what the world record is for holding your breath under water?"

Small patches of light appeared in the seating as some members of the audience got out their phones to Google it. A few shouted guesses came from those without phones and Klunn shook his head at each attempt.

"Eleven minutes, thirty-five seconds!" came a shout from a teenage girl near the back.

"Correct!" Klunn applauded. "A record held by Branko Petrovic from Serbia since October 2014. But tonight, in front of your very eyes, you will witness me break that record. I will immerse myself in the tank, sealed in by a lid and smash that record right here in Bristol!"

Sam listened to the murmur of anticipation passing through the crowd and shook her head.

"But before we start: does anyone in the audience hate clowns?" Klunn hollered.

A few laughs sounded but no one shouted up.

"Come on! Someone must hate clowns!"

This time a few shouts answered him, and Klunn ran around the ring looking at those who had shouted.

"You, Sir!" Klunn announced happily, pointing at a huge man who had answered his question, beckoning him into the ring. "If you can sit on the lid to stop me getting out, you'll get twenty pounds. Payable either by the undertaker or by me!"

The man cautiously followed Klunn, who fetched a stout ladder and placed it against the water-filled tank. Three stagehands ran out, one to steady the ladder, one to remove the lid, and one to start the giant stopwatch. Klunn climbed the ladder and gently lowered himself in the glass tank, displacing gallons of water as he did so.

"Once the lid is replaced, my large clown-hating friend here will sit on it until the stopwatch gets to twelve minutes. Only then will he release me, or my corpse, and claim his twenty pounds!" Klunn shouted from the tank, this time without the loud hailer.

The man nodded and climbed unsteadily up the ladder, assisted by one of the stagehands.

"Go!" yelled Klunn, fully submerging himself.

The heavy lid was placed over the top of the tank and the large man gingerly sat on it. Below him the clown could be clearly seen, theatrically holding his breath and waving underwater. As the applause quietened, the theme from the film *Titanic* blared from the public-address system and a few appreciative cheers sounded. Then one of the Bulgarian jugglers ran into the ring, expertly juggling four large clubs to entertain the crowd as the seconds turned into minutes. But all eyes remained on the glass tank, and the clown who continued to wave and hold his breath.

Sam paced anxiously, unaware that Klunn had any ability to hold his breath at all. She could see no trick; it was clear that Klunn had no pipe to breathe through and nothing to stop him drowning. As the stopwatch passed three minutes the *Titanic* theme restarted, and the audience became increasingly hushed. At six minutes the theme started for the third time, and Klunn's waving became weaker and more sporadic. Each second felt like a minute to Sam, unsure as to what she should do. She moved towards a fire extinguisher, thinking that breaking the glass tank would be the quickest way to get Klunn out if she needed to act quickly. After nine minutes Celine Dion again stopped singing and silence filled the tent. The seconds now passed in silence until some of the audience started to count down the seconds for the final minute. The majority were counting with thirty-seconds to go, and by ten seconds to go every member of the audience and staff were counting as one. Sam rushed forward, seeing the blank expression on Klunn's face as a few small bubbles lazily rose from beneath the small red nose.

The count reached zero and the huge man quickly scrambled off the lid, a worried look on his broad face. The audience broke into a rapturous applause and loud cheering as two of the stagehands reached down into the tank to pull out the clown's limp body. Sam watched in horror; astonished at what Klunn had done, and even more astonished that she had just stood there and let him do it.

"Klunn!" she yelled, kneeling over the prone body. She quickly put Klunn's head back and leaned in to give CPR.

"Not so fast!" spluttered Klunn, twisting his head away. "We're no longer together, remember? You'll have to go on your on-line dating sites to get that now."

Sam sat up in shock and the crowd went wild, cheering and applauding and shouting for more. Klunn staggered to his feet, water squirting out of his overlong clown shoes, and bowed deeply to the three sides of the ring. He picked up his loud hailer and moved back to the centre.

"Ladies and Gentlemen—now you know who holds the record for holding their breath underwater; Klunn the Clown! And you saw it here tonight at Victoria Park, Bristol, at Chello Circus! We're here all week, and I will add an extra five seconds to the record each night!"

After a further deep bow, Klunn waddled out of the ring, dripping as he went, leaving Sam the Ringmaster speechless. She ran after the clown, catching him as he walked through the tunnel to the backstage area.

"Aren't you going to announce us?" asked Bruno from the Flying Bulgarian Trapeze act as Sam stormed past.

"Announce yourself!" she shot back, grabbing hold of Klunn's wet arm.

Klunn pulled free and continued walking.

"What the hell are you doing?!" Sam demanded, blocking the clown's path.

Klunn stopped and regarded the Ringmaster angrily. "I'm trying to save Chello Circus, but as usual I can never do anything right for you. You broke my heart when you dumped me, and now you want to take away my job. But I now have Karpescu's lost film; the golden grail for a clown. Most clowns would give their right arm to watch it, to help them perform the greatest acts of the trade. The film will make me the ultimate performer around, but even that is not good enough for you. We both know that whatever I try to do, it will never be good enough!"

Sam stood blinking at her ex-lover, shocked at his outburst. "No, it's not like that," she stuttered.

"Sure," said Klunn bitterly. "Just keep telling yourself that."

"Come on, Klunn," Sam started. "We split up because it just wasn't working. Neither of us was getting what we wanted; we just weren't right for each other!"

"And no matter what I did to change, you were having none of it!"

"But I didn't want you to change," Sam countered. "It's pointless being in a relationship if you can't be yourself. I was hoping you'd find somebody who'd be better for you."

"And being in a touring circus it's so easy to find the right person and settle down!" Klunn snorted bitterly.

"Either way, us splitting up was to allow us both to find the right person," Sam explained. "I still have feelings for you, Klunn, which is why you've got to stop this madness that will end up getting you killed!"

"There you go again; whatever I do to please you it's never right."

Sam shook her head. "That's not true."

"Well, we've got just under five more weeks before my contract ends, and then I'll be out of your life forever," Klunn sneered. "But you wanted Cirque de Soleil and Circus of Horrors, and that is exactly what me and Karpescu are giving to you. As we open in each new town I'm going to add something new to my act; I'll make Chello

Circus famous, although I know it still won't be good enough for you!"

"What I'm struggling with is your obsession with some old clown film, which seems to have taken over your whole life."

Klunn rounded angrily on her, his eyes blazing. *"Some old clown film"*! That just shows how little you know about clowns and the circus in general; you've no idea how important this film is."

"I come from a circus family, I've spent my whole life in circuses, and yet I've never heard of this Karpescu. So, forgive me if I can't understand this self-destructive fixation of yours, I just don't want anything bad to happen to you."

Klunn shook his head tiredly, his anger suddenly dissipating. "Look, Karpescu is the master. This lost film shows how a clown can truly achieve greatness, this is my chance to put everything right."

"But at what cost?" countered Sam. "Damn this Karpescu!"

Klunn regarded her blankly for an instant, then frowned darkly. "Too late for that."

***

Over the coming weeks Klunn avoided all contact with Sam, shutting himself in his tiny caravan between shows and watching the film time and time again. She could see the flickering light from images at the edges of curtained windows, seemingly constantly on. A couple of times she managed to get an obscured glimpse of the screen by peering in through a crack in the curtains, but each time it appeared the grainy black and white footage was paused. A soon as she moved away the flickering began again, as if the film would only let

Klunn view it.

On stage, Klunn was as good as his word, adding a fresh element to his act on the opening night at each new town. In Worcester he got a stagehand to drop a dozen sharp knives on him from high on the upper ropewalk; and each night each knife miraculously missed him by only fractions of an inch. In Wolverhampton he was hoisted to the top of the tent in a straight-jacket on a burning rope; escaping every night just a few seconds before the rope parted and grabbing a stanchion with his free arm to prevent a fall. In Jackson he climbed into a coffin shaped cardboard box and the three circus elephants were driven over it four times at speed; and not once did one tread on the box. By the time the circus reached Nottingham, the final week of Klunn's contract, it was less of a circus and more of a show dominated by one single act, which lasted over an hour. But the media and the crowds loved it. The first night in Nottingham was sold out by the start of the previous week, and all tickets for the remaining days quickly went. Chello Circus had never been so popular, but Sam knew it could all end on the last night. Klunn continued to avoid her, and even when Sam sought him out the clown refused point blank to talk.

The excited media attention led to dozens of requests for local TV and radio interviews, and Klunn happily gave them all. He loved the attention, always playing up for the cameras or the microphones, and always giving a great performance. There were so many hits on the circus's website that the hosting company had to install it on a bigger server. Takings soared, and for the first time in months the accounts were well and truly out of the red.

Klunn headlined the opening night in Nottingham by juggling six razor-sharp bowie knives, executing complicated swops and fancy feigns whilst riding a high-speed hoverboard. Despite being clearly fatigued by doing all the acts one after the other in the same show, he did not even get a scratch. After the final show on the last night in Nottingham the crowds gave him a five-minute standing ovation and were joined by all the other performers and circus staff. Klunn was a sensation.

The only person not clapping was Sam, who watched sullenly from the wings. After a few minutes of the rapturous applause she could stand it no longer and retired to her caravan; knowing that sooner or later Klunn would have to show to claim his final pay. It turned into a long wait, as Klunn proceeded to hold court with interviews and people asking for autographs. By the time the knock came on the caravan door Sam was both annoyed and tired.

"Come in!" Sam shouted irately.

"I've come for my wages," Klunn said, walking in still dressed in his clown outfit.

"So, finally you can spare me a word?" said Sam, standing to meet him.

"I had interviews with BBC Radio Nottingham, and will be on tomorrow's East Midlands Today," boasted Klunn. "The guy from Derby Evening Telegraph called me "Britain's best clown"."

"I've been trying to talk to you for weeks," muttered Sam.

Klunn sneered at her. "I wanted to show you how hard it is when someone shuts you out."

"I've never shut you out, Klunn," Sam sighed. "We just grew apart. And what has happened over the last six weeks with that damn film just goes to show how little I knew you even when we shared a bed."

"We didn't grow apart, you just got bored of me and kicked me out!" Klunn shot back accusingly.

"I'm very sorry you feel that way," said Sam, holding up her hands, "and I'm sorry you want to leave Chello

Circus. Your act over the last six weeks has been unbelievable; you've been carrying the whole show by yourself. I've tried so many times to talk to you about staying, but you just blanked me every time."

"Again," said Klunn, "I wanted to show you how hard it is when someone shuts you out."

"Well, you've succeeded. I'm sorry that you think I shut you out, and I wish there was something I could do to make you stay on. But now you're a star I'm guessing you've no shortage of great offers, and I truly wish you all the best for the future."

"There is no future," laughed Klunn bitterly. "My ability to do death-defying stunts ends tonight. In order to view Karpescu's film you have to make a pact, and the deal doesn't last forever."

"What?"

"All I ever wanted was you, Sam. To be with you, to be your partner." Klunn whispered. "When I realised that was not to be, my world was over. But instead of suicide I made a deal with Karpescu."

"Karpescu?" asked Sam in confusion. "Surely he must be long dead?"

"He came to me with a pact; a soul in exchange for the film, which would make me the best circus performer in the world. But the deal would only last six weeks."

"I don't understand," said Sam. She took a deep breath, frustrated yet again by Klunn's irrational behaviour and by his inability to let the relationship go. "Look, we were good together, but it just didn't work. All this nonsense with the stupid film has confused things even further. I'm sorry but I don't love you, Klunn, and no relationship can last without love."

Klunn tearfully bowed his head. Sam stepped forward to hug him but as she did so immediately felt a searing pain rip through her abdomen. She looked down in bewilderment, seeing Klunn twist and yank one of the large juggling bowie knives from her torn stomach. Blood jetted from the gaping wound and she dropped to her knees, coughing up blood from ripped and filling lungs.

"I knew that would be your answer," hissed Klunn. "Which is why I sold Karpescu your soul instead of mine."

# From the Darkness Within
## C. Bailey-Bacchus

Harry gripped the front page of the Financial Times and sighed in resignation. Brexit was a terrible idea. He was sure of it. But there was no time to consider the point. The arctic wind that had pursued him all day was gusting again. He crumpled the page into a ball and forced it into his jacket. His heart sank. In his mind, the Financial Times had gone from representing the pinnacle of his career to cementing him inescapably at rock bottom.

Still, nothing was ever gained from self-pity.

Harry winced as he pulled up his hood. It brought with it a faint waft of stale alcohol and decay. Though, by the way those he encountered covered their noses as he approached, he supposed his scent was far more pungent than that.

The streak of peach light at the horizon was thinning. Soon, it would be dark enough to go to the park and settle down for the night. During the day, Cannon Park belonged to mollycoddling mothers and their screeching children.  But at night, it was the dominion of the unwanted, those who subsisted on desolation and alienation. Those like Harry.

His back ached in protest as he bent to pick up the tattered rucksack containing his worldly goods.

Something juddered in his periphery. He froze. His heart pounded and his mouth dried. Standing steadfast he tried to see through the mist created by his involuntary deep breaths. A further step stirred the thing beside him. He turned just as the grotesque figure squared up to him.  His mouth flopped open, but the scream got lost in his throat. Then the cold left him as the pure white heat of shame crackled across his skin.

Confronted by his own reflection, he was sickened by the hunched fragment of his former self struggling to stand straight. The rest had been ravaged by alcohol and devoured by guilt. He stepped away from the shop front.

Harry should cry, he wanted to cry, but he didn't have that depth of emotion anymore. He had grieved the loss of what he had and who he was long ago. He had no capacity for sorrow now.

The need for sanctuary and rest motivated him to move.

The Victorian grandeur of Cannon Park had, like Harry, suffered a decline. Walking along the cracked pathways, sporadically littered by piles of dog faeces, he looked across the stunted yellow grass to the diseased trees. No doubt, the landscapers would weep were they to see what had become of their masterpiece. But Harry smiled, he was home.

Then, in the perpetual haze of drunkenness and disappointment, Harry heard jeering voices. He turned to see two young men stumbling behind.

"Down it! Down it!" One loudly chanted as the other held the bottle up to his mouth. Judging by the large wet stains on their shirts they had been playing this game all evening.

Harry looked away, making eye contact ensured reprisal for daring to exist. He hurried as fast as his weak knees would carry him.

Intuitively, he expected the thud to the back of the head, but not the degree of pain that passed through his skull. Blinded for a moment, he fell to the ground. In the confusion, a green beer bottle rattled past him. His hand slipped toward the bottle, greedy for the dregs within. But at the sound of approaching footsteps, his hands instinctively snapped back to protect his head.

"Dirty tramp!" one man shouted. Harry held his head tighter and rolled into a ball. "Kick him!"

Harry braced himself, but the blow didn't come. He looked up to see a young woman by his side with tousled hair and an oversized coat, struggling to pull him up. The stranger's grip was too strong to repel.

"Get up!" she said as he stumbled to his feet.

"Oh my god! Look, there's two of them! The tramp's got a girlfriend!" Another beer bottle flew between them.

Harry was unable to fathom how his feet were moving so quickly, but he did nothing to stop them as the raucous shouting of the men gained distance. The woman stopped when they reached the footbridge over the pond.

"Down here!" she said, pointing at the ditch that led beneath it. Frustration and reticence swelled through the dizziness. He just wanted to be left alone.

"No." He resisted her pull.

"It's ok, we'll be safe here," she said.

It was the sense of urgency in her eyes that allowed him to follow. The metallic arch of the bridge was like a cave, etched in intricate Victorian detail. The walls were alight with a dancing luminance. It gave the impression that the black lacquered walls were silently flexing. He held his hand up to catch the reflection of the silvery ripples that flared across the walls.

A ragged duffle bag was tucked beneath one of the struts. *Oh no my bag!* Before he could voice his concern, she threw his bag down next to hers. He rushed to open it and make sure everything was accounted for.

"Are you alright?" She reached to pull his hood back.

He cringed away and cradled his bag.

"I'm sorry, I just wanted to check you weren't cut," she said. "Maybe we should get you to the hospital. They hit you pretty hard."

It had been so long since he'd seen it; he didn't recognise the look on her face. *Is it compassion?* "Don't worry." His voice was quiet and croaky. He also couldn't remember the last time he had spoken. He cleared his throat. "I'm fine, honestly."

"Will you wait with me until they go? I have this…" She scrabbled to open her bag and pulled out a large bottle of whisky.

Something dark and insatiable and cruel stirred within him. He took the bottle and drank greedily. The thoughts he battled every waking moment started to abate and his eyes flickered slowly as he found himself slipping somewhere safe and familiar.

"Where did you get this?" He wheezed.

"I stole it." She held her hand out.

He reluctantly passed her the bottle and took her in properly for the first time. Her face was round and framed by long, thick, messy black hair. Her caramel skin was flawless. He looked into her big brown eyes, so dark they appeared black, and knew she had not been on the streets for long. They still had life in them. She took a sip and spluttered, then handed the bottle back to him.

"What's your name?" he said.

"Zoë."

"I'm Harry." He watched her closely and took another swig. The rush flowed through his veins. "You haven't been on the streets for long, have you?" he said.

She looked down. Her delicate features pouting like a child denied chocolate. She shook her head. "Two weeks."

"The first rule is not to trust anyone, especially other homeless people," he said.

Her face relaxed then contorted in fear.

"Don't worry. You're safe. I'm not that kind of guy." He smiled. "Besides, I owe you one for helping me back there and for this." he said waving the bottle. He settled back. The sky was clear and the full moon reflected mesmerising silver ripples across the pond.

"How did you end up sleeping rough?" she said.

"Rule two of being homeless." He looked down at her. "Never ask for a life story."

She smiled up at him. His stomach sank. The things they would do to her. All that innocence and kindness made her weak. She was like a lost little lamb and the wolves would come circling soon. She was not cut out for this. He hoped she realised that before it was too late. *Silly girl.* "What about you? Did you have an argument with someone, your parents? It's been two weeks; they'll be worried sick. All will be forgotten."

"No argument. I just don't have anywhere to go."

"Who did you live with?"

"Rule two." She smiled. "I lived by myself." She looked at him quizzically. "You speak proper posh. Don't see a lot of people like you out here."

*Posh?* He looked down at his frayed coat and scoffed.

"You must have family or house or something," she said.

"I did." Those errant thoughts began to spring to his mind again. "But now I have nothing." He took another gulp of whisky to quell them. "This is no life for a young girl like you."

"I did a terrible thing. I don't deserve any better."

"We've all done terrible things, but your life is at the start," he said. Zoë pulled her knees to her chest and wrapped her arms around them. She suddenly seemed so much younger. "How old are you?"

"Nineteen." She shivered. He passed her the bottle and she took a sip. Her eyes were locked on his, full of expectation for a conversation.

He couldn't remember the last time he'd had one. He probably wasn't up to it, but he could listen, or at least drink whilst she spoke.

"You tell me your story first," she said.

His story was a burden that had snaked itself around him, constricting him. Pulling that little bit tighter every day. He could never break free from it, he could never tell. She moved closer to him and took his arm. The touch of another was alien to him. His breath quickened as he felt the warmth.

"Let's make a pact. Whatever is said now, whatever was done, it stays between us," she said.

"Okay," he lied. "But you go first." Those hooligans would have left, and he'd have finished the bottle by then.

"My mum died when I was fourteen and I never knew my dad." Zoë looked away so wistfully that Harry's eyes involuntarily followed hers across the moonlit pond. "I lived with my Gran, but when she passed away, I couldn't pay the rent."

"I'm sure there are lots of programmes to help people like you. You should go to the council tomorrow. I'm sure they'll be able to help you."

"I'm not sure I want their help. I deserve this," she said.

Harry understood that feeling, but didn't believe for one second she was culpable of the horrific acts he was. "I can't believe that's true."

Her smile didn't reach her eyes. "About a year ago Gran got sick, then my hours got cut at work and money became tight really quickly. She felt like a burden and she wanted to help." Zoë fixed Harry with her warm chocolate eyes, and shuffled to sit against his shoulder. "I know how its sounds, but she had always believed she was a medium."

"She thought she could see ghosts?" He couldn't help but lace every word with derision.

"Like I said, I know how its sounds. But she was known for it. She used to say the gift runs in our family and she was sure I had it… I never saw anything though. But she told me all about it. It's not like most people imagine or like the films. The ghosts she saw would sometimes find her or sometimes they would come when called for. But they all came with a purpose, and they couldn't see anything beyond it. I don't think she saw that in the beginning.

"At first, those that Gran saw wanted to tell their families that they loved them, or they had messages like where to find their old bonus bonds and stuff. But then she was tricked." Tears bobbed gently along her eye-line.

Harry had to fight the sudden urge to wipe them away. "You don't have to tell me anymore." He offered her the bottle again, but she declined with a shake of her head.

Zoë cleared her throat and rested her hand on her chest. Her sigh was deep and rueful. "I don't have anyone to talk to, I want to tell you." Little dimples formed in her cheeks as she smiled at him. "Gran used to do séances at home."

"That was so dangerous," he said.

"It wasn't as bad as it sounds. It all worked by word of mouth. The people who came were generally her friends, or friends of a friend. You know, widows who wanted to speak to their husbands who had passed on, that kind of thing. I'd sit in with her, take the money and make cups of tea." She absentmindedly kneaded her knee with her palm.

His head began to sway. He had to force himself to concentrate on her words.

"One day, she was doing a reading for a lady called Mrs Morris and her granddaughter, Mona. Mrs Morris wanted to speak to her son because he'd died in a motorcycle accident. I should have known something wasn't right. I swear, as soon as my Gran sat down, she said that a young guy had appeared. That had never happened before.

"She described him to us. Blonde hair, blue eyes, Mrs Morris practically jumped out of her chair. She was sure it was him. So my Gran asked him if he had a message, and apparently he said, *tell her Danny says Rick has his watch*.

"So Gran passes the message on, but Mrs Morris doesn't know anyone called Danny or Rick. She gets really angry when my Gran explains that was all he said before leaving.

"Mrs Morris ripped the money out of my hand, and then stormed out, calling my Gran a fraud and a joke. Gran said that she had never experienced anything like it before. But she just brushed it off and carried on with her next client. A couple of days later, the police were knocking on the door."

"The woman called the police? Because she had been given a false reading from a medium?" Harry slurred, even though the whisky in his veins was starting to make its presence known, he knew without doubt the story was hyperbole. He momentarily wondered where she was going with it before wishing she would stop.

Another sip of whisky soon soothed his objections.

Oblivious to his mockery, Zoë continued. "It turned out the message was for Mrs Morris's granddaughter Mona. Until the day the police turned up, I never really believed my Gran was for real." A single tear found its way over Zoë's eye line.

As Harry tracked the tear's path down her cheek, it incited guilt. "What happened?"

"Mona never said a word when she was there, not one. But she'd had a secret boyfriend. He was a lot older than her. His name was Danny and he'd died. The police thought he had been stabbed during a mugging. Three years later, they still had no leads, no idea who had done it. But then Danny visited Gran." She looked up at Harry and confusion sullied her brow.

Harry realised he had externalised his doubt, it was written on his face, and Zoë had perceptively read it clearly.

"You don't believe me," Zoë said solemnly.

"No, it's not that," He said, taking another sip of whisky. "It's just a little…" Harry searched for an inoffensive way to say preposterous. "…out there."

"Out there?" Zoë's face relaxed. "Like crazy?"

"Well…" He started.

"Harry, you haven't even heard what happened yet." Her smile was weak. "When Mona left that day, she went to see Danny's best friend Rick. He was surprised to see her after all those years, but he invited her in. I don't really know what she wanted to happen. Something bad, I guess, because she had taken a hammer with her. Without warning, when he turned his back, she took it out of her bag and thumped him over the head with it. He fell to the ground bleeding."

"Seriously?" Harry asked. This really was getting preposterous.

"Yeah, Mona confessed everything. She knew Rick could easily overpower her, so she had to put him out of action. She refused to get him help until he told her what happened.

"Rick and Danny had been smoking skunk at a party, and on the way home something…paranoia I guess, caused them to fight. Danny pulled a knife on Rick, and in the struggle Rick stabbed him. He panicked and took Danny's watch and wallet to make it look a mugging." Tears fell freely as Zoë struggled to stifle her sobs.

"Hey," Harry said gently, stroking her arm. "It's alright, I know she assaulted him but he was ok, wasn't he? He was still speaking at least."

"That wasn't the end of it. She made him tell her where the watch was, and then left him there. It was three days before his mum called the police because she couldn't get hold of him. He had bled out."

It was like Zoë steered the elements, falling raindrops mimicked her tears. Harry watched as each droplet created an expanding circle in the stillness of the pond. He didn't have the strength to sit upright anymore and flopped back against the wall.

He had given up trying to find some reasonable explanation in his raging doubt. He just didn't want to upset her further. "None of it was your fault." He said.

She stifled a sob and wiped her face. "I should have stopped my Gran. If I had, she wouldn't be…" Her lips puckered into a pout again.

*Poor girl!* He took her hand. "…in prison?" He attempted to finish her sentence.

"No." She squeezed his hand. "The police came and questioned her. But she was already ill and the stress of it all… it was all too much… her heart gave out," She sobbed.

Harry soaked up her pain. His exhausted body felt it.

The heart he thought incapable of feeling anything, felt it. It was the sort of pain only someone like him could understand. He took three large gulps of whiskey. It was the pain spawned from abject guilt.

"Tell me," she said. "How did you end up here?"

The question sent his mind into a frenzy of muddled thoughts.

"You're a good man, I can tell, it can't be that bad."

He looked into her eyes, and though he tried to look away, he couldn't. "Good men don't end up like this."

"But you weren't always like this. What happened?"

Her insistence stirred the dark, greedy, rotten thing within him. "Aren't you scared?"

"Of you?" She scoffed.

His temper erupted. He felt that rotten thing reach his mouth. "Yes, of me! Are you stupid? Really, are you? Why would you even think you should approach someone like me?" Zoë recoiled, her mouth agape. The fear in her eyes fed the rotten thing. "You're right to be scared. That day something woke in me, something terrible. It's always there now. A poison seeping into everything and everyone I meet. This won't end well for you."

She shifted away. "What day?" Despite her best efforts he heard her voice tremble.

"The day my wife died"

"Your wife is dead? What happened?"

He sensed the apprehension in her voice. She had seen the monster he kept within. It had swallowed her confidence. She was doused in fear. He looked at the bottle in his hand and took another swig. The warm sticky whisky trickled down his throat. His temper soothed. He lost his train of thought.

"Anna, my wife, and I worked at an investment bank in the city. I was a Finance Controller, she worked in securities. We were polar opposites. I was quiet and reserved, and she was loud and gregarious…the life and soul of the party."

An image of Anna, the one of her in his old t-shirt and a pair of jogging bottoms flashed in front of him. She was painting the bedroom that awful pink colour. The paint had dripped on her hair and cheek. She smiled when he walked into the room. Had she ever looked more beautiful?

"From the moment I laid eyes on her I knew there was never going to be anyone else. She was so beautiful, and when she smiled at me—I felt so… special. I used to watch her sleep and think how lucky I was that a woman like her could love a man like me. But she took me for a fool… because I was one."

His face and demeanour hardened as those supressed memories began to reach the surface. "They used to snigger about me… the people that I worked with. I'd walk into a room and they would fall silent. I used to talk to Anna about it. She would reassure me and say that I had been mistaken, that they all liked me." Harry massaged his forehead in a vain attempt to stop the pain. *Take another sip of whiskey.*

"Then one day, she told me she didn't feel well. So I left her at home and went to work. I was at my desk when I got a call from the bank." A giggle of lingering disbelief rose from his throat. "She didn't realise there was a clause on our joint account. If more than five thousand pounds was removed from our account, the other person would be notified."

"How much did she take?" Zoë moved closer to him.

"Fifty thousand. At the time, I thought it had been a mistake. I remember turning to my assistant and saying it had to be fraud."

Harry saw Anna standing at the top of the stairs scowling. The image was so vivid it was like she was there in front of him. Harry pounded his fist on his lap.

"Damn it! I was so bloody stupid." He gasped for air. "My assistant just looked sheepish. She told me Anna was having an affair with a colleague, John, a smarmy little prick. She had wanted to tell me but couldn't find a way. Everyone knew...Everyone but me."

"What did you do?" He could tell Zoë was beginning to put something together in her mind.

"I went home, half expecting her to be gone. But she had other plans. When I got home she was upstairs packing her things. I have no words to explain the pain I felt. I was utterly devastated. She was so shocked to see me. She thought that she had all day to take my life from me. I confronted her, told her to go, but that she couldn't take the money.

"She laughed at me… laughed right in my face" He balled his fists. "She told me the first thing she did was hide the money. She picked up her case and headed to the stairs. At the last minute she turned. The look in her eyes… it was like I was nothing…nothing to her at all. She called me pathetic. Told me that she never loved me, that he was twice the man I was." He wiped the burgeoning tears from his eyes.

"It happened so quickly. She tripped on her case and tumbled down the stairs. I froze at the top, staring at her… she was like a rag doll… lying lifeless at the bottom. I ran to her, but she was gone. " He fell into great sobs.

Zoë pulled him down until his head rested on her lap. "It was an accident, you didn't do anything wrong." She gently brushed the hair away from his forehead in long slow strokes. He looked out across the rain battered pond.

"I didn't tell you everything before." Her voice was barely audible over the pounding rain. "The night after my Gran was arrested she came into my room and woke me. I was so happy to see her. I asked if they'd charged her. But she looked at me with this smile, and said *see*. Then she left the room."

Harry knew that he'd had too much to drink. She wasn't making sense to him anymore.

"You see, I had the gift… well it's more like a curse. The ability to see those that remain comes from the darkness within, and listening to those who remain, brings nothing but darkness to the lives they touch. I suppose you could say I manifest their evil…that's how I know you're lying." Her words were murmured as though they were a profession of love.

He looked up and saw that she was certain of his guilt. She had known it all along, there was no doubt. Harry struggled to move from her lap. He rolled onto the ground. "What?" Harry groaned as he tried to sit up.

From beneath the seductive charm; menace crept across Zoë's face. Her full lips thinned as she smiled. Her eyes were wide and glittering. "You're lying. About your wife, I mean."

"What?" His mind raced. Everything about her had changed. Her face was hard and unfeeling.

"Let me help you." Zoë smiled. "She lay at the bottom of the stairs, but she wasn't lifeless. Was she?"

Her words were like a blow to the stomach. He struggled to breathe. He couldn't understand what was happening. "Yes, she was," he mumbled.

"Was she?" Zoë's metallic echoes reverberated through his chest.

"Yes," he whimpered and he pushed himself to his knees. *Whisky*. He reached for the last dregs but she pulled the bottle away and smashed it against the ground.

"She lay at the bottom of the stairs, broken and unconscious, but not dead. You didn't help, did you?"

"I thought she was dead." He sobbed. He tried to

stand but his knees buckled.

"Liar! What did you do?"

He cupped his ears with his hands. He couldn't hear anymore. Zoë pulled them away. "What did you do?" she screamed.

"I was so angry…" he heaved and sobbed, his lungs fought to take air.

"You were so angry that you did what?"

"I put my hand over her mouth and nose," he cried.

"You killed her and then you ran."

"Yes!"

She looked and spoke to the emptiness. "Have you heard enough?" She nodded. "Are you sure this is what you want?"

Though he was certain no one was there, he turned to see to whom they were addressed. "There's no one there. Who—" Harry said.

"Shush, come," Zoë, said pulling him towards her. His body flopped without permission into her arms. "It's going to be fine," she whispered into his ear.

He inhaled sharply as a searing pain radiated through his chest. Confusion quickly became horror when he looked down to see the shaft of a knife protruding from his side. He reached down. But his pace was too slow. His fingers merely grazed the metal as she drew the knife out.

Harry reached up and brought a closed fist against her eye socket. The blow caused her to drop the knife and clasp her cheek. It took the length of two breaths for her pain to surface. She screeched, and broke down in sobs.

As the blood poured from his wound, Harry clutched his side and scrambled to his feet. He was at the edge of the bridge when he heard her roar. The instinct to turn overwhelmed him. Zoë plunged the knife into his shoulder the moment after he did. He screamed, and clutched her throat. But she had already pulled the knife out and was slashing at every piece of his exposed skin. Then finally, his fingers had no strength to hold her. His arms slipped from her neck.

Harry felt dizzy. The dancing ripples blurred. He convulsed downwards and rolled onto his back. Zoë loomed over him until she filled his sight with the same look of disdain Anna reserved for him. He couldn't bear it, his eyes blinked to a slow close. Tiredness fell upon him. No more pain. No more cold.

"Where's the money?" Zoë said.

"Do you know the Crown Hotel on the high street? I hid it room 20. If you stand on the toilet and move the ceiling tile above, you'll find the money in a plastic bag."

Harry opened his eyes and forced himself upwards. That voice was familiar. It was a voice he never thought he'd hear again.

"Anna?"

Harry stood in the bleakness and stared at her. In that moment, it was not hatred, but excitement he felt. It was his Anna, the woman he had made the sincerest of vows to, the woman that death could not even part him from. He had prayed for this moment. That somehow she would come back to him.

His eyes flitted between the two women staring back at him, and he realised that neither had any joy or excitement at the sight of him.

Instantly sober, his mind had never been clearer, but he still couldn't understand what was happening. He followed Zoë's pointing finger to the ground and fell to his knees. An otherworldly numbness took hold of him as he looked at his body slumped across the ground.

Zoë pulled a cloth from her pocket and wiped the handle of the bloody blade in her hand and threw it into the pond. She shrugged off her blood stained coat and pulled a leather jacket from her bag.

"What is happening? What have you done?" Harry's pleas went unheeded as Zoë kicked off her dirty trainers and slipped her feet into spotless boots.

Anna's guttural snickers filled the air as she bounced up and down excitedly. "She's done what I paid her to do." She smiled sweetly.

"You did this?" he said.

"You didn't think I'd let you get away with murdering me, did you?" Anna seemed downcast because he hadn't realised she had been the architect of this plot.

He succumbed to her disappointment. "I'm so sorry."

Anna laughed. "Fuck you, and your fucking sorry."

Zoë forced everything into her bag and threw it over her shoulder. She looked from Anna to Harry. "It is a wicked, wicked thing you have done to each other and yourselves." She picked up his rucksack and threw it against his body.

Harry stumbled. "We're wicked? You did this for money!"

Zoë paused for a moment before a wry half smile curled. "You're right…oh well!"

"What would your Grandmother say?" he shouted.

Confusion briefly crossed her face before she smiled. "Come on, you're sober now. You can't seriously still believe that nonsense!"

"It was a lie?"

"Most of it." The smile became pity. "Goodbye Harry… and good luck." She turned and walked away.

"Wait!" Harry shouted. He moved towards her, but something clamped his wrist so hard he couldn't take another step.

"No, you wait," Anna said.

# Mr. Elvid
## Justin Boote

The dark swept away the last few remnants of its counterpart, claiming the sky for its own. With it came a mild breeze and, as though some ethereal bodyguard, blew away the tendrils of cloud that still hung like ghostly cob-webs allowing its greatest ally—the moon—to show itself in full view.

Beneath its welcoming embrace, devout followers began to stir in whatever represented a resting place. For some a hole in the ground, others a hole in a tree or for the larger adepts of night, an abandoned barn or shed, while for others it signalled a time to seek their fortune amongst the bright lights and secluded alleys that criss-crossed the many towns and suburbs of Manchester.

For Mr. Elvid, no such commodity was necessary. Only a tranquil spot to rest and contemplate while awaiting the burning rays of the sun to fade away and allow him to continue his mission.

***

"Hey, you! You can't drink alcohol on the bus! You'll have to get off!" said the irate driver.

"I beg your pardon, young man. Am I bothering anybody in some way? As far as I am aware, no complaint has been made concerning my behaviour. May I suggest that you relax a little and continue your journey?" the man replied.

"What you talking about? I don't care if anyone has complained or not. You can't drink on the bus, so get off. Now!" The young drivers" face was beginning to turn a bright shade of red, provoked even more by the man's manner of speech. He felt like he was being patronized, and he didn't like it.

"I'm not moving until you get off the bus," he repeated.

"Dear fellow, I suspect you are over-reacting slightly about my choice of beverage. You could provoke that delicate heart of yours into having a relapse."

"Look. Stop talking like a yuppie and get off my damn bus. If not, I'll kick you off myself." Although he was staring intensely at the man, trying to impose authority, inside he was starting to feel nervous. There was something about him that didn't feel right. He was tall and lean, well over six-feet, and impeccably dressed in an all-black suit; shirt and tie included.

The driver looked at the man's face to ascertain age and failed. He figured that he could be early forties or late fifties, as no wrinkles disfigured his lean, tanned face even while smiling, yet his eyes suggested a knowledge far beyond the years that accredited him. They were dark, he couldn't be sure if brown or dark green, and an ominous flicker of light seemed to emanate from them that had nothing to do with the fluorescents hanging from the ceiling. His hair was jet-black, not a strand misplaced, yet no gel or cream appeared to have been used to maintain order. To all intents and purposes, the driver thought, he could have been a successful funeral director save the incessant smile fixed to his face.

Using all possible will power to maintain his stance, the driver realized that the threat was going to have to be put into practice. He'd expected the man to leave the bus in the interest of everyone, yet he'd called his bluff. After threatening to use force to remove him, the man's features had not shown the slightest twitch, the smile never wavered, and his arms remained passively by his side.

Beginning to regret his threat, he sighed and opened the door that separated him from the passengers, yet before he even had time to step out of the cubicle, the man was upon him. It seemed impossible that he could have approached so quickly. As the driver looked up into his face, sweat dripping from his forehead, he suddenly felt rather than saw as two fingers were thrust deeply up into his nostrils. He let out a shriek of both pain and shock as he grabbed at the man's arm with both hands and tried to free the grip. It was impossible. The man's grip was ironclad and there was no way of budging it. He looked towards the other passengers for help, yet all were either half-asleep or submerged in their smart phones.

Suddenly, he felt a sharper pain as something began pressing against the inside of his nose. The driver screamed as blood started to trickle and two long, sharp fingernails burst through the skin like some mutant insect hatching from its shell, and raked down his nose, splitting it in two, leaving it flapping like some abhorrent disfiguration. Blood spewed around the driver's face and surroundings, yet strangely not a single drop landed on the man's suit or arm as he pulled it away.

The driver slid to the floor screaming and clutching his now disfigured face. The man looked down at him, tutting and shaking his head as though scolding a naughty child.

"Dear oh dear. What a mess you've caused yourself, young man. You should really show more respect for your elders, you know. Or perhaps there's just no hope for some." He sighed again and, before the now startled passengers could react, turned and left the bus. By the time the first passenger arrived to help the driver, Mr. Elvid had already disappeared.

***

Dave looked around the street. There was no one in sight, which indicated a perfect time to carry out his employment obligations. He'd been watching the gas station for a few days and had memorized the shift changes. The only person working there now was a young teenager that would remain there alone for the next six hours.

That it was a youngster behind the till was completely irrelevant to him. He would have walked in had it been Rambo. He'd performed the same operation on countless occasions and the fearful look he employed to frighten his victims, coupled with the pistol he carried in his pocket ensured that each robbery had been a complete success. And now was a great time for the next. His head was throbbing, and a mildly trembling body informed him that he was already in need of another fix. If he didn't go in now, his body would soon begin screaming for mercy and he'd have to take bigger risks. Time to go to work.

"Give me the fucking money, quick!"

The shocked attendant looked up from the skin magazine he was studying, and looked aghast first at the man's face and then the pistol that was being pointed at him. Deciding that life was still too valuable to lose for a few pounds, without hesitating he opened the till and threw the money towards him.

"Good boy," Dave said. "Say a fucking word and I'll be back for you." The boy believed him.

Dave left and walked off trying to look as calm as possible. He'd had to use considerable will power to keep the gun from wobbling in his increasingly nervous state, and was thankful the kid hadn't challenged him. Now, it was time to spend his hard-earned profits on something useful.

As he crossed the road, he was alerted to somebody standing by a shop door. His heart beginning to pump a little faster, he gripped the gun and prepared himself for a confrontation should it be a cop. He'd been in prison before for robbery and returning was not on his list of priorities.

"Excuse me, young man, may I have a word if you wouldn't mind?" said the stranger.

"The fuck d'ya want? I'm in a hurry," he replied. The posh way the man spoke suggested no officer of the law, so he relaxed a little; probably some perv looking for company, but still, he had no time now for niceties.

"Please, what disgusting language! I would just like to discuss the matter of your actions a few moments ago. I must say it seemed ever so rude of you to intrude in that manner upon the young boy."

"The fuck's it got to do with you? You a cop or something, because I ain't got time to fuck about, so get lost or get shot."

"Oh my oh my! What is the world coming to these days? Such aggressiveness, such violence! I would like to suggest you return the money you stole from the poor boy and thus, continue your journey free of any reprimand on my behalf."

Dave was shell-shocked. He couldn't work out if the guy was drunk, drugged, ridiculing him or just plain mad. He certainly didn't seem any of the above; he wasn't swaying, slurring, or drooling at the mouth. Therefore, he must be a passer-by who obviously fancied himself as some kind of modern-day superhero. He decided aggression was the best policy and removed the pistol, aiming it straight at the man's chest.

"You fucking with me, or you just wanna die, "cause right now I ain't got time for playing around?"

"Sshh! Young man, young man. You know violence is not the answer. Why don't you remove the implement you are holding, and we can discuss the situation like two rational human beings?" he said, raising his index finger to his mouth as if to add effect.

Dave became more agitated. This was not ordinary behaviour from somebody with a gun aimed at them. His body was screaming for its fix, yet there was something about the situation that held his curiosity. He wanted to know who had the courage to challenge him so blatantly.

"You gonna make me?" he asked defiantly. "'Cause you wouldn't be the first to receive a bullet. In fact, you're starting to really piss me off. In fact, old man, I think I should just shoot you right now and be done with it." He cocked the lever and aimed it at his face, yet before he could even think about firing, the man, with a sudden, unnatural burst of speed, emerged from the shadows and had a hand around his throat. With the other he grabbed the gun from his trembling hand and pointed it back at him.

Mr. Elvid tutted. "You humans really do seem to have an awful time controlling your tempers, don't you? I do believe a lesson in good manners is required," he said.

With a force and speed unrivalled by any known creature on earth, Mr. Elvid spun him around with one hand

and bent him over a garbage bin. With his other hand, he put aside the gun and forced down his trousers. With Dave's glory in full view, Elvid picked up the gun and forced it hard into Dave's rectum, causing an immense scream of pain to erupt from him.

"Now, every time you sit down to perform your rather disgusting toiletry operation, I would be most grateful if you would consider that somewhat derisory attitude of yours and think about the harm you have caused to others. You may find somewhere deep in your soul that there is a good boy just dying to get out. Good day to you, Mr. Dave."

Mr. Elvid patted him gently on the back, shook his head in disapproval and walked away. Even after he had reached the corner at the far end of the street, Dave's screams could still be heard.

***

Mr. Elvid sat in the corner of the coffee shop sipping at his hot tea. He was tired. Even in his privileged position, age held no bias. The years still affected him in the same manner as those that he sought to re-conduct. And his work appeared to be increasing rather than the opposite. Everywhere he went, looked, and listened, the same derogatory attitude and behaviour was present in those around him. He often considered retiring to warmer climates and leaving the work for his adepts, but their methods were often less graceful than his, and subsequently, on many occasions they had been caught and trapped by those that pursued them.

He leaned back in the chair and put his hands behind his head, revelling in the cosiness and warmth. Not too long ago—although to humanity it would appear an eternity—he had been the one to inflict pain and fear, as had been decreed by the Rules. However, the events of the last few centuries had left him somewhat perturbed and, if he had to admit, almost irrelevant in the new age. The humans did not need unworldly entities anymore to carry out their acts of death and destruction. They were more than capable of doing it on their own without his help, he had come to realize. Who needs demons when it seemed that almost every human being on the planet has their own private one to do their work for him? And far more potent and resilient than he could ever strive to be. Yet, a job was a job and until he could dissuade his Mentor above to release him from his duties, he was bound by Him to continue.

***

John Perkins closed the newspaper and felt his adrenaline begin to rise. His theory had been proven right. The person he was looking for was back after so long and was apparently circling the outer suburbs of Manchester. The bus driver had been savagely attacked at the north, in Ramsbottom, near to St. Andrews Church, by what witnesses described as a tall, thin man with a highly snobby English accent who had disappeared before anyone could even attempt to stop him. Then, two days later, a known criminal had also been found in the same area, in what had been described as bizarre circumstances; 'violated' was the term the press had used, but through his contacts at the police department, John had been given the complete story, and the descriptions matched. And they had told him an amusing anecdote; while in hospital, the victim—Dave Winters—had stated that he wished to become a member of the church and seek penance for his crimes.

Five other horrific attacks had taken place in Chadderton, in the town of Oldham, a few miles or so to the east. Logic told him that he would now probably be heading towards one of the towns to the south in Stockport. This was his usual routine, he knew. He picks a large town or city and would circle the area choosing a handful of victims and then moving on before the police could catch him.

John folded the newspaper and finished his coffee. He would have to move fast. The last time he had come close was a year ago, and had actually seen him in action—but the man was quick, abnormally so, and here no normal weaponry would suffice to finish the job he desperately wanted to resolve.

He knew that the creature he was looking for would be hiding or resting during the daylight hours. Experience told him they all, no matter in which guise, still relished the commodity and safety of the dark, so he allowed himself a few moments to ponder over his plan of action before heading into southern Manchester. There, he would contact those that kept him informed of any particularly outrageous attacks, and begin the search that he hoped would bring a final outcome to his thirty-year mission.

***

Dellboy dragged the girl down the dark alley that led off the main drag; a refuge from prying eyes and stalking cops who regularly patrolled the prostitute's zone. The swirling waters of the River Mersey that flowed beneath it provided a welcome distraction to any noise that may hinder certain activities.

He threw her against the wall and produced the switchblade he always carried, both for protection and as an implement of threat.

"So where's the rest of the fucking money, bitch?"

he spat at her. The girl, Sharon, squirmed against the force of his hand at her throat and the knife that was teasingly close to her cheek.

"I ain't got no more money, Dell. I gave you it all," she blurted. "I promise!"

"Fucking liar! I saw you get in the car with your regular. What are you telling me, you work for free now or what?"

"He just wanted to talk. He gave me ten quid and left, I swear!" she insisted. She knew from past experience that trying to trick him and keep back some of her earnings for herself could cause serious trouble if he found out; that knife was not just for show.

"What have I told you before about stealing my cash, bitch? You think I'm fucking stupid or what?" he asked. Dellboy knew about the few quid they often tried to keep back; five here, on a good night, maybe ten. If you didn't keep a good reign on them, they'd keep the fucking lot. And then before you knew it, they were trying to leave the city and become freelance.

He pressed the knife harder against her cheek provoking a thin gash.

"I want the money now, or the only business you'll have will be from the fucking blind," he threatened.

"Oh dear, well what have we got here?" said a voice from behind.

Dellboy spun around, in the process unwittingly slicing Sharon's cheek. She screamed and slid to the floor, clutching her bloodied face.

"Who the fuck are you?" he asked.

"Oh you poor girl," he replied, ignoring the question. He produced a handkerchief and held it out to her. Dellboy swatted his arm away and held up the knife. "I said, who the fuck are you? This ain't your business, so get out of here."

"Young man, I do believe you have caused considerable

harm to the young lady here. I think it would be most appropriate if you apologised," he said.

"The fuck you talking about?" Dellboy took a step towards him, the knife at throat level. "If you don't fuck off right now, you'll get the same."

The man didn't even flinch, which began to make Dellboy nervous.

"I think it would be in your best interest to remove that knife from my face or I may be forced to cut out your tongue with it," he replied.

"Yeah, go on, kill the bastard!" Sharon shouted. With his tension levels at maximum, Dellboy launched at Elvid, but before he could even bring the knife down, Elvid grabbed his arm and twisted it, the knife falling to the floor and a loud crack echoed down the alley as his arm broke. Dellboy screamed at the sudden pain, but again, before his screams could alert any passers-by, Elvid picked up the knife and forced it into his open mouth. Dellboy's screams were cut off and became liquid garbles as his tongue fell to the floor.

Elvin knelt down, stepping onto the slain tongue and lifted up Dellboy's bloodied face.

"Now, every time you clean your teeth, assuming that you do of course, I would like you to reflect on this little to-do that we have just had. Maybe you should consider a career less, umm, conflictive, shall we say."

Dellboy rolled around the floor clutching at his face, oblivious to the advice offered by Elvid. Later, in hospital, he would indeed reflect on his choice of employment, but not because of the damage he had suffered, but because Elvid's face and words would reverberate in his head every time he considered retaliation. The phrase "Good Samaritan" would resonate inside him like a broken record.

Elvid approached Sharon as she stared disbelievingly

up at him. This seemingly harmless old man had just single-handedly wrought justice a thousand others much bigger and stronger had failed to achieve. She was in awe.

As he held out the handkerchief once again, a series of words brought him to a stop. He fell back against the floor as though he had just been kicked. His head swam and throbbed with pain as the words tore apart his senses. No sound came from his lips, but the whites of his eyes and the terrible grimace on his face told multitude of truths.

Holding his hands to his ears, he looked up to see a man standing before him with what appeared to be a scroll in his hands. He was chanting words over and over while he looked directly at him.

Finally, he stopped.

"So, at last I've found you. It's taken a long time, but I knew I'd catch up with you at some point. My only concern was that I might die of old-age before you do, but then you don't die do you?"

Still reeling from the verbal attack, Mr. Elvid looked up at the person before him. Even though the verse the man had spoken had caused him great pain, he didn't consider this man to be of any considerable threat. He could have killed him right there and then if he so desired, but he was curious as to the identity and motives of his presence.

"May I be so bold as to enquire your name, young man?" he asked.

"My name is Paul Jenkins. I'm a demonologist, and I do believe that I have the Father of all demons right before me. Am I not right?"

"Well, actually, that's not quite true. There is another who boasts such a title, one who a long time ago was actually a friend of mine, until we had a mild discussion and He sent me to, umm, warmer climates, shall we say. And right now He has a lot more followers than I."

"Ah, the Prince of Lies, Lord of Deceit."

"Well, I suppose at one point I had many names, and they may have been two of them, but I fear young friend, that you may be mildly mistaken in your belief of what I am and do."

"I know what you do and what you've been doing for many centuries. I have followed your journey for many years, studied the reports of your depravity in journals and newspapers. Only one could possibly act out these atrocities. And fortunately, I have in my possession the one weapon that can send you back to your dank, decrepit land once and for all."

John lifted up the scroll; a relic he had obtained in Jerusalem many years previous and written in Aramaic. It was considered to be a rite for expulsing demons from the Holy Land, written by one of Jesus' followers themselves. He had used his experience and contacts to obtain a copy of the scroll and, by using methods Elvid might have been proud of, procured a translated version for himself.

"Well, I must congratulate you on your perseverance, dear John, but I think you have misunderstood my intentions. Of all the names I possess, perhaps you could now, in fact call me the 'Good Samaritan'. Quite ironic when you think about it."

"Oh really? You consider defiling and torturing people Christian behaviour, Lord of Flies?"

"Actually, that is the last resort. And in many cases, my actions have had a 'therapeutic' affect, you might say. Why don't you sit with me here and I will tell you a story? You think I am here of free will? Believe me, with the hate and evil that runs through your world, in mine it is positively heavenly. I would be the first to rejoice if given the opportunity to return home."

John stared at Elvid for a few seconds, unsure whether he was being tricked and should banish him right now, or whether to listen to what he had to say. He certainly seemed harmless enough there on the floor, but he knew him for what he was and that appearances, more often than not, were deceiving. He decided to listen but kept a distance.

"Okay, I'm listening," he said.

"Jolly good." Elvid positively beamed at the chance to explain his motives. He had been roaming Earth for centuries carrying out his obligations and here he had a chance to perhaps redeem himself and be concerted a release from his sentence.

"Do you not wonder why towards the end of the twentieth century, my 'employees' began to reduce their visits to your world? Only sporadic appearances in cases of extreme necessity?"

"Well, certainly accounts of possession have tailed off these last fifty years or so, but that's because new developments in medicine and science were able to distinguish between real possession and illness of the mind, but even so, there are still reports throughout the world," he said.

"Yes, that is true. I do after all have to train new adepts, but that is not the real reason, my friend."

"I am not your friend," replied John. He almost had to pinch himself to confirm that he wasn't dreaming, yet was actually having an apparently civilized conversation with the master of dark himself.

Elvid ignored the comment. "The reason that my Legion has moved to…alternative areas of work, shall we say, is that I fear we have become almost out-dated, unnecessary. What could I possibly order my workers to do that was worse or more terrifying that what you are already doing yourselves. Every day I read the newspapers and I see a… demon, for want of a better word, is doing my work for me. The demons you all carry within you consider it necessary and amusing to drop bombs upon hundreds of innocents, youngsters find it interesting to walk into school and shoot their fellow companions and teachers. How can I compete with that?"

"That's not because they are possessed. It's because they are mentally ill or power-hungry and vengeful. They kill others for their own benefit or belief regardless of who may get in their way."

"Well, is that not the same thing then? When I claimed souls for my own benefits, do you think I cared about others? When Behemoth orders a soul to be taken for his collection, is he doing no worse than your Lieutenants and Sergeants? Those who blatantly shoot another to preserve their own life under the premise of 'I was receiving orders'?"

"There are a lot of evil people out there with no understanding of empathy or guilt. They kill for their own personal gain," said John. He was beginning to feel uncomfortable. He had an idea where this was going and, he thought, his arguments were rapidly becoming futile.

"And ever more and more, young man. Ever more and more. Which brings me to my real purpose here. Despite what you may believe, I am not here of my free will. I would love to leave this ghastly land right now, but I have been obliged to carry out a job, so that some-day I may be allowed to return to my rightful home with my Brother."

"What job, and who is your brother?"

"Oh, I think you know very well who He is. He is the one that your ridiculous race prays to everyday in naïve hope, and usually while at the same time they are ordering another attack on some helpless country. As to my mission, let's say that once upon a time, your God, tired of the constant bickering and fighting, ordered a clean start by washing away all life and starting again. Several thousand years later, unfortunately it has gotten worse and He has become fatigued with it all, so He and I made a deal. If I could release the demon that many carry inside and convert them to His ways, He would allow me to come home, and all my workers and co-leaders would be given eternal peace. Hell would be closed for refurbishing, you might say."

Elvid smiled at the connotation. He was feeling rather pleased with himself. John stared at him, unsure what to say or think. The whole theory of this thing's story seemed preposterous, and yet, was there not some logic towards it?

He wasn't a strong believer in God, at least not as a physical entity, yet many of the things he had seen during his time as demonologist suggested a power other than those found on Earth. And of course, if one believes in God, one had to believe in the Devil as well. And apparently, here he was right before him.

"So why do you have to perform such terrible acts to convince them? Why not just show them yourself as you really are? Surely that would be convincing enough?"

"My dear friend, were I to do that, the sheer shock would be too much. They would probably die from it or remain incapacitated forever, and like that no gain could be achieved. And remember I have never actually killed anyone while trying to 'convert'. Just a little teaser to give them something to think about."

"So the devil himself has become a Good Samaritan?"

"Exactly, just as I said earlier! Yes, I suppose that is what it has come to. All very sad, don't you think? Who would have thought? Now why you don't put away that nasty piece of paper, and perhaps you could join me? Become one of my disciples as it were."

John looked once more at the scroll in his hands. His shoulders drooped and he sighed. He felt depleted. Years of dedication, of investigation. Trying in his own way, to be a Good Samaritan and rid the world of the evils that plagued the land. Evils that many considered a hoax or invention of those seeking to earn riches through the naivety of others.

And the man before him—the Master of Lies—had been telling the truth in that he had never actually killed any of his victims. Would the devil not want the souls of those he tormented? If not, then to what purpose his actions? Had he not actually saved the young girl right now from a more sinister fate?

And was it not true all he had said also? Exactly who were the real demons? Those that he sought to destroy through exorcism or those that strolled through life daily, happily causing destructions to thousands without a whim or pity?

Paul stared at the scroll in his hands, and then at the thing before him.

"Fuck it," he said, tore the scroll in half, threw it to the floor and walked away.

Sharon, who had been listening to the entire conversation, rose to her feet and slowly began to edge away from Elvid.

"Don't look at me like that. I've already decided. I'm going to join the nunnery," she said and headed off in the opposite direction.

Elvid stood up, brushed the dust from his trousers, and smiled.

"Still so much to do, so much to do," he said to himself and wandered out back into the street to search among the busy, thriving streets for a new convert.

# Formaldehyde
## Munib Haroon

The stench of formaldehyde, though foul, is more bearable than the noisome, nauseating stink it represses and which would seep out in its absence from an anatomy dissecting room. And though the unwelcome presence of this preservative clings to your clothes, nestles beneath your nails, and lingers on your lips—when you eat your food or when you kiss your lover—as a medical student you quickly become accustomed to its presence, learn to ignore it. Ignorance is bliss—as they say—however, ignorance is seldom wise.

I, for one, cannot habituate to the smell. Perhaps, if I had a lifetime—and ordinary circumstances—to get used to it, maybe it would be a different matter and I would just be like every other doctor who passes through, forgetting their brief sojourn in such a charnel house. But I do not have a lifetime. I do not have years, months, weeks or even days.

All I have is now—a now that consists of minutes, if not seconds. And maybe, just maybe, there is enough time to tell my story…

It began with the three of us clustered around a metal dissecting table: Bob, Doug and myself. We wore identical white lab coats on our backs and identical expressions on our faces—bravado mixed with disgust—but otherwise we were very different in appearance. Bob was tall and as lean as a cadaver—trust me, I've seen cadavers—whilst beside him, Doug was like a gingerbread man scraped together from Bob's leftovers and left baking too long. I suppose, if we continue the fairy tale theme, I was like Goldilocks: fair and neither tall like Bob, nor squat like Doug—something in between, maybe just right.

We were closeted away—over a hundred and fifty of us—in the dissecting room of the Leeds Medical School building—that granite-grey, poke-in-the-eye of West Yorkshire's collective face. And though the room was cool, I could feel the sweat slicking my brow and staining the t-shirt beneath my lab coat. My mouth felt like it was stuffed with cotton wool. I sneaked a glance at the other two. Seemed we were all avoiding eye contact. I suppose it wasn't a surprise; after all, it was our first day among the dead.

Behind us there was a loud clatter as a kidney dish fell to the hard floor. I turned to see a girl—mousy hair, and waxy, white facial features—fainting and falling to the floor.

I winced and watched her anatomy partners and a few others crowd around her.

"Is there a doctor in the house?" someone joked.

One idiot—gallant, but an idiot nevertheless—tried to help her sit up, except she kept flopping back like a rag dog; his persistence led to her twitching and jerking.

Suddenly Professor Keating, Head of Anatomy, was beside the mass of perturbed medical students.

"Leave her on the floor, you morons, let gravity do its job, and get on and do yours."

Professor Keating was one of those round-shouldered, *rugger-bugger* types who seemed like a tough bastard and spoke like a tough bastard, but we knew he was talking sense.

Someone cradled the girl's head with their hands, and after a moment we could see signs of blood returning to her face—turning it rosy red like the dawn—and with it came the first flickers of consciousness. Her eyes opened, and— startled and embarrassed—she looked around in panic.

I glanced away, not wanting to make her feel worse, and saw the other two doing the same.

My gaze drifted past white coats and frowns towards the back of the room where dog-eared embryology posters, showing the different stages of foetal life, hung from the walls; glass jars filled with deformed, cancerous kidneys and cirrhotic livers sat cheek by jowl upon dark, dusty shelves.

After a moment my eyes were drawn back to the table: opaque, under plastic sheeting was the still form of a cadaver.

"There's a dead, bad smell coming from underneath that sheet isn't there?" joked Bob.

I smiled at the gallows humour. It was the only way to get through it, but Bob didn't know his limits. He started it.

By then, we'd only known each other a week. Medical school commenced the first week of October and we'd found ourselves drawn around a lab table because our surnames all began with H. That's why we also ended up together in anatomy with the same cadaver. But we came from very different backgrounds: Bob went to Oakham, a posh school in Leicestershire, where the annual fees were probably more than my mum's salary; Doug was a common comprehensive boy like me, but his parents were actors on a BBC soap. I was Leeds born and bred, the first boy in the family to go to University. I was hungry to succeed, but destiny left me sharing a body with Bob and Doug.

Frank's body.

Now, cadavers don't turn up with a name on a toe-tag, and that impersonal aspect works well for many medical students. For others, it seems easier to remember that a cadaver was once a living, breathing person, someone who has performed one last great service to humanity by donating their body to science. If you feel like that, it's almost comforting to refer to the body as *Bill* or *Jess*, which is how some cadavers end up with names.

Personally, I belonged to the former, impersonal camp; but it was Bob who came up with the idea for a name.

Wait...I'm getting ahead of myself. I feel pressed for time, and my head is hurting. Before we'd named 'Frank', somebody helped the fallen medical student outside. She didn't return that day— didn't, in fact, return at all; maybe she was the lucky one.

Then, Keating told everyone to gather 'round, and we did. We clustered tightly around him—asteroids around a planet—as he lectured about our *sacred duty towards those who had bequeathed their bodies to science* and how we would be for the *high jump* if we were disrespectful in any way to our *dead teachers*.

We returned to our tables and pulled back the thick plastic sheets...

I tried not to flinch or betray any revulsion. I held my breath and sucked in my stomach at the sight and smell—at what felt like a full-frontal assault on my senses. I'm not sure what came first: the hammer-like blow of formaldehyde that flooded my brain—leaving me reeling and dizzy—or the visceral vision of a once-living thing, which, now, shorn of soul, seemed to mock its vestigial humanity with a fixed rictus grin. Its skin was like leather left outside to soak in the rain.

A dull thumping caught my attention—I looked around and listened carefully, only to realise it was the throbbing of my heart, the activation of my sympathetic nervous system. But I should have recognised it for what it was: a drum beat, a signal, a warning.

I glanced up at Doug and Bob. Doug was pallid and still, but Bob was smiling. He turned to me and winked.

"He looks like my uncle Frank," he said.

"Maybe he is your uncle," said Doug.

"Nah. The greedy bugger would never lend anything to anyone, let alone his body."

I stayed silent, staring down at the body, wondering what had made it smile in its final moments, wondering how many others died with such an expression on their faces.

"Let's call him Frank," said Bob, cheerily: "In honour of my late uncle."

I gazed at Frank. Let my eyes rove over the pale, papier-mâché skin, along the shoulder; down the forearm—on the right hand was a small tattoo. I leaned in to look closer—it was clearly a word, but the letters were foreign, strange, in a language I did not recognise—though, I now know their import and that they were written in Cyrillic. I wish I'd known their meaning then.

I settled into medical life. The first weeks passed in a blur of lectures: anatomy, biochemistry, psychology and physiology. In the evenings I stayed until late, befriending the journals and textbooks in the medical library, often not leaving until nine when the medical school was locked. Sometimes, instead of the well-lit warmth of the library, I would retire to the lab and sit at my bench, a reading light my only illumination; the rest of the surroundings sat in the shadows. It was here, one night, as I pored over Grey's Anatomy, trying to memorise the relationship of the brachial plexus to the surrounding tissues—and wondering why the hell we had to go through this, when only a hand surgeon would need to know this much information in this much depth—that I decided the only way I would get a proper feel for things would be to go back up to the dissecting room and examine some of the prosections. (Prosections were dissections, done by trainee surgeons attached to the medical school, on specific cadavers to illustrate certain anatomical areas.)

I opened my locker, donned a fresh white lab coat and left the lab. It was eight in the evening and a hush pervaded the school. Most members of staff, including the cleaners, had long since departed. Security staff would be skulking around somewhere, waiting to lock up, but there was so sign of anyone. As I headed upstairs, the echo of footsteps broke the silence of the stairwell like a series of thrown stones smiting the stillness of a lake's surface.

Even if I had gotten lost, I would have known I was on the right level from the smell. As soon as I pushed open the thick fire doors to step inside the main corridor, which coiled around the anatomy department, I was assaulted by the smell of formaldehyde. It was like it had been hanging there, all evening, waiting for my arrival. I wrinkled my nose and headed to the dissection room.

The cadavers were reposed on their metal beds, behind two sets of thick, double doors which you had to heave open to get inside. You could come and go pretty much as you pleased while the school was open—provided, a class wasn't taking place—but the *open-all-hours* service wasn't taken up by many, at least not until the last few weeks before exams, when everyone would flock together like migratory birds arriving for a spell of Winter-sun.

I came expecting to be alone with my 'dead-teacher' and the rest of his 'faculty.'"'But at the back of the room, nestled around Frank, beyond the dozens of tables housing their silent residents, stood two bowed and bent figures: Bob and Doug.

Though their backs were turned to me, I recognised them by their builds. Besides, who else but them would be up at this time, bent over Frank? I must say, however, I was surprised: at eight o'clock on a Friday evening, shouldn't they be doing a pub-crawl around Leeds or something?

Perhaps they had decided late on in the day to put in some extra hours of study. I couldn't help feeling a little hurt at the thought that, despite being their lab partner, they hadn't felt to include me in this arrangement of theirs.

I decided to surprise them. It would serve them right.

I stalked up quietly on tiptoes.

"And what do think you're doing here?"

Doug gasped, stepped back suddenly from Bob's side, and turned towards me, his eyes bulging like headlights. But Bob stood stone still, not moving even when Doug finally drew breath and spoke.

"Jesus! You scared us!" said Doug

"Sorry." I stepped around to see what they had been doing.

I froze at the sight before me.

Bob stood with a saw in hand, the blade sunk into Frank's flesh, performing what was clearly an unorthodox dissecting manoeuvre. The blade sat still now, three quarters of the way through slicing off the hand at the wrist.

A loose ribbon of skin curled across the forearm like a tiny worm.

"What are you doing?" I breathed.

Bob stared at me, held my gaze without speaking, and then turned to Doug.

"Go on…tell him," said Doug.

"Look," said Bob, "it's just a bit of harmless fun. We had a bit of a dare. That we could borrow a hand and take it out with us to the pub. Take some pictures as proof. Give Frank a proper send-off and then return him before anyone found out he was missing."

This was madness. This was grounds for expulsion from medical school.

I faced a dilemma. Well, it would only be a dilemma if they made good on the dare. I had to convince them it was a bad idea.

"If someone finds out, you'll never graduate."

Bob looked at me, a wry smile upon his lips.

"No one but the three of us knows."

"Yes…but…"

"You won't say anything." It wasn't a question.

"No?" I said.

"No," said Bob. "And do you know why?"

"I don't. Why don't you tell me, Einstein?"

"You're not the snitching sort. And besides, we're all in this together now. You're here watching me saw off Frank's hand, and if you tittle-tattle, I can easily implicate you."

"I could go and find security now…"

"Come on," cut in Doug, spinning a ring nervously on his middle finger. "You're not going to do that. Honestly, no one else needs to know. No one's going to get hurt. It's just a bit of fun. To help relieve the pressure."

When Bob saw the doubt on my face, he piped up.

"Doug's right. And besides, we're not the first to pull one of these pranks. You've heard the stories; medical students are always pulling crap like this. Look, if you're so worried about Frank's hand, come along with us for the evening; make sure we don't get up to any mischief. Be the angel on my shoulder."

I nodded.

I should have put a stop to it there and then.

I didn't.

I stood on guard, watching Bob sweat, watching him saw off Frank's hand. As he sliced through the last bit of sinew and skin, I watched the hand land with a soft thunk on the table. Then, Bob pulled out a plastic Morrison's shopping bag from the pocket of his lab coat and placed the hand inside it. The two of them covered up Frank, and we all left quietly and quickly; thieves in the night.

We went and sat in the Faversham. Filled with cigarette smoke and the stale smell of beer, it heaved with the sounds of raucous laughter, chatter, and football commentary from an overhead television. The place was filled with medical students and other life-science undergraduates.

Our tiny cabal of three—plus a hand—found a table where we weren't going to be observed from all sides. Doug and I sat down together while Bob went to buy us all a round.

He came back with three bottles and a satisfied look. When he sat, I leaned over. "Have you still got it?"

He patted his parka and smiled. "Relax. Safe as houses, right here."

"And you're just going to keep it there?" My voice was incredulous; if the plan was to walk around with a dead-man's hand in your pocket, then I didn't see the point.

"No. I'm just getting used to having it around," Bob said. "Besides we're only here to have a drink, there's too many people who'd recognise us here."

His response both worried and reassured me. On the one hand, there was more to this after all, but I felt better knowing he was concerned about getting caught; perhaps this would modulate his behaviour.

We sat drinking; our first round turned into our second, then third. I was only having orange juice and Bob appeared to handle his liquor well, but Doug seemed to be tolerating it poorly and grew progressively louder as the evening progressed.

"Come on, get it out," he said, making nearby heads turn. "Let's see it, pull it out!"

"Doug, be quiet!" I said. I placed my hand on his shoulder but he shrugged it off.

"It's okay, I'm only joking, I'm not pissed," he insisted.

Bob stared at Doug, silently admonishing him with a shake of the head, then draining the dregs of his drink, he stood up.

"Come on, let's go."

We stalked off into Leeds city centre, a good ten minutes away. The other two were engaged in some sort of animated discussion, whilst I kept my thoughts to myself. I wasn't particularly interested in what they were talking about; I had come along just to see that they didn't get up to too much mischief with the hand.

We passed the Town Hall. Suddenly, Bob shot off ahead and dashed up the broad steps to the sculpted stone lions sitting on either side of the grand entrance. He turned to look down at us, where we'd stopped, staring up at him.

"Right, boys, let's take a picture here!" Bob said. "Me, Aslan, Aslan's twin and the hand!"

He put his hand in his coat pocket and pulled out the Morrison's bag. He fumbled inside and drew out the hand by its fingertips.

I stood back and watched as Doug guffawed and pulled out a tiny instant camera from his pocket; he took a couple of shots in quick succession. Then Bob put the hand back in the bag and pointed towards town.

As we set off again, I sidled up to Bob. "Is this what you're going to do all night long? Take a series of pictures featuring our friend in your pocket?"

Bob smiled. "Yes, it's like a memento of our time in anatomy. In years to come we'll look back and have a good laugh."

I shook my head. It was a memento to stupidity. But at least—or so I supposed at the time—it was harmless.

We played the same stupid game all evening. We'd traipse into a pub, find ourselves a quiet spot, and then Bob would surreptitiously take out the hand and Doug would snap him a photo. Then, we'd do it all again. Mostly, Bob just held the hand up before him, but a couple of times—I think after the beer had begun to take hold—he would pose with the hand on his shoulder or grip it in a handshake. It was during these last few pictures that I got a good look at the tattoo seared into the skin. I memorised its appearance and made a mental note to ask my girlfriend about it later the following day.

Eventually, we hobbled out of the last pub to wander around for several minutes, trying to hail a cab. Once we managed to flag one down, we all piled into the back and told the driver to take us to Chapel Allerton—a quiet suburb in North Leeds—where I still lived with my parents.

As we drew to a halt outside my house, I turned to Bob.

"Are you going to be okay getting back safely?"

"Yes, mother," Doug sniggered.

Bob looked at me through tired, swollen eyes; he patted my shoulder and nodded wearily. I dug in my pockets for my wallet—my share of the bill—but Bob gestured that it wasn't necessary; and so, in the end, we parted on good terms.

For that, at least, I'm glad.

I stepped out of the car and felt the first blast of a cruel wind smite my face. Swaying a little, I hurried to the front door and paused just long enough to see the taxi's brake lights flitting—once, twice—before merging with the darkness. I went inside and tried to forget about the evening.

The next day my parents interrogated me over the breakfast table about my late evening out. All that was missing from their Gestapo act was the leather jacket and spotlight. This hastened my departure from home, and so I was not around to take a series of increasingly fraught phone calls from Doug. It was late evening before I became aware that something was amiss.

I headed over to see my girlfriend, Caroline. She was up from Trinity College, Cambridge—she was studying Russian and French—and we spent the afternoon cozied up on her sofa watching television. My urge to confess, to tell her everything about last night, warred with my lingering sense of guilt that I hadn't tried harder to prevent the antics, no matter how much I insisted to myself that I hadn't played a hand in the removal of a body part from the medical school.

Eventually, sensing that something was amiss, Caroline crawled onto my lap, flicked her dark hair behind a shoulder, and, fixing me with her dark brown eyes, said, "I can tell something's not right. Is this about us? You…you don't want to break up with me, do you?"

I laughed, laughed out loud; she looked at me as if I was going mad, and I clasped hold of her arms and kissed her.

"No, no I don't want to break up with you. Not at all. I think it's just the work that's getting to me, that's all."

"I'm so relieved!" She cried, then checked herself.

"Oh, but I don't mean I'm relieved about work getting to you, of course….do you want to talk about it?"

"No." I said. "But there is something you could maybe help me with. Do you have some paper and a pen?"

She disappeared for a moment, returned with a small notebook and pencil, and sat down next to me. She watched as I wrote out, from memory, the letters on Frank's tattoo. I held out the notebook to her.

"Do you know what this means?"

She peered at it for a second before shaking her head. "Where did you see this?"

"On a tattoo."

"A tattoo? Whose? Where?"

"On a cadaver named Frank."

"A cadaver? Do they have names?"

I interrupted the train of conversation before it went any further off the rails.

"Do you recognise the language?"

She peered at me with a frown and spoke. "The letters look Cyrillic, but I don't understand what the word means. I can ask around if you'd like."

"If you could," I nodded. "I'm curious."

We spent all day together, and when I finally left, all thoughts of the previous night had been firmly put to bed. However, this idyllic state of mind did not last long, because as soon as I stepped through the front door, at home, I found my mother waiting for me.

"Someone named Doug has called five times," she said.

"Oh," was all I could think of to respond.

"He asked that you call him back as soon as you got home."

I felt a faint flutter of panic, like a butterfly banging against my rib cage, as if it were a windowpane.

"Did he mention what it was about?" I tried to keep my voice casual.

"No. But he said it was urgent."

When Doug answered the phone, his voice was breathless, agitated.

"Doug, Doug, calm down, calm down. What's going on?"

"We lost it!" he said. "I don't know where, but it's lost. We're in so much shit!"

*We're?* I thought.

"Slow down and tell me what's lost," I said this, even though I knew. I knew what he was on about.

"The hand! The bloody hand! I don't know how we lost it, or where, but we left the taxi at my flat, and Bob checked his pockets just before he left my place to get into his car—and it wasn't there. IT WASN'T THERE! Bob called up the cab company to tell them we had lost something valuable but when I rang this morning they had nothing to report. We might have dropped it anywhere… It could be anywhere…"

"Okay, let's just stay calm," I said to him, whilst trying to keep myself in-check. "Have you called Bob? What did he say?"

"I don't know," said Doug. "He hasn't answered his phone all day."

We talked for a few minutes more, most of which consisted of me trying to calm Doug. After I hung up, I was consumed with thoughts of what was going to happen first thing on Monday morning.

I would never have guessed.

The phone rang just after midnight. I'm a light sleeper and after the first few rings I was on my feet, ambling towards my bedroom door. I wanted to get there before my parents; nobody would be calling for them at this time of night, unless it was bad news, in which case I still wanted to get there before them.

"Hello?" I said, picking the receiver.

"It's Doug, can I speak to—oh it's you! The police were just here!"

"The police?"

"Yes. Something happened… Jesus, I don't know why he did it! I really don't…Jesus!"

I couldn't understand what he was talking about and tried to get him to make some sense.

"Doug! Doug! Shut the hell up, will you? Quieten down, so I can hear myself think!" I was trying to keep my voice down and failing, and soon I heard footsteps above me, then my mother's voice on the landing.

"You're being very loud, dear."

"Sorry," I said. "I'll keep it down."

I waited until she had gone back to her room. "Doug, you're not making any sense. What's happened? Why are the police involved? What's going on?"

There was a pause, and I was going to ask if he was still there, but then his voice came out, accompanied by a burst of sobs.

"It's B-B-Bob! He jumped—or fell—off his balcony this evening! He's dead!"

"Jesus Christ! Are you sure?"

"Yes, of course I'm fucking sure. I just had the police round here. My calls showed up on his answering machine—they traced me."

"What did they want to know?"

"What his state of mind was last night. Was he okay… did he have any enemies."

*State of mind? Enemies?* That didn't sound like they were convinced he had fallen. It sounded like they thought he could have jumped… or been pushed.

I felt a wave of nausea building up beneath my ribcage as I listened. My stomach was suddenly a roiling sea of acid and my mouth tasted sharp and bitter. I wanted to stand and chat, but I also wanted to lie down in bed and sink into unconsciousness. I wanted to not wake up, and to not have to worry about what was coming.

"Look…" I said, trying to think on the spot, trying to cloak myself in calm. "There's nothing you can do now. It was probably an accident—so there's probably nothing you could have done then, either."

"No, no," cried Doug. "You didn't see his face when he realised we'd lost the hand. He looked awful. Like he was going to cry. He jumped!"

I took a deep breath. "It's not your fault."

"It *is* my fault," said Doug. "I encouraged him with the dare."

We talked a little longer, until the sobs had subsided, and I was convinced Doug was not going to go and follow Bob over the balcony. But I slept uneasily that night, and in the morning, before dawn, I called Doug. He answered on the first call—as if he had spent the night sitting by the bed awaiting further bad news.

After speaking a while we decided to go and eat breakfast.

"I think I can smell sausages," I said to him, trying to sound jovial.

"I wish I could," he spat. "But all I can smell is the dissecting room. Fucking formaldehyde."

Then, Sunday being my day for a long run, I dressed in shorts and a long top and went out for a ten-mile run. I returned, my head buzzed with endorphins, my legs felt like every sinew had been stretched. I showered and sat down to study some physiology, and before long it was evening. The waves of exhaustion had been creeping over me like a slowly building tide and by the time I realized it, I was submerged. I fell asleep without checking on Doug.

Monday morning ushered in a flurry of bad weather: fierce winds shepherded in huge rain-bearing clouds that sat penned in over Leeds for the rest of the morning.

The long walk from the bus stop left me drenched through by the time I got to the medical school. Still soaked, I had just wandered out of the lift and was turning to enter the lecture theatre when a hand tugged me by the elbow. I turned around expecting to see Doug but instead was greeted by the scowling face of Professor Keating.

"Oh, Professor, hello," I said.

The Professor grimaced before speaking. "Could I have a word with you in private?"

We took the lift up to level nine and stepped inside his cramped office. It was a tight fit with all the office furniture—desk, shelves, coffee table and chairs. A narrow window offered views onto a grey and grim morning.

Hunkered down in a corner seat was a moustachioed man wearing a Mackintosh.

"DS Garside," said the Professor. "This is the student I was telling you about."

*Shit. Shit. Shit. The police are here?* I thought.

I stared down at the man; he regarded me coolly and gestured towards the empty seat close by.

I sat down and gazed at the ceiling, tried to compose myself, gathered my thoughts, told myself: *deny everything, deny everything.*

"It's okay, you're not in trouble," began DS Garside. "I'm just hoping that you can shed some light on what is turning into quite a serious matter..."

"I'll do what I can to help, Sir," I said, trying to sound helpful. I smiled at him.

"Good, excellent. Well, something has gone missing from this floor, and given the nature of it, I don't think it would have just gotten up and walked out of its own accord."

I could tell he was toying with me, trying to rattle me, playing coy, to see if I would somehow let something slip—and then he would have me.

"Oh?" I said. I tried to sound surprised, whilst keeping my words in check. I knew it never did any good to say too much.

"And our missing object seems to be linked to a number of students: Bob Andrews, Douglas Banks and you."

I tried my best at playing dumb. I frowned, knitted my brows together, shrugged, shook my head; I looked from DS Garside to the Professor and back again to Garside.

"If it becomes public knowledge that things can disappear like this, from here, it will damage the reputation of the medical school and its students very severely; no one wants that to happen. It's also a criminal offense. So, you can see why everyone is anxious."

"Yes..."

"Now. We can't speak to your friend Bob Andrews because—"

"I know. I heard."

"Well I'm sure it came as dreadful news. I can tell from your expression that the two of you were close."

I nodded. There seemed little sense in trying to correct him. The mere mention of his death now made my pulse pound. Beads of sweat began forming on my forehead, and my hands were suddenly clammy. I was starting to lose my composure.

"D-do you know how it happened?" I asked, unable to contain myself.

"Hard to know for certain, but the fall looks accidental. Although it seems as if something scared him first… made him run out onto the balcony… he'd knocked over a chair and an ashtray on the way out. But then there was no sign of an intruder. It's odd…"

I stared down at my brogues. Tried to make sense of what he was saying.

*So, it wasn't suicide? But then what scared him? Might drink or drugs have been involved? They'll find out when they do a post-mortem...Post mortem—Jesus! Seems grim that Bob's going to end up dead in the cutting room...like Frank.*

Suddenly an image flashed into my head. The rictus grin of Frank. I shook the thought away.

"Are you okay, lad?" said Keating.

"Yes, I'm fine. I'm just shook-up."

Keating nodded.

"I can see this is a lot to take in," Garside said kindly. "But I'm afraid there's more—would you like a glass of water, first?"

*More?* I thought.

"Last night our men were called out to the student accommodation at Devonshire Hall."

*Devonshire Hall? Isn't that's where Doug lives?* I thought.

"I can tell you—because we've already notified the next of kin—but…well, there isn't an easy way to say this…we found Douglas Bank, dead in his room and—"

*Dead? Doug? Fuck…! How has this happened?* I managed to keep silent, but just barely.

Garside was still talking, but I had tuned out. I was dimly aware of his words, but it was as if I was listening to him from underwater. I focussed at the wall behind Garside's head, at flakes of peeling, white paint; at dirt marks, at a trapped bristle from a paintbrush; the near-emptiness was like a snowfield, and then suddenly out of the snow-scene a face seemed to emerge. That rictus grin—stretching back until the hind teeth showed. Frank! It was Frank's face and he was laughing. Laughing his head off.

"Are you okay there, lad? Lad?"

"What?" I gasped, snapping back to the present and turned to face Garside.

"I said, are you okay? You looked like you were going to be sick."

I couldn't take it any longer. I couldn't keep this to myself. I couldn't play dumb. It was getting to me. It was killing me.

"Look," I stared Garside dead in the eyes and it all came spewing out. "It wasn't my idea. I tried to stop them both… taking the hand… It was such a stupid idea."

Garside flashed a glance in the direction of Keating. Something unspoken seemed to pass between them—I didn't know what—but when Garside then turned to looked at me; it was with a cold expression. The earlier warmth had gone like a doused flame.

"Hand?" He said. "What are you talking about?"

"The hand. The missing hand?"

Garside frowned and assessed me for a moment. Then with a decisive nod, he stood. "Professor, do you think we can wander over to the dissecting rooms? It may help shed some light on what our friend here is talking about."

We made our way down the corridor, the formaldehyde floating in the air, through the double doors and into the dissection room. It was quiet. Keating led the way, and Garside brought up the rear. We passed one table and then the next; row after row of silent witnesses watched our progress.

I knew where we were heading—towards Frank.

I knew what we would find.

I knew I would be unable to keep what had happened to myself.

I knew this was my last day at medical school.

I tried to picture the scene: telling my parents that my

childhood dream—their dream—was over.

Keating came to a halt before Frank's table. I stared up at a wall, steeled myself, watched out of the corner of my eye as Keating gripped some of the sheeting and with the practiced flourish of a stage magician pulled back the sheets.

I gasped.

*Fuck! Fuck! Fuck!* I thought.

All eyes were on me: Garside's, Keating's.

All eyes, except mine. My eyes stared down at the metal table.

Frank's table.

An empty metal table.

Frank's cadaver was gone.

Garside, or maybe Keating—I wasn't sure who—was saying something, but I felt as though I was underwater again. My vision was swimming. I heard a clatter of metal, my hand flailed for the table and knocked over a kidney dish. I hit the ground and remembered no more.

They let me out of hospital after a period of observation. Garside came and visited me, before I left, to tell me that he had no further questions for me at this point in time, but that he would be in touch. He left a box of chocolates by the bedside. I thought my fainting spell had more than convinced him that I knew nothing about the missing body.

I returned home on Tuesday morning to an empty house—my parents had left on Sunday night to go and visit a sick cousin in Dorset, and I had opted to not tell them about my accident. It would wait. Besides, it was small fry compared to the other conversation we'd probably be having once Garside's investigation had concluded. However, it remained to be seen what exactly he would conclude. He had two dead medical students and one missing cadaver. How did those things all fit together?

I ate a hasty breakfast and sat down to try to make sense

of it all. But try as I might, there seemed no rational explanation for the weekend's events.

They were easy to state, just hard to explain. We'd stolen the hand belonging to a cadaver and then lost it. Then, one of us, Bob, had jumped, or fallen, out of a balcony to his death; a second, Douglas, had been found dead in his room—I did not know the exact circumstances of Douglas's death, although one of the last things that Doug said to me kept coming back to haunt me. He'd told me he could smell formaldehyde.

The morning mutated into an afternoon that melded with the evening. I drifted upstairs into the study. I took some aspirin for my still-throbbing, swollen temple and tried to go over the events of the day, but all I could see were the dead bodies of my lab partners; Bob, a mess on the concrete outside his flat, Doug, dead in his flat. Then, once more—except that this time he wasn't dead—I saw the face of Frank—a living, breathing, inanely grinning Frank: he stared at me, opened his mouth and started laughing, laughing, laughing...

The phone went off.

I jerked upright, realising I'd fallen asleep at my desk, and grabbed at the black melamine receiver.

"Hello?"

"Hey, it's Caroline."

"Oh, Caroline!" I exclaimed, relieved to be drawn from the dream; relieved to hear her voice.

"I was just watching the news," she said.

"Ah…"

"Those two dead medical students. Was I imagining it, or were they your lab partners?"

I broke down on the phone. Right there and then. Broke down and sobbed and let out all the fear and shock I had been suppressing. Told her my fears about medical school.

"So, listen," she said after a while. "I'm going to speak to my tutor tomorrow and catch the train up to Leeds."

"No, Caroline, it's okay," I said. "Really, I'll be fine."

"You don't sound fine to me."

"It's just shock, that's all. Honest."

"Sure?" She sounded doubtful.

"Sure." I tried my best to sound certain.

There was a pause on the line.

"Caroline…?"

"I'm here," she said. "I'm just debating with myself whether I should tell you some superstitious mumbo-jumbo I heard today; I don't know if it will make things worse after what has happened."

Superstitious mumbo-jumbo sounded better than all the crap I had had to put up with…

"It's okay. Tell me," I said.

"It's about the wording of that tattoo. I spoke to one of the tutors here and it seems that there's a history behind it all."

"Oh?"

"It's a tribal thing originating on the Steppes. Certain tribes were very twitchy about their children being snatched and murdered, so they branded them in childhood with a tattoo - that very same tattoo on the cadaver. It's a curse. The idea is that if the child was snatched and killed, their spirit would return to wreak revenge. I thought it was rather funny, but then this has happened… I know it's just coincidental… but…"

We talked for a few more minutes and then I hung up and went to bed.

I was tired, my eyes and my head hurt, and I drifted off quickly into an unsound sleep interspersed with images of my lab partners carving away at a cadaver. I drew closer to see what it was they were dissecting; I expected to see the familiar form of Frank.

But it was a different face.

A familiar face.

It wasn't Frank they were dissecting.

It was me.

That's when I woke up.

That image of one's dead self is not something you sleep through.

I was drenched in sweat and my heart was thumping against my rib cage. I took a deep breath and that's when the acrid smell hit me; I could feel it flooding my airways, permeating my airways and sinuses, making my head throb.

Formaldehyde…

I reached out for the bedside lamp, knocking something onto the floor. It landed with a thump. Flailing, my fingers finally found the switch and flicked it on.

An arc of light pushed back against the encroaching darkness. I blinked, looked down at the ground, stared at what had just fallen.

It was a hand—bloodied and severed at the wrist; its fingers splayed, flattened, and twisted—as if something had taken them with great force. But what seized me with terror, what made me choke, was the gleaming band of gold on the middle finger of the hand.

It was Doug's hand.

Here we are.

I hear a floorboard creak and a shadow falls across me. Then, stepping out of the darkness the form emerges. I recognised the face, the spreading rictus grin.

Frank.

He laughs.

I look down. In place of a bloody stump—where we had taken his hand—is Doug's other hand. The hand holds a scalpel.

Now I understand. Frank has come for revenge. He's come to take the hands of those who robbed him of his.

I scream, inhaling formaldehyde with my final breath.

# Foundations
## Lex H Jones

The old turret had stood in the sloping fields of Walliston since before the first house in the village was built. Despite its age, the turret was in good condition and hadn't actually needed any shoring up or reinforcement as such ancient structures often did. The turret stood close to fifteen feet high, with a complete diameter of around seven feet. A man could comfortably lay down in it with his feet touching one of the interior walls, but there'd be little room for much else. Part of the turret had—at some lost point in time—collapsed inwards, with some of the black stones still being present where they'd fallen inside. These loose stones had, rather curiously, become far more weathered than those still part of the circular structure, as though the complete shape somehow kept them more immune from the elements. The local witchcraft and herbalist shop would often tell tourists that this was because there was power in the shape of a circle, before going on to selling them some expensive trinket or other.

Nobody quite knew the purpose of the turret. Whilst its age and mystery did attract a steady stream of tourists, it certainly was nowhere near the status of something like Stonehenge. Archaeologists had taken samples of the stone and studied the history of the area and estimated that it must be at least a thousand years old. The church in the village was four centuries old, and the oldest farmhouse was three centuries. That is to say the oldest farmhouse that was still in possession of its original stonework. Many had been knocked down and rebuilt on the same site in the same appearance, of course.

The half-millennia gap between the oldest structure and the turret had caused much speculation amongst historians, and no less than three twelve separate applications had been put in since the early twentieth century to excavate the area around the turret to see what lay beneath it. All twelve had been rejected by the Walliston village council, on the grounds that an excavation might disturb the foundations and damage the turret. The so-called experts on the matter would argue each subsequent time that the archaeological methods and technology had improved since the time of the last request, and that the structure was quite safe. But, being under no obligation to accept the excavation request, and the matter not being of large enough media interest to attract any pressure from local government, the Walliston village council stuck to their guns and the turret remained untouched. Its origin and purpose remain a mystery.

Connor Randall had worked at the Walliston village shop since leaving school. His father had owned it before him, and his grandfather before that. Before then it had been a candle maker's, but once the Randall family had taken over they diversified the shop to cover a wider clientele, selling everything from newspapers to groceries to souvenirs and gifts. In recent years Connor had even sold such modern amenities as mobile phone top ups and DVD rentals. That had been his wife's idea. Abigail had always been that perfect mix of respecting the old but embracing the modern. Perhaps it was because she was ten years younger than him, only twenty years old when they first met. She was a little closer to the pulse of the modern world, as Connor would put it. She hadn't been born and raised in this village like he had, but she had become a part of it nonetheless. The locals had embraced her when they'd wed and had mourned almost as strongly as Connor himself when Cancer took her—aged only twenty-eight. That was three years ago now, but people still gave Connor that little tilt of the head, with a sympathetic tone asking him how he was coping, whenever they came by the shop.

"I'm fine, thank you. Getting by." Connor would answer with a polite smile. He'd never got tired of the question. It was meant well and he appreciated that the village had never forgotten Abigail. She was still a part of the village, and he believed they felt that too. The conversation opened much the same way on a chilly day in October when the local butcher, Morgan Truscott came by.

"Do you think about getting out there and meeting someone else?" he asked. "You can do it all by computer now, so I'm told."

"I don't think so. Abigail will always be a part of me, and that's enough."

"Long as you're not lonely, lad." Morgan smiled as he folded the newspaper he'd just purchased and slid it under his arm. "Didn't see you at the village meeting this month."

"Bad timing for me, was busy with restocking. Did I miss anything good, or just the usual gripes and moans?"

"Oh, plenty of those," Morgan chuckled. "Couple of other things though. There's been some complaints about water supply. Apparently some folk have been seeing it come through black, intermittently. They think the pipes might have corroded a little, so the water authority is coming out to have a look. And there's some documentary crew coming out here to film too, end of this week."

"Oh really? Countryfile or something like that, is it?" Connor enquired, sipping tea from a big white mug as he stood behind the counter.

"No, I think it's some history thing. They want to look at the turret and talk to people about what they know."

"Well that'll be a fun programme to watch, what with everyone saying that don't have a bloody clue what it was for." Connor laughed.

"I know, but you've seen these programmes. They'll fluff it out with made up nonsense and speculation and get a three-parter out of it."

"Brings a nice bit of money to the village, I suppose." Connor suggested. "You best get some of that good game in. Those TV sorts are fancy, they'll like the expensive stuff."

"You're a sharp businessman, Connor Randall, I'll give you that. Might have to put a few quid extra on the price of the steaks, too." Morgan said with a wink. "Mind how you go, lad."

"Have a good day, Morgan."

Connor watched Morgan go and then walked through the door behind the shop counter and into the small bathroom beyond it. He turned the tap on and let the water run, then stood and watched it. The tap started to judder slightly and then the water turned black and thick. It was at this point that Connor put his hands under it, washing them carefully as though covering them in soap. The black water ran over his hands and soaked in as easily as if they were sponge. He shuddered slightly and looked in the mirror. The veins in his eyes around the pupils were now black instead of red, and the edges of his vision were black and inky as though countless tiny black fingers were reaching towards his eyes.

"I'll come tonight." He said into the mirror.

***

It was after midnight when Connor left his home. It had fallen dark several hours before, but if he left too early there was always the chance of dog-walkers out in the fields. From his house, Connor followed the path that led up the hill into the surrounding fields of green grass and dry stone walls. About halfway up the hill he left the path and hopped over the low wall, then continued the rest of the way through the grass. The turret came in sight before long, illuminated partly by the moonlight reflecting from the damp outer stones. Connor stepped inside the turret via the partially collapsed section and looked up to see the crescent moon directly above him.

"I'm here." He said, then knowingly took a step back.

The earth that filled the inside of the turret rumbled and shifted as though being disturbed from below, and then opened up to reveal the top of a spiral stone staircase. Connor walked immediately down the staircase, seemingly untroubled by the pitch black that surrounded him. The first few times he had come here he had brought a pocket torch along to help him see, but now he no longer needed it. She had seen to that. The dark, the cold, even his old hip injury no longer impeded him.

The staircase was tight and narrow; it would have been impossible for two people to walk down it at the same time. Even a person traversing it alone would have struggled if they'd been a lot larger in frame than Connor was. By now though, he knew the twists and turns, knew when to duck and which steps were angled awkwardly. Before long he had reached the bottom of the staircase and found himself at the base of the turret, which actually went far deeper into the earth than anyone had suspected. Nor was it even close to the entirety of the structure either, for down here, below the earth could be seen more black stone walls, stretching out to form whatever castle or temple had long since been swallowed by the earth. Much of the black stone was now covered in soil and roots, but enough was still visible that it would be quickly discovered if the permission to excavate was ever granted. Connor sometimes hoped that it would. He almost wanted them to know. But she didn't. She liked the quiet. And she came first. She had always come first.

Connor walked along a tunnel lined by a wall of black stone that was still largely visible. The ground felt solid beneath his feet, with several black stones peeking through the dirt. The tunnel soon opened into a much wider expanse, which might have at first been mistaken for a cave save for the black stone pillars and surprisingly well-preserved stone archways around the ceiling. Connor had thought that this must have been some form of church, clearly built long before the Christians arrived on the island of Britannia with their new god. This place was surely built to worship something long forgotten, although now it had a new being to be worshipped and loved. Or perhaps it didn't, Connor sometimes wondered in his darker moments. Perhaps it was the same thing as that had always been here, now hidden in its own church. Except now it wore a different face. But no. No, it was her. It was definitely her.

The ebony walls inside the sunken church writhed and moved like an oil slick being pushed back and forwards by a gentle tide. Connor had been greatly disturbed by this the first time he had come, when the voice had woken him from his sleep and led him here. He might even have screamed, he couldn't quite recall. But now the moving walls relaxed him, like an animal feeling its mother's heartbeat. He actually touched his hand against the nearest wall, spreading his fingers so his palm was as close to it as he could press it. The black pulsed, some of it spreading around the tips of his fingers and thumb in an embracing, numb cold.

"There's people coming, to film the area." Connor spoke to the empty church. "I won't let them discover you. I know you like the quiet. But I need help. Morgan. I trust Morgan. Can you show him the way, so that he helps?"

Whilst no audible answer came, Connor knew that he had been heard. And that his request would be granted. She always listened.

***

Morgan Truscott sighed as he lowered himself into the hot bath water. Carrying the heavy boxes of meat had made his bones ache all the more since arriving at the age of fifty, and the soothing effects of a hot bath were like Heaven to him. His wife had suggested using bath salts to help with the aches, but he didn't like the smell, so he'd always opted for simple soapy water instead. As he rested his head back against the inflatable bath pillow behind him, Morgan frowned at the realisation that the water wasn't quite as warm as it could be. He'd left it too long before getting in. A delicate operation, running the perfect bath.

With a sigh and a groan he sat up and leaned forward to turn on the hot tap. Nothing happened, and then the tap started to shake slightly. Before Morgan could turn it back off, thick black water started to gush from it.

"Jesus!" he exclaimed, clambering out of the bath.

As he grabbed the towel to wipe himself off, Morgan noticed that the black water had splashed over much of his face and chest. He furiously wiped it away, but not quick enough to stop much of it seeping into his skin. A wave of dizziness swept over him, causing Morgan to grab the edge of the bath to keep from falling headfirst to the floor. He took several deep breaths to try and fight off the nausea, then felt something writhing beneath his skin. Moving to the mirror, leaning against the sink now for balance, Morgan wiped the steam from the mirror and studied himself. His face was covered with tiny black fungoid polyps, moving this way and that like tree branches in a breeze. He yelled out and fell back, his feet slipping on the bath mat so that he ended up falling into a seated position on the toilet lid behind him.

"Have you got the water too hot again, pet?" Mrs Truscott called from downstairs.

Morgan didn't answer, but cautiously approached the mirror once again. He was afraid to look this time, but knew that he must. He breathed a massive sigh of relief when he saw that the polyps had now gone. His breathing and heart rate slowed, and he smiled at himself in the mirror. Why had he been so scared a moment ago? There was nothing wrong. Nothing to be scared of. Nothing at all.

Climbing back into the bath, Morgan closed his eyes and relaxed. His body no longer ached, not even slightly. He felt better than he had in years. As his mind let him drift into a dozing state, he dreamt of a beautiful woman caressing his face and welcoming him to her family. She was pale, slender but not skinny, and with black hair that passed her shoulders. Morgan thought he recognised her, but in his dreamlike state he couldn't place it at first. Then his memory caught up, and he smiled as he lay in the bath, speaking softly to the empty room with his eyes still closed:

"Hello Abigail."

***

"Oh this is perfect." Libby Clarke announced as she climbed out of the van and admired the surrounding fields. "It feels old. Doesn't it feel old?"

"Cold? Yeah, it's very cold. Thankfully carrying all this heavy shit should help with that." Nathan Wickes replied, carefully exiting the van with a camera in one hand, a metal box full of cables in the other, and a boom mic folded and tucked under his arm.

"You know we couldn't get the network to agree to send a full crew for this, so it's just you and me. And when this pays off and becomes the next Life on Earth, or Time Team…."

"I'll still be carrying all your shit."

"We'll get a newer camera. A smaller one. Is that better?" Libby suggested.

"There's a shop over there," Nathan pointed with his forehead. "Let's go there first and get supplies before we check in at the B+B. Might have hot drinks too."

The bell above the door rang as Libby and Nathan entered, looking around them in awe at the time-locked little store.

"It's like Open All Hours!" Libby exclaimed gleefully.

"They got DVDs, though." Nathan replied, picking

up a film and reading the back.

"Hello there." Connor announced himself as he walked behind the counter from the back room.

"Oh, hi. We're here to film the documentary. About the history of the area? I'm not sure if you've heard." Libby explained.

"I've heard." Connor replied, forcing a smile and making it as genuine as he could manage.

"Can you tell us anything about the turret? That's going to be our focus really, but we'll loop in any old ghost stories or interesting historical stuff from the wider area as well."

"I don't know anything about the turret. Nobody does. That's part of its charm," said Connor.

"We're thinking of filming up there tonight. There's a full moon due, so that should be perfect." Libby explained excitedly, causing Connor to suspect she hadn't really listened to his answer.

"I'll go with you, if you like."

"You will?"

"I can tell you what little there is to say about the local knowledge. Spice it up a little, if you want. I know how these TV shows work. You don't want outright lies, but it's got to hold the interest hasn't it?"

"You want a job, mate?" Nathan called over from the DVD rack. "You sound qualified."

"If you're happy to come and do an interview by the turret tonight, we'd really appreciate it." Libby gushed. "That's so nice of you."

"Happy to help. Can be dangerous up there. Lot of loose ground and tripping hazards, so it's safer to go with someone that knows it."

"Thank you so much." Libby beamed. "We need to go and check in and dump our stuff at the B+B. Where can we find you at about 8ish?"

"I'll be here. Shop stays open long as I can be bothered

to stay, really. But I'll wait."

Libby and Nathan departed after Nathan bought a cup of tea in a Styrofoam cup, and several large bags of crisps and multipacks of chocolate bars. Not long after they'd left, the shop bell rang again and Morgan Truscott entered. He and Connor exchanged a knowing look, and Connor immediately understood that Morgan had seen her. Felt her. He understood now, just as Connor had requested.

"They're filming up at the turret tonight." Connor explained. "I'm going with them. I'll make sure they don't find anything."

"If you need any help, I have a big slab and plenty of sharp tools."

"It shouldn't come to that. I'll just distract them with some fairy tales and nonsense to make the turret seem less interesting."

"Right you are. You know I want to help though, if you need me."

"I know, my friend."

"We have to protect her. We have to keep her safe." Morgan said firmly.

"Yes, yes we do."

***

"How's the light, is it good?" Libby asked as she stood with her back to the turret.

"Yeah, it's alright. Getting a bit of glare off the stone though." Nathan replied, adjusting the miniature floodlight he'd set up at his side.

"That's odd, I haven't noticed it raining." Libby remarked, walking over to the turret to get a closer lock.

"Could just be damp in the air." Connor suggested, standing with his hands in his pockets as he waited to start his interview.

"No wait, it's like some sort of black lichen covering the stones. It seems to be slightly bioluminescent," said Libby, studying the turret stones with the light from her mobile phone. "Nathan, it's a bit like the cave fungus we filmed in North America. The one that was affecting those bats."

"Oh for fucks sake, I'm not doing another documentary about fungus. I'll take that job filming Celebrity Juice first." Nathan announced.

"Fungus?" asked Connor.

"Don't even ask, mate. We had to do a whole bloody four part series about different types of fungus for Discovery. And no fucker watched it. Why would they? Who wants to watch that? I could have told them that and saved us several damp and disgusting visits to the biggest moist shit holes on the planet."

"It was interesting!" Libby said defensively as Nathan and Connor joined her at the wall.

"Bloody wasn't." said Nathan.

"Did you know there's some forms of fungus that can affect behaviour? They get inside an animal's brain and alter the way they think, the way they act." Libby explained to Connor.

"Why would it do that?" asked Connor.

"To propagate itself far and wide. To spread its influence. It makes these creatures, usually insects but not exclusively, carry its spore as far or as high as it can, so it grows further than it could ever reach alone."

"Not everything wants to be spread far and wide. Some things like being left alone." Connor pointed out.

"Not fungus. Its purpose is always to expand its reach."

"Not that one in that cave where I shat myself." Nathan pointed out. Connor frowned at him so he added, "I'd eaten a bad burrito."

"We witnessed some adaptive behaviour in advanced

lichen cultures, it's true. The one Nathan means had been getting trodden on constantly out in the open so had adapted to hide in the dark corners of cave systems. It had literally changed its behaviour to survive and grow."

"See, so some fungus does want to be left alone." Nathan gave a satisfied nod. "What type is that on them stones, then?"

"I have no idea. I'm not touching it though, it could be hallucinogenic." Libby moved away from the wall and dusted off her hands, more out of caution than anything else since she hadn't actually touched the wall.

"Like that one those Indians were putting in their soup."

"Native Americans." Libby corrected him.

"Whatever. Yeah mate, they had this fungus, right." Nathan said to Connor, whose face was halfway between confusion and annoyance at this stage. "And they'd eat it, or sometimes bathe in it, and they said it let them see the spirit world. Let them see the Gods, or some shit. I just think they were tripping balls."

"Maybe our eyes can't normally see what's around us without help?" Connor suggested.

"Thank you, Connor, that was what I said." Libby beamed, then scowled at Nathan. "Right, shall we get started?"

"So we're not filming another fungus show then?" asked Nathan, returning to his camera rig.

"No, Nathan."

"Thank fuck for that."

"Ok, go in one…two…" Libby stood next to Connor, brought a honed professional smile to her face, then began, "I'm here with Mr Connor Randall, local village shop owner, whose family has lived in the village of Walliston for generations. Mr Randall, what can you tell us about this mysterious turret standing alone in this field?"

"Well my dad used to say it was probably an old medieval corn silo or something like that. Nothing too interesting. Local lads said it was haunted by the ghost of a farmer who got his head cut off by his own plough."

"Oh really, can you tell us about that?" Libby beamed, knowing she'd just struck documentary gold.

Connor smiled and continued with his entirely fabricated story, feeling a growing warmth inside him at the knowledge that he was successfully keeping her safe by moving their focus away from the turret.

***

Morgan Truscott answered the doorbell to see a smiling man in a set of blue overalls, holding a grey toolbox at his side and a plastic ID card raised to face-level in the other.

"Hello, Mr Truscott, I'm here to check your water pipes, my name's Eli."

"There's nothing wrong with the pipes." Morgan replied, not yet fully opening the door.

"Yours might be alright, but I've been going door to door checking each one and I'm afraid I do have to check yours, Mr Truscott."

"What for?"

"Well if I can see how many homes are affected, that will give me an indication what sort of problem we're looking at. Is it a corrosion of the mains, or just of the direct pipes in each home, or is there a leak somewhere letting an outside pollutant in? Whatever the cause, I need to find it as quickly as I can for health and safety reasons."

"Alright." Morgan agreed, not able to think of a reason quick enough that might prevent the man from coming inside.

"Have you had any problems with your supply lately?

Discolouration, pressure, temperature fluctuation?"

"Not that I've noticed."

"What about that bath you had the other night? You said the water went cold." Mrs Truscott called from the living room.

"Thank you, dear." Morgan called back through gritted teeth. "Yes, she's right. I forgot. The bath."

"Ok I'll start with those pipes first then, if I could get a look at the taps?"

Morgan nodded and led Eli upstairs to the bathroom. The plumber then sat down besides the bath and started taking tools from his toolbox.

"Would you like a brew?" Morgan asked.

"Tea would be lovely." Eli smiled. "Two sugars, please."

Morgan went downstairs leaving Eli to his work. He put the kettle on, placed a teabag in the mug, and slid a large steak knife into the waistband of his jeans as he waited for the water to boil. Once it had, he covered the knife with his jumper, mashed the tea, then called into the living room:

"He's got to shut the water off. You'll have to go round to Mary's for your bath. Best do it now before he shuts hers off too."

"Alright. Have you made him a cup of tea?"

"I'm doing it now, I'm not a savage." Morgan called back. He listened for the sound of his wife leaving the house, then returned upstairs, taking care not to spill the tea.

When he arrived back at the bathroom, a thick solvent smell greeted his nose; strong enough that it actually burnt the inside of his nostrils. He leaned round the door and could see Eli, wearing a plastic mask over his nose and face, pouring a jug full of thick, yellowish liquid down the plughole at the end of the bath using the measuring jug he had found under the sink.

"Can't buy this in the shops." Eli lifted the empty sachet, which he'd mixed with water to make the cleaning agent and held it up so Morgan could see. "Probably best stay out of here until I've aired it out a bit, mate. Strong stuff."

"I have your tea."

"Brilliant, just leave it outside the door if you would." Eli said with a thumbs up, pouring the last of the liquid down the drain. "I found some traces of black mould or something in the taps, so was best to clean the pipes through with this. Not saying that'll stop it completely, but it certainly won't hurt."

The ringing in the back of Morgan's head suggested otherwise. It was hurting. It was hurting her. He wasn't protecting her. He was failing.

"I think you've dropped your ID card in the bath, Eli." Morgan said, pointing at the bath.

"Oops." Eli turned to look in the bath. He was immediately puzzled when he couldn't see the ID card anywhere in the bath but didn't get chance to question it before the knife blade plunged through the back of his neck and out the front of his throat.

"Hope you brought some more of those sachets." Morgan remarked as Eli slumped forward, his blood pooling into the bathtub. "I just cleaned that bath this morning."

***

Connor found himself back at the Turret late that night. He'd made up enough local legends and half-true historical tales to make it seem as if the whole area was ripe for filming, taking focus from being aimed solely at the turret. He knew they'd still want to film it, of course, but now they were less likely to try and apply for yet another excavation. What was beneath them needed to stay buried. More importantly, it *wanted* to. *She* wanted to. Connor stepped inside the turret via the broken section, then felt his phone buzzing against his back pocket. Morgan's name flashed up on the screen as he held it up to see who was calling.

"I've killed the waterboard man." Morgan announced as Connor answered the phone.

"What? Why?"

"He was hurting her. Didn't you feel it?"

"I got a ringing in my head, I had to take some tablets. Is that what that was?"

"He poured something down the drain. He was going to keep looking, he might have found her. Or at least poured more of it down. I had to stop him. For her."

"You did right. What about the body? And his car?"

"I got him chopped up and bagged. To look at it's no different than any of my other offal back here, so I'll take it to the incinerator tomorrow. And I drove the car out of the village and set fire to it. Smashed it up a bit so it looks like somebody was joyriding in it, too."

"They'll come looking for him."

"Not immediately. His diary said he was booked to be out here for a week."

"Alright. Get rid of any evidence. Tell anyone that asks that he didn't find anything wrong with the pipes and left."

"What about you, how did it go with the film crew?"

"I think they'll leave the turret mostly alone. I'm going there now, I think we need Ciara. They're staying at her B+B, so that way she'll keep an eye on them for us."

"Give her my love."

Morgan ended the call and put the phone back in his

pocket. He then stepped forwards and watched as the ground opened before him, revealing the hidden staircase. With a jaunty whistle he ventured down into the blackness.

***

Ciara Wright walked into the lounge area of her Bed and Breakfast. It had once been the smoking room, but since that was now illegal in such establishments, it had been renamed the lounge area. The smell of smoke still clung to some of the vintage furniture she insisted on keeping, but she'd usually use enough *Febreeze* that it was mostly covered. Having just taken a shower and refreshed herself in time for the afternoon meal, already over the momentary panic from the water turning black, she decided to check in on her current guests.

"And how are we both this afternoon?" she asked, finding Nathan and Libby seated in the lounge area with their respective laptops.

"Looking forward to that roast later." Nathan said with a wink.

"So you should. Its locally sourced meat, the butchery done by a local, and then cooked by me. You won't find better in one of those fancy London restaurants."

"I told you I was vegetarian, right?" Libby asked, suddenly concerned that this may have been forgotten.

"So fucking awkward." Nathan said with a roll of his eyes.

"Hush, you." Ciara said playfully, then turned back to Libby, "You did, dear, yes. I've done you a nice nutroast. Cooked in a different tray and before the meat so there's no juice run off or anything like that."

"That's very considerate, thank you." Libby blushed. "See, Nathan, not everyone has to be an arsehole about it."

"So how is the documentary coming? Getting some

interesting stories?" Libby asked, perching on the arm of the lounge chair which Nathan's large frame currently filled.

"We spoke with Mr Truscott yesterday and got some interesting stories. Hoping to get some more today. The weather has been against us this morning, and we want to film mostly outside to really showcase how beautiful the area is. So whilst the rain stops we've been doing a bit of research via your Wi-Fi."

"Faster than you'd think, isn't it?" Ciara smiled. "What is it you're researching?"

"Fungus. Again." Nathan said with a deliberately exaggerated sigh.

"Fungus?"

"We found some weird lichen on the turret, and the way it seemed to shine suggested a degree of bioluminescence." Libby explained.

"I didn't think you were doing a nature documentary, dear," said Ciara.

"Oh we're not, but it's the implication of that discovery which matters. Fungus with qualities like that grows in caves, or underground. Since there's no caves near here, it must have spread from some subterranean source. Which means..."

"That turret goes deeper down to some bigger structure under the earth. And we want to find out what it is." Nathan grinned.

"Thanks for cutting me off."

"I like to do the big reveal, sue me." Nathan shrugged.

"They've tried to get excavation rights for that thing before, dear. Never been agreed." said Ciara.

"No, but this time there'll be TV crews. And TV money. Local government will be keen and the village council will probably get overruled even if they're not happy."

"I don't think they'd be happy about that at all. And I'm not sure the locals would be either."

"It'll all be done very respectfully, taking every care to not to damage anything." Libby assured her, "This will put Walliston on the map. The tourism trade it will bring... You'd be fully booked all year round, Ciara!"

"Some things are more important than money, dear. Some things need to be safeguarded."

"I agree. But don't you see, this will help that. If we can prove there's an actual, ancient structure down there, it'll be an actual piece of pre-Christian architecture. It'll get government funding to protect it, it'll be listed and preserved."

"Well, good luck with it all." Ciara forced a smile.

***

Connor, Morgan and Ciara met at the turret that night, beneath the light of the not-quite-full moon. Ciara had delivered the news about the documentary crew's change of plans, and it was accepted as gravely as she'd known it would be.

"We need to kill them." Morgan suggested.

"It's not like killing a plumber. These are TV people. They'd be missed quicker." Connor replied.

"You killed a plumber?" asked Ciara.

"He was hurting her." Morgan explained.

"Then good riddance to him. We can't let her be hurt. And this documentary will hurt her, even if they don't realise it or intend it."

"We must speak with her." Connor insisted, "She'll know what to do."

The three of them descended as the stairway appeared before them, Connor leading the way as the others had yet to actually make the pilgrimage themselves. They felt no apprehension or nerves, but a sense of eager anticipation grew in them. This trip to her church might mean they actually got to see her. Once into the cavern-like sunken church, Connor stood in the centre and spoke up to the ceiling. Morgan and Ciara followed his gaze to see he was staring at a writhing mass of black lichen that clung to the dirt and the protruding rafters.

"Abigail, my love. We need your help. We are doing what we can to protect you from them, but these latest ones are so determined. They're from the television, and they're likely to get a permit to dig if we don't stop them. We need your guidance, my love."

The cavern rumbled slightly, and then the black lichen peeled away from the ceiling and reached downwards, somewhere between a serpent and a stalactite. The twisting, gelatinous black column almost reached the ground now, then stopped just in front of Connor's face.

The layers of black peeled away, revealing the naked, porcelain and perfectly preserved form of Abigail Randall. She didn't look sick with cancer now. She looked as whole and beautiful and fresh as the day Connor had met her. When first he had seen her here, Connor wondered how her body might have been brought down here. Had it been plucked from the hill where she was buried, restored and given life once more? And why her? Or was something else simply speaking through her restored corpse like a twisted marionette? No, he'd assured himself. It had to be her. It was her.

"Connor, my love." She purred, her voice soft yet echoing through the cave. She reached for his face and his whole body tingled at her touch. Morgan and Ciara smiled but inwardly were envious of her touching him.

"How can we stop this, Abigail? What can we do? Can you share your love with them?"

"I can no longer reach them through the water. The damage done by the man with his chemicals was too much. It will take time before I can extend myself that way again."

"Then how can we stop them?"

"Bring them here. Let me see them."

"They might be frightened."

"I will give you the strength to make them come." Abigail smiled, then took Connor's face in both hands and kissed him passionately. As she did this, Connor felt his body infused with power. It was like that very first time, when the black water had fallen into his sink and splashed him, only a thousand times stronger. There was no fear this time, though. Just power, and a renewed sense of purpose.

"I will bring them here for you, my love." Connor swore, stepping back to let the others approach. His eyes were now obsidian black, as were the pulsing veins on his face and hands.

He watched as his wife embraced both Ciara and then Morgan, giving them each the strength that she had just shared with her husband. Connor smiled and felt happier than he had for a while. He could protect his wife now. He'd failed before, when the cancer came. But he wouldn't fail now.

***

"Attendance has been fairly constant really. I know it's dropped off a lot in bigger towns and cities, but we've been lucky here in that people still have room for God in their lives." Joshua Claxton, the local vicar, said into the camera.

"And what do you think to the turret up there, then? The best guesses about it say it's older even than this church, which was itself the first Christian structure built for miles around." Asked Libby.

"I love history and I'm in no denial that the world existed before people heard Christ's teachings. I'm not one of those who says the earth is six thousand years old or that dinosaurs aren't real." The vicar laughed. "I'd be as interested as anyone to see what the origin of that structure really is."

"So you're not as reluctant as some of the other villagers, then?"

"I think they're worried about the turret, or the local landscape, being damaged. I share that concern, but I also trust that the people who will want to excavate know what they're doing. I think it's important to learn about our past. Some things just shouldn't stay buried."

The doors to the church swung open and three figures stood rigid in the doorway, one woman and two men.

"Hello chaps. And chapette." Nathan waved, stopping the record button on the camera. "Are you here for prayers or something? If so could we just finish up with the vicar, if you don't mind?"

"She needs to see you." Said Connor, his voice deeper and scratchier than it ought to be.

"Who does? Wait, are you alright, mate?"

"Morgan, your wife called last night when you didn't come. Have all three of you been out all night? Is everything alright?" asked the vicar, his voice increasingly concerned as the three figures approached. As they got closer, their pallid skin, black eyes and pulsing black veins were clearly visible.

"Fucking hell!" Nathan yelled as Connor grabbed his arm. He tried to break free but the grip was impossibly strong. For a moment Nathan was reminded of that time at school when the other boys had clamped his arm in a vice during a woodwork lesson. Ciara grabbed Libby, and Morgan took hold of the vicar.

"What about him?" asked Morgan.

"You'll have to bring him too."

All three hostages struggled, kicked and fought as best they could, before a single blow to each of their heads rendered them limp and docile. When next they awoke they were inside a sunken church, staring up at a moving black mass that approached them from the ceiling, revealing the beautiful pale figure hidden within.

***

### *Epilogue 1:*

"What we have here, whilst the subject of much local myth and mystery, is most likely nothing more than a medieval grain silo." Libby explained, gaining a thumbs up from Nathan as he stood facing her with the camera. "That's not to say there's nothing of interest to be found in Walliston, of course. There's a few interesting ghost stories that are sure to make you pull the covers up over your head when you go to sleep tonight. We'll let the locals tell you themselves."

"And cut." Nathan announced, lowering the camera. "Brilliant, now we'll edit in the story Connor told, and then get some more from anyone else that has one."

"That should keep her safe." Libby agreed.

"So should my idea to extend her reach to the local government."

"She's not strong enough to travel that far yet."

"She will be. She hasn't been awake that long. Give her time." Nathan said confidently. "Right, lunch time I think. Let's see if Morgan has any of those roast pork sandwiches left. And some lettuce for you."

"Fuck off, Nathan."

*****

### *Epilogue 2:*

"I saw his van drive up last week. Never saw the man himself, though." Connor shrugged as he spoke over the counter to the blue-overall wearing man.

"We're understandably a bit worried about him, that's all. Eli is usually fairly punctual at filing his reports."

"I understand. Do you have one of those tracking things in his car, perhaps?"

"Oh we found his car. Abandoned and burned out. Joyriders got it, from the looks of things."

"Bloody bastards. They always come to the quiet villages to have their fun, the shites." Connor said in dismay.

"Folk like that ruin everything, don't they? Still, it doesn't stop me worrying about Eli. We might have to get the police involved, I think."

"Excuse me, was it the plumber gentleman you were looking for?" came Joshua Claxton's voice as he approached the counter with a newspaper and a bag of sweets. "Hello, by the way, I'm Joshua, the local vicar."

"Hello there. And yes, that's him. Have you seen him?"

"Well the last I knew he'd taken a look at some pipes in a few houses, and deduced that the problem was with the main pipe leading out of the village. There's an old access point right by that turret up on the hill, so that's probably where he's been working. I can take you if you like?"

"Oh that'd be grand, thank you." The man smiled, shaking the vicar's hand.

Joshua paid for his paper and led the man out of the

shop, but not before turning and giving a knowing smile and nod to Connor. The bell rang as the shop door closed, leaving Connor alone once more. Except he was never alone now, not really. He felt her presence constantly, and he adored that. Connor looked at his wedding ring, then kissed it softly.

"They won't hurt you, my love. Nobody will." He promised.

End.

# After Midnight
## Michael Byrne

<u>1</u>

When Charlie Ross complained that there was something creeping around his room at night, he was chastised by his son for trying to inspire guilt. Guilt for having moved so far away with his family. Charlie tried to protest his innocence. That at night he genuinely did see a shadow appear in the corner of the room, diminutive at first but growing into the shape of a small human in a short space of time. Always in the same corner of the room and always at the same time of night. Midnight. The routine was eerily predicable. Charlie would often cry himself to sleep, isolated as he was now that his son lived abroad. He would then wake, stirred by an unknown force in time to see it manifest, wandering his room aimlessly before directing its attention toward him. Prone as he was under the covers like a terrified child. His nerve broken he would turn on the bedside light as it reached for him, only for it to disappear.

Staff at Redleaf care home listened to what Charlie described, causing a wave of relief to wash over him, assuming that they took his fears seriously and would help find out who the intruder was. But the day after his revelation he was met by a psychiatrist. His heart sinking when, after polite but clinical interrogation, an incantation of medical terms came forth from the doctor, followed by a concoction of suggested medications to help with sleep and to alleviate psychosis.

Only Charlie's neighbour, Owen, seemed to believe him. He lapped up every detail that Charlie had to offer, writing them down in a bulging notebook. He said he had done similar investigations with others at the home before they passed away, a thought that perturbed Charlie. Looking for reassurance he asked Owen if this meant he was going to die. A shrug was his only response. One thing was certain however; if Charlie were to take the medication prescribed he wouldn't get the answers he sought and would never find out what was lurking in his room after midnight. And so Charlie took Owen's advice and delayed the consumption of the sedatives, deciding instead to wait at night for the thing to re-emerge and then confront it with the help of Owen, who would arrive later so as to not disrupt his 'experiment'.

It did not take long for the conditions to be perfect. Charlie had been expecting a Birthday call from his grandchildren but nothing came and so he retired that night tearful and heartbroken. Lying in bed he felt foolish, wondering if in fact this was all in his head and brought on by stress or depression as diagnosed, and considered whether he should not just take the medicine after all. The thoughts were fleeting as once more in the corner of his small bedroom he saw the shadowy mass begin to form. Charlie instinctively reached for his bedside lamp but stopped, remembering the advice from Owen. Instead he looked at his alarm clock. The time read five past midnight. The intruder was fully formed now and Charlie split his attention between it and the door, whispering Owen's name, unsure why he had not arrived yet to witness the phenomenon. But Owen was falling toward a deep, painkiller induced sleep, only to be revived by the whimpers from Charlie's room, a noise familiar in the home since his family left. Realising his tardiness Owen made his way to Charlie as quickly as his wheelchair would allow him. It was twenty past midnight and his hand shook as he reached the door handle, bracing himself before entering.

<u>2</u>

"There comes a time in your life," Gregor father had said. "That regrets outweigh hopes, love makes way for despair and you wake each morning wondering if this is your last twenty-four hours on earth."

A week later he was dead. One minute holding a cup of tea at the kitchen table, the next, keeled over underneath it. Stiff like marble. Gregor had found him on his way home from school. That was sixty years ago. Now an age far beyond what his Father had reached, Gregor had had more time to think on this philosophy, the words never far from his conscious. Like an unwanted guest they would appear from thin air at his most treasured moments. His graduation as a police officer for Merseyside Constabulary, the first time he saw Rose, his wife to be, and the birth of his children; Mark followed by Jane a few years later. Each jubilation would stir a cocktail of the sweetest of feelings but with the sobering millstone of mortality still echoing from his father's lips. At times the words would be so powerful in his mind that he would have to take Aspirin to stop the throbbing headaches that accompanied them. Rose would rub his shoulders and hold him until the feelings ran their course and the pain receded. But sometimes they would not relent, and he would stand and stare out of the window of his home, across the deep soulless dark of the Mersey until dawn broke. In these moments, though he never admitted it to Rose, he could have sworn that the words themselves had oozed from his brain into the material world around him, standing in a corner, chittering away like a madman, gaining power from the night.

"Churchill called it his 'Black Dog.'" Rose once remarked after she woke to find he had sat in the garden since four in the morning. Gregor said nothing.

On occasion these bouts would cause tension if not full-blown arguments. Rose would chide Gregor for being locked away in his thoughts, for ignoring the kids" and her needs for weeks on end. He would respond by snapping an insult and leaving for hours, taking long walks to anywhere, to nowhere, before coming home to a scene of indifference, as if the whole argument had been imagined. Once Rose, while held in Gregor arms, suggested that his job could be making it worse. That being surrounded by crime scenes and convicts could hardly be good for his health. Yet it was at work where Gregor had felt the clearest in mind and where he felt his father's words had no power over him. Staring at his first death had brought with it a sense of purification. A young woman, no more than thirty, had not paid her rent for two weeks and the landlord decided to let himself in. He found her naked in the bathtub, her wrists smiling from two thin cuts that had diluted the water crimson. Gregor had seen how the other constables had reacted to the scene, bashful and mortified in equal measure and wondered if this was his father's gift to him. To see and deal with the worst life can present with sober indifference. The feeling was no different toward personal tragedy. At his mother's funeral he shed no tears while the coffin rolled toward the furnace, nor did he let his emotions cloud his responsibility as a father when he came home to find Rose crying in the bedroom. A letter lay ripped in half next to her. The words were a blur as he read them but their meaning was unmistakable. Rose fought on for another six months despite the doctor's predictions. An irrational fear of being buried alive, she too followed his mother on the same small conveyor belt in the crematorium. Again no tears wetted his cheeks as the beige curtains hid the coffin from view, a fact his daughter noted and ruminated upon until at the wake her silent treatment let up and she spoke behind the bravado of four double whiskies.

"Would it kill you to show some fucking emotion?" she had said. He gave no reply. Returning to his silent home, Gregor was not surprised to find his father's words waiting for him in the darkness.

Jane was married now, with children of her own. They would visit him at his house at first and then at Redleaf after his old home had become too cavernous a space. Redleaf was three miles or so from Ellesmere Port, on a quiet stretch of country road, which was succumbing to the green tide of grass and tree branches. Not close enough to hear the sea but still within reach of the sea mist that aged the relatively new building's external walls prematurely. Despite now being closer to Jane geographically, Gregor had noticed visits wane. One Christmas his grandson gifted him a mobile phone. It sat in a box for three months until they visited again to show him how it worked. It was only a matter of time before visits were replaced by phone calls and then phone calls with text messages. Gregor could have rallied against the changes, have demanded more face to face visits, but his grandchildren were maturing at preternatural speed and his daughter's relationship with him was stoic at best. He recognised a lost cause when he saw one.

But there were some conversations that had to be done in person. Some that needed Gregor to raise from a shallow rest in the early hours to leave unseen and walk through country lane and field before reaching his daughter's house. Gregor walked to the back door on the western wall of the house, a small wooden gate easily unlatched to access the overgrown garden. Though he had a key he didn't need it as the door was unlocked and so, mindful of the time, he crept inside, locking the door behind him. He stood for a moment in the kitchen, the unearthly light of dawn casting a pink hue over its contents. A bowl for washing up in the sink was clearly increasing as the days multiplied. A pizza box, maw open, contents devoured next to a half drunk bottle of red. Gregor moved from the kitchen up the stairs, his eyes straining in the half-light, before he came to the landing and the bedroom of Jane and her husband. The smell of cigarettes rose from the bottom of the door. She had been eighteen when Gregor found her smoking for the first time. He should have stopped her then, he thought as he entered the room to find Jane asleep in the bed bathed in the light of a bedside lamp. Gregor took a moment to watch her sleep. Even in slumber her face seemed furrowed with tension. *Even her dreams caused her pain,* Gregor thought. Maybe it was the frown or the light, but Gregor noted she looked much older than he remembered, the crow's feet and weathered cheeks making her appear middle aged. Then there was the hair, once a vibrant gold it now seemed to be fading to silver. Questions arose in Gregor mind. Was he sure this was his daughter? Had he entered the wrong house instead? He stood motionless, looming over the sleeping woman while he retraced his steps. He was certain this was the right house, his key worked after all. But then who was this before him? Where was Nigel, her husband? Where were the kids? Concern grew to frustration as Gregor sat on the edge of the bed and nudged the woman firmly. At first she did not stir, but Gregor was unrelenting and shook her, calling out as he did so. Finally, she woke, bleary eyed, and turned to face Gregor who peered back at her. They stared at each other and despite the woman's unfamiliar appearance he could feel a connection between them. He went to speak, to ask her who she was, but she drowned him out with a long loud sigh before looking at her alarm clock.

"I've got work tomorrow, for God's sake," she said. Gregor was taken aback and repeated his questioning.

"Who are you? What have you done with Jane?" but she was ignoring him, already on her phone to Redleaf.

"Yeah, morning. This is Jane Callaghan. He's here again…" Gregor stared at Jane while she continued to berate the person on the other end of the phone. *How was it that she had got so old?* Eventually he had to look away, clinging to some semblance of understanding. Jane put down the phone, rubbing her eyes and face.

"Apparently someone called in sick and agency staff never showed," she nudged Gregor with her foot. "Not that it matters how many staff are on with you."

"I've done this before?" Gregor asked but it was more a statement of fact, he knew that he had. Jane nodded, raising three fingers.

"Including today. Sometimes I wonder what they get paid for over there."

"I could only remember you as twenty five." Gregor

said. Jane laughed, and Gregor could have sworn there was a menace to its tone if he could have sworn to anything anymore before turning his attention to the empty side of the bed.

"Nigel? The kids?"

"Over a year ago. I've told you all this already." Gregor nodded, the faint memory of Jane coming to visit him in tears. Not about Nigel, but her children who were old enough now to choose who to live with. And they had chosen him.

"I'm sorry, Jane," Gregor wrung his hands, "I remember bits and bobs…and only then sometimes." Jane stood out of bed, shimmied some jeans on under her nightdress and threw on a jumper that lay crumpled on the floor.

"If I don't get you back there now I'll be late for work." Gregor stood from the bed also as Jane rummaged for her car keys in her jeans pocket.

"Wait," he said, "I had something to tell you."

"You don't." Jane said but Gregor insisted.

"It's about your brother…I got a call, he's been in an accident. I'm so sorry…he's…" The words faded from his lips. Jane's attention focused squarely on him.

"Dad. Mark's been dead twenty years. You tell me every time you turn up." Gregor looked away to the floor as the memories returned. His mind reconstructing a blurred memory his son inside a coffin on the same conveyor belt as Gregor mother had lain years before. The same conveyor belt Rose would lay on two years later. A conveyor belt he would no doubt soon rest on. Jane walked with him to the car and they drove back toward Redleaf.

At this stage no one was sure if it was the cancer or the medication that was causing the onset of confusion, a jigsaw puzzle of memory with pieces missing altogether while others had been wedged into the wrong place. Hallucinations were not uncommon for him either and Jane reminded him how last week he had thought he was in a pub with Mark when in fact he was sat in an armchair conversing with a lamp. A saving grace was that thus far moments of confusion came in sporadic bouts. That and for now he was still physically fit despite the illness, though to Jane this was a mixed blessing as without his mobility Gregor fondness for travel would have been stymied. The car drove into the nursing home's grounds, under two silver birch trees that had knotted their branches to create a natural threshold. Gregor mind burned with concentration as he reflected on his excursion. Despite having relayed the same message to Jane three times he could barely remember any of it and the more he tried to focus the more it slipped away. By the time he gave up he was stood outside the home with a nurse by his side, Jane's car driving off into the distance. She had said goodbye several times before leaving. He hoped his lack of response was not too upsetting.

"What time is it?" he asked and was told nine in the morning. A tiredness enveloped him, more often than not he found himself sleeping during the day now more than night. The night bothered him. The night was when his father's words visited. Gregor made his way back to his room but as soon as he sat on his bed there was a knock at his door. He opened it slightly and saw Owen staring up. Owen nodded at his friend, his hands taught around the grip of his wheelchair.

"It got Charlie." He said.

<u>3</u>

Owen Browne was better known to staff at Redleaf as 'Limerick', despite actually being from Cork. Gregor, however, chose to call him the 'Professor'. Not just for the fact that he had a PHD in History but because he was genuinely the smartest man he had ever known. Yet despite his accomplishments, Owen's gaunt body and strong Irish accent had presented to those around him a figure to be taken lightly, if not disregarded completely. People's internal prejudices working against him to the point that they barely accepted anything he said beyond being creative confabulation. The fact very few people paid much attention to Owen was the reason he confided in Gregor so much, counting him one of his only true friends. His other confidante was Lilly, a gentle soul who was new to the home but not shy as a result. Gregor had noted to himself when he first saw her how vibrant her eyes were; as if time could consume her external form but her inner beauty would live forever. Gregor thought of Lilly's eyes often and how they complemented her smile. That of a twenty-year-old, he had said to her once, which caused her to blush. Owen's eyes on the other hand had been left for dead by age, sunken and yellow at the edges. As the three sat in the TV room the contrast was unmistakable. At least Owen's pain medication kept the more visceral part of his illness at bay, allowing for some moderate respite and keeping his mind clear to theorise on the events around him.

"Charlie had been crying himself to sleep this past month," Owen spoke in hushed tones to the others, looking over his shoulder every so often as he spoke. "Ever since his family moved to Canada, you know?" Gregor nodded, remembering how the sound would roll through the home at night, through the darkness of the corridors before reaching his room.

"Charlie always was a sensitive soul." Gregor said, half distracted by the TV.

"That may be," Owen paused to stop his excitement increasing his volume. "But when he lost control of his emotions he painted a big target on his back. Just like Mary before him when she broke her hip. And Maggie when she stopped eating." Lilly tried to change the trajectory of the conversation,

"Has anyone got through to his family yet?" her voice was loud, and Limerick winced, checking to see if her volume had brought any unwanted attention. Gregor responded, hoping to reassure her.

"I think I heard that one of the nurses called. Would it be the afternoon in Canada now?" Owen watched, awe struck as the conversation collapsed into triviality. To what part of Canada Charlie's family lived, if any one of them would visit, how cold it must be there, until at last his patience wore out and his whispered tone became an involuntary roar.

"Oh to hell with Canada! To Hell with Charlie!" Attention fell on the trio, gasps and tuts echoing about them while Owen tried to shrink within his wheelchair before he returned to his muttering. "All I mean is there is more pressing matters than whether Charlie's kin live in Labrador or bloody Toronto."

"And what might they be then?" Lilly began. "That somehow, despite being here in Heaven's waiting room, it's suddenly suspicious that people pass away? And that someone just *has* to be responsible?" Owen stared at Lilly and Gregor for a moment before replying,

"Not someone. Something."

Lilly shook her head and laughed. "Of course, this thing you saw, that you can't describe or explain but you know is in here with us."

"Again, not that I *can't* describe it. That it is *indescribable*."

Now it was Lilly's turn to be exasperated. "That's the same bloody thing!" But Owen shook his head.

"How do you describe what air looks like? Or the

sound of still water? How do you describe something outside of your normal parameters of reference? Outside of your normal senses?" Owen looked to the sunlight through the window, shimmering through the fingers of tree branches. "That thing I saw was something other. Something I wasn't supposed to see. That I shouldn't have been able to see at all. But I could see it. Standing over Charlie. As I'm sure it stood over Maggie. As I'm sure it stood over Mary." Limerick returned his attention to Gregor and Lilly. "And while I don't much care for what happens to me, I'll be damned to see it hanging over you two." The group fell silent and eventually Lilly sighed, smiling at Owen and Gregor.

"You know sometimes I wonder if when I go to bed at night I won't wake up again. Or worse, wake up trapped in my own body, not able to speak or feed myself," Owen tried to protest but Lilly continued to speak, calmly but with a majestic authority. "But I don't see the point of spending my last years worrying about that, or some bogeyman coming to get me in the middle of the night." She stood slowly from her armchair, her frame fragile but still lithe for her age. "I raised two kids on my own with barely any money to my name. I've done all my worrying for one lifetime." Lilly paused for a moment. "And I've had my fill of fairy tales as well." Gregor smiled at Lilly as she left, watching her disappear out of the lounge back to her room. Owen however focused on Gregor and scoffed aloud.

"You must have been a florist in a past life." Gregor turned to face him.

"What do you mean by that?"

"Nothing really…" Owen trailed off, "Your wife was called Rose, no? Lilly? Rose?"

"Give over!" Gregor snapped, causing Owen to chuckle before Gregor fell back into his stoic persona.

"How did your travels go this time?" Owen asked hoping to open him up again. Gregor shrugged.

"Lucky I didn't break my ankle," he said. Owen nodded, tapping his wheelchair. "One of these would help with that."

"I wouldn't much mind these walkabouts if it didn't upset Jane. I could walk off into the Mersey for all I care now. But to keep going to her house. Goin' over old ground…"

"Who'd look after Lilly though? I mean if you went paddling?" Owen asked, his voice stoic to Gregor plight.

"Lilly's all right," Gregor said, thinking on her eyes. "She's got family to come see her."

"Aye. Gives her a reason to keep on living. Keeps whatever it is at bay I reckon." Owens words acted as bait and Gregor, though aware of the game being played, bit into it willingly.

"My mind's buggered, Owen," he began. "but what you're saying sounds mad even to me. I mean what exactly is this thing supposed to be anyway?" Owen processed Gregor words before replying.

"I'm not sure, not just yet. But I know what it looks for in a victim." Raising three bony fingers he continued. "Mary, Maggie, Charlie. All dealing with prolonged sadness reaching apex. Whatever the specifics, they were in the throes of despair and I think that's what it looks for in people. Feeding not just on those near death but those who have nothing to live for."

"Very creative, Professor," Gregor tried to laugh but part of him had been carried on the story unfolding before him. "But I'd need to see evidence before just taking your word for it."

Owen groaned. "Naturally, constable, naturally."

Gregor turned and saw Lilly returning to the lounge,

by her side a little girl who held her hand tightly; her granddaughter. The room lit up with affection toward the child as she made her way to a row of empty seats by the windows. Lilly beckoned them both over but Owen declined, reaching out to Gregor as he accepted the invitation.

"Give me some time," he began. "Then meet me in my room. At midnight." his eyes focused and stern. "I'll get that evidence for you." Gregor watched as Owen left before his attention was drawn to a voice next to him. A nurse had taken him by the arm. He turned to look at Lilly whose face was frozen with concern. He felt light headed, as if he had been stood still on the spot for hours. The Sun seemed lower in the sky than it had been just moments ago. He saw the nurse was talking to him but the words came a second later than when they were spoken. It was another sudden bout of delirium. Passing nearly as soon as it arrived. As he sat down next to Lilly he processed what the young nurse had been saying.

"Don't listen to Limerick." was the advice. "He's always making up stories."

<u>4</u>

It had been raining for hours, the light from the lampposts dancing in the puddles. It was late but still balmy—Gregor uniform sticking to his body in the July heat. Ahead of him he could see a car crushed against the wall of a corner shop, as if trying to occupy the same physical space as the bricks and cement in front of it. A lethal embrace frozen in time. The left indicator winked at Gregor as he approached, and the smell of petrol pinched at his nose. Past the rising mist and the glaring reflections of neon lights, Gregor was able to make out a figure in the driver's seat. Blood congealed like a crown on their head and they wore a grimace, as if they had caught a glimpse of themselves post mortem. The driver's window had shattered on impact and Gregor crushed the shards under foot as he examined the body. It was as he had expected. It was his son. At the time Gregor remembered a feeling akin to being shot in the stomach. A shortness of breath that left his chest feeling ready to collapse in on itself as a myriad of synapses flared off all manner of responses and instructions. But despite the smells and sounds, despite feeling the sweat on his brow and the iron of adrenaline in his mouth he knew that the image before him was a phantasm of memories past. To test his theory and his own confidence Gregor spoke aloud. "This isn't real." he said, voice trembling through the silence. Mark, his son, had been driving too fast that night and lost control of his car. If it had been a hedge, he probably would have survived. But the force of energy created on hitting a brick wall at seventy miles per hour needed to go somewhere and so it soared through him, shattering bone and tearing muscle as it did. He was dead instantly. Despite his injuries, however, Mark's eyes opened at his father's words and, his face maintaining its contortion, began to speak.

"It's ten to midnight." His voice was shallow. Gregor shuddered. He hoped for an exit from this memory but found himself stuck within its grasp. He steeled himself before getting closer to his son's body, a faint humming on the horizon becoming gradually louder. Gently he took Mark's hand in his.

"I'm sorry, Mark." But Mark didn't respond, just watched as Gregor stood up, shielding himself from the bright yellow light that descended with the increasing volume of the hum. Blinded now, Gregor heard Mark speak once more before the hum was overpowering;

"Owen is waiting." is all he said.

Gregor found himself in his room, the light and hum emanating from the opened fridge, a carton of milk warming in his hands. He thought about retracing his steps to try and remember what it was he was doing, but frustration got the better of him and so he slammed the fridge shut, rattling the contents inside. He looked across the room and saw his wall clock showing five past midnight. A week had passed since he had spoken to Owen about his research, and tonight he had finally requested Gregor presence to present the findings he now spoke so boldly about.

The hallway between Gregor and Owen's rooms glowed from the light of a distant TV in the lounge. For some reason Gregor felt like a teenager sneaking out of his room despite having full liberty to leave. Maybe it was the thought that if they saw him, staff would try to persuade him to return to bed for fear of him going on yet another late night ramble. Another piece of evidence to give to the doctor that would seal his fate and revoke his basic rights of independence for fear that it would cause him irreversible harm.

Gregor let himself in without knocking. He found Owen sat in his wheelchair looking out at the garden. The light of the nursing home reaching vainly into the darkness beyond so that only shadows of trees could be seen. Their branches stretched forward like fingers, ready to smother the building in retaliation for its encroachment into nature.

"I thought you'd be in bed." Gregor said, walking over to Owen.

"I'm like yourself there." Owen refocused his gaze from the trees to his own reflection. "Night time is when I'm most active." Gregor sat down, Owen peering at him over his shoulder. "Did you let anyone see you come in?" he asked.

"No." Gregor paused, "For some reason I didn't."

"Good. Best not to take any chances."

Gregor let the words sink in before chuckling.

"So you think staff are doing us in then?" Owen wheeled over to his bookshelf that was bursting with notes and worn leather hardbacks as Gregor protested on behalf of Releases workers. "Is this because they call you 'Limerick'?" Owen eyed Gregor for a moment before turning back to the bookshelf, pulling out a large tome, a peeling faded red spine hiding the gold leaf lettering that made the book's title. Owen placed it next to Gregor and even then he had to hold it close to his face to make out its name; *Myths and Legends of Ireland*.

"Oh that it was as simple as mere animosity on my part, *Constable*." Owen said, tapping the tip of the bookmark rapidly until Gregor took the hint and opened the book to the relevant page. Despite the size of the book the font was small, suggesting that no stone had been left unturned in the author's quest to create the most comprehensive book of Irish folklore there was. To read even the first page would be exhausting so Gregor looked instead for the most obvious clue which came in the form of the chapter's title; *The Darker Side of Sidhe*. Pre-empting Gregor line of questioning, Owen began to speak.

"Over here you'd call them Fairy Folk. Pixies, which sort of thing," Gregor scanned the pages as Owen continued "but to imagine little fellas with wings would be rudimentary. In Irish lore a fey creature can take on all manner of forms. Tiny, giant, corporeal, incorporeal, beautiful and monstrous. Whatever you can imagine there's a Sidhe for it." Gregor flipped slowly through the pages, stopping at the name of one such Sidhe. A fairy whose purpose it was to escort the dying when their time had come, the *Dullahan* would never have to leave Redleaf to get its fill. Half joking Gregor proposed this to Owen.

"Just look out for a tall lad carrying a scythe, right?" Owen smiled and nodded.

"I thought that at first as well," he said, his face retuning to a serious composure. "But new-borns die, children die. Dullahan has as much reason to be by the side of a road waiting for a speeding drunk as it does in a nursing home." Owen realised the crassness of his words as he said them. He thought about apologising for his clumsy analogy but he was too invested in his pontificating and so he pressed on, moving the book forward six or so pages until the name of another Sidhe stood out in bold type face.

"Remember what we're looking for is something that doesn't just feed on waning life but on the despair and sadness that latches itself to people at such times." Gregor looked down at the new page Owen had turned the book to. "Charlie had lost all hope when his family moved away, he knew then all he was waiting for was death. More than likely he'd never see them again. Death is easy but the hopelessness Charlie felt—that people feel in a place like this is a beacon to those who hunger for it." The page's subheading read *Sluagh*. Gregor tried and failed to pronounce it, leading Owen to provide its other title; *The Host*.

"Stories vary, naturally," Owen went on. "Some report that The Host were once human, only able to exist on the souls of the dying to replenish their own darkness. There's mention of them appearing as a flock of ravens and other birds too. But unless you count the sparrows on the bird feeder as a portent of evil I think this may be make believe." Until then Gregor had found himself carried on by the spell Owen had cast, his hushed tones and lyrical voice ensnaring the susceptible part of Gregor nature. A ghost story for bedtime. Nothing more. But hearing him split hairs about what was real and what wasn't in the composition of the Sluagh snapped him back to cold, scientific reality. Closing the book, he noted the title page and its author and sighed.

"Did you sell many copies then?" Owen took a moment before taking the book back.

"It was a scholarly book, not for sale to general public. But in academic circles it was warmly received."

"It's a great story," Gregor spoke with warmth in his voice, he did not want to hurt his friend's pride. "But isn't it going a little too far now? I mean you were close to Charlie, seems an odd way to remember him." Owen nodded.

"I was close to him yes, close enough to be the only one who believed him when he said someone was in his room at night that shouldn't have been."

"And conveniently it was this creature *you* wrote about, that happened to kill him?" Owen nodded with a faux naivety that made Gregor curse.

"So why here then? Why choose this place where you happen to live, eh? I mean how the hell did it get here from Ireland for one thing?"

"Same way I did?" Owen said. "It's only a hundred and fifty miles from Dublin. Not exactly other side of the world. And who said anything about this being an isolated incident? Truth is these things could be in every care home and hospice across the country, doing what they need to do to survive. Unseen. Until now."

"Exactly." Slipped easily back into his police officer's persona. "*Unseen.* You said to me that you had proof of whatever it was you think's going on but you've shown me bugger all." Owen nodded his head at the protest.

"Well that's why I asked you here at midnight, the hinterland between life and death, when the spirits are more active. And more likely to accept a sacrifice." Gregor laughed, looking over his shoulder.

"Sacrifice? Should I be worried, Professor?" But Owen smiled shaking his head. "It is said that the Sluagh's intended target can be saved if another takes their place." Reaching across to Gregor, Owen placed an empty bottle in his hand.

"I thought to test that theory." Gregor looked at the bottle momentarily, reading the name of the medication that it once stored before he looked back at Owen.

"What have you done?"

"Only what was coming anyway." Owen's voice quivered slightly but he regained his composure with lightning speed. "My liver's a time bomb. I don't want to spend the rest of my days doped up on painkillers. Hopefully my theory is right and it will leave to find pastures new."

"Pastures new?" Gregor stood from the bed, realisation igniting his mind. "Christ you're going to top yourself for a bloody fairy-tale!" Gregor moved as swiftly as he could to the door, eager to get help but Owen shouted of him to stop.

"Whatever happens," His voice was still. "Make sure you see it for yourself. Then leave this place for good."

Gregor pushed Owen's door open and hurried toward the lounge. A young nurse was sitting in the dark, the glare of the TV casting her in a florescent haze. She turned her head, eyes still fixed on the television screen as Gregor spoke, the words tumbling out of order but clear enough to relay the urgency of the matter. The nurse moved with purpose and Gregor noted how for someone so youthful in appearance she was able to keep her composure—her movements fluid as she rushed down the corridor. Owen looked up as the two entered his room and he barked with anger at the betrayal. The Nurse reached for the pill bottle, before turning to Gregor to go and call an ambulance, her voice void of emotion. Gregor did as he was instructed, returning to his room where his mobile lay while Owen's protests echoed behind him. Once inside his room he snatched at his phone from the kitchen side and turned back to face the door only to see it slam shut and lock of its own accord. Gregor muscles seized in fright making him drop the phone and it was a few hesitant seconds before he bent to pick it up again fearful of removing his attention from in front of him. His confidence returned, Gregor tried the door but found it to be locked only by the latch. Yet when he pulled at the lock or at the door itself it felt as if was welded shut. He could still hear Owen's tirade at the nurse and this reassured him somewhat but when he turned to his phone to call an ambulance he felt a sudden change in the atmosphere, as if a pulse of static energy reverberated through the rooms of the nursing home. The emergency operator's voice, faint and crackling on the phone, pleaded with Gregor to respond. But he was concentrating too hard on the noise from Owen that had slipped from a shout to a dreadful whimper in a matter of seconds. Gregor pulled at the bolt again, throwing the phone to the ground to use both hands and all his strength before it eventually released, tearing the side of his palm open on the twisted metal of the lock. Ignoring the pain, Gregor pushed himself to return through the corridor, still illuminated as ever by the TV. The static feeling from before becoming denser as he reached Owen's room. *This isn't real*, Gregor thought to himself as he had done earlier that night, but it gave no comfort and as he opened Owen's door all further reassurance fell from his mind. Owen lay on his bed, unconscious and in pain, his chest rising and falling in quick staccato impulses. The final symphony of a dying man. Over him stood the nurse from before. There was nothing horrifying about her as such. She did not sprout wings or bite at her victim with razor sharp fangs. Nor did she screech at the night like some brimstone devil. Yet the more Gregor looked at her the more her mask of humanity fell apart. She appeared half made up, the way an alien might draw a human from faded recollection. Her skin was porcelain and looked smooth to the touch, missing lashes and eyebrows. Her face lacked the contours and lines of someone who had never smiled, eaten, or frowned even once.

Gregor noticed her hands as they pressed on Owen's chest and how they seemed abnormally long, each digit equal in length. A solitary index finger tapping rapidly on Owen's bare flesh, creating a hollow thud that echoed around the room. But it was the eyes that turned to look at Gregor that startled him the most, reflecting an opaque yellow in the half light. Ignoring Gregor, the nurse continued her bizarre ritual, pressing her palm harder onto Owen's chest, his breathing now nothing but a faint sigh every ten seconds or so. Unable to stand by any longer, Gregor looked for a makeshift weapon but finding nothing resorted to trying to pry the nurse from Owen himself. The Nurse made a hollow growl, clearly frustrated at being disturbed from her meal. The sandpaper rough palms of her hands leaving abrasions on the skin. Holding both her wrists as she struggled, Gregor threw her to the ground and she called out in pain. A moment later Gregor felt arms envelope him from behind. He turned his head and saw it was one of the care workers restraining him from further violence.

"She's killing him!" he screamed and nodded in the direction of the nurse who was back on her feet and performing CPR on Owen, all preternatural elements obfuscated from view. Still he protested as he was dragged from the room to allow more staff to support the nurse in her attempts to revive Owen. Gregor struggled as he was led to his room, the sound of sirens becoming ever louder. Once deposited he stood alone in the corner, finding his Father's memories waiting for him as they always did but now with little effect. He had seen something that surpassed their horror.

<u>5</u>

The Police and ambulance arrived in quick succession and some of the residents stirred at the maelstrom of activity coming from Owen's room. Many lamented his passing in great swells of agony, not just for his own sake but for the feeling that they too now shuffled further toward mortality's cliff edge. Had Gregor witnessed their tears and sorrow he would have seen nothing more than further victims in waiting to The Host. The cycle of grief may not have been started by the thing he saw but it was certainly perpetuated by it. Naturally when he described the thing to the staff that escorted him to his room he suffered the same fate as Charlie and was reminded of how his medication and illness could cause delusions. He was losing his mind slowly, this was true. But the very fact that he himself wished what he saw to be a hallucination was enough to convince him of its reality. Despite this he knew he would soon be at the mercy of medical scrutiny so when a gentle knock came to his door he prepared himself to be interrogated by a wall of professionals. It was with relief and pity that he saw Lilly standing in the doorway instead. Relief to see a friendly face after such horrors, pity to see her eyes sore from tears. Gregor touched her shoulder as she came into his room.

"I can't believe he'd do something so stupid." Lilly said, her face still damp. Gregor said nothing, watching as she looked around his room for some hidden reason in the night's events. "I mean was he really in that much pain? That depressed? I feel like I let him down somehow. I should have noticed." Gregor shook his head as she started to cry again.

"Owen was stubborn, and that's putting it mildly. And he was an arrogant sod when he wanted to be too." Gregor met Lilly's gaze for a moment, "But he wasn't depressed, and you certainly didn't let him down." Lilly smiled and placed her palm on Gregor cheek. He closed his eyes as his mind reflected on stolen kisses and the awkward, exciting fumblings of his teens. The vision was so sweet it was hard to pry his eyes open again, feeling a glow in him from Lilly's touch, rejuvenating his soul. "You need to leave." He said, "*We* need to leave." Lilly looked confused and attempted to speak but Gregor continued. "This home, this place. It's dangerous." Lilly moved her hand from Gregor face.

"What do you mean 'dangerous?'" her voice taking on a tone of concern. "Is this something to do with Owen?" Gregor head suddenly felt heavy, the idea of lifting it to speak too much for his neck to bear. So instead he stared at the ground.

"I saw it, Lilly." He said. "I saw it kill Owen." Lilly sat back in her chair. Gregor felt a tension build between them as he went on. "He took his pills to lure it out, to prove to me it was real. He said that I should leave this place in case it targets me." Gregor looked up, a sudden surge of fragile optimism spurring him on. "That *we* should leave this place"

"Gregor." Lilly's voice was cushioned with tenderness but still it weighed on Gregor chest like an anvil. "What you're saying about Owen, about this creature you saw," she paused while she searched for the words. "None of it is real and I think deep down you know that." But Gregor shook his head.

"When I left his room to get help he was talking, shouting at me for calling the nurse. How does a man go from being belligerent to near death in thirty seconds?" Lilly shuddered at the image. "Owen said this creature feeds on despair, waiting for when you're at your lowest." Gregor stopped suddenly, thinking back through his years of battling his own demons. "I've been fighting this thing my whole life."

"No," Lilly said. "No, what you fought tonight was a nurse trying to do CPR on our friend." Gregor shook his head but Lilly continued. "Which means more than likely someone's going to come along to lock you up while these hallucinations continue to get worse."

"I know the difference between what's in my head and what's out there," he said, pointing to his window. "How do you know it was thirty seconds?" Lilly asked. "You said in thirty seconds Owen went from shouting to near death—well how do you know?"

Gregor shrugged "I just know."

"Like in the lounge when you lost track of time and stood staring at me for five minutes. You *just knew* then it had only been a couple of seconds." Gregor attempted a rebuttal but nothing came as he pondered Lilly's words. Was he now remembering standing motionless in his room for half an hour because it happened or because Lilly had suggested it? Had he seen The Host because Owen told him he would see it or because he now lived between sanity and madness, allowing such things to reveal themselves? His confidence imploding, he turned to Lilly for support.

"I…I just don't want to die here alone," Gregor said flatly and Lilly held him tight to her.

"But you're not alone though," she reassured him. "I'll be here with you." Gregor smiled and nodded, thanking Lilly for her generosity and for the sudden offer of a multitude of days out, social gatherings and the like. To be welcome in her world. To find a semblance of meaning and happiness. She responded to his thanks by giving him a peck on the cheek. But the kiss lingered and Gregor moved his head slowly so that their lips met in a tender, fragile kiss. It was brief and Lilly removed herself from further affection before getting up.

"Get some rest," she said. Gregor smiled and nodded though inside he was an eruption of unsaid things. His mind wondered from how to convince her of The Host's existence to seeing himself sat with her and her family, laughing, joking and happy. A way of keeping The Host at bay. Moreover, a reason to live. But then he remembered his condition and the fantasy faded away. He, like Owen, had a death sentence hanging over him more impending than most. For Gregor it was not matter of slowing down the onset of death but choosing where to greet it. And one thing was for certain; it would not be at Redleaf.

***

An hour later Lilly was restless in her bed, the previous conversation sitting with her. Defeated, she sat up, turning to her bedside table and a framed photo of her grandchildren. Their smiles piercing the darkness of her room. At first she went to the lavatory but then, standing by her front door a compulsion gripped her and she succumbed to it begrudgingly. She walked quietly to Gregor room. Once inside, it was as she expected. Gregor was gone. As she walked back to her room a staff member asked how Gregor was doing, and if he had settled since the incident before. Immediately she responded.

"He's sleeping," she said.

## 6

A ship's horn bellowed in the distance as Gregor arrived at Jane's house. The port was beginning to stir at the break of dawn a few miles west. The journey had taken longer than he remembered last time, finding himself lost where before he would have walked the route without hesitation. Light rain had combined with muddy paths to result in his clothes becoming sodden and caked in soil. Under a fledgling sun he examined himself, no longer surprised at his false memories of having dressed appropriately seeing he was still in his slippers, now weeping water as he walked the last part of his journey. At least one memory resonated within him, anchoring him to his mission. He knew that what he had seen in Owen's room was not a hallucination. He would tell Jane and whether she believed him or not he would be resolute in his demands. If he was to die, which was surely soon, it would be with her, in her house; in a safe place with a loved one to help usher in eternity. Far from loss and loneliness. Far from what had happened to Owen and the others. Once again Gregor tried his key for the door on the western wall and once more found it unlocked. But the similarities to his last excursion ended there. Where before in the kitchen Gregor saw plates, utensils and food, he now only saw cardboard boxes and large heavy-duty laundry bags, bursting with contents. Examining the living room Gregor found a similar scene, furniture moved to one side to make space for packed up belongings; a box marked 'Charity Shop', giving away its secrets as a cuddly toy peered from within. As he ascended the stairs he saw the spaces on the wall where framed pictures once hung, void of dust. The spare bedrooms were towering cityscapes of boxes, some filled while others lay dormant awaiting their purpose. Finally, Gregor slunk into Jane's room, taking a moment to recognise her as she slumbered, forever in his mind a young woman. Maintaining his faculties for once he sat on the edge of the bed, as he always did, placing a hand gently on her shoulder. "Jane," he whispered but she did not stir and so he nudged her. Jane grunted slightly and repositioned herself in bed so that she lay on her back, her arm flopping out of the covers as she moved. Gregor went to take her hand, to move her arm back into bed so it would not go numb. But when he reached down he paused, rendered motionless by the large raw scar that run the length of Jane's wrist. Sanguine in colour and tender to the touch, Gregor stroked its outline with his fingers, remembering the woman in the bathtub he had encountered all those years ago. The same lines torn into her flesh as those now healed on his daughter. Suddenly he felt Jane stir and her arm slipped from his grasp and back under the covers. He looked up and saw her staring at him.

"You shouldn't be here." Gregor said, noting the deepness of the lacerations. Jane looked away from her father.

"No, you shouldn't be here! I'm sick to death of you sneaking into my house!"

Gregor nodded but refused for the subject to be changed.

"Why, love?" his voice quiet. Jane sat up in bed, wiped the amassing tears from her eyes.

"The kids," half laughing at how simple it sounded out loud. "I missed them." Gregor looked at the boxes piled in the bedroom.

"So you're moving closer to them?" Jane nodded then sighed.

"It's not just that, Dad." her words were hesitant. "I can't keep doing this. I can't keep seeing you get worse and worse. I'm terrified if I leave the back door locked I'll find you asleep outside one night. Or worse." Gregor looked down at his muddy feet, his footprints leading to the stairs. He felt like a shamed dog not quite knowing what it was being chided for but sad all the same. "I'm going to be here until they make more secure arrangements at the home, so you don't scare any new tenants," she laughed but again it was muted.

"And then?" Gregor asked.

"I'll still visit, call you and that." The words were as subdued as her laughter and Gregor recognised how empty they were. He thought about confessing why he had come this morning, or what had happened to Owen. But it was clear that this would only work as evidence of further deterioration. Instead he tried to summon some wise words to impart, a gift forty odd years delayed. But all he could provide was a solitary sentence.

"I'm sorry I was such a closed book all these years." Jane said nothing, a silence deepening where tenderness and comfort should have existed. But any chance of a connection was severed at the sound of the doorbell. Both Jane and Gregor looked at each in confusion. It was just past six in the morning and no one was expected. Jane yawned and emerged from bed, leaving Gregor sat as she walked down stairs and opened the door. Slowly he moved to the stairs, the sound of murmuring conversation from below becoming clearer. As he descended he saw Jane come round the corner with another person and Gregor stopped in his tracks. It was the young nurse from before. The one he had seen with Owen. She smiled up at him, her lips like spider's silk. He could hear Jane talking, explaining how the nurse had volunteered to collect him and bring him back at the end of her shift, how they had checked on him to see how he was and found him gone again. Gregor senses were elevated, his heart surging. Despite being a few feet away, Jane's voice sounded distant. He couldn't be sure but she sounded nervous, fearful even. He then thought on her scars.

"Have you come for me or my daughter?" He asked, moving in front of Jane. Stifled laughter emerged from the two women.

"You'll do for now," the nurse said.

"And if I go with you now, you won't come back?" Jane tried to reassure him but the nurse intervened.

"I don't see why I'd need to," she said, still smiling. Gregor felt a weight lift from him only for another to take its place; the thought of leaving with the nurse petrified him but Jane had to be protected. Slowly the nurse raised her hand to Gregor, a gentle gesture which did nothing to reassure him, feeling like a convict on his day of execution. The nurse began to walk Gregor out to her car but he stopped at the threshold of the house and looked at Jane, he knew for the last time.

"Keep them close. The kids," he began. "Don't let them drift away like I did with you." It was the first time Jane had ever seen her father cry.

Gregor sat in the passenger's seat staring ahead. Light-hearted Pop music whispered on low volume from the radio, the nurse tapping her index finger to the beat. He looked out of the window to his side, the sun now fully birthed from the horizon. He closed his eyes to its brightness, its glow illuminating the blood vessels in his eyelids. Then he felt the nurse's hand take his. Gentle but firm.

"A Poor Soul burdened with a corpse." Her voice was sharp glass. Gregor didn't understand the quote; he was tired from the night's excursion and just wanted to sleep. And so he did.

# Mirrored Evil
## Guy N. Smith

"It needs a lot doing to it," Karen Alker surveyed the detached house on the edge of the remote Welsh village, brushed her long blonde hair back with one hand, clasped her 11-year-old daughter, Skye, with the other. "It hasn't been lived in since the last owner sold up five years ago."

"All it needs is some TLC," Darren, her husband, gave a reassuring smile. "We got it at a knockdown price and don't forget I'm a builder, so there won't be any wages to pay. Structurally, it's sound so I reckon I can do a real good job."

"I'm just surprised that it's stood unsold for so long," Karen had an uneasy feeling about their new home. "Why hasn't some building firm bought it, done it up and made a good profit?"

"Dunno," Darren smiled, shrugged his shoulders. "Let's just say that we've been lucky. We can start moving in next week. We'll have to put up with a bit of inconvenience for a few weeks until I get it sorted."

"I don't like it," Skye pouted her lips. "It's…it's creepy. Why couldn't we have stayed in Lichfield?"

"Don't be silly, darling," Karen smiled. "It'll be much more relaxed living in the countryside, away from all the traffic and the hustle and bustle. When Daddy's got it sorted you'll love it. Likewise, your new school, just twenty pupils instead of that crowded classroom…"

"I won't," Skye folded her arms and screwed up her face.

"You will, just you see," Darren ruffled her hair. "And I'm going to make you the cosiest home you'll ever have."

Karen found herself tensing and a little shiver ran up her spine. There was some truth in what Skye had said. That house was sinister but there was no logical explanation. Just an ordinary house, she attempted to convince herself. It would be altogether different once Darren had smartened it up.

***

"Well, how has school been today?" Darren broke an uneasy silence as the three of them sat down to their evening meal.

"It's all right," Skye did not look up from her beans on toast.

"We told you so. Anyway, as soon as you've finished your tea, it's bedtime."

"I've finished your room today, wall papered, really nice." Darren speared another slice of cold pork.

"I don't like it, Daddy."

"That's because it was so scruffy. It isn't now."

"It gives me the shivers."

"It won't now. I've got the radiator working properly so

you'll be warm and cosy."

Somewhat reluctantly Skye followed her mother upstairs. Darren filled and lit his pipe.

Shortly afterwards Karen returned and began clearing the table.

"Skye's really spooked," she shook her head. "It's really smart now, smarter than her room at the old house. She'll get used to it."

"Let's hope so. Anyway, I suggest we have an early night tonight; I've had one helluva day trying to get the kitchen cleaned up. God, what a mess!"

"An early night sounds great," he blew a cloud of smoke up towards the ceiling. "As the saying goes, tomorrow is another day."

By eleven o'clock they were both asleep in bed. It was sometime after midnight when Darren was awoken by Karen shaking his shoulder.

"Uh-huh," he grunted, "What's the matter?"

"Darren, wake up. Skye's shouting for us."

"Oh, blimey. She doesn't like her room," he groaned, threw back the bedclothes. "We'd better go and quieten her down."

They shrugged into their dressing gowns, hurried out on to the landing. As they did so the door of the small bedroom was already opening and a white faced, trembling Skye was rushing to meet them.

"Skye, whatever's the matter?" Karen clasped her daughter to her, felt how she shook in every limb.

"Mummy…mummy…there's…there is a …lady in my room!"

There was a stunned silence. Darren and Karen looked at each other, dumbstruck.

"That's nonsense," Darren grunted. "You've been dreaming, Skye."

"No!" the child shrieked. *"She's horrible, she's in*

*the mirror!"*

He pushed past them, flung the bedroom door wide, flicked the light switch. The mirror faced him on the dressing table, a relic of a former owner of the house, standing in a gilt frame, in excellent condition he had retained it rather than throwing it out with numerous other items. It reflected his own image in its recently polished glass. Nothing else.

"There's nothing in the mirror except my own ugly mug," he laughed, tried to make light of his daughter's terror. "Like I said, you've been dreaming, Skye, had a nightmare."

*"It was real,"* she shouted. *"A horrible woman with eyes that hated me, watched me. She meant me harm. I didn't dream it!"*

"All right," he tried to calm her. "You go and sleep with Mummy, Skye. I'll sleep in your bed and if that woman shows up I'll give her a rough time."

Skye nodded, clung to her mother. Darren went into the small bedroom, closed the door behind him, and stretched out on the bed. That mirror was too good to junk. If it really troubled his daughter then he would move it into their own bedroom.

In the meantime he was exhausted. He switched off the light, and in a few minutes had drifted into a deep sleep. The night passed peacefully, there were no further disturbances.

***

Skye was obviously still troubled at breakfast the next morning. Karen took her to school and then returned to continue cleaning the small lounge. Darren busied himself re-papering and decorating the main bedroom.

"I think maybe it would be a good idea if Skye slept with

you tonight," he said as they shared a sandwich lunch. "Maybe for a couple of nights, I'll sleep in her bedroom. After that I'll move that mirror which seems to be troubling her, put it somewhere else. Of course, she had a nightmare last night, nothing to do with the mirror itself. Then, hopefully, everything will settle down."

"Good idea," his wife nodded. "But I have to say there's something strange about that room. I can't place it but it gives me the prickles. Like there's somebody in there that I can't see."

"Well, I'll fix it, whatever it is," he laughed. "We can't have a spooky bedroom in the house."

Later that evening she escorted Skye up to the parental bedroom. "I'll be up to join you later," she promised." And Daddy will sleep in your room. Just for a couple of nights.  After that we'll move that mirror somewhere else as it seems to trouble you, maybe even get rid of it altogether."

Skye nodded, smiled, and started to undress.

***

Later that evening Darren climbed into the small single bed. He found himself staring at the mirror on the dresser. In its own way it was attractive, probably made in the thirties. If it came to the crunch he would scrap it, which seemed a pity. Probably, though, Skye had had a nightmare. It couldn't be anything else.

In a matter of minutes he drifted into an exhausted sleep.

Sometime later he stirred restlessly. It was like he wasn't alone in the room. It was aglow and the ethereal light was coming from that mirror. He sat up.

*What the hell was happening? Within that gilt frame the glass was lit up by a glow that steadily brightened and revealed a face; female features that were decidedly attractive but in a disturbing way. The wide brow was furrowed, strands of auburn hair spilling down on to it as though trying to hide the eyes which glowed red. Thin lips parted in an unmistakable snarl of sheer hatred revealing even white teeth tightly clenched. Watching him intently, those orbs boring into him. He could almost feel their venom. It had been no childish nightmare which Skye had experienced. The terror was there before his very own eyes.*

Shock and fear but the latter was only temporary. Darren had never been truly scared of anything since childhood. He froze then, with a supreme effort, pulled himself together.

"Damn you!" he snarled. "I'm not going to stand for this nonsense in my own house. Sod off!"

Those red orbs flickered depicting a burning hatred. The lips curled into a snarl, but no sound came from them.

"You might scare a child, but you don't scare me!"

For a second that mouth closed. Darren interpreted it as a hint of fear. It was just a reflection, nothing more. Whatever it was it was trapped in that mirror. The advantage was his.

His fingers scrabbled on the bedside table, located a book belonging to his daughter. It was a paperback, he would have preferred a heavier hardback, but it would have to do. He grasped it, his arm went back and he flung it with every ounce of strength, which he could muster.

His aim was true. It hit that mirror with a thud and a fluttering of pages.

"Take that!" He shouted.

On impact those fearful features in the weird reflection seemed to come to life as though they had felt the impact. The mouth opened, a silent scream of rage.

Then a hand appeared, slim female fingers clutching what was undoubtedly a kitchen knife. Its heavy eight-inch blade was thick with a scarlet fluid, which slowly dripped. *Blood!*

*Jesus Christ!* He recoiled; his instinct was to flee the room. Then suddenly the mirror went blank like a television set that had been switched off. It was tottering from the impact of the missile, which had struck it, almost as though that fearsome image was attempting to vacate it, swaying back and forth.

Darren yelled at it and then it fell forward, crashed on the floor, lay still. With shaking fingers, he switched on the bedside light. Miraculously the glass had not smashed; to all intents and purposes it was just an ordinary mirror that had somehow toppled from its resting place.

"Darren, are you all right? What's going on?"

As he swung off the bed the door opened to reveal Karen with Skye cringing behind her.

"Nothing to worry about," he did not want to alarm his daughter. "The mirror fell off the dressing table. I guess it was perched rather precariously and I must've knocked it when I drew the curtains."

"It was that awful woman again!" Skye shrieked. "I know it was."

"Nonsense. Anyway after all the distress that it's caused Skye, I'm going to junk it tomorrow. I'll take it to the refuse tip, get it out of the house altogether, then you will be able to sleep in your room without worrying about it. How will that suit you, Skye?"

"I don't like this room," his daughter muttered. "It's… creepy."

"Well, it won't be once that mirror's gone. Now, let's all get back to sleep. You've got school tomorrow and your mother and I have got a busy day ahead of us."

***

Darren heard Karen driving away to take Skye to school. He was both uneasy and angry as he went upstairs and fetched the mirror. Damn the bloody thing, good riddance to it.

He carried it out onto the back yard then fetched a sledgehammer from his tool shed. He was trembling slightly; last night had been a frightening experience for which there was no logical explanation. Well, it would soon be over.

He propped the mirror up against the wall, swung the heavy tool above his head and brought it crashing down with every ounce of strength, which he could muster. The glass splintered into fragments and the frame cracked. Another blow just to make sure.

"Take that, whatever you are!" He grunted.

He fetched an empty cardboard box and a broom, began sweeping up the debris. Then he loaded it into the back of his van. The council's refuse tip was a few miles beyond the village. It was with a sense of anger and relief when he hurled the box onto a pile of household rubbish, which would be collected and transferred elsewhere. Thus the mirror would be gone for good.

Only then did he experience a sense of relief.

***

On his return home he recalled a job he had done for a guy named Paul Adams down in Limbury, near Luton, a year or so ago. Paul was an exceptionally nice guy and they had kept in touch ever since. The other was involved in occult research; having written several books on the subject and had also appeared in a television programme. A thought occurred to Darren that it might be worth having a word with his friend to find out if he could throw any light on the recent strange happenings.

Karen had mentioned that she might drive into town and do some shopping after dropping Skye off at school so there was no time like the present to phone Paul. It was preferable that Skye did not know anything about it.

Paul was at home and answered Darren's call almost immediately.

"Hi Paul, some strange goings-on here and I'd feel easier if I spoke to you about them." He related the recent happenings with the mirror and Skye's reluctance to sleep in her bedroom.

"Hmm," Paul replied. "It would seem to me that this relates to something that has gone on there in the past. You say that the house has been unoccupied and just in the hands of an estate agent for a few years. First of all, I would suggest a basic exorcism, which you can do yourself. You will need a saucer of salt, a bible and a crucifix. Place them by the mirror, shut the room up and let your daughter continue to sleep with yourselves for the time being. After a few nights I suggest that you sleep in that bedroom and see if anything happens."

"There's just one problem, Paul."

"What's that?"

"I smashed the mirror up this morning and took it to the council dump. I wanted it out of the house."

"Oh dear, that's the worst thing you could have done. Whatever is haunting that bedroom was focused in the mirror, existed there."

"But surely it has gone with the remnants of the mirror?"

"I would like to think so. Anyway, all I can suggest is that you go ahead with the exorcism in the manner I have explained, placing the items on the dressing table where the mirror stood. Possibly, hopefully, you have driven this spirit, which was undoubtedly evil, from your house. Let us hope so. If it returns, then I will arrange for some of my contacts to come up and conduct a full exorcism in the house. That's all I can suggest at the moment. Try it and give me a call in a few days to inform me of any events. I just hope that there will not be any."

Darren sighed as he replaced the receiver. He had no option other than to take Paul's advice and hope that everything worked out.

***

A sudden idea crossed his mind as he began sorting out his tools for the day's work ahead. So far neither he nor Karen had made contact with any of their neighbours in the village; their move here had been carried out at short notice. Maybe somebody living in the vicinity knew something about the history of the house.

He went down to the bottom of the short tarmac drive. A few houses away a man was forking the front border. Darren walked down towards him.

"Good morning. My name's Darren Alker, we've just moved into the end house."

The other straightened up with some difficulty, a man in his late seventies, jammed the fork into the ground and stroked his grizzled chin.

"Pleased to meet you. George Jones, I used to be in the police force, in the days when they had village bobbies. Nowadays if you see a copper around here he's in a car whizzing by. Sign of the times."

"I guess so."

"So you've bought number twenty," Jones glanced down towards the house in question. "Lotta work needs doing to it. Nobody's lived there for some time, the property agents have had it on the market for years. No luck understandably." He cleared his throat, was quick to add, "The weather forecast's good, there'll be holidaymakers flocking here, every B&B booked up…"

"About my house…"

Jones cleared his throat, deliberately avoided the other's gaze. "I'd rather not be the one to tell you if nobody else has. The agent didn't because you probably wouldn't have bought the place if he had."

"Rumoured to be haunted?" Darren pressed.

"Not that I know of, Mister Alker but…" he hesitated again. "There…there was a double murder there sometime back in the seventies."

"What?!"

"I was involved in the case but I'd rather not talk about it. The villagers certainly won't. Bad for the holiday trade. Tell you what, now you've asked me, go to the library in town, browse the local papers for those years. It was front-page news at the time. I'd rather leave it at that if you don't mind."

Darren tensed, speechless for the moment. Then he nodded. "Thank you, Mister Jones. I…I'll do that."

"Wish I hadn't told you," the other turned away, picked up his fork. "But I guess you'd've found out in due course. A lot of properties these days have been the scene of murders and folks just live in 'me. Best to forget all about it."

Darren returned home, left a note on the table for Karen to the effect that he had gone to town to buy some paint. Then he went back outside to his van.

***

The small library was under notice for closure, like many others the length and breadth of the country. A thought crossed his mind that it would have been preferable if it had already shut down. That way he would have been spared the awful knowledge of the macabre history of their home. No, he *had* to know.

The reading room was deserted. The young librarian brought him a pile of copies of 'The Star' from the 1970s. He nodded his thanks and began to browse them with trembling fingers.

The March 13th issue blazoned the murder in bold front-page headlines. 'Double Murder in Village. Local Woman Arrested.'

Darren pursed his lips, read on.

"On the evening of March 10th, a double murder occurred in a village house on the Welsh coast. Frederick Allport, aged 32 stabbed his 6-year old daughter and then attacked his wife, Cynthia, aged 30. Mrs Allport grabbed a kitchen knife and delivered a single thrust to her husband's heart.

"Hearing the screams, neighbours called the police and Mrs Allport was taken into custody and is due to appear before magistrates on Friday."

Further reading revealed that the case had gone to Crown Court a month later. There were several reports of her trial over the following two weeks.

It was revealed that the Allport's" daughter, unknown to Frederick, had been conceived in an affair which Cynthia had had shortly after their marriage. Years later he discovered that their daughter was not his own and in a fit of rage he killed her in her bedroom and then attempted to murder his wife. Mrs Allport grabbed a kitchen knife and murdered her husband.

A further report stated that she had been sentenced to 15 years in prison.

There was a photograph of Cynthia Allport alongside the report. That was when Darren tensed, the fingers holding the open page shaking uncontrollably.

*There was no mistaking the features portrayed; they were those, which had appeared in that mirror the previous night, the likeness unmistakable. Jesus Christ!*

He left the pile of newspapers on the table, went back outside, took several deep breaths. The mirror on the dressing table had somehow retained the reflection of the murder committed in the small bedroom and Cynthia Allport had become a living entity within it.

He tried to convince himself that smashing it and removing it from the house had destroyed it once and for all. Right now he needed to speak to Paul Adams.

"You've been a long time," Karen greeted him in the kitchen where she was busy preparing a sandwich for lunch.

He seated himself at the table, recounted falteringly that which he had discovered at the library.

"Oh my God!" She buried her face in her hands. "Darren, we've got to sell up and move. We can't live here with…with *that*!"

"First I need to get Paul's opinion," he replied. "I'm going to call him now. Whatever he says, Skye must never know. I'm going to sort that small room out next to ours, the box room, turn it into a bedroom for her. In the meantime she'll have to sleep in with us. God, I don't believe all this."

***

"There is no logical explanation," Paul told him. "I've visited numerous buildings which have been haunted after a specific happening, ghosts which appear at intervals, usually harmless. On this occasion Cynthia Allport's spirit has been trapped in that mirror which reflected the murder. But I've also done some research on the case. *A year or so before she was due for release from prison, she died.* Hence her spirit returned to the scene of her daughter's death and the murder of her husband. Somehow, and there's no explanation for it, it became trapped in that mirror. Her spirit is still desperate for revenge…on somebody."

"Incredible! Darren's voice shook. "But how do I now get rid of it from our house?"

"Only time will tell. You've carried out a basic exorcism in the room but you've destroyed the mirror, which was the focal point of the haunting. I only wish that you had left the mirror in there, then I would feel more confident of a good result from the exorcism. So, what happens to Mrs Allport's spirit now we may never know. Hopefully you have set it free from its incarceration in the mirror and it will rest in peace. Give me a call in a week or so, earlier if anything happens."

I'll do that, and thanks for your help." Darren sighed and replaced the receiver.

***

"I'm going up to bed," Karen rose from the armchair where she had spent most of the evening. "Skye was sleeping peacefully when I checked on her earlier. Let's hope she stays that way. See you later."

Shortly afterwards, just as Darren was considering retiring for the night, there came a knocking on the front door. Three sharp raps.

"Who the hell can that be?" He muttered to himself, crossing the room and switching on the outside light. He experienced a sense of apprehension as he opened the door.

"Good evening. What can I do for you?"

He saw his visitor, a tall woman with auburn hair, strands spilling across her pallid features. She was not wearing a coat, simply a frayed dress which fluttered in the breeze revealing a shapely pair of legs.

It was when they made eye contact that he stiffened with shock; saw a pair of orbs that dimly glowed red. The lips drew back, an unmistakable snarl.

*Oh, Jesus, there was no mistaking her likeness to that photograph of Cynthia Allport, which he had seen in the newspaper earlier that day. Her hand raised slowly, and he saw that she clutched a blood stained kitchen knife.*

*"I've come for Frederick, my husband."* Her voice was soft, threatening, a kind of whispered echo.

Darren swayed, clutched at the open door for support, thought for a moment that he might faint.

"He…he," he stuttered. "Frederick Allport doesn't live here…any longer. Hasn't for…for several years. We…we bought this house, have only moved in recently."

The red in those eyes dimmed. The woman's arm fell to her side, the knife dangling like she might drop it. A nod as though she understood. Darren gripped the door, would have slammed it shut except that his foot caught against it. He lowered his gaze, momentarily afraid to look upon the awesome, terrible nocturnal caller.

One final glance as he freed the door and started to close it, as though she had commanded him to look upon her.

*There was nobody there; the driveway and the street opposite were empty. There was no sign of anybody, human or…*

Finally he managed to close the door, locked it and leant up against it. His shaking legs struggled to hold him upright. Jumbled thoughts: Maybe he had freed her from her incarceration in that awful mirror. One final visit to the house of those dreadful murders so long ago had proved fruitless.

He prayed that Cynthia Allport was gone forever,

that she would now find peace of mind beyond the grave. Only time would tell.

# Yobs
## Kevin J Kennedy

"Haw, doll. C'mere," a voice called out.

Kelly picked up her pace as she passed the young team, knowing she should have went the longer way home but in the end deciding it was too cold. Her heels clicked on the pavement as she sped up.

"Haw. A said c'mere, ya wee slut," the voice came again.

She knew the voice. It was Ringo, the self-appointed leader of the group of *bams* that had been hanging about her area for the last few months.

They called themselves a *Young Team,* but half of them were in their late twenties now. Sure, there were still lads as young as ten and eleven hanging around with them but these days the group consisted mainly of older guys who should have been out working; instead they mainly just hung around the lane, drinking and causing trouble.

It had never been like that when her brother had lived at home. Kelly knew that her brother had been far from an angel, but he was never a terror to people walking down the street. He had chosen a less than savoury path, selling drugs from the age of twelve. It had been a massive disappointment to her parents when they found out. Her family had never been particularly well-to-do, but they had brought their children up well, with good morals and guidance.

Billy had always been a child filled with initiative and it often got him into trouble. When the police brought him home that night and his parents asked him what he was thinking, he had explained he only planned to do it up until he was sixteen and then his police record would be wiped anyway, so it didn't even matter that he had been caught. Kelly had been watching from the doorway and was shocked to see her parents speechless. Billy went on to tell them that he was going to save up the money and use it to start his own business at sixteen. While her parents were furious with Billy, Kelly could sense that in a strange way her father seemed to be almost proud of him. Her father had wanted Billy to be tough from a young age. He had been put into a boxing class at the age of four and had taken to it like a duck to water. He had kept it up and while all his friends were out drinking and trying drugs, Billy was instead training and selling them drugs.

There was only a year in it between Billy and Kelly, with him being the elder of the two, but they had always had a great relationship. He was a very protective big brother and everyone knew who his sister was and that you didn't go near her. Until Billy moved into his own place she had never had a bad word said to her, but she knew with the Young Tea, it was out of sight, out of mind. He no longer sold them drugs either, so she supposed that was another reason they wouldn't be too worried about upsetting him.

The last few times she had passed the group they had done nothing but shout vile slurs at her. She could handle the name-calling but she had no plans of getting any closer to them than she had to.

"A said fuckin' c'mere, ya wee bitch."

She could hear the footsteps approaching as she tried to move even quicker in her heels, knowing her dress was blowing in the wind and just hoping she wasn't giving the little pricks a good look. She was just around the corner from her house. If she could just get there, at least her father could offer her some protection. He was too old to be getting involved in trouble, but he had always been a tough man. He wasn't the type to stand and take shit from a few little pricks. Her father's mantra was "you have to be tough in a tough world". It was funny though. Kelly wasn't tough and it was because of the men in her family she had never needed to be.

Kelly felt a hand go around her arm and swing her round. She instantly smelled the drink on Ringo's breath, *Buckfast*, it smelled vile. He wore the same grey, hooded tracksuit that he seemed to have on most days. Most of the boys in the group wore the same clothes daily. She knew that they were a product of bad parenting, or in some cases no parenting, but that did not help her feel any sympathy for a group who terrorized people. Only last week a fourteen year old boy had been stabbed and bled to death in the street. Everyone knew it had been the Young Team but there were no arrests because no one would speak to the police. The rumour was that he had been stabbed because he wouldn't give one of them a cigarette. The boy didn't even smoke.

"Did you no" hear me or something! Need they pretty little ears cleaned oot!" Ringo said, leaning in and licking her lobe.

Kelly pulled back in disgust. "Just leave me alone. I'm in a hurry. My dad's expecting me."

"Ooh, her dads expecting her, lads. Better let her go, eh?" one of the younger lads sang in a mocking tone.

The small crowd laughed way more than necessary. Especially Ringo—he was a full-blown psycho—fourteen years old and never convicted but already suspected of two murders. He was a wee *chib merchant*, always carrying a blade or something similar. Kelly had never heard of him being in a single fight and doubted that he would last long considering he was built like a butcher's pencil but everyone was scared of him due to his unpredictability. She was positive there was a minefield of undiagnosed issues buried in that little guy's brain but doubted he would ever receive the help he needed.

There was no real leader to the gang but there were a few older, harder lads that were known to be able to handle themselves, but it always seemed to be Ringo in the middle of everything, winding it up.

"When we shout you over, you come fucking over," Ringo said, spit flying everywhere as he spoke. "Understand?"

She nodded in submission, keeping her eyes on the ground. Although the street lamps lit the walk way she felt surrounded by darkness.

"Do you think you're special or something? "Cause you're Billy Henderson's sister? Or is it "cause big Mick's yer da? "Cause if ye 'hink we care, ye have another fucking 'hing comin', hen," Ringo went on.

She noticed he used *we* rather than *I*. She knew they had a group mentality and couldn't function on their own. Her brother had explained it to her when they were younger, how bullies always travelled in packs and were rarely as big mouthed or brave if you ever got them on their own. But she didn't feel like she was in a position to educate the boys.

"Your brother is a fuckin" nobody now 'n we run these streets," Ringo said, finishing his rant and sounding like a character from a bad eighties movie.

"Look, just let me go. I never bother any of you and I'm already late. Please!" Kelly begged.

"I'm late!" one of the other younger boys called Skinz mimicked.

They all laughed again. It seemed that when anyone said anything snide, everyone in the group had to join in for the big laugh whether it was funny or not.

Kelly wrapped her arms around herself thinking that it was a really stupid idea not to wear a jacket.

"You can come over and sit on the stairs wae us for a while and have a wee drink. Nobody will miss you," Ringo said, taking her arm harder than anyone had ever manhandled her before. She tried to pull out of his grip but was surprised that he was far stronger than he looked.

"Daaaaaad!" Kelly screamed at the top of her lungs, thinking he would never hear her with the wind blowing so strongly, but not knowing what else to do. She was absolutely terrified and knew something bad was going to happen. As she screamed, Ringo spun and rattled her across the jaw with the back of his hand. "Shut it, slut!" Ringo continued dragging her towards the stairs leading to the lane they all drank in.

Just as Kelly thought all hope was lost she heard a car screech to a halt and a door slam. She looked over her shoulder in hope, as she felt Ringo's fingers dig even deeper into her arm. She had prayed to God a million times for a million different things and he had never answered, so when she saw her big brother striding towards them, she thought she must be dreaming.

A lad of fourteen called Dizzy stepped into her

brother's path before he reached the group. Billy still hadn't said a word and held a steady pace as he approached. Dizzy was a bulky lad for his age and had always been known as a bit of a fighter, but he wasn't the sharpest pencil in the box, hence the name.

"It's awright, Billy. We were just having a wee laugh wae her," as Dizzy finished his sentence, Billy's fist smashed across the bottom of his jaw with a well-placed cross, knocking him out cold before he even started his fall.

A few more steps after the punch and a few elbows flung had separated the crowd enough so that he was standing in front of Ringo and one of the bigger lads named Slice, who had been in the Young Team since they started out.

Billy looked from one to the other and back. Slice was lot taller than Ringo and a lot better built. Billy knew he could fight, having run around with him a little in his younger days, but he had never been a part of their team as they liked to think of themselves.

"Who the fuck do you think you are, prick? You'll get yersel' killed coming down here actin'' aw hard like that. Your days of thinking yer the man are long gone, Billy," Ringo raged, stepping forward and poking Billy in the chest. The flurry of punches that Billy landed on Ringo's face happened in less than a second but it was five solid hits that not only put the little guy out but left his face a smashed wreck of blood, cuts and lumps.

"Ye haven't lost it, Billy," Slice said, one side of his mouth turning up.

"Naw! A fuckin' haven't, mate. What the fuck are you doing wae ma sister?"

"Listen, Billy. Ye know these young lads. They do what they want. Am no their da. You're no aboot any more so they think yer sister is fair game. Ye know a cannae let ye put two of ma boys down and just let ye walk away, don't you?" Slice said, looking almost sad.

"Am no goin' anywhere, mate," Billy said taking his jacket off. "Kelly. Home. Now!"

Kelly took off running as best she could in her heels. None of the boys made a move to stop her. Billy's stare had made sure they knew better. There were only two guys in the whole team that had hung around when Billy did, but they had all heard of him by reputation.

"Naebody jump in," Slice said, giving an order that was rarely given amongst these particular guys, the normal fight situation being more similar to a pack of jackals attacking a small antelope. Billy wasn't sure if Slice had done this out of an old respect they held for each other, or simply because he had always wanted to fight Billy to see who was toughest but had never been afforded the opportunity.

The fight went on for over twenty minutes and although no one jumped in, several kicks came from the younger lads when Billy was getting the better of Slice. At the end both men stood up, a few broken ribs between them, a few less teeth, both of their faces looking like they had been in a car crash and their clothes in tatters. They stood a few steps apart, looking into each other's eyes and Slice smiled.

"Man, you can fuckin" go, Billy! That's the best work out av had in years. Fair play lad."

Billy knew that was it. They had fought, nobody had won but that was enough for Slice. He knew that Slice was no leader of men, but he also doubted there were many lads in the group that would want to feel Slice's wrath.

"That us cool? Nobody goes near ma sister again?" Billy asked.

"Aye. We're cool," Slice said genuinely. "You's aw hear me? Naebody goes near his sis fae now on or you's will have me tae answer tae. Awright?"

There were murmurs among the lads, but nobody wanted to say yes. As Slice looked around them, a few nodded as they caught his eye, but Billy knew that was it.

As Billy walked back to his car, Dizzy was awake but struggling with his balance and Ringo was still out cold.

***

Ringo had just finished smashing up his mother's flat for the third time that day, not that anyone would notice the difference—the only people who ever saw the inside of the place were her junkie friends and they didn't know if they were coming or going. His temper would not settle, the pain in his jaw making sure of that.

"Fucking did nothing, that prick Slice. Not a fucking thing!" There was no one else in the flat. Ringo was talking to himself as he often did, not just when he was angry. He was on his second 99p bottle of *Silver Strike* cider and had done several speed bombs by the time the clock struck ten in the morning. "I'll fucking show them aw who's top boy round here. Think 'cause they can fight they're hard. I'll fuckin' show them hard."

Ringo had always liked to get a buzz on before doing anything really crazy. When he was fucked up he had no fear, he could do anything. He had watched films where guys playing Wall Street stockbrokers spoke about coke and how they felt on top of the world doing it. No way would he spend that kind of money on a daft gram. You could get a quarter of speed for the same price and still have money for a few bottles of cider to go with it. It lasted a lot longer too.

***

"Am scared, Billy," Kelly said down the phone.

"I told you last night that that's it sorted."

"But you didn't come by."

Billy hadn't wanted to let his sister or parents see him in the state he was in. It was a long time since he had arrived at their door after a fight and he didn't want to drag up old memories.

"I'm fine, Kel, I just remembered I had somewhere to be. It's all sorted out. None of them will bother you now."

"Dad wants to go and speak to their parents," Kelly said, trailing off.

"Are you joking? Most of their parents are alkies or junkies. Tell him to phone me before he does anything stupid."

"Okay."

"Kelly, it's okay. I promise."

"Okay, love you."

"Love you too, pal, see you soon, okay."

***

Ringo sat parked down the street from the Five Aces gym, happy that it was in a shitty area and the streetlights had all been smashed out. The people that used this gym weren't the type of guys who got mugged so it probably hadn't been reported. Most of the patrons probably preferred moving around in the dark anyway. He had followed Billy here from his flat, keeping a safe distance but as he was driving a stolen car he wasn't too worried about being recognised and doubted anyone would be looking for it yet. Billy had been inside for a few hours, but it was no big deal. Ringo just sat smoking weed and thinking about getting his revenge. His jaw still ached but the weed he had was pretty powerful, he was half-drunk from earlier, and the speed was still buzzing through his system.

As Billy stepped outside the club, Ringo started up the engine, put the car into gear and started to slowly pick up speed. By the time Billy heard him coming and turned around, Ringo had already smashed the car into his legs, flipping him up onto the bonnet. The windscreen cracked but not too bad, he planned to pick up another car later anyway. Ringo was up and out of the car like lightning. Billy had left the club himself but who knew how long it would be before someone else came out. He dragged Billy to the back of the car, opened the boot and with some difficulty managed to get him inside. Billy was still awake but dazed and his legs were in bad shape.

***

Billy was tied to a chair in one of the old lock-up garages. He had come round fully now and knew he was tied tight. His legs were agony and Ringo kept kicking him, which didn't help.

"Do you know why you're here, Billy?"

The gag that had been tied in Billy's mouth prevented him from answering.

"I'll tell ye why yer here, will a? Yer here 'cause I've decided that a don't much like ye. It's been years since ye've been on the streets and a kinda respected ye from aw they stories av heard aboot ye, but now yer back and am no' havin' it. Slice is fuckin' dead as well. I'll be the top man around here come the morra 'n' there's fuck aw you or anybody else can dae aboot it. Understand?"

As Ringo finished his sentence he smashed Billy's knee with a hammer that had been hanging on the wall. Billy screamed into his gag until his throat felt like it was on fire. If his legs weren't already ruined, they were now. He had never felt pain like it in his life. He was on the brink of passing out when Ringo slapped him hard and then poured a freezing bucket of rainwater over him that had been sitting under a small hole in the roof.

"Don't pass out on me now, Billy. We've got a lot to talk about. Like what I'm gonna dae tae yer family when am done wae Slice. Ooft! It's gonna be special. Shame you'll no be able to help them. Eh?"

Billy's focus was coming and going due to the pain in his legs. He tried to speak through the gag but it was useless.

"Listen, mate. Am no' interested in yer pish. Am away tae sort oot that bam Slice then I'll go and see yer folks. If am still feeling energetic a might swing back here and show ye some pics of ma work, I'll take on ma camera phone. That sound good, buddy? Thought so. Don't you go dying on me. No' just yet anyway."

As Ringo walked out of the lock-up wearing the same grey hooded tracksuit he had been wearing for the last three weeks, he shouted over his shoulder, "The good guy doesnae always win mate. That's just in the fuckin' movies."

***

The music blared from inside Slice's flat. Ringo knew that meant he was shaggin' some wee dirty. He always played the same Bonkers album—the first one. He told everybody all the time if you come round and that's playing don't come in.

The good thing about Slice though was that he never locked his door. Ringo tried the handle and found it was open, as he expected. He slipped inside quietly, not that there was really a need. The flat was in darkness but he could see a sliver of light creeping out from under Slice's bedroom door. This was going to be easier than

Ringo had expected. He slipped his hunting knife out of the back of his trousers and crept towards the door. He decided he would just throw the door open and run straight in. Slice was a big guy so he wanted to get him before he knew what was going on. He pushed the room handle down very slowly then rushed into the room.

*It was empty.*

He turned round quickly. Slice was standing in the doorway. He had been hiding in the toilet right next door to his room, waiting for him.

"How'd you fuckin" know?" Ringo raged.

"You never even thought to go through Billy's pockets ya dumb cunt! Ye left him wae his mobile. The minute he managed to get a hand free he got me on Facebook through his phone and sent me a message. You really need to be careful what you overlook in this day and age, mate. Cunt hasn't had ma number in years n he still managed tae get a hold ay me just cause you're that fuckin' dumb."

Slice had been shouting over the music but as he was speaking the music had been turned all the way down, from the other room. "You've become a problem, mate, a big fuckin' problem."

As Slice stopped talking, the rest of the Young Team filed into the hall behind him.

"Sorry, wee man. Ye know how it is."

He walked back into the living room and turned the music up full blast to drown out the noise. The Bonkers album had finished. Ultra Sonic's Annihilating Rhythm clicked on and pumped out of the speakers as he turned and nodded to the lads. As the lads went to work on Ringo his screams almost drowned out the music... Almost.

***

Billy spent a few weeks in the hospital, his family a

constant reminder that he was back where they didn't want him to be, fighting with thugs in the street. He hadn't argued, he knew they couldn't help being scared when things like this happened. He would always walk with a limp but that wasn't what bothered him the most. It was the fact that he didn't get to deal with that little prick Ringo himself.

Slice had come to visit him in the hospital and told him that Ringo was gone. He hadn't elaborated on the details, but Billy knew that he meant for good.

"Lads were sick of him." Slice had told Billy. "Was time for him to go. Cunt was a liability. Fuck, I was always half expecting the wee dick to stab me when he was around anyway," Slice said with a chuckle.

Slice had come to visit Billy every day. He had even made a joke about how he wouldn't have broken Billy's ribs if he knew he was going to get hit with a car and his knee smashed with a hammer, which was the closest Slice had ever come to giving an apology. He didn't really regret the fight. It was something he had needed to get out of his system but it had reminded him why he liked Billy so much. Billy wasn't like the other guys. He was a real fighter, a true warrior but he just didn't feel the need to shout about it. He never wanted to hurt others or prove he was tough. He just went about his life, minding his own business but when it came down to it he was one tough fucker.

"So, you're in charge of the lads now?" Billy asked.

"Mate, no one will ever be in charge of those lads. Most of them are already too far gone, but I'll keep an eye on them and make sure they stay away from you and your family."

When Billy got out of the hospital he never saw Slice again. They didn't become life-long friends or get together at the weekends, but Slice stuck to his word.

The Young Team disappeared from his neighbourhood and his sister was never bothered again. Occasionally Billy would meet one of them from time to time when he was out drinking but they would always just give him a nod or offer to buy him a drink. It seemed in some way that getting rid of Ringo had quietened the group down or maybe it was just the fact that they had watched him and Slice batter each other close to death and get up and walk away from it. Billy didn't know, and he really didn't care. All he did know was that he fucking hated wee yobs.

# The Devil's Tree
## Lee Franklin

Kari enjoyed the warm glow of the Yorkshire sun on her back, as she watched the children racing around in the playground, making the most of their summer holidays outside. It was a child on the far side of the playground, and in the field beyond, well away from the frantic energy of the others that caught her eye. Wearing a hideous orange cardigan, the boy looked lonely as he knelt on the floor looking out towards a large old oak. Curiosity got the better of Kari, stretching her legs and she went to check on him.

As a backpacker, working in a day care centre certainly beat picking fruit and, yes, at times the kids could be painful, but it paid quite well. It was pure luck she landed the job. She had planned to meet up with her backpacker friend, Judy, in the village on her way through to York. Apparently, Judy worked for a week and then, failed to show up for work just a few days before Kari came looking for her. Kari was disappointed but not overly concerned as Judy was generally spontaneous and irresponsible.

Walking over to the boy, Kari noticed that he was sat in the dirt looking at a football that was resting up against the trunk of the old oak. Kari called out encouragingly, "C'mon, little man, go get your ball."

The boy turned around and looked at her, his little blue eyes wide and red with dread. He shook his head.

"I can't go near the tree, miss, it doesn't want me too. It's bad." Kari tried hard to hide her laugh as she approached him, such a serious little face and his cute lilting accent was too adorable.

"Don't be silly now, it's just a tree."

"No, Miss Kari. It's evil. Everyone knows that."

Kari looked at the tree properly for the first time. Yes, it certainly did look spooky. A large, grey mottled twisted trunk and easily twenty metres tall, it looked half dead, unlike the other trees around the playground. Not a patch of green grass grew underneath it and whilst the other children climbed and played under the other trees in the park, this one was left well alone. Come to think of it, Kari could not remember ever seeing any children even come this close to it. But the country folk were known for their superstitions. She patted the boy on the back as he wiped off his tears with the cuff of his very pumpkin coloured looking cardigan.

"What's your name, little man?" Kari asked, furiously trying to remember him from the seething mass of children at breakfast.

"Thomas, Thomas Crosswell, Miss," he sniffed.

"It's just a tree, Thomas, but if you are scared I will go and get your ball for you."

Thomas grabbed onto her hand as she started walking towards the tree. "No, Miss, I appreciate it, but the ball is lost now. It belongs to the tree and I don't want to get too close. Miss, you must not go over there. It's dangerous. Please I beg you don't go there."

Kari turned and smiled at him, his face was a pale mask of dread and he had started trembling.

"I'm Australian mate, I'll be safe, kiddo. No tree should come between a boy and his ball."

Dropping Thomas's hand and ignoring his protests, she walked towards the tree. Stepping under the tree's canopy, Kari suddenly felt a feeling of dread grip her heart and a chill in her blood that almost made her hesitate. Kari felt Thomas's eyes burning nervously into her back. Taking a deep breath, Kari relaxed her shoulders and shook her head at her own silliness. With every step closer to the trunk a distinctive smell of mould and rot rose from the ground and assaulted her senses. *It would smell like this under such a massive canopy.*

Kari had only smelt death once. Long ago, Kari found the half-rotting corpse of the family cat, Albert. Albert had been missing for close to three weeks and it was Kari that found him, crushed under the stack of timber. The image of Albert with his exploded stomach, infested with maggots and insects came uninvited to her mind. Empty eye sockets looked at her as ants marched in and out of his nose. The image stuck in her nightmares for a long time, but it was the smell Kari could never forget and that is what she smelled now—a sulphurous eruption of spoiled intestines and decaying flesh.

Moving quicker now, her skin prickled in fear. No, it's just cooler in the shade, she told herself. Kari reached down and picked up the old leather ball, she noticed that her feet were sinking as the ground was almost bog like and huge chunks of mud clung to the cuffs of her jeans. Annoyed, Kari leaned against the tree to flick it off, wondering how it got there. Under her hand, the trunk felt warm and soft like human flesh. She shuddered and instantly removed her hand, pulling off pieces of bark with it. Kari suppressed a shriek and told herself not to be ridiculous. Feeling his blue eyes boring into her back in terror, she turned to force a smile and waved at Thomas, letting him know that she was all right. Quite a crowd had gathered close around him, but still a good distance from the tree, their little voices twittering in nervous anticipation. The other staff whispered nervously to each other, looking serious and grim as they watched Kari under the tree.

Uneasy tension clenched her stomach, Kari laughed as she tried to shake it off. Silly superstitions. With a startled shriek, Kari fell face first in the boggy mud around the tree. Somebody from the crowd screamed, Kari felt the smack to her forehead as she hit the dirt. It was like she had smashed her face into Albert's rotting body, the stench, the damp was horrifying, and she could taste the blood that trickled down from her brow.

Kari heard a moan of agony from behind her.

"Help me, help me." Terror rippled through her body as she struggled to stand up. Her left leg was trapped and being dragged back towards the tree. Flailing momentarily, she managed to shake it loose and scramble to her feet.

Trying to maintain a calm demeanour for the children's sake, Kari finally emerged from underneath the tree canopy; it was only when she was a few metres from the group when her co-worker Helen rushed towards her "What are you doing? You mad woman. Are you all right?" as she offered a tissue which Kari used to stem the blood flowing from her forehead.

"I went to get the ball for Thomas," Kari explained, looking in the hovering crowd for the young redheaded boy.

"We don't have a Thomas, and you don't have a ball," Helen hissed through her clenched teeth and faked a smile of reassurance for the throng of on-looking children.

"What? I was just speaking to him," Kari mumbled, the pain in her head starting a heavy throb.

"Why don't you go and get cleaned up?" Helen suggested warmly as she herded Kari towards the old school building. Kari grimaced in response and felt herself get swept up in the jostling group that headed back to the building. But the whispered conversations around her were not lost on her.

"Miss Kari is so brave."

"No, she's not, she's stupid. Nobody goes near the Devil's Tree."

"I can't believe Miss Kari survived."

"Aye, maybe for now, but the Devil always get those who go near his tree," said a young boy as he made a sign of the cross.

"No, it's just a story to scare us kids."

"Ni, it's true, my Daddy told me it's the door to hell," insisted another boy.

"My nan told me it's where the little people take the babies."

"My nan told me…"

Miss Helen shouted, clapping the children away. "Okay, children, that is enough, be gone, go play. Leave Miss Kari alone from your nonsense. Miss Kari, I think you had best see Ms. Crosswell, the school nurse," Helen said pointedly, looking at the growing lump on Kari's head.

"Crosswell, Thomas Crosswell, that was the boy's surname," Kari whispered, weak kneed with the screaming roar in her head.

Helen shook her head softly and thoughtfully. "We haven't had a Thomas Crosswell at the school for decades. The last boy with that name was Ms. Croswell's younger brother who went missing around this area a long, long, time ago."

"Please do not upset Ms. Crosswell with this silly story," Kari whispered.

"Oh, sorry, Helen, one more thing. What is this Devil's tree thing the children were talking about?" Kari mumbled, the words sounding wrong on her tongue.

"It's nothing, just an old local superstition. Don't get ol' Ms Crosswell started on it either." Helen answered.

Ms. Crosswell quickly swept into the nurse's room, the limp of her left leg from a childhood injury was barely noticeable as speed and grace belied her age of anywhere between fifty and eighty years of age. Her silver grey hair was slicked back into a neat bun and she still wore a pinafore on top of her nurse's uniform. Ms. Crosswell looked carefully at the wound on Kari's head.

"You've done a fine job here, Miss, I'll have to give it a good clean out and maybe a couple of stitches."

"Shouldn't I go to a hospital for that, Ms. Crosswell?" Kari asked nervously

"Why would you go bother them, a three-hour round trip, it'll heal itself before you get there. Besides, I've been sewing wounds before half those doctors were a twinkle in their father's eye," she stated matter-of-factly as she began to prepare her tray of bandages and ointments.

"Miss Helen, can you please bring me a cup of boiled water so that I may prepare Miss Kari a tea to ease the pain."

"Yes, Ma'am" Helen whispered as she gratefully slipped out of the room.

"How did you do it? Miss, you smell like you tripped on a cow carcass." Ms. Crosswell tittered as she dabbed a foul-smelling antiseptic on Kari's wound.

"Oh, I fell over under the old oak, fetching a ball for young Thom ... um, a young boy," Kari explained, feeling foolish for already forgetting Helen's warning.

Ms. Crosswell dropped the tweezers she was holding into the tray and fumbled trying to pick them up again. Kari looked up into her face and saw a mixture of fear and sorrow in her eyes and a shake in her hand that wasn't there before.

Helen slipped back into the room with the cup, exchanged a knowing look with Ms. Crosswell before excusing herself to get back to work.

"Not you as well, Ms. Crosswell. What is it with that tree that has everyone so afraid?" Kari asked, trying to sit up before searing pain forced her to lie back down. Ms. Crosswell pulled up a chair and took Kari's hands in her own, her watery grey eyes hard as steel as she stared into Kari's eyes with all seriousness.

"Now, child, you listen to me, and you listen to me good. You stay well clear of that tree. It is full of bad spirits. Some people say it was planted after the angels fell from heaven to keep them locked in the fires of hell. The fallen angels thrust their swords through the earth to kill the man-folk that planted the tree, their blood was the first watering that tree ever received, the pile of their bodies was the tree's sole sustenance for generations.

"Other folks say it's where the faerie folk used to hide the stolen babies and the wee bairns would cry and scream from the cold and loneliness until they died. Them babies are always looking for a mummy or a daddy—and the tree, it steals folks to look after them."

"Whatever the story is, it could well be anything like that because that tree is evil and brings badness to all those that go near it."

Ms. Croswell's eyes narrowed as she continued,

"Some folks around here think that is indeed what happened to your friend, Miss Judy."

"Do you believe the tree took your younger brother, Thomas?" Kari asked hesitantly.

"Yes, I believe it did. How did you know about my brother? Who told you?" Ms. Crosswell asked, her tone still light, yet her features hardened.

Still a painful subject, Kari instantly regretted raising the subject.

"A boy was there at the tree, Miss. He said his name was Thomas, Thomas Crosswell. It was his ball I went to fetch. He warned me not to go," Kari explained. Ms. Crosswell face seemed to soften and faded off into a daydream with a faint smile on her lips. Kari then sipped at the bitter tea concoction that had been prepared for her.

"Ms. Crosswell," Kari asked curiously. "If the tree is so evil, why has it not been dug out or cut down?"

Ms. Crosswell then smiled wryly. "Would you risk opening the door to hell, Miss Kari?"

"I guess not. But why build a school near it?"

"Because the children, like the animals, just know it is evil and stay away from it. No birds sing there, no dog lifts its leg there. All animals avoid it. We don't have to tell the children or watch them as they know, as only the innocent do, that it's an evil place. Adults on the other hand," Ms. Crosswell looked pointedly at Kari, "Can't help but meddle and interfere, and go places that they shouldn't."

Ms. Croswell's face softened suddenly. "You honestly believe you saw my Thomas? I can't believe he is still around after all these years."

It felt foike glass was breaking behind Kari's eyes as the pain in her head intensified. "Well, I honestly just thought it was one of the children here. He said his name was Thomas, Thomas Crosswell. He had bright orange hair and blue eyes. He was so very upset about his ball."

Ms. Crosswell smiled broadly and chuckled to herself. "What is that child up to?"

"Sorry, Ma'am, were you talking to me?" Kari asked starting to feel extremely tired and groggy. Ms. Crosswell just smiled and patted her arm as she looked out of the window.

Kari was now beyond smiling, as the pain in her head pulsated as though it had a life of its own. She groaned involuntarily as Ms. Crosswell covered her in blankets. "You have a wee rest now, Miss Kari. That's it, off to sleep, child, it'll be over soon."

Kari slipped off the edge into a deep sleep that she didn't know was waiting for her.

Kari startled awake, her heart thrumming in her chest. It was already getting dark outside and the shrieks and laughter of the children had faded into silence. What was the time? How long had she been asleep? There was a note pinned to her blanket. "Best to let you sleep. Please lock up on your way out," written in an elegant cursive signed by Ms. Crosswell. Kari sighed as she struggled to sit up. Her head still felt clouded in a murky fog, that her thoughts stumbled through with heavy feet and she momentarily considered making the three-hour round trip to the local hospital.

Struggling to pull on her damp and muddy joggers that still reeked of the bog from down near the tree, she checked her phone and finding it completely flat, knew she wouldn't be getting a taxi anywhere and would be facing a 15-minute walk back to the cottage she was staying at. After finding her coat she headed outside. Although it was summer, the night had a chill to it that made Kari shiver as she pulled her coat closer around her shoulders. A fog had set in making it harder to see more than fifty metres ahead, but she could still make out the oak tree in the distance, she could feel it watching her. Shaking off her silliness, Kari set off through the playground deliberately going in the opposite direction of the tree.

Head down, Kari marched on across the field waiting to feel the crunch of the drive way underfoot. It wasn't long until a familiar chilliness froze her insides and a smell began to rise from the ground around her. *What the hell?* she thought, as she looked up, found herself but metres from the huge oak.

Disoriented Kari once again set out away from the tree, but the smell grew thicker, making gorge rise in her stomach and her eyes water. Looking up again she found herself only a few metres from the trunk of the great oak and her feet already deep in the boggy earth. Turning around made the world spin as Kari's headache started to roar behind her eyes as whispered screams and voices filled the dark night around her.

The putrid earth continued to suck at Kari's feet as her senses were overwhelmed with the smell of putrefaction and the roar of voices screaming and shrieking blew like a gale in her ears as she struggled to see anything other than the trunk, fog, and blackness of a starless night. Kari cried helplessly against the trunk. The screams suddenly stopped, but the sound of a child crying seemed to come from the tree. Kari looked closely at the trunk of the tree, where she saw the crying face of a child, then another and another. She touched the trunk of the tree and felt the movement of the child's face, the wetness of the tears. Then, it was like somebody turned the volume up, as an ear-splitting wail broke free of the tree.

In shock and ankle deep in bog, she fell backwards trembling and crying out in fear. Kari rolled onto her stomach, wrenching her feet free of the bog and tried crawling away from the tree. The putrid scent of death filled her nose and the coppery taste of blood flooded her mouth. Shivers ran up and down her spine as her bladder released sudden warmth against the cold clammy mud. All the time the wailing and crying of the children and babies increased in intensity.

Muscles aching with effort, Kari tried to pull herself from the loathsome bog and away from the tree when she felt a tree root wrap itself around her foot. Screaming, she was pulled over as it dragged her back towards the trunk. Kari's screams turned into body wracking sobs as she fought to breathe, fighting and kicking out as hard as she could. Her hands grasping at the rank sodden earth whilst it just crumbled away between her fingers.

A bright flash of orange blinded Kari as a fire roared to life in front of her. Between the fog and the smoke, Kari could barely make out several shapes floating hypnotically, their shadows flickered and swayed with the flame of the fire. Still, the tree pulled her back towards the trunk, her leg feeling as though it was being crushed and shredded as it was dragged into the actual trunk of the tree. Kari's screams of agony were lost in amongst the desperate wailing of the babies and children from the tree. Rippling shadows from the fire drew closer to the tree Kari could make out human voices. Torn and fragmented as the tree chewed on her body Kari was pulled into it, the agony and a burning heat leaving her breathless. In desperation, her fingertips clutched the splintered maw and pushed her face back towards the night outside. Outside, she could see the fire was larger and the figures more clearly human, with lit torches standing around the tree. Their mouths moving, but the words were lost in a roaring wind in her ears amidst the screams of the children.

Inside the tree, Kari's body felt like it was burning,

needles of pain stabbed all over her body. Scorching hot gusts of wind circled around behind her carrying the screams of terror and now a visceral cackling laughter. The babies cried relentlessly in her ears, sobbing she felt their pain, their hunger, their loneliness. Her fingers so desperately torn and split she almost let go.

"Hold on, lass, don't let go, whatever you do. Don't let go and do not look behind you."

Kari screamed as she tried to pull herself out of the trunk, the crushing and splintering sensation that ripped at her body with any movement backwards or forwards. A raspy, desperate voice screeched in her ear.

"Help, help me please, please help me," it cried jerking at her sleeve like a demanding child.

"Don't leave me here, please don't leave me here." Kari's arms felt like jelly as the effort of pulling herself free, took its toll, her fingers were bleeding, nails split and torn with only her nose and mouth visible from the outside.

Until that point, Kari had no thought to look behind her, but, the desire grew like an itch that demanded to be scratched. Momentarily Kari's fingers slipped until only her nose was outside of the tree. In front of her she saw a red ball of fire that stretched forever. All around her were beasts of nightmares, tearing apart and eating the babies within the burning fiery hell of the tree. Kari tried to draw a breath to scream in horror, but her lungs exploded in fire and her throat burned raw.

Kari found her grip again and pulled her face back into the real world. Sucking in the cool night air against her razored throat she saw the people and Ms. Crosswell stabbing at the earth with their torches, simultaneously the crushing hold of the tree loosened its grip on her body. Pushing forward with unknown energy, she surged out of the tree with half her body, without looking backwards she cried out to the voice behind her.

"Hang on, if you want to come with me." Within seconds, she felt desperate hands grabbing onto her body. "Now push," she commanded driving her body through the trunk until only one leg was left inside.

Looking down she saw a bundle of twig like fingers clutching desperately onto her jacket. Terrified, she pulled herself the rest of the way out; tumbling behind her, clutching desperately to Kari's jacket, was Judy, almost unrecognisable. Kari's jaw fell slack. Judy was alive! A flash of light and Kari's eyes blinked away the smoke to see that Judy resembled less herself then a half-finished hand-carved puppet. Some parts of her looked smooth, carved and sanded to perfection, while twisted knots and gnarls scarred the rest. Kari screamed and shook Judy off; the other woman looked to be in agony and moved awkwardly and slow like a marionette.

Kari scrambled to get away, leaving the wooden woman behind, trying to ignore the pleading and begging from her friend's mutilated form. Exhausted, Kari stumbled and fell between the people with their torches, singing their incantations. She did not stop until she was far away from the tree. Collapsing onto the cool earth in relief, Kari briefly glimpsed the people laying their torch to the abomination that was once Judy. Judy's wooden body exploded into fire, while her tortured voice screamed in agony, echoing across the paddocks.

Kari covered her smoke scorched eyes in horror, her chest heaving with effort and her mouth dry. The smell of smoke, of burning flesh filled her nose and made her empty her stomach onto the leaf littered ground below her.

"Miss, you must get away now," a voice whispered urgently to her from the darkness.

"You must, Miss, you must leave right now, Miss. RUN, MISS, RUN!" the voice implored, shouting in desperation. Through the haze of her eyes, Kari could just make Thomas out, his little body shimmering amidst the moonlight and wavering light of the fire behind him.

"RUN, MISS! RUN! They are coming to get you," he shouted, his eyes lighting up with fear as he tugged desperately on her jacket. Kari turned to look over her shoulder where she could see the people with torches slowly approaching her.

"But they saved me," she wheezed, exhausted and numb with shock.

"No, Miss, you must get up. My sister, she is evil, she will feed you to the tree," he said insistently. Confused, but instinctively trusting Thomas, Kari stumbled to her feet; her left foot feeling as though she had rolled it. Moaning in pain, Kari barely made it more than a few steps when she heard a whistling sound through the air and her world went black.

The sun was shining through the window of the nurse's office when Kari woke up. Her head pounded fiercely like the worst hangover in history, her body felt bruised and every nerve ached in agony. Kari tried to sit up but found herself handcuffed to the bed. What she thought were blankets, were instead a variety of thick ropes and a few bicycle chain locks. Kari jerked on the chains hoping to free herself, instead she felt like her skin was blistered raw.

"Help, help me! Hello, is anybody there? Help me," she cried out her throat feeling raw like she had smoked a packet of non-filtered cigarettes. Ms. Crosswell came into the room keeping her distance from the bed, her eyes examining Kari's every movement.

"Oh, Ms. Crosswell, what is happening here, please get me out of these cuffs," Kari begged. Ms. Crosswell sighed and sipped from the cup of tea she held in her hand.

"Do you remember last night, child?"

"Last night?" Kari answered vague memories flew through her mind, the last; Thomas's desperate pleading with her to run.

"I don't remember, I feel like I've been hit by a train, I don't understand why I am here, handcuffed, tied up like this!"

"I'm sorry about the handcuffs, but sometimes we have to take precautions. The ropes and chains are crude, yet seem to be effective," Ms. Crosswell observed calmly. "See, my friends and I…"

"That was you! It really was you, you saved me, but I don't understand why I am tied up, I have done nothing wrong," Kari panicked.

"Let me finish, child," Ms. Croswell's eyes flashed angrily.

"My friends and I practice the old ways, the ways of what you would call witchcraft or druids. Anyway, we have managed to save a few souls from that tree, but it was only after Thomas, we realised that though we may have saved them bodily from the tree, we did not necessarily save their souls. Did you at any stage breathe inside the tree, child?"

Kari paused, remembering the breath that felt like she had swallowed a fireball; her throat was raspy and felt like she was swallowing razorblades but all the same she answered with a firm no.

"You see," Ms. Crosswell stood up and began pacing around the bed. "We found that if you breathed in the breath of the devil, that you would always be bodily linked to the tree. It was not until you told me about Thomas that I realised that we can still save your soul."

Ms. Crosswell pulled back the blankets off Kari's feet to reveal her left foot was wooden. A knot of twisted branches with splintered ends, it felt bruised and uncomfortably hot, but still very much like her own foot. Kari gasped in shock and horror.

"What is it? Oh my God! What is wrong with me?" She shrieked hysteria rising like a wave that threatened to drown her. Ms. Crosswell ignored her and continued her story.

"You see, Thomas was the first one we managed to save from the tree. The very first. I wrapped him up in blankets and took him home as if nothing had happened. He was not well and in quite a bit of pain at the time, but he was alive and mostly seemed himself. Then about one week later, I came home from school and found him."

"My nine-year-old brother, sweet and funny little Thomas, had slaughtered our Mother by slashing her neck while she was feeding our baby sister, Mary. My Father had been hacked to death in bed by a hatchet as he slept off his night shift. Mary, oh poor little baby Mary," Ms. Crosswell paused and dabbed at her eyes that were wet with tears.

"I found them together, Thomas and the babe, he was gnawing on her leg, my poor baby sister, still alive…"

Ms. Crosswell rounded on Kari with the fire of anger and hatred in her eyes.

"That tree, that damned evil tree, turned my sweet little brother into the Devil himself. He didn't even hear me as I came home. I noticed then, the first time free of his blankets that he was indeed half wooden, looking like one of those marionettes, puppets, very much like your foot here."

Kari's eyes grew wide as she realised that the bed was on wheels and Ms. Crosswell— grunting with the effort— pushed it through the school, around the back of the old building to where the incinerator sat hungrily flickering away.

"Ms. Crosswell, what the hell are you doing? Why are you doing this, stop this please, it doesn't make sense your brother was trying to help me to keep me from the tree. Help, help me!" Kari screamed, her voice hoarse with fire. Ms. Crosswell froze at the mention of her brother.

"Thomas was there at the tree, pulling me out. Please, Ms. Crosswell, you don't need to do this." Kari pleaded

Ms. Crosswell ignored her. "The only way to get rid of wood is to burn it and so I did, the whole house, my mother, my father and wee lil Mary all went up in flames that day. They never found the body of Thomas in that fire, the authorities believed he had been kidnapped and the house had been burned to destroy evidence."

Kari screamed trying to break free of the handcuffs that bound her to the bed. "Please don't do this, Ms. Crosswell. You don't need to do this, oh please God, don't do this! Help, help, help me somebody please!" Kari sobbed.

"You're a liar, Nora," shouted the angry voice of Thomas from beside Kari's head. "It's you, you evil witch, you feed the tree, you made a deal with the devil, you killed our Mary, our Mummy and Daddy."

Ms. Crosswell recoiled, frozen at the sight of her angry little brother.

"Thomas? No, it cannot be," she said shaking her head. "I fed you to the Tree."

"Yes, to save yourself, and you have done so ever since."

"I had to, I had no choice. I told you not to follow me. I told you to leave me be."

"No, I'm a child, your brother, but you didn't hesitate to feed me to the tree to save yourself. I escaped though, and ran home, nobody would believe me. I was locked in the cellar for telling stories when you burned the house down. You gave them our Mary, you wicked witch, that poor babe, you killed our parents."

"But, last night she saved me," she gasped trying to

make sense of it all.

"Only to continue to trick her friends. She intends to feed you to the tree and tell them you left the village terrified. She's done it before, she will do it again. That's how she stays alive so long," Thomas glowered at his aged sister.

"Release her! You will feed that tree no more," Thomas demanded.

"But, she has breathed the breath of the Devil, she must go to the flames," Ms. Crosswell answered angrily before quickly pulling out a milk bottle filled with a clear liquid and started splashing it over Kari, the strong smelling vapor of petrol filled the air. Kari roared as she fought to escape; straining so hard on her restraints, the cuffs tore into her flesh drawing blood and she almost tipped the trolley over.

Thomas ran towards his older sister and pushed her hard in the stomach, forcing her to take a few steps back towards the incinerator. Ms. Crosswell bent over gasping for air.

"Why, Thomas? Why now, after all these years have you come?"

"Because, Kari can see me and that makes me strong. You're old, the time of the old ways has gone, your time is up," he shouted grabbing the bottle of fuel from Ms. Crosswell and splashing the liquid into her eyes. Ms. Crosswell shrieked as the liquid burnt and took yet another step back, shrieking in pain. With strength beyond that of any normal child, Thomas charged and pushed her so that her body slammed into the incinerator.

It took mere seconds for the flames to catch her dress as Ms. Crosswell scrambled around on fire, screaming trying to pat the flames out. The fuel on her hands and face convulsed in ripples of flame as it melted the flesh away from her skin and soon she was a ball of fire, laying limply on the ground, her body jerking as the fire consumed the gases that escaped her old body. It was then Kari noticed her left leg sticking out oddly, all but wooden, misshapen and gnarled like the limb of a tree.

Kari sobbed at all that had just happened. The smell of burning flesh and hair filled her nostrils, the acrid taste burning the back of her throat forcing her to bring up an acidic flux of bile.

"It's okay now, Miss. Now I'm not lonely and we will be here together, forever. Now, you are the Keeper of the Tree. We needed, someone brave like you, not tainted by the old ways. You have a lot to learn, but I will show you the ways, and well…we have lots of time to fill." Thomas spoke softly as he slid his little hand into hers, his hand that felt both coarse and soft like the timber of a tree.

The End

# Sisters of Solicited
## David Owain Hughes

*"We walk right past each other, every single day.*
*Like cold machines, we're marching on and on and…"*
–Alice Cooper

"Unsolicited," Wendy uttered. The word was ugly, heavy, when spoken aloud. It was cheerless, with sharp edges, like the world had become.

Her grip on the steering wheel intensified.

*It sounds like it means someone who isn't represented by a solicitor*, she thought. *Fucking snowflakes*. A smile pulled across her face as she peered out the van's tinted windshield; its engine idled in readiness.

"It's on the snowflakes' crest, you know, Wends," Capri chirped as though reading her friend's mind.

"The snowflakes?"

"Uh-huh."

"Aye, I know. It's also in their fucking mantra, too." Wendy stared out the window with intent. "What time do these dried-up old fucks meet? It's now ten-past two."

"Two. Let's just hope for their sake they're getting the sticks surgically removed from their arses."

"They're as tardy as they are wretched."

"Not that it'll matter soon!"

Wendy turned and looked at Capri. "True."

Capri, like Wendy, had worked in the modelling industry (twenty years of service between them) before the world went to shit and turned itself into a cold, mindless utopia of robotic madness.

The spiral started off slow between 2010 and 2018. Stories about sex scandals and rape hit the news and were splashed across the papers' headlines; celebrities and the ilk—directors, sports doctors, authors, musicians, footballers, studio executives, actors—were named, shamed, and sent to prison.

It had been triggered by the 'unsolicited dick pics' and *#MeToo* movements, which gained traction fast. The government clamped down with immediate effect.

But then *everyone* seemed to have a tale to tell regarding rape and molestation that spanned ten years or more.

It was hard to know who was lying.

Many jumped on the bandwagon.

Careers and reputations were left in smouldering ashes.

*A lot of innocent men got their arses fucked in jail!* Wendy thought.

Of course, the ones who deserved it got what they so richly deserved. Wendy believed this, and so did her Sisters of Solicited. They were all for the empowerment and equality of women. Wendy wanted her sisters, globally speaking, to have the same opportunity, pay, and standard of work conditions and respect (to a rational degree) as their male counterparts.

For a while, it worked. And, had it not been for the liars and the oh-so-easily offended who saw an opportunity to ram their views down everybody's throats, it would have continued to do so.

The women who'd fought for fairness, building on what the Suffragettes and countless other female organisations had done over the years, slotted into place.

The world *was* changing.

Men and women of an old-fashioned way altered their behaviour, practices and thinking. Workplaces, and indeed the streets, became safer—a no-nonsense tolerance towards lewd and unfitting behaviour was introduced.

However, the power went to some people's heads through their victories. And the more ground they took, the more they wanted.

High horses were mounted.

Snobbery shot down the nostrils of the well-to-do and arrogant.

This rational, disciplined, and proper way individuals started conforming to was pushed that bit further to the brink of psychosis, when activists wanted the good ship Morals to be battened down further.

They saw to the banning of lap dancing joints, strips clubs, prostitution, modelling, escorting and any other form of 'degradation;' of the human form where it was exploited for money.

A public outcry erupted.

Women and men lost good-paying jobs, and, in turn, their houses and families.

Their complaining and ranting was shut down, closed off.

The government stepped in and supported the maniacal

do-gooders. Why wouldn't they? They were supporting the people to suppress the people. It was a win-win situation. No more money wasted on 'eyes in the skies', Big Brother, subliminal messages, phone, radio and Internet tapping; the snowflakes were doing it for them.

Instead, the extra money was used to build walls and put extra teams of police, who ruled with iron fists and cattle prods, on the streets.

People were kept in line, too scared to look at each other, let alone offer a smile or greeting. They became cold machines.

And if that wasn't bad enough, the lunacy went a step further.

No wolf whistling.

No lewd jokes.

No banter.

No comments or anything of the sort.

Short skirts, heels and any other form of sexy clothing and underwear were also outlawed.

Flirting became a capital crime with a *stiff* punishment: men were castrated, women bunged.

All derogative music, film, books, words from the dictionary, porn, art and images were banned. Removed. Burned.

Creativity no longer existed.

The freethinker was hobbled.

Wendy watched the world implode on TV.

"The world's gone PC mad! You're nothing but a bunch of prudish cry-babies!" argued one lady on a panel show of men and women ranging from the far left and right parties, to those who sat on the fence and everything in between.

"I guess any and all types of behaviour goes after Auschwitz, eh?!" a man yelled back.

The snowflakes thought they'd won.

The masses were cowed, held in place and laying dormant with the fight burnt out of them.

It seemed only Wendy and her friends could see what was happening. How the downfall of society was occurring. The human race was speeding towards its impending annihilation on a tidal wave of over-the-top principles and foolishness.

When Wendy lost her glam modelling/stripping/posing career, along with Capri and a dozen other girls, they stuck together through thick and thin, forming an underground society by the name of Sisters of Solicited, or SS for short, which resembled lightning strikes on their crest.

It was yes to fun.

Yes to acting wild.

Yes to being their *own* woman.

Yes to fighting back.

Yes to male attention.

And yes to everything else they'd been stripped of.

They weren't just sisters doing it for themselves, but for all women, men and growing children.

It was time to take back some of the control.


*Funny*, she thought, *how they've taken away the very thing they were fighting for: to give women a voice. They said we could be anything we wanted to be—but within reason, of course.*

"It's not just *their* fault, Wendy," Capri said, again reading her friend's thoughts.

"Never said it was, Sister."

Both women laughed.


After forming their secret group on the agreement of striking back with force and not just sitting around on their hands talking issues through, they found themselves a clubhouse, a place where they could sharpen their knives, strategize, and organise.

The first target on the list was the Houses of Parliament. The Sisters wanted to try and take out as many thick-headed, power-hungry pricks as they could in one hit. Cut off the monster's head, so to speak. With them gone, the reins of power would be left flapping in the wind like cow's ears.

Rules and regulations would fold.

It would give someone the chance to step in and take over. A person who wanted to revert to how it was before the crazy train smashed through its final stop and hurtled towards hell.

Or so they hoped.

Wendy, along with her women, trained to use various weapons and learned bomb-making skills from within the shadows. As luck would have it, there was still a black market, a fence in the system, for certain people to acquire specific goods, which went unmonitored.

Thanks to the money they'd saved whilst working, the Sisters managed to lay their hands on all kinds of hard merchandise: machine guns, handguns, shotguns, grenades, sniper rifles. They built themselves a well-stocked arsenal that rivalled Arnie.

It was surprisingly easy for them to pull off the attack on the Houses of Parliament. Over three hundred were reported to have lost their lives in the blast the Sisters detonated.

It wasn't just politicians and the like killed, but people who'd been close to the building at the time. Tumbling rubble crushed skulls and snapped necks; shrapnel tore out eyes and ripped flesh and veins open.

The streets ran red with liquefied bodies.

Guts, innards, and body parts bobbed along the crimson waters.

A stench of charred remains clung to the air, and a

number of neighbouring structures were left scorched, blackened.

Screaming was heard for miles around.

The swift, brutal assault was carried out after a month of planning. No stone was left unturned. They were to go through the sewers and plant enough explosives to cripple the building twice over.

Kegs of gunpowder, sticks of dynamite, cans of fuel, and grenades were planted over the course of a week.

Wendy thought for sure they would be found out, that a sweep of the sewers would expose their trap.

But it never happened.

The powerful had become comfortable in the knowledge that they were safe. Untouchable. That their war machine had crushed everything in its path and that their people were in full support. They had been seen as 'doing something'.

How gullible one becomes on a pedestal of power.

*Did they honestly think their ivory tower was impenetrable? They were wrong.*

On the day of the attack, Wendy and her crew were gifted with an upheaval that broke out on the streets outside the Houses of Parliament: snowflakes clashed with protesters, involving a large amount of armed and mounted police.

Tear gas was deployed.

Water cannons were sent in. Beatings were vicious, tenfold. Hospitals filled up and ran over.

The perfect distraction.

And even though Wendy thought some of their own would be killed in the strike, she knew it had to be carried out.

It was all in the name of liberty.

There was a lot at stake. Not just for her and their few, but for the generations to come.

*That was if things got that far*, she thought. *And the way it was going...*

As the riot raged on, Wendy and two of her Sisters went beneath the city and carried out their plot by running a lengthy fuse from their mountain of explosives. When Wendy set it alight, they ran out of the sewers, collected the rest of their gang, and hightailed it out of the city.

The blast was seen from two miles away.

A mushroom cloud consisting of human remains, blood, guts, dust and debris ascended into the sky and spread, dotting out the sun for the briefest, blackest of moments.

Afterwards, Wendy and her Sisters sent a message via video link to those still left standing in office.

They wore Guy Fawkes masks.

*"No longer will we sit back and watch as you and the many destroy mankind with your child-like feelings and musings. There will be random attacks on you and your like until you have either backed down or reverted..."*

Wendy's message had stretched several minutes, demanding change.

She'd given them a month.

*"If there's no revolution by then, consider your death warrants signed!"*

Not the slightest of difference came.

When a new leader was placed in charge, their extensive communication was returned: *"We will not be bullied into indecency and a Neanderthal way of living by scare tactics and cowardly assault. We will stand defiant in its face. You are nothing but common thugs, Nazi sympathisers and terrorists of the worst kind..."*

They went on.

And on.

The Sisters had taken great pleasure from the rant in

their hangout.

"The guy sounds like he needs to find his fucking sack!" Candy blurted, causing the other women to laugh.

"What type of faggot-arse fella speaks in such a way?" Pip wanted to know.

"A she-male!" another Sister chirped, bringing a fresh roar of laughter to the room.

"Okay, ladies—that's enough. We need to get down to action."

"That's what my husband used to say!" Pip confessed.

More laughter.

Wendy chuckled. "Yeah, back when *fucking* wasn't a crime."

"We should have seen it *coming* when they took our dildos away," Capri said. "Bunch of fucking wankers."

"They took everything away. Can't remember the last time a fella grabbed my arse."

"Ladies, ladies, please! We must start planning our missions."

"I say we hit the Welsh Assembly next," Pip suggested.

"And take out our new president over in London," Capri said.

"Yes," Wendy confirmed. "Also, in a few weeks' time, there's a meeting of minds in Scotland."

"The one with the world leaders?" Candy asked.

Wendy nodded. "That will take some planning. In the meantime, let's hit the Welsh Assembly and go from there. We should be able to take them out with ease."


For the next six months the Sisters lay dormant.

They recruited ex-lawyers, nurses, doctors, scientists, page three girls, dancers, firefighters, soldiers, and more. They also planned, modified, and restructured, bought vehicles and tactical clothing and constructed a large assault course within their base (which was an old aircraft hangar).

When the media thought Wendy and her Sisters were never going to act again after such a lengthy period of time, they started whipping up stories in their tabloids: *Terrorist Captured, Tortured and Executed at Tower of London! Houses of Parliament Bombers Cleared Out!*

This riled some of the women.

It ignited Wendy. "Let it stoke your fire for war, ladies, but don't let it blind you. This is what we wanted. It will make them drop their guard."

Quiet murmurs of "yes" and "she's right" rippled through her troops.

Heads nodded, guns were cocked, and knives were drawn; teeth-exposing smiles gleamed in steel.

As the Welsh politicians and leaders gathered at their place of work on a sunny June morning—exactly eight months after the annihilation of the Houses of Parliament—ten large four-by-fours screeched to a halt at the curb, kicking up dust and gravel.

Supporters who had congregated outside the important, immaculate building displayed placards adorned with slogans of support: 'We're all with you!' 'United in terror' and Wendy's favourite, 'Snowflakes not Sinners!'

The blackened windows to the jeeps rolled down and out popped a dozen or so machine guns. Uzis and AK-47s, mostly.

Sisters popped out of sunroofs.

Others got out.

Hand grenades were tossed.

Bullets rattled off in the hundreds.

Empty casings spat, spinning into the air before crashing into a heap of spent brass.

Bodies were riddled and ripped apart.

Blood jettisoned.

Screaming blared over the clatter of automatic firepower.

"Cease fire!" Wendy called, who was one of the ladies poking out of a sunroof.

"*Ooh*, fuck!" someone screamed.

Wendy turned her head and saw Capri slumped against her jeep. She had a hand between her legs. "Are you hit?"

"N-n-no," she panted. "The damn thing gave me an orgasm!"

"Fuck sake. Hit the tape, will you."

Capri nodded and ducked into her jeep. Wendy's modified voice boomed from the speakers mounted on the vehicle.

*"You think we'd back down? The Sisters of Solicited will crush the snowflakes, their leaders, and supporters. If your ignorance continues, we will be forced to roll over you like a tidal wave—we will stop at nothing. As long as we have fight in our bodies, we will press on until the last of us is standing..."*

The message continued to play as the jeeps rolled away.

Many of the perforated crawled and clawed themselves from the carnage.

Many lay dead.

Only a few politicians had been wiped out in the attack, but it didn't matter—the message had been sent.


At the time of the Welsh Assembly ambush, some four hundred miles away, another section of Wendy's organisation was dealing white-hot justice in the form of an assassination from a rooftop overlooking the world leaders' meeting in Scotland.

They thought they were secure.

But, just like the slaughter in Cardiff, this assault also had people on the inside who'd paid the guards off and replaced the bulletproof windows with regular glass.

When the sniper rifle slugs started flying, *nobody* was safe inside the building.

The US president was the first to go.

"He's nothing but a jumped-up, half-witted celebrity with a bad complexion!" Wendy had stated.

He was followed into the afterlife by the French and German leaders, who some had said were nothing other than androids or cyborgs or some shit.

"I guess I can confirm that," Carpi said as she loaded another round into the high-velocity gun and watched the aforementioned presidents frazzle, fire and spit blue sparks.

She put three more rounds into each.

"Got to make sure." She raised her fist and yelled, "Liberty!" The wind flapped her unbuttoned, camouflaged shirt, exposing her *Tank Girl* t-shirt underneath.

As she put her eye to the scope once more, she snapped her bubble gum. "Come to mama, babies."

A bullet barrel-rolled out of her gun's muzzle, smashing through the face of another country's front-person, spreading their brains all over a wall.

"You say something, C?" Abigail called over. She wore her hat back to front—a fat cigar jutted from her mouth.

"Nah—*woah*! Did you see that fucker's head come apart?"

"*Help*!" one of the leaders screamed from inside the room that was quickly starting to resemble an abattoir. He banged on the door, but it was futile. They'd been locked in by the Sisters' insiders.

"You want that fucker banging to get out?" Abigail called over, rolling her cigar from one side of her mouth to the other.

"Bet you thirty quid I can shoot the toupee off his head without killing him!" Capri said, turning to look at her comrade. "What you say, sugar tits?"

"Thirty quid plus a rug-munching and you're on."

Capri's bullet went wide, taking a chunk of the fat man's ear.

"Ugh-*argh*!" he squealed like a pig with a slashed throat, his hands going to his boo-boo.

"Ah, *fuck*!" Capri slapped her fingerless-glove-covered hand to the side of her rifle. She loaded another round but was too slow: Abigail's bullet tore through the back of the man's head, spraying the door with blood, bone, and gore.

"Would you like to face-fuck me here, my place, yours or the hangout?" Abigail smiled as she stood, her hands going to her belt buckle and zipper.

"How about I buy us some beers out of the thirty and take you back to mine later tonight?"

"Deal."

Shortly after this attack and the one in Cardiff, the establishment found itself chopped off at the knees, with the world's most powerful, prestigious leaders dead.

Allied countries distanced themselves.

Soon, they turned their backs on the imps and strove for a fairer ground for the common people.

The tide had indeed turned, thanks to Wendy's efforts.

When photos of the android leaders hit headlines on a global scale, the snowflakes lost a monumental amount of support, exposing the few that stood between Wendy and her victory, as they tried to get the Man back on board.

"We will help protect you!" had been the snowflakes' bargaining chip.

"They have superior members of the police, Army and many others of influential power in their pockets," was the reply, but it wasn't spelled out in such a pretty way.

A couple of weeks after arriving home from their successful mission in Scotland, Capri and Abigail were pleased with the news Wendy had to share with them and the rest of the Sisters.

"I received word this morning that the government wants us to back down. That—"

"How did they find out about us?" Pip wanted to know.

"They have no idea who they are dealing with. The message was sent via a dark channel in hopes it would reach our ears. And it has. They're calling for peace and are happy to agree to any demands we may have."

"Why do I feel like there's a 'but' coming?" Capri said.

"There is. However, it's a good one. Something you ladies will love." A smile spread across Wendy's face.

"Didn't take much to get them to back down!" Abigail said.

"Only a few dead world leaders and a truck full of dead politicians," chirped Candy, winking.

"They're scared. Not only have they lost the support of allied countries, but also political ground, finance and, since Brexit, trade deals and everything else that comes along with it. Britain is in turmoil, with no great dominant force to take control. Until someone does, the UK is a lost cause. We've hit them where it hurts, ladies."

"Going back to accounting after this is going to be some challenge!" Abigail said.

Others laughed.

"What's the 'but'?" Candy asked, pushing aside her pink-coloured dreads which were blocking her field of vision.

"There's a large group of snowflakes standing in the

way of the government being able to change the course of their thinking. They want us to remove them."

"Who are 'they'?" Candy asked.

"An all-female activist group. They were among some of the first to trigger this whole fucking war," Wendy said. "They got what they wanted and pushed for more, doing tons more harm than good."

"Yeah!" the Sisters said in unison.

"How do we take them?"

"Through the government. I have a place, date, and time."

"And if we do this?" Capri spoke.

"Then we get what we want, within reason. They're willing to take on our changes, or 'demands', as they call them, and work them into a new way of living. One that fits all. Of course, we get to say whether we like it or not."

"And if we don't?" Capri wanted to know.

"Then we continue the war!"

The Sisters raised their hands and yelled in agreement.

"So, do we take them up on their offer? All those in favour, let me hear you!"

The entire hangar erupted in yells, whoops, and cheers.

Two days later, Wendy replied to the deal, which was sent back through the underground channel.

Her message was simple: '*We accept.*'

A response came containing the required information and instructions Wendy would need to complete her task. Within, she found a note scribbled on a piece of paper:

*Once a month, the bigwigs of this outfit put in an appearance to discuss matters at hand. It is the only time they are all in one place, giving you the opportunity to kill them in one. With them gone, we will be free to negotiate.*

Over the next few weeks leading up to what they hoped would be their final mission, Wendy pushed the girls hard during training and went over their plan until everybody knew it inside out, back to front, and upside down.

At exactly one-thirty pm, Wendy and her crew pulled up outside their targets' HQ. The building looked rundown, disused. A couple of the windows were bricked-up and the large double-doors were weather-worn and tired-looking. Slate was missing from the roof and birds were nesting in the chimneys.

The joint looked beat up. Abused.

Graffiti coloured most of the walls and pavement.

Of course, Wendy knew it was the perfect ruse to avoid unwanted attention.

"Hey, look at that," Capri said, pointing out a massive, multi-coloured dick and balls. Underneath the cartoon-sized prick were the words *Home of the Anti-Cock and Ball-Busting Brigade*.

"Ha! Love it. These camel-toe-sucking bitches won't know what's hit 'em in their pompous morals by the time we're finished."

The streets were dead.

Nobody came or went.

"Almost two-thirty now…" Wendy muttered.

Both ladies were decked out in black clothing, with balaclavas in place to pull down over their faces when the time was right.

"We should have blown the place up, dude. It would have been easier, and safer. I don't like this at all."

"Relax. We have Sisters all around us if the brown sticky stuff should hit the fan. Besides, this way sends a stern message." Wendy looked over at her bleached-blonde friend and saw that her knee was bobbing and her jaw was working a piece of gum overtime. "Chill, yeah? You don't think I'd let anything happen to my ladies, do you?"

"Nah, course not. But there are some right sneaky fucks out there."

"Not as sly as us, babe." Wendy winked, patting her friend's knee.

Twenty minutes later, the scratched, in-need-of-a-paint-job doors to the building swung outwards and the first of the young women appeared.

They didn't seem nervous or panicked, as they spoke and laughed among themselves.

More women piled out and into the streets.

"Capri, unleash the Jets. Let's give these bitches something to really fucking scream about. Take away our rights, will they? Not if we've got something to say about it."

"You got it, *amigo*." Capri opened her door and got out.

Wendy's hands tightened on the steering wheel as she eyed the women in detail. Some wore pins and button badges that showed their support for hard feminism. Others held placards demanding respect among men and women.

"It ends here." Wendy got out of the van, grabbed her AK-47, and made her way around to Capri, who was unlocking the door to the trailer attached to their vehicle.

"They sound wild in there, Wendy. Starving them and shooting them full of drugs has done the trick."

"When you throw the door, make sure you get out of the way."

Capri nodded.

Wendy turned to the other vans and signalled the drivers and passengers into action.

"We're good to go," Capri said, feeling the door of the trailer being pushed from the other side. "I'm not going to be able to hold them much longer."

"One second." Wendy checked to make sure the other Sisters were in place. They were. She raised her hand and brought it down. "*Now!*"

Capri ran from the door and jumped behind Wendy, who fired her gun into the air.

The trailer gate burst open, slamming against the box itself as six black horses stampeded out. They snorted, brayed and whinnied, nostrils flaring. Their shoed hooves made a thunderous racket as they crashed down the street towards the female congregation.

More horses shot past Wendy and Capri.

Screams filled the streets, followed by that of bones snapping and bodies twisting, overpowering the sounds created by the beasts themselves.

Wendy waved her hand. "Move in," she ordered, brandishing her machine gun. She strolled down the road with Capri by her side and a small army of Sisters at her back. "Club the wounded to death. Spare nobody."

By the time Wendy and her crew reached the trampled women, the horses were long gone.

"P-p-please!" one of the women begged, holding a bloodied hand out to Wendy.

Capri stepped in and staved her head in with the butt of her shotgun. "Fuck you!"

Wendy spat, her phlegm spattering the woman's smashed-in skull. "Told you there was nothing to worry about," she said, casting her eyes over the dead, dying and crawling before her.

In the distance, the sound of heavy helicopter blades split the afternoon air asunder. Out of the dark clouds chugged a gunship, its side door open. A robust, fifty-calibre machine gun mounted there was trained on Wendy.

Before she had time to think, formidable bullets ripped into the concrete around them like a meteor shower on steroids.

"Run!" Wendy raged, throwing herself under a nearby car.

"It's a fucking double—" was all Capri managed to say before being riddled with bullets. Her arm was torn off, her face chewed up. Squibs of blood splashed in all directions.

All around Wendy, Sisters hit the deck.

*Fuckers are trying to kill two birds with one*— Her thought derailed as the chopper fragmented into twisted, burning chunks that rained down to earth. The stench of cordite filled her nostrils.

"Wendy? Wendy?!" she heard a Sister call.

"Candy?" Wendy rolled from beneath her car and clapped her eyes on the pint-sized lady with pink hair, who held a smoking bazooka. "Ain't you a sight for sore eyes?!"

"You got it, sugar tits."

"Gather the girls. We need to hit the bricks back to base."

"What do we do now?" Candy asked.

"Now we crush the bushwhacking fucks into the ground!"

Back at HQ, Abigail was screaming and panting as the throes of a fifth and final orgasm washed over her. She placed her hands to the back of Candy's head and kept her face buried between her legs, the woman's tongue lashing her sensitive bead hidden within the holy hood of her pussy, her thighs wet and sticky.

"Oh, God—don't stop—C-Candy!" Abigail panted, slapping Candy's arse whilst imagining it was Capri munching away at her shaven kingdom. But then she felt bad. *Candy was good enough to uphold—Jesus, this girl has a mean tongue!* And then reality kicked in. *This could be my last fuck ever. We'll be at war tomorrow—boo-yaa!—and I might not make it back.* The thought galvanised her, making her last bout of pleasure that little better.

And then an alarm blared within their hideout—it was the ten-minute warning.

Candy pulled away. "Our night went fast," she said, looking at her watch. It was almost six a.m. "We need to get our arse over to the war room, Abi. It's time to rock and roll, babe."

Both women got off the bed, kissed, fondled each other and hugged. "When we finish the bastards off and get back here, it's my turn to do you," Abigail said with a wink, throwing a tee on and grabbing her boots and gear.

Candy did the same, slipping a stick of gum in her mouth. "Fucking-A. I can't wait to kill me some more government fucks, Sister."

As they walked out of the bedroom, they high-fived, laughed and headed towards the hideout's war room, where all Sisters were to report ahead of the day's mission.

"Ready, ladies?" Wendy asked, rallying her troops. She was met by choruses of enthusiastic yeses. "Then let's roll, Sisters!" Wendy raised her fist, opened the door to the hangar, and jumped behind the wheel of her four-by-four. It was time to take out the rest of those who stood between them and liberty.

# To Put a Price on Love
## J.C. Michael

"Fair? Are you fucking serious? I offered you what was fair and you had to go for more. Twenty grand you've taken me for. That's over a grand for each year we were together. It's…" he stuttered for a second as his mind did the calculations he'd done so many times before, "It's over a hundred quid a month. Twenty-five pounds a week I've effectively been charged for the pleasure of being with you and when you've paid for a woman you know what that makes her don't you?"

She glared at him, "There's no need for that, you need to calm down and stop behaving like this. It's why we've ended up this way in the first place."

"No, it isn't."

"Look, I'm not doing this again. All I've done is make sure everything was done properly. I can't help what the law says."

"Fuck the law. You didn't have to go for what the law says you can. You could've done the right thing and that would've been that. But no, you had to listen to your solicitor didn't y'?"

"Well, that is what I was paying her for." Her voice was drenched in resignation that however much she wanted to avoid an argument she was getting one away.

"Oh yeah, it was wasn't it. Like she gives a rats arse if we never speak to each other again. Or how all this affects Diana."

"I wondered when you'd drag her into it. You can't use her as a weapon, Geoff. She's a child."

"I know she's a bloody child. My child. A child who cries every time she sees me because she doesn't understand why Mum and Dad can't stand the fucking sight of each other anymore."

"Well I don't feel like that but if you do…"

The argument paused. It had been a storm lingering on the horizon for months and now that the divorce was finally complete the dark clouds of bitterness that had built and festered had been unable to contain themselves any longer.

"You left me," Geoff's voice was calmer now but not without an edge, "and all you had to do was let me buy you out of the house and leave it at that."

"That's not how it works. The agreement had to be acceptable to the court."

He sighed, "Well it might have been. Besides, it isn't like you're going to give me the extra back, is it? If this was all about getting things signed off you could pay me back the extra twenty K, but I don't suppose that's an option is it?"

Carol made an effort to smile, experience telling her that the storm was passing and her ex-husband was calming down. "It's time I was going. I think that's everything picked up now and you can do what you like with anything of mine that's left." She opened the kitchen door and started down the path towards her car. "I think it'd be best if we drop it now. Like you say,

Diana needs help through this. Speaking of which, my mam's at work at seven so I'd best get a wriggle on and pick her up. I'll drop her off on Saturday."

"Alright then."

It was the best Geoff could manage. Inside he was two-thirds beaten, a third furious. Furious with how she'd happily spent the money she'd earned, which was as much per month as he, while leaving him to pay the bills. Furious about the affairs that had betrayed his trust. Furious that when the truth came out she'd refused to try and save their marriage, choosing instead to waltz away to a new life and leave him in the ruins of the old. Furious that half of his savings had now been stolen away from him by a legal system that had held him to his vow of for richer, for poorer yet paid no heed to the way Carol had abandoned their vows of fidelity. And furious that he still loved her regardless.

Her hand was on the handle of the car door and although she paused she didn't turn back to him when she said, "I'll see you Saturday."

"Shame you had to move so far away." He spoke to the ground, his head down as if in defeat. "I'm heading up there myself later, well, a bit further up the country but I'll be passing. I've got a meeting on Monday morning."

"Well enjoy the drive, but it's supposed to rain, at long last."

"Yeah." And that was that. No goodbyes. The car engine started and as she pulled away from the kerb, Geoff headed back into the home they'd established together and which was now his alone. They'd been loading the car with the last of her possessions when the argument had started, the unintended consequence of which was the bag left in the middle of the kitchen floor. He kicked it out of his way and winced at the sound of breaking glass. Everything had been carefully packed when he'd reduced her influence on their home décor to a collection of suitcases and carriers in the spare room but as he moved the bag, more carefully this time, and the crunch of glass sounded again, he couldn't help but think how wrapping her wine glasses so carefully in left behind socks and bras had clearly turned out as big a waste of time as the past fifteen years. "Fuck it," he muttered as he collected his own keys from the kitchen counter. He was glad that he too would soon be driving away from the home that felt too empty these days.

***

His mood had improved by the time he reached the cottage he'd rented for the night. The woman he was meeting the next morning had sounded nice on the phone when they'd spoken about a new Box Office ticketing system earlier in the week, and a night away at his work's expense was a welcome break from routine. The drive had been okay for a Sunday afternoon running into early evening even though the hot weather of the previous six weeks had finally broken and the last half hour had been spent driving through sheets of rain. He made a mental note to avoid the ford he'd driven through a mile or so before reaching the cottage if the rain continued, and although his back ached after four hours straight behind the wheel his mind felt clear of the mornings somewhat tense visit from Carol.

Making a second mental note, this one to thank his P.A, Katya, for finding this place, he surveyed his surroundings. She'd done well to hunt it out on one of those rental sites as *Harrison's Hideaway* was not only cheaper than any of the local hotels, but it also promised to be far nicer. It sat at the far end of a quiet farmyard not two miles from the small market town of

Kirkbymoorside where his meeting was scheduled for 9 am the next day and was the traditional picture postcard image of a small stone built structure covered in climbing roses. The rain-enhanced aroma of the flowers welcomed him as he operated the lockbox by the door to obtain the key that would get him inside. There was a single kitchen/living room downstairs, the fire laid in the grate ready for a match should the night come in cold. Milk and fresh eggs had been placed waiting for him in the fridge. A half-bottle of wine and a homemade cake sat on the kitchen table to complete the welcome pack.

The lack of an all you can eat breakfast cooked ready for him in the morning was a slight disappointment when comparing the cottage to his usual Premier Inn or similar, but he'd packed bread and bacon anyway. At the thought of food he patted his stomach, and the extra pounds he'd packed on since Carol had left reminded him that at some point he really should start eating healthily again. His diet since the break up had fluctuated between poor and abysmal, as had his attitude toward his health in general. So long as he lived long enough to get Diana through school, and hopefully Uni after that, he'd be content. He had no interest in ending up a burden to her, and if he shuffled off before retirement she'd get his double salary death in service benefit, pension fund, and anything else he managed to squirrel away between now and then.

Retirement would just be a cost, a waste of money, and the last thing he wanted was to be a vegetable sat rotting away in an old folks home. He shook his head. His mood had shifted slightly the past few weeks, away from such thoughts, and it was time to move on, time to be more positive. Diana needed him and who knew, maybe one day he'd be a grandfather as well as a father. *I'll start eating healthier now the divorce is done, and cut down on the drink too,* he thought as he looked at the wine and considered the bottle of Bells in his bag, *but not tonight*.

In the end, he decided to skip the wine and pack it in his case; it'd make a good prize in the next school raffle. Besides, a drop of Bells after a quick meal of cheese on toast was far more in line with his usual tastes. He lit the fire, and for the first time in an age, a feeling of contentment wrapped itself around him. It was an unusual, yet entirely welcome feeling. He checked his emails and ran through his presentation, a standard sales pitch he'd done a hundred times, but it never hurt to make sure it came across as though it had been prepared just for the client in question. The TV sat silent in the corner, a stack of DVD's beside it along with a slightly taller pile of paperbacks keeping it company. At a touch over ten, it was too late to start reading a novel, so he cast his eyes over the DVD's, mentally ticking them off one by one as either seen or didn't care for. He tutted as his eyes reached the bottom of the stack and was about to settle for flicking through the TV channels with one hand while scrolling through Facebook with the other, when the book on the top of the pile on which the TV remote sat caught his eye, 'Tales and Legends of the North York Moors'.

***

Settled in the overstuffed leather armchair by the fire with his glass of Bells on the small side table to his right, he opened the book. There was a map spread over the first two pages, and he soon found Kirkbymoorside and then, half an inch to the left and roughly where he thought he was staying he noticed another name, Kirkdale. The name rang a bell, a road sign he'd passed only minutes before his Sat Nav had safely delivered him to the cottage and not far from the shallow ford he'd driven through. His fingers flicked the pages from front to back and he scanned the index finding that while Kirkbymoorside was unlisted, Kirkdale had an entry. His digits danced back through the pages to page 33 and, pausing only to take a sip of his whisky, he began to read:

*The valley of **Kirkdale**, a part of Bransdale along with the adjacent Sleightholmedale, carries Hodge Beck from its moorland source near Cockayne to the River Dove and then into the Rye, which gives its name to the wider area, Ryedale, in which Kirkdale sits. An aquifer swallows a good deal of the water from the beck resulting in it running beneath the frequently dry riverbed, particularly evident in the dry summer months, before re-emerging further downstream.*

*The area is also part of the Vale of Pickering, of which the limestone outcrops found at Kirkdale are typical. Within the limestone escarpment of a small quarry there is a cave noted for the prehistoric bones found there, and which was at one time a hyena's den.*

*Historically Kirkdale was the centre of a large parish despite the puzzling fact that there is no village in the dale, and only scattered farms in the surrounding area. A parish church dating back to the Saxon period, St. Gregory's Minster, sits not far from the beck and the present structure, built pre-conquest in 1055 and on the site of previous structures, is renowned for the 11th-century sundial and Old English inscription above the door. Recorded in the Doomsday Book Kirkdale translates as Church Valley, which pretty much sums up what is a delightful place to visit and where the modern world can feel a million miles away.*

Geoff took another drink, the warmth in his belly matched by the warmth of the fire. He checked his watch; it was getting late, and continued to read.

*It is this sense of the remote that has likely led to the*

*feeling amongst locals that Kirkdale is a place certain to be haunted, even if details of any such hauntings are scarce. The tales told in the local schoolyards include the legend that should a shilling be placed upon one of the graves at midnight, and then walked around three times, a hand will rise and take the coin, and this method of summoning, the three times around at midnight, with the added stipulation that this be carried out in a counter-clockwise rotation, is replicated in the legend of the Green Lady. This ghostly female can be called upon should the church itself be walked around in this fashion, but unfortunately any further details on the Green Lady, who she was, or indeed is, don't appear to be part of the story. This only adds to the mysterious nature of this corner of rural Ryedale, and gives added excitement to the Scout troops who frequently use the field adjacent to the church for their summer camps.*

He put the book down, feeling cheated by its promises, and sharing in the disappointment of the author. There'd been more on the history of the area than the scarcely worth mentioning legends that were little more than the kind of playground stories you'd likely find in every school in England. The book was clearly old, and checking the publication details he saw that it had been written in the 1950's when factual detail and honesty were clearly the order of the day rather than the more modern compulsion to throw in some Horrible Histories style blood and guts on every page. Standing, he looked outside as he took another drink. The rain was easing slightly, and the mystery of the Green Lady, vague as it was, tugged at his thoughts.

***

"Well, it was worth a shot," he said to himself as he

took one last look back at the church. There was no denying that his heart hadn't been going ten to the dozen as he'd walked around it as the bell tolled its twelve rings and the rain poured down upon him, but there had been no apparition waiting for him once his circuits were complete. Although he had felt a tinge of disappointment it was hardly a surprise when he didn't even believe in ghosts.

The rain continued as Geoff walked back to the cottage and the fire he hoped would still be dancing in the grate. He shivered as he walked over the narrow footbridge that crossed the ford that was now running at double the depth it had been when he'd driven through earlier. The dark shadow of the nearby viaduct that provided a third, and far grander crossing of the river, plunged the road he needed to take back up the hill and out of the valley into a darkness devoid of the comfort of the light of the moon. Instead, he relied on the light from his phone and spent the journey fretting about the amount of water that was falling on a device worth the best part of a fortnights wage.

By the time he got back, he was drenched from head to toe and feeling stupid for having turned out in such dreadful weather. As soon as he was through the door he began to undress—boots, coat, jumper, shirt, trousers were scattered in a pile around him as the warmth of the fire beckoned his virtually naked body. He stepped towards the fire and heard a noise upstairs. *It'll be nothing, just the kind of creaks and groans old houses make* he thought as he reached the fire and hunkered down. The sound again, like footsteps on the stairs. *Don't be fucking stupid; you've given yourself the willies with all these thoughts of ghosts.* Another noise. Another step. His heart pumped. He put his hand on the poker as if to stoke the fire, as if in preparation for whatever was coming down the stairs. *It's just the weather, a change in pressure or something.* He knew it wasn't, it was footsteps, soft and light. His heart hammered in his chest and he felt dizzy from the heat of the fire and adrenaline. A floorboard creaked; he stood and spun around, the poker in his hand, and promptly dropped it to the floor in shock.

***

She was beautiful. Her green dress flowed like sunlight over the shape of her body while her red hair flowed down over her shoulders. Her skin was alabaster pale, her feet bare beneath the hem of the dress, which sat ankle height at the front but trailed on the floor behind her. Her arms were bare too but for the gold arm rings that circled her slight biceps. She was a head shorter than he, but her eyes made him feel disorientated as if they were looking down on him from an angle of imperious dominance. He stumbled over the words he wanted to say, his tongue too thick in his mouth as his mind demanded a rational explanation, but his spirit told him that this was exactly what it appeared to be, the Green Lady of legend, and a being not of this world.

"Erm, hello, can I help you?" A pathetic piece of dialogue for such a situation but then what on earth would be appropriate? It wasn't like his life to that point had in any way prepared him for anything like this, and it was all he could do not to simply flop into the nearby armchair and stare at the woman his mouth agape.

"Possibly, but I can certainly help you," her words were as assured as his had been faltering and her accent as sweet and seductive as any he had ever heard.

He swallowed, the lump in his throat barely moving as he croaked out a simple, "You can?"

"Yes, I can."

She stepped toward him and he suddenly remembered that he was standing there in nothing but a pair of saggy boxers he'd owned for at least four years.

"I know how the sound of silence weighs heavy upon the shoulders of the lonely. You don't need to be alone tonight, not now that you have summoned me."

Geoff blinked. He knew he wasn't dreaming, and it didn't feel like a hallucination. That only left two options; he'd gone mad, or this was really happening. He feared the former and couldn't accept the latter. "I don't understand."

"You don't need to," she said, almost to him.

He hadn't even noticed her cross the room. The fire was warm on his skin as he took an instinctive half step back, but he felt even hotter facing her, as though the woman standing before him was a flame herself.

"All I would recommend is that you take full advantage of what I'm offering. Let me heal your body. Let me free your soul."

Her hands were upon him, as soft as mist yet infused with a static charge. She began to massage his shoulders and guided him to the armchair. He sat, and she sat upon his lap her dress as smooth as silk across his skin.

She talked softly and largely listened, as the night stretched into the early hours and he unburdened himself in a way he had never felt possible, not even to his wife before the betrayal. He now found himself speaking with an openness he had failed to achieve since the day the envelope of pictures sent by her lover had landed on his desk at work. He felt like he had known the green goddess in his arms forever, and as sleep took him he wished with all his heart she would still be there come the morning.

****

They were rutting like animals on a wooden floor, their bodies slick with sweat and the floor wet with something else, something thicker, redder. Her green dress was torn and ripped further as he pulled it from her pale body to expose everything she had to him. As he thrust himself into her she began to change beneath him, biting his ear and whispering that she could be anyone he wanted, anyone he had ever wanted. He continued to pound into her as her features rippled and deformed into a multitude of faces from his past—each of which represented a fantasy, some forgotten, like the mother of his best friend that had been his first crush, to others he had craved for years. Ex-girlfriends, colleagues he'd lusted after in secret, movie stars and teenage pop stars. Carol. He pulled away.

"Don't you still want me?" she asked with a serpent's smile.

"No."

"Good. Forget her. Love me." and she was the Green Lady once more. But different. Darker. Sinister. Everything around him was getting darker and claustrophobically closing in as he turned and tried to run but slipped on the blood on the floor, falling flat on his face in front of two corpses that had been savagely torn apart as if by a wild animal—bodies barely recognizable as those of his wife and her lover. He looked up and saw himself standing behind them, his own body naked and caked in blood with a smile beaming forth from a face wet with tears. He held a knife in his hand. A knife he brought to his own throat— he watched himself smile and slice, with a single life-ending stroke.

***

He awoke, covered in sweat. The fire had burned down but the embers still glowed. There was a clock on the mantlepiece, 4:30 am. She was still there. Sat, her head to one side, watching him like a hawk watches its prey. He felt exposed. He felt sick. He stood up. "I need to get dressed."

"You had a nightmare."

"I guess so." His wet clothes were still by the door. His bag was upstairs with everything he would need but he was reluctant to turn his back on the Green Lady. "Who are you?" he asked.

"I'll tell you who I was, who I am, once you tell me who you saw me as just then. In your dream." She came toward him and he shied away. The memory of the blood lingered, the thought that he was losing his mind pushing for acceptance as she rested her hand on his chest.

"You were everyone."

She smiled "Was I her? Your wife?"

"It's ex-wife." Not a real answer but she paid no mind.

"Do you still love her?"

"No."

Her breath was warm on his face as she looked up at him causing him to fall into her eyes as she spoke, as she touched him. "Do you wish for retribution?"

"No." His voice weak, a murmur, which escaped from his lips—her own, full of allure and promise.

"Yes, you do, it's understandable. You've wished for her to pay. You've thought how things would be easier were she to have an accident. To vanish from your life like smoke in the wind. It would have solved your problems. You could have saved your money. Diana would be yours." She kissed his cheek, her lips cold on his skin, a feeling that lingered as she drew away and continued her seduction. "We all have such thoughts. Perhaps I can grant them to you. Tell me what you desire."

"No. It's over. I've no need to punish her." It took all his force of will to rest his hands on her shoulders and gently push her away from him. It was difficult to breathe.

Hard to focus. He felt drunk or drugged. His thoughts clouded and confused.

"Come now," she twisted her hair in her fingers and smiled her seductive smile, "I can sense it, the fury within. You want to hurt her." Her hand ran down her front over her body, everything she did serving to hold Geoff in her thrall. "Why didn't you? Why didn't you hit her like you threatened? Why didn't you use that poem she'd written? The one about her depression that you found when clearing her belongings from your house. It was written in her hand and would've been accepted as a suicide note if you'd given her the nudge to do it, or a helping hand."

She was using what he'd spoken about earlier against him. Twisting things. Manipulating his words, his deeds, his thoughts. "Shut up."

She pouted and shrugged her bare shoulders. "If you're sure. But I know you aren't. I'm letting you accept the truth, Geoff. It's time you saw things for what they are and decide which path to take. I can help you. Or not."

"Who are you? What are you?"

"Get dressed and I'll show you, it's time the night reached the final act."

***

"What are you doing?" she asked.

He'd come downstairs dressed and ready to go out, but force of habit had caused him to grab and then check his phone. There'd been a text that must have been delayed by the poor reception in the area. A simple two words, "Goodnight, Daddy," sent from Diana on Carol's number. A moment of clarity had hit him when he'd read it, and he'd composed a reply when she'd spoken, causing him to look up from the screen. What the hell was he doing? Losing his mind?

"Leave that, you've no need for it, put it to the side," she continued before Geoff had answered her initial question.

His finger hovered over send.

"Come along."

Obediently, he let her lead the way out of the house, but not before slipping the phone in his pocket. For all that he was bewitched, he'd been taken for a fool once before by a woman, and somewhere deep inside his damaged psyche, his mistrust refused to be entirely erased by the charms of the woman in green.

****

They walked through the churchyard; Geoff two paces behind the woman who appeared to have taken control of his life and deeds.

"Were you buried here?" he asked, wondering as he spoke if a more correct question would have begun with 'are.'

"Not quite. I am buried on the outside of the wall and where the sunlight never falls. But at least he buried me, or rather what was left."

"Who? And why?"

"So many questions. Come." She opened the door of the church and as they entered, the candles burst aflame with a spectral green light, illuminating everything as though it were being viewed through the kind of night vision goggles you see on TV.

The interior of the church was small, perhaps a dozen rows of pews, an altar at one end, as would be expected, and a font at the other. It felt cold and damp in the eerie green light and Geoff felt that they shouldn't be there, that she, in particular, shouldn't be there, and that the green was the colour of sickness—her resurrection far less holy than that of the Christ who looked at them from the cross suspended in front of the far window. Removing the lid of the font she beckoned him closer, and as he approached he heard her muttering words that sounded not dissimilar to English, but older, coarser.

"Look into the water," she said, and as he did he saw it turn cloudy, like green-tinged milk, before it cleared, and he was looking at the valley from above. The image was as focused and clear as a T.V screen, and he could see the river running through the fields between the steep tree-lined banks of the valley sides, but the church was of wood, not stone, and other timber-framed buildings surrounded it. "That is my time, now watch, as I tell you my story.

"I was claimed as a young maiden by the Lord of this land, and all was good until men came from across the sea and made our land their own. There was an uneasy peace, but one, which nobody expected to last, and one day my husband invited the leader of these Norsemen—their Jarl—to feast with us. He was a man of brutish and pagan nature, a giant of a man of whom my husband's men were afraid." As she spoke, Geoff saw the man in the waters of the font, a warrior dressed in furs and mail with a sword in his belt and an axe across his back.

"The feast consumed, my husband left us alone, called away by his servants on some business or other, and this man, this beast took me on the floor like the head of the pack takes a cur. And then he left me, bruised and torn on the packed earth floor of our hall."

Geoff tried to turn his head, and when he couldn't, attempted to close his eyes. Viewing the scenes in the font was not optional, and he watched as the woman beside him, her husband—her rapist—enacted everything she described in such a brutally realistic way, he had no doubt he was not watching a mere representation of the past, but was viewing the past itself.

"When my husband returned I begged him to avenge me, yet he dare not. Instead he sent me to the cunning woman for plants only she could identify and prepare, and then he convinced me to go the Jarl's own hall and to offer myself to him again," her voice cracked slightly as she spoke, and then she pressed on as Geoff continued to watch the scenes play out as reflections on the surface of the water. "My shame reaffirmed I provided for his other thirsts, a horn of beer, poisoned by my own hand," she was speaking quicker now. "And he died a painful and horrible death. Once he was gone I expected my husband to come for me, as arranged, but he did not, and instead, the Jarl's followers took me. They beat me, they abused me, and then they dragged me through the dirt to the hanging tree. I called for my husband, but he had forsaken me, sending instead his servant who condemned me yet further as I sat awaiting the noose. He said that my husband disowned me, claiming that I had gone to the Jarl's bed driven by lust and then killed him out of malice. As the mob gathered I called to the only force left that I hoped could provide me with clemency, my God, but my prayers went unanswered as they sat me on the Jarl's steed and put the rope around my neck before striking the horse upon his flank. When the horse bolted I dropped, and swung in the air kicking and twisting in my torn green dress as my shoes fell from my feet."

Geoff felt sick as he watched the illusion in the stone bowl show each and every action as it was described. A medieval snuff movie of which there was more to come.

"Look," she whispered in his ear. "Look as I swing and choke and try to call out to God and Christ, our savior, to save me through a rapidly constricting throat. Desperate to shout out to a saviour as silent as he is now on that cross over there." She spat in the water, the ripples momentarily disturbing the image. "But there, see, the old woman, she knew I had been betrayed. Deceived. And with her, to her left, can you see Him, the hooded man? Do you know what he said to me? He said, "Your god won't save you, you have lain with the heathen willingly, and you have killed. But I pity you, and I am not a cruel master. I will forfeit my claim to your soul. For a price." I could hear him in my head as the darkness closed in and my life ebbed away. The jeers of the mob sounded far away, but his voice was as clear as an angel's calling me to Heaven. I wanted to ask, "What price?" and although I could not, He heard me regardless "There is no time for that, your last breath is spent. Do you accept my offer?" I could not say it, but I thought it, and with that thought, that single word, "Yes", I was damned."

The image in the font began to disappear and Geoff finally felt able to move. He turned and saw the tears in her eyes, a weariness upon her perfect face born of pain and suffering. A centuries-old torment that had left her damaged, and alone.

"I've more to tell if you will listen."

He took her hands in his and held them, albeit that they were as cold as the grave. "That's why I'm here."

"Later that day I stood with the hooded man as a raven took my eyes before leaving me to the crows who feasted on the carrion I'd become. The Jarl's men cut me down and left what remained of me at my husband's door. He shed no tears, and the burden of his betrayal has weighed heavily upon me ever since. He buried me as I watched, though it was less than the Christian burial I deserved, and then wed the Jarls widow thus gaining his lands. Not that there was to be a happy ending for him, as I believe that although my God would not save my own life he was prepared to punish my husband for the wrong he did unto me. His new bride died in childbirth, and our own sons were slain in battle. Convinced God had forsaken him, and rightly so, he built a new church and razed the village to the ground in penance. The villagers scattered to the four winds and I was left the sole resident of the valley. I believe he himself went to war in the East, but his fate has been lost in the mists of time."

"So that was the price you paid? To be trapped here?"

She smiled, "Oh, Geoff, you are so sweet to believe such a price would be all that was expected. The price is that unless I have a companion, someone to stay with me, someone who will love me, someone who will do anything for me, my soul will be called to Hell. That is the price, a price I cannot pay, but which someone else must pay for me. It is much to ask but…" she stopped and turned away. "No I will not ask you, it is too much to ask, and perhaps it is time after all these years that I accepted my fate."

"There must be another way," said Geoff, gently turning her head back toward him.

"No, there is not. There are only two paths to me. One leads to damnation in Hell, the other is my damnation here, but with a willing companion, someone who must willingly give themselves to me, and whose selflessness will be repaid, in any way I can."

Geoff felt a vibration in his pocket, a simple enough action but one, which distracted him for a second from the intensity of the moment. Why did he feel so compelled to agree to what this woman was suggesting despite his unease? And what exactly did she mean by willingly give themselves? He shook his head as if the enchantment he was under could be shaken off like water from freshly washed hair. His thoughts solidified a little, enough to question what was happening even if still insufficient to break free of the spell that was binding him. "And you've been waiting all this time before having to pay this debt? Like a thousand years?"

"I'd be lying if I said yes, my love, and I have sinned enough, in life, and in death where I have helped avenge those who have been wronged, those like you, without the need to compound such sin with deceit. There have been those who have come before and paid the debt for me, men who have chosen to stay with me, to comfort me, and I them. But eternity is a long time. Those who stay eventually fade and move on, some after years, some after decades. Even when you're not alone this is a lonely place to haunt, and although I am resigned to forever inhabit this valley, or be dragged to the depths of Hell, Heaven awaits those who decide to wait a while by my side."

She turned and began to walk away from him, pausing only briefly at the Church door to say; "You need to decide—it's almost dawn. Give your life to save me from the Pit and I can repay you with unimaginable pleasures, and your revenge, if you wish. Or choose to walk away back to your current life and never think of me again."

There was no choice to make. His life was a mess and for all she had told him, had shown him, her allure was irresistible. He followed her outside almost at a run and was surprised at how far away she had managed to get from him in no time at all. The rain pounded down, making it slippery underfoot but he scampered after her like a puppy chasing a child, the water feeling fresh on skin that was burning as if he was consumed by fever. In no time at all he was climbing through the trees toward the viaduct which spanned the valley, the green-clad spectre, whose name had neither been asked for nor given, always keeping ahead, her walking pace matching the speed he himself could run. At the top of the hill he reached an old railway line, the tracks long gone but the cinders still marking an arrow straight trail of grey through the trees. He sprinted along the cinders, which crunched, beneath his shoes, delighted to see that she had at last stopped. Stopped to step up onto the side of the viaduct, the wind blowing her sodden dress around her as she turned to him. The wet fabric clung to her body exposing the shape of her breasts, the curve of her hips. She held her arms open to him without saying a word. His pocket vibrated again.

Geoff stopped. *What the fuck am I doing*, he thought, *I have a child*. He hadn't spoken, but the woman had heard him.

"Diana will be well cared for. I know you've considered how she may be better off without you. Provided for by what you leave behind and free to grow up without the confusion of a splintered family."

"That's only one way of looking at it," he said, his phone continuing to vibrate, continuing to ground him in a reality beyond the madness of the night that was coming to an end as the first light of dawn began to creep over the horizon, "I'm her father, she needs me."

"Accept it, Geoff, you're just a problem, a legacy of the old when Diana could be free to live with her new family, a new father who will care for her like his own. She's young enough to adapt, and she'll remember your kind smile rather than the bitterness that will etch itself upon your face as she grows and drifts away from you."

His phone stopped, the caller either giving up, or the call linking to voicemail, and thoughts of mobile phones, thoughts of Diana, thoughts of the real world, they all ebbed away. All that mattered was the lady in green. Someone who wanted him. Someone who needed him. He walked towards her and she fell silent, the smile of someone who has won playing across her full red lips.

Barely realising it, he stepped up onto the brick parapet and looked down. It would be easy to walk off. He paused, one last shred of sanity holding him back from the brink.

"Don't deny it, you've thought of ending your life plenty of times," she was giving him the encouragement he needed, the slightest nudge that would take him over the edge. "Numerous times before you even met me. All I'm doing is offering you a way to do it with pleasure at the end, not oblivion." He closed his eyes. It was true. He had. He'd thought of just taking his hands from the wheel and running off the road. Or swallowing a load of pills and booze and slipping away.

"Geoff, get down."

He recognised a voice that sounded so far away, yet so close.

"Geoff, please."

Carol? It was Carol. What the hell was she doing here? What the hell was he doing here? He tried to turn.

"She doesn't want you, Geoff, but I do," a second voice, a voice as sweet as honey, laden with seduction, deadly as venom.

"Geoff, listen to me, please."

"I can't, it's her," it took all of his willpower to croak out those four words—all of his mental strength—not to step off into the void.

"It's who, Geoff? Come down and tell me about it."

He wobbled in the wind, slipping on the wet brickwork but regaining his physical balance even as his mental balance threatened to tip over, with or without his body. The rain lashed at his face and he began to cry. "I don't know what's going on, Carol. She wants me to hurt myself."

"Who does, Geoff, who wants you to hurt yourself?"

"I don't want to hurt you, Geoff," the second voice,

the one in his head. "I want to set you free. Release you from this conniving bitch that betrayed you. How did she even find you? Does she spy on you, Geoff? Does she still want to control you? Manipulate you?"

The voice had a point. "How did you find me, Carol? Why are you here?"

The reply came from close by, not as close as the voice inside him—the voice telling him to take one little step, the voice getting increasingly demanding and desperate, the voice that just wouldn't shut the fuck up. "Your text, it said, 'help me', which is so unlike you I had to come right away."

"Sneaky interfering slut, tracking you down, following you," the voice was showing its true colours now.

"You set up *find my phone*—remember—for both of us, in case our phones were stolen. I used that to find you, Geoff. I tried ringing. I could tell you needed someone," Carol was beside him. Her hand on his arm. But the voice was still in his head and wouldn't let go.

"There's only one way to be rid of her, Geoff. One of you has to die. Take a step or throw her off this bridge. One or the other, Geoff. I don't care which."

"I thought you loved me," he wasn't even sure which voice he was addressing, but both replied.

"I'll always care for you," said one.

"I love you, prove you love me," said the other.

"Someone needs to die before dawn, and it's almost too late."

A third voice. A deeper voice. A voice of torment and torture that made Geoff's blood run cold.

"Geoff? Geoff?" Carol was shouting but Geoff was paralyzed with fear. The hooded man was stood before him. Floating in the air as the rain came down and the sun rose at his back. His hood was empty of anything but shadows, shadows that were as deep as Hades itself.

"Jump," screamed the voice of the Green Lady in his head.

"Step down," said Carol. "I'll help you. You're soaked to the bone. We can work this out, come on."

But all he could do was stare at Death, or the Devil, or whoever the hooded figure was.

"Make him do it or you're coming with me," the words rumbled from the faceless hood causing Geoff to wet himself with fear. "You know what has to happen. His soul in lieu of yours. If he doesn't die, I'll drag you to hell where your Viking and his kin have been waiting 2,000 years for you. He'll fuck you and kill you over and over again for all eternity."

Carol grabbed his hand, saying, "What is it, Geoff, what do you see?" The voice of the Green Lady continued to yell and plead in the background, begging him not to betray her, to save her soul from damnation, and threatened to take his life herself if he should fail to give it willingly.

He could feel the terror on his face, the look of abject misery that his ex-wife could read but couldn't understand, as she stood in the rain, unaware of the spectral forces at play. "I'm sorry."

***

There was a bright light and his head felt heavy, but he tried to pull away from the light. He hadn't wanted to jump, but the banshee-shrill wail in his head had been so intense he'd stumbled, and Carol had caught him. She had saved him. But his memory was returning piece by piece. Carol had saved him, pulled him back from the edge, and held him tight, but then, but then…

"Who the hell is she?"

He remembered those words, spoken softly to him as

she began to guide him down from the ledge after saving his life.

The Green Lady had returned, revealing herself to his wife whose confusion was clear in her voice. "Geoff?"

The ghost had finally left his head, where she had taken refuge when Carol had arrived, and was now stood on the viaduct. All pretence was gone, her plan to make Geoff appear insane abandoned, as there was no time for any more games. Her eyes had blazed with green fire and her hair had been wild. Behind her stood the hooded figure, although Carol had made no mention of him, and perhaps his presence was still veiled from her perception, but inside his hood he was laughing, a fact Geoff had sensed despite having no way of knowing such a thing. And then she had run at them, her arms outstretched as she had launched herself at Geoff and Carol, and all three had fallen. Down, down, down, as the rain fell on his face and the sky began to brighten with a new day and then nothing. Nothing until the light.

"Mr. Manchester? Mr. Manchester? Can you hear me?" It was a man in a white coat next to a woman in a blue blouse. "You're in hospital, Mr. Manchester, and you've been very lucky."

"What happened?"

"Well, I'd expect you to have a better idea of the details once you've come around a tad more but suffice to say you took a nasty fall from Kirkdale viaduct."

"Then, how…"

"How come you're in bed here and not…" the doctor caught himself and the nurse shot him a glance that suggested he'd been about to say something inappropriate, like 'in the morgue.' 'The flash flood,' he continued, leaving his previous sentence hanging. "The fall would've killed you if the river hadn't been in full flow. And even then, you were damn lucky the fire service was dealing with a car stuck in the ford not a half-mile downstream. That's who pulled you out, grabbed you, in fact, as you were being swept by. You gave them quite a shock and were remarkably fortunate."

"My wife?" Geoff croaked, a memory of Carol falling beside him, still holding his hand as they hit the water suddenly slamming itself into the forefront of his thoughts.

"If that's the lady with the blonde hair and blue eyes she's safe too. Shaken up, and a few broken bones, but stable. You can see her soon."

"Thank God for that," said Geoff, and meant it literally as with the Devil on one side they must have had God on theirs.

"I have to ask though," the nurse shot the doctor another glance, but he continued. "Was there anyone else with you? A green dress was pulled from the river a few miles further downriver and both you and your wife were fully clothed when you were pulled out."

Geoff didn't answer. All he could do was stare at the figure in the shadows that wasn't really there. The figure with a finger to his lips.

"Mr. Manchester? Are you still with us?"

Geoff nodded but closed his eyes.

"Well, that's good. The Police will no doubt want to chat later but it's best you get some rest now."

He kept his eyes closed and listened as the doctor and nurse left the room, and as he laid there he was glad that Carol was alive and glad that he too was alive. He also knew that he would deny any knowledge of a green dress and that no one would ever hear him speak of exactly what had happened that night. He would never tell a soul, even if it meant the Green Lady would be free to return and encourage some other unfortunate individual to sacrifice their own life for hers. Because when the Devil tells you to keep a secret, only a fool would betray his trust.

***

The moonlight danced across the shallow pools, which dotted the otherwise dry riverbed as it snaked beneath the viaduct. Looking down made him feel dizzy, as though the rocks and boulders were drawing him toward them. He edged forward, the toe ends of his trainers now projecting over empty space rather than standing firmly upon Victorian brickwork. She should be up here. They should be doing this together. *She wouldn't trick me, would she?* he thought as he looked down at her. She'd said she would follow on, and then they could be together. Forever. She'd told him that she had to wait for him to jump first, to make sure his life ended quickly and without pain. And if it didn't? She would finish the job and then take the leap herself. Down into his open dead arms. A whisper in his mind begged him to see sense, to see how this wasn't the answer. Another voice called to him, a siren's song to drown out the logical side of his consciousness and bring him back under her spell. The embarrassment he had felt at the party would soon be gone. The cruel rejection of the girl he'd held a candle for over the past term would be forgotten. How lucky he had been to find her as he had wandered home with tears in his eyes, the girl in green. *His* girl in green. She understood him. She would be the companion he longed for and take him away from all his teenage trials and troubles. He took a breath and fixed his gaze on the horizon as the sun began to rise. She called to him, a single word—his name, William—never sounding sweeter. He took a step and plummeted down into the waiting embrace of the hooded figure who had taken the place of his beloved.

# Childe Abbas
### Bill Davidson

The girl tried to be silent, as she climbed the stairs of an unfamiliar house. The house would have been unexceptional were it not for the manic scribbling that crawled across wallpaper and paintwork.

The writing was in biro and felt tip and lipstick. It was big and small and black and coloured and, as she climbed, the girl found the words thickening and massing, like huge and hectic insects. One short phrase only, over and over; I am Tilly.

The name meant nothing to her, even when she tried it out in her mouth. In a room at the top of the stairs, surrounded by writing that teemed like it would boil off the walls, she found the ragged girl.

***

Three months earlier.

On the drive South, Tilly's mom kept saying things would be better in Childe Abbas. She turned all the way round in her seat, holding Tilly's gaze.

"I know you don't like it when things change, Hon. But, this will be good for all of us. I promise."

Entering the little town, her mom was still doing that bright and brittle thing, wide eyed and grinning, putting too much into it.

"Look, Tills. Actual thatched cottages!"

Short for eight, Tilly slumped as low as she could go, heavy glasses disappearing behind her long dark hair. Still, she couldn't help but see the town square with its old stone buildings and brightly coloured shops, and there, rising like a spooky ruin from Dr. Who or something, the deep red sandstone Abbey that gave the town its name.

Her dad pointed, adopting his informative voice. "There it is, Childe Abbey, right slap bang in the middle of town. One of the oldest is England, but it didn't stop Henry VIII sacking it in 1537."

"1539." She corrected, sitting up. "Destroyed during The Dissolution. Abbott de Beres…" She dried mid flow, seeing a tall old man on the wide pavement in front of the Abbey, coming to a halt as he saw their Volvo crawl past. He smiled in recognition, his hand rising in greeting.

Her mom was instantly animated again, waving. "That's Councillor Beresford!"

Tall and craggy in his tweed jacket and old-style red cravat, Beresford looked somehow fitting in the shadow of the Abbey. It felt as if he was looking, not at her parents, but at her.

Once he had been left safely behind, she asked, "What's a c-c- c…" Took a moment. "A Councillor?"

Her mom twisted in her seat. "A local politician. Normally they don't have much influence, but I'm not sure we would've been allowed to come here without his seal of approval." Quickly adding, "That's a joke, Tilly."

She patted her daughter's knee. "He was so pleased to hear about you. The more kids the better, he said." Her attention suddenly bounced away.

"Look, a play park! I've not seen one like that since I was a little girl."

Tilly didn't look, and, turning into Breslaw Avenue, her mom bounced in her seat, even waving her arms above her head. "To think, we live here now!"

Tilly snorted, but even she could see how pretty it was, with tall elms, and solid Victorian houses set behind mature gardens. The sun flickered on the windscreen and birds sang as they drove the last few yards to where the removal van stood waiting.

***

Tilly staked her claim on the loft room as soon as she saw it. Taking up the whole second floor, it was twice the size of her old room, and full of odd angles.

Her mom, holding a Solar System poster for Tilly to tack in place, grinned wide, still trying hard enough to irritate. "Come on, admit it! This is so cool. You want to keep that awful mirror?"

The previous owners had left a full-length mirror, screwed to the wall, so that she would encounter her own reflection whenever she entered her bedroom. Tilly, seeing how much her mom disliked it, asked for it to be left.

"Ok. I think it's creepy, but it's your room. I'm going to help the removal men. God knows what your Dad is telling them."

Left alone, Tilly wandered to the window and looked across the long rear lawn, seeing trees and houses, and, in the distance, the looming bulk of the Abbey. Two gardens down, she noticed a blue trampoline, and the familiar feeling of panic swelled in her chest. What if those kids weren't nice? Ran behind her, shouting, "T-T-Tilly the w-w-weirdo"?

She understood her dad's new job would bring in more money. The way he explained it, "State schools simply don't work for you, Hon. There's a fantastic private school not far from Childe Abbas, with a talented and gifted program. But it's not cheap. This way, you get what you need, and it won't bust the bank."

Now she watched a bald man with a big face cutting his hedge and, further along, a couple on sun loungers, reading. Turning back, she found Big Face staring at her, shears open in front of him. She ducked below the window and waited, after a few moments, the clipping resumed.

Later, they ate fish and chips straight from the wrappers and Tilly helped push furniture around, hiding a smile when her dad said, "I don't know why we bothered with those removal men."

Later still, lying in the strangely quiet bedroom with its alien attic angles, she let herself cry, thinking she would not sleep in this place. Then drifted awake to find her mom, coming in with a rustle of clothes and bending for her usual goodnight kiss.

When she had gone, Tilly breathed in her mom's perfume, and closed her eyes.

***

The following morning, they spent a while exploring their new town, the country walk, the old chapel, the big market. Late morning found them crossing a lush recreation ground, with a pristine cricket pavilion in white. The Abbey, as always, loomed damply in the background.

Tilly's dad picked her up and whirled her round, making her squeal and giggle. Then he threw a Frisbee for her, threw it over and over, even though she could never catch it.

They continued into town and her mom exclaimed over the Purple Bead Shop, the Village Bakery, and the Tea Room. She pointed to a poster showing the dark silhouette of a cloaked and top hatted man.

"Look, Tills. The famous Childe Abbas ghost walk! First Friday of the month, eight pm at the town pump. Children go free. That's tomorrow!"

"My bed time is eight-thirty."

"We'll make a special exception. But right now, let's try the Abbas café."

"It's called Abbas Tea Rooms."

The place was busy but the curvy blonde, flower printed owner (call me Jan) made space and it seemed everyone wanted to say hello to their new neighbours. Tilly listened, leaning in when the ghost walk came up.

Jan nodded, enthusiastic. "It's for tourists, mainly, but locals have to go at least once. It's the law! Councillor Beresford does it. What he knows about the history of this place!" She shook her head, like the man's knowledge was a great mystery.

"He's entertaining as well, though." Smiling now at Tilly. "You're a lovely little one, aren't you? Look at those big dark eyes! You will love it, hon."

On the way home, her mom said, "It's like stepping back in time."

Her dad laughed. "About two hundred years. Everybody is just so…"

She finished for him. "Friendly."

The play park was still empty, but Tilly walked on, spurning the childish suggestion of swings. Glancing back, though, she was surprised to see a boy of around her age, sitting on the seesaw and eating what looked like an entire sponge cake. An incredibly dirty boy. He froze, staring at her with wide eyes.

They regarded each other for a few seconds, then she twisted away and hurried to catch her parents.

"You see that kid?"

Her mom turned. "What kid?"

The park was empty again. Tilly told them, "He was there, though." What she didn't say— he's the only kid I've seen all day.

Two doors from their new home, a nervy woman left her garden to shake hands. "Pleased to meet you, neighbour! I'm Pauline."

"I'm Margaret, this is David. Have you lived here long? In Childe Abbas?"

"Mike and I moved from London, oh, about a year ago. But this town! So friendly."

"We noticed! It has to be just the best place to bring up kids."

Pauline shrugged. "We don't have children ourselves, but I'm sure you're right."

Tilly had been listening, hoping to find out about the users of the trampoline, and now found herself asking about it.

Pauline looked at her for the first time, frowning. "A trampoline?"

"In your back garden."

The woman shook her head, "Not our garden, no."

That night, as Tilly closed her curtains, she stopped to watch Pauline, deadheading roses. Placing the cuttings on the trampoline.

***

The evening of the ghost walk arrived, and Tilly gave

up pretending she wasn't excited. A knot of seven people, including a boy and girl of around Tilly's age, was already waiting at the old town pump. Tilly looked away, avoiding the children, but soon Councillor Beresford was striding towards them. His voice fitted his appearance.

"A grand turnout! Hello again, David, Margaret. And this must be Tilly, the memory girl."

He was shaking hands with her parents and now turned to her, and she thought she did *not* want him to touch her. But, oh look, her hand was already in his.

He had bent right down, but now he straightened and turned to the others, his voice loud and his presence huge. He was wearing a long coat with proper tails, and again the deep red cravat, high about his neck. As Tilly watched, he fired a match and lit an old glass lantern, which glowed yellow in the fading light.

"First, a word about Childe Abbas, one of the oldest towns in Britain, folks. A Roman settlement, in fact. Any idea when that would be?"

He asked the question generally but was looking at Tilly.

"AD 67."

"Ex-unctly! You've read my pamphlet, I bet. Even before that, this place was settled. Those ridges on the hill above the town, that's an Iron Age fort, would you believe? It was the pagan capital of Mercia. So, this place has plenty of history. Plenty conflict, sacrifice, sword-fighting and so there are plenty of..."

He raised his hands expectantly, and the little group did not disappoint. "Ghosts!" They cried, laughing. All except Tilly.

"Let's get cracking. First stop, Gallows Cross!"

It hadn't seemed obvious, or possible, that he had been holding anything behind his back. Yet, with a flourish, a shiny top hat appeared and was settled, high on his head.

Beresford turned out to be a master showman; funny, knowledgeable and quick witted. He took them to Gallows Cross, Hangman's Cottage, and the Black Pool, telling of murders and betrayals. Showing them the green man, carved into the stone of the old chapel, and the runes above the door.

"See, they pretended to be Christian, in the early days. Stopped them being burned alive. But they never gave up being pagans."

By the time they entered the Abbey graveyard, it was full dark, and the lantern threw shadows behind the gravestones, and across Beresford's craggy face. The other kids had been ostentatiously brave but now Tilly noticed them drift beside their parents. Even the adults seemed on edge.

Beresford suddenly stopped dead, staring hard at a gravestone, and Tilly could swear he winked at her, before walking on. Coming abreast of the stone, Tilly could see nothing. Then there he was, peeking round, the dirty boy. He stared at her with huge, watery eyes, shook his head once, and was gone.

The group halted before the shattered entrance to the Abbey as Beresford raised his lantern.

"See. The Green Man again. And look here, hidden in plain sight. The Pentagram. The Horned God. Even when the place was sacked, they couldn't have noticed these, or they would have destroyed them. Makes you wonder why, doesn't it?"

They filed past the broken doorway, with its faded symbols, and entered the Abbey, ruined walls rising high around them, massive and somehow still stately. Beresford did a little twirl. "Smells kinda green, doesn't it? We're standing in the Narthex, where Abbot de Beres committed suicide, rather than permit himself to be executed. Slit his own throat."

He held the lantern up and closed his eyes, inching his finger across the cravat, his expression close to ecstasy. Tilly looked at her parents, wondering, do they think that's ok? Really?

Talking constantly, he took them through one ruined site after another - the gloomy Choir, the Cloisters and the High Altar. At a grassed area he called the Garth, he pointed to a low stone circle, looking something like a well.

"This is the exact centre of the town, even today. The heart of Childe Abbas, if you will. You can still read the inscription cut into the stone. Latin, naturally."

He turned to Tilly, his eyes so intense that she took a step back. "Can you read it? I'd be ever so grateful."

She didn't want to, but her parents were acting like she'd been chosen for something special, so she walked the circle with Beresford and his lamp, reading as she went.

"Sinite par...parvulos...et nol...nolite eos prohib...prohibere ad me venire."

Beresford stood up to his full height, his expression one of deep satisfaction. Satisfaction in his voice as well.

"Suffer the little children to come unto me and forbid them not. Well done."

There was something disturbing about how he said it. The way he emphasized, come unto *me*. For a moment, it seemed as though the earth tilted under Tilly's feet, or something, someplace loosened. She looked round, but nobody else seemed to have noticed anything, and Beresford was speaking again.

"Do you see the grating over the well?"

Everyone crowded round, and Tilly's dad tapped the

rusty iron, making a dull clang. "Is it a well, then?"

"Actually, it's a bottle dungeon. Once you're in, you can't climb out."

"Oh, ok."

"The chronicles of Sir John Newell, Henry VIII"s Commissioner, tells how disgusted he was by what he found here, before he razed it to the ground. Depravity beyond imagining. Little children, born out of wedlock, the issue of Monks and Nuns. Evidence of Pagan Rituals, as if the place never had a thing to do with Christianity. He even called Abbot de Beres…" He struck a noble pose and intoned loudly, "…a parasitical creature of the Devil."

"Was Newell going to execute him?"

"He was indeed. It's said de Beres cursed Newell. Cursed the town. Said the very souls of its children were forfeit to him, and he would haunt it forever."

Tilly, suddenly anxious, asked, "Like the child snatcher, from Chitty-Chitty-Bang-Bang? But snatching souls?"

Beresford considered this. "Now look here. You can't just snatch a soul, like someone's purse, young lady. It would be altogether too large. No, my view is that it would have to be sipped gradually, savoured over time." He made a sucking, sipping noise, earning a laugh. The he winked at Tilly, his face stone.

"It wouldn't go down, all in one bite."

Then he held his lantern above the grating and everybody strained to see inside.

Tilly's dad asked, "What did Newell do with the kids?"

Saying nothing, but looking grim, Beresford pointed to the hole.

"And then what?"

"And then… nothing." He bent, and stage whispered, "Listen."

They became quiet, hardly breathing, and, when a crow broke the silence with its rough caw, the spell was broken, and everyone was laughing and clapping their hands, saying well done, good show. Beresford didn't laugh. He just looked at Tilly.

***

Tilly's father started work, and they settled into a new routine. Tilly, coming down to breakfast, admitted to her mother that the house was cool. And the garden was great, but not today, she thought, under a dismal layer of mist. It looked like the colour had been washed out of everything.

"But I don't like the Abbey. And I've still not seen any kids."

Her mother shrugged. "It's the holidays."

Tilly had only ever seen one child, the one she thought of as the dirty boy, and him only twice after that time on the swings. Once, he had been standing in the café, eating fries, straight from an old lady's plate. The second time he had been right outside, staring at Pauline's house. There had been a third time, but she didn't count that, because she wasn't sure if that was real.

Her father grabbed a slice of toast, in a hurry to get to work. She called, "Remember to get my new Lava lamp!"

"Oh, yea. I keep forgetting!"

"I've stuck a note in your car."

"Well, I'll be sure to remember, then."

So, when her father's car splashed into the driveway that evening, she ran to meet him. "Did you get it?"

He frowned at her. "Get what?"

"My lamp?"

"What lamp?"

Tilly giggled and poked him in the stomach. "Where

is it, silly?"

"No really, where's what?"

"I p-p-put the s-s-sign in your car!"

"There's no s-s-sign in my car."

Tilly rocked back, eyes wide. "Dad!"

He threw up his hands, leaving her to trail him into the house. "What's wrong now?"

"You made fun of my s-stutter!"

"I would never do that. What a thing to say!"

Tilly turned away and ran to look into the car. Her sign was right there, unmissable on the dashboard. They were acting weird, both of them, and it got no better when, coming into the house, she found her parents kissing. They were kissing properly, as though they were eating each other's faces.

"Gross!"

Her mother looked around, confused, but her father's hand was still squeezing her bottom. Her mother pushed his chest, stepping away from him. "Hey, it's Friday!"

Tilly. "S-s-so what?"

Her mother answered her father, as though it had been he who had spoken. "So, it's the end of your first week. Let's go to the pub!"

Tilly, her voice rising to a squeak, shouted, "I don't want to go to the p-p-pub."

Her father. "Great idea!"

Tilly stormed out of the room. "Great! I c-c-can't even g-g-g-*go* to the pub!"

Nobody followed her, so she stormed back, shouting about nobody caring about what *she* wanted to do. Her mother looked at her, her expression that of someone working on a puzzle. "What's wrong?"

"I can't go to the p-pub!"

It took a moment, but suddenly her mother smiled and held out her arms. "Of course not, Hon. It was just an idea.

We'll order pizza."

***

"Do you have to look into *every* window, every day?" Tilly was bored of the dense rows of low houses, and of the little town Square, the shops looking so much less cheerful on rainy days like this. In fact, Tilly thought, they were tatty and downright miserable.

Her mother tutted, irritable this morning. "Let's go to the tea room."

Hurrying ahead, Tilly looked through the window and found herself face to face with a man, eating an egg sandwich. At first, she thought he was staring at her, then realized he was looking through her, completely inside his own eggy world. She stuck her tongue out but stopped when the egg man still failed to notice her. He took another bite and munched on.

They found a seat and Jan bustled up. "Margaret! With you in a sec."

Tilly smiled, but Jan didn't smile back, and she reddened, thinking she had been spotted, making faces at customers. Her mother ordered for herself and, when Jan left, Tilly shook her arm, her voice tiny. "Am I not getting anything?"

Irritable again. "What?"

Tears brimmed in Tilly's eyes. "Am I not g-g-g... not getting anything?"

Her Mother threw her hands up in frustration. "For goodness sake! Jan!"

Tilly looked away, freezing when she found her eyes locking with those of Councillor Beresford. He was sitting beside a couple who were paying him no attention, smiling widely at her. As she watched, he took a couple of fries from the lady's plate, hitting a dim note in her memory. Hadn't she seen someone do just that? She could recall.

Her mother, Beresford's biggest fan, hadn't even mentioned him. It gave her a strange and frightening feeling, as though she and he were the only people in the café.

***

"Pauline! I love your kitchen!"

Saturday morning, and it seemed that her mother and Pauline could talk forever about wallpaper and gardens. Tilly wandered through her neighbour's oppressively tidy home, stopping in front of a framed photo of Pauline with a baby on her knee and a grinning boy of perhaps six. She frowned at the photograph, thinking hard—then she had it. Clean and happy, he was just recognizable. The dirty boy.

The third time she had seen the dirty boy, the time that might not have happened, she had been dozing on a sun lounger when a shadow fell over her. She opened her eyes to find his face, inches away. He whispered, "Are you a ghost?"

Then, he wasn't there anymore, and even the memory was hard to catch onto, making her think it must have been a dream. Now, Tilly let her gaze slide from the photograph and wandered into the garden. After a while, bored, she walked back into the house, surprised to find it empty and quiet. Hearing her own breathing, shaky in her throat, she tiptoed the silent rooms until a sudden deep thump from upstairs made her jump. She sprinted to the front door, scrabbling at the lock until it clicked open.

Tilly ran out onto the pavement and to her own house, pulling the door open to hurry inside. She went room to room, still out of breath, and found her parents relaxing over coffee in their kitchen. She ran screaming up to her

Mother. "You left me!"

Her Father looked up, annoyed, as Tilly ran into her Mother's lap, crying. Her Father tutted, and shook his head, then went back to his newspaper.

The next morning was Sunday, full breakfast day, the day it wasn't necessary to have Cheerios. She let herself doze to the sound of clattering dishes, watching rain make patterns on the window, before crawling out of bed. Her parents were already finishing their meal, when she walked into the kitchen.

She stalled, jaw hanging open. "Why d-d-d-didn't you wake me?"

Her father looked round, like he had heard something outside, then bent back to his plate, while her mother squinted across the table and exclaimed, "Tilly!"

As though she was surprised.

Her mother put together a cold and greasy breakfast, which Tilly ate grumpily while staring out at the dripping garden. That night, she fell into bed, strangely exhausted, coming awake much later, hearing her parents talking loudly as they came upstairs. They didn't check on her, didn't come in for a kiss, and, when the landing light clicked off, she pulled the covers over her head.

The next morning, Tilly woke late and wandered downstairs to find her mother cleaning the kitchen. She stood watching for a while, before asking, "Can I have breakfast?"

When her mother didn't answer, she asked again, louder. Her mother whipped round, her hand at her throat and her eyes wide. Later, Tilly wondered if a second had passed before she said, "Oh. It's just you."

It was a day of grey drizzle from a sky the colour of milk, and Tilly had to be cajoled into walking into town but was counting puddles when Pauline's Smart car stopped across the street from them. She stepped behind her mother as Pauline leaned out to say, "Hi, Margaret, I was just about to go to Poole. Fancy tagging along?"

Her mother was suddenly animated. "Why not?" She walked to the tiny two-seat car, as Tilly called, "Where will I s-s-s..."

Her mother was climbing in, laughing at something Pauline was saying. Tilly hurried in front of the car. "Wh-wh-where w-w-w..."

She was shouting now because both doors had closed. "Sit! Where will I *sit*?" Then she had to jump out of the car's way, landing on the curb before scrambling back to her feet and screaming, "Mommy! Mommy!"

All Tilly could do was stand there as the Smart car drove away. After a while, Jan appeared, walking fast along the pavement with her umbrella and raincoat. Tilly shouted to her, saying her Mom had left her. But Jan kept walking.

Eventually, Tilly wandered home, sheltering as best she could. After what seemed like many hours, her mother arrived, humming happily and carrying an armful of shopping bags.

Tilly, drenched and furious, ran at her, screaming, "You left me!"

Her mother looked confused. "What's that?"

"You left me!"

She threw herself at her mother and beat at her with her fists, shouting, "Why won't you hug me?"

Her mother was backing off, bags protectively in front of her. "Mom? Hug me. *Please*! Mommy!"

Now her mother was folding her in and holding her tight, saying don't cry, don't cry, Tilly. Tilly did cry. She cried for what was left of the afternoon, lying still wet in her mother's arms.

She said, "There's-s-s-something wrong with this place. I've never seen another kid. Not one. Not once."

She must have fallen asleep because she came awake lying on the couch, aware that her father was home and dinner was being made. She lay still, the familiar sounds soothing her, before walking into the kitchen.

Her father chewed and looked at Tilly as she walked in the room but didn't speak.

"Has Mom told you what she did today?"

He pointed his fork at his wife, his thoughtful face in place. "Think we should get Sky TV?"

"Dad!"

"What?" He looked around as though searching a crowded room.

"Never mind!"

As Tilly stormed off, she heard her mother say, "I went to Poole today. With Pauline."

The next morning, Tilly woke early, feeling that everything was wrong, and went to tell her father about it. He was reading a paper in the kitchen, eating toast, and didn't look up when she walked in. Didn't kiss her head.

Tilly sat beside him, watching him eat for a while. "Dad?"

Nothing.

Getting scared, Tilly shouted at him, but he bit his toast and read on. Then her mother walked in, asking, "Want another cup?"

"Go on then."

"Dad's ignoring me."

Her mother stepped past Tilly and picked up the kettle. "You're right about Sky."

Tilly screamed, a spontaneous shriek that hurt her own ears. Her father nodded and smiled. "I'll check out what deals there are."

Hysterical, Tilly threw herself at her mother, slapping and kicking. It was like trying to fight against a barrage balloon. Her mother rubbed a reddened cheek and said, "I'll do something about the back room today. All those boxes."

Tilly backed away, breathing hard. "Wh-what have I d-d-done? Why are you d-d-doing this?"

She followed her mother round for most of the day. At one point, she picked up a glass and threw it at the wall. Her Mother tutted absently before cleaning it up.

In the evening, her parents ate an amiable meal, setting the table for two, before watching television. Tilly had stopped shouting. If she was quiet, she could almost believe everything was normal.

Finally, she ran upstairs. Throwing her door open, she screamed in fright. A wild-eyed girl was right there in her room, staring at her. She sank to her knees, then looked up, replaying the terrifying moment when she hadn't recognized her own reflection. She smiled weakly to herself, wondering if she was looking somehow thinner, less substantial. She stepped forward until her spectacles clicked against the glass, and mirror fingers touched. Whispered, "I'm not a ghost."

Tilly went to bed with the hope that, when she awoke the next morning, the spell would be broken.

It wasn't. She snatched up the landline receiver and dialled a number from memory, ranting down the phone to her Grandmother, who said, "Hello? Is anybody there?"

She slammed the phone down and ran into town, but nobody answered her when she spoke. She walked into the teashop and, hungry, began eating from someone's plate. She lifted a bowl of soup and threw it at the wall, splashing an oblivious couple sitting nearby.

On her way back, she had to pass the Abbey. Beresford was standing amongst the gravestones, staring. No question, he was staring *at* her, smiling broadly. He raised a hand and, when it dropped, it landed on the shoulder of a small and dirty boy she had somehow failed to notice.

The boy wasn't looking at anything. It struck her then that this was the first time she had ever seen another kid in Childe Abbas. She backed away from Beresford, shaking her head at him. Then she turned and ran.

Back at the house, she sat at the bottom of the stairs and thought about that moment, the one where she opened the door and screamed at the wild-eyed girl. Then she picked up a biro and wrote, right there on the new Laura Ashley wallpaper, *I am Tilly*.

Weeks trailed into months and, one day, Tilly climbed the stairs of a strange house, where the walls were covered in a frenzy of writing. The words meant nothing, even when she tried them out in her mouth.

At the top of the stairs, she met a filthy and wild-eyed girl, her hair matted, and her heavy spectacles cracked. She raised her hand in greeting, and the girls moved together, fingers meeting in a cold and glassy touch, spectacles clicking. They whispered, conspiratorial, asking, "Are you a ghost?"

Then they turned away and were forgotten.


THE END

# The Swarm
## James H Longmore

Everyone said that Tommy Johnson was a born leader, a kid who displayed more natural charisma in his little finger than a gas chamber full of televangelists. He hailed from a nice, posh town just outside of London, raised within the luxurious bosom of upper middle class white suburbia by his well educated, professional parents, Steven and Janet.

There a certain *je ne sais quoi* about the kid, who at the grand old age of seventeen had declared to the entire school during assembly, in between the solemn hymns and prayers—his was a Church of England school, and this was long before the forced separation of church and state—that from that day forward he was to be known as Pete Puke and that all teachers were nothing more than bourgeois, mind controlling cunts. And such was Tommy Johnson's charisma, even the teachers joined in with the applause at his impromptu speech.

Tommy – *Pete Puke* – was ever the trailblazer, a pioneer of the new amongst his friends, a beacon of inspiration to everyone who knew him, or even knew *of* him. He was the first to pierce his ear himself with a safety pin he'd heated up over his Mother's ciggie lighter – an anniversary gift from his father (the Dunhill, not the pin) – an adornment that was followed some days later by an even larger pin through his nose. He was the first, too, to embrace the new wave of music that was sweeping through the country with a more ruthless efficiency than the Great Plague back in the sixteen hundreds; raw, vicious, *angry* tunes that were spat out in stinking flea pits across the green and pleasant land by kids who had no real idea as to just what they were supposed to be angry about. Even so, the new era of punk was welcomed by the younger generation, as it kicked aside the insipid stench of disco and the dying remnants of glam rock that were still hanging on for dear life long after the Bee Gees had pissed all over it.

This was 1977 – Tommy's year – a time of great changes that swept through the once great empire country that was the United Kingdom in a tidal wave of discontent and resentment. It was the year of Sham 69, Siouxsie Soux, Generation X and, of course the band that kicked the whole revolution off—the incomparable Sex Pistols. It was also the year of the Yorkshire Ripper—who was happily enjoying the middle of his murderous spree amongst the county's ladies of the night—the Queen's silver jubilee, of Johnny Rotten and the boys serenading her on the occasion of such a monumental Royal milestone from a barge in the middle of the Thames with their own, very special rendition of *God Save the Queen* – followed hastily by Her Majesty's insistence upon their arrest and an outright ban from the BBC.

Ungrateful bitch.

And it was one Sunday evening in that wonderful, yet fateful year, that for Pete Puke – *nee*, Tommy Johnson – that in keeping with the great insurrection that was happening all around him, everything changed.

"But, Dad!" Tommy protested, his fingers tugging absently at the fat head of the nappy pin in his left ear. "*Even* Flakey's going, and he's a fucking metalhead!"

"Tommy!" Janet Johnson gasped, really not used to hearing such profanity from her son. Seventeen or no, he was still her baby boychild, and she remembered forcing his huge head out of the vagina he'd wrecked like it was only yesterday.

"I've said no, and I mean *no*!" Steven Johnson maintained his voice at somewhere above slightly raised and parentally firm. "And I don't give a damn about what your idiot friend does – or doesn't do."

The Flakey in question was Tommy's best mate, they'd been friends since middle school and much to the Johnson's chagrin, the kid's parents appeared to be far more gung-ho about their son's upbringing that Steven and Janet. The boy's real name was Gerard Burke, but everyone called him Flakey on account of his severe eczema affliction – an unfortunate medical condition that was never more obvious than when the boy was headbanging to Motorhead, Black Sabbath, or his own personal favorite – AC/DC. Some days it was like a miniature snowstorm was dusting the dance floor beneath Flakey's head.

Tommy ground his teeth together and pulled hard on the pin in his ear, the pain sending hot, white flashes across the periphery of his vision. "You can't say no, it's a free country," he said in calm, carefully measured words. Tommy maintained eye contact with his father, a defiant stare that served only to further inflame the tension between the two.

"You are under age and living under our roof," Mr. Johnson growled back, his face reddening. "So you will do as we damn well say."

Tommy groaned at the age-old cliché, and at the fact that his father clearly thought that it put the whole gig thing to bed; Tommy *would not* be going, and that was pretty much that.

Or was it?

Tommy had been looking forward to going to see *Sodomy for Cash* ever since their gig had been announced via clandestinely circulated flyers all around the high school. They were a local band made good – they'd started life as a Clash tribute the year before and quickly graduated to writing and performing their own brand of hate-filled, venomous songs. Tommy had procured himself a bootleg copy of their album, *Buggering the Dog* on cassette, his favorite number being the less than melodious *I Fucked my Sister*. It was perhaps because of said song – along with many more like it – and its underlying venom that Tommy's parents had forbade him from going to the gig, even if Flakey was going.

"It's not *fucking* fair!" Tommy wailed, his steely resolve crumbling beneath his father's icy glare. "I fucking hate you!"

"Tommy!" Janet cried, tears rolling down her plump cheeks, which were still flushed pink from the half-bottle of red wine she'd guzzled during dinner.

"Mind your damn language, boy," Steven Johnson warned. *Damn* was a serious word for the man to be using; Tommy's dad never, ever swore, so for him to be pulling out the big guns meant that Tommy was getting in far deeper than was good for him.

"It's only a gig, Daddy," Tommy's sister, Veronica

piped up, ever the one to attempt to keep the peace in the Johnson household. For every grain of unadulterated magnetism that her brother exuded, fifteen-year-old Veronica Johnson matched it with Kissinger-level diplomacy, although she was not above a little mischief herself – having snuck in to see Saturday Night Fever with her best friend in the world, Tracey Mellor who, according to Dad, was *all big hair and tits.* "And it's at the Old Barn Dance Hall, it's not like it's too far to go."

"Keep out of this, Ve'," Mr. Johnson spat. "This has nothing to do with you."

Tommy shot a sideways glance at his little sister, still unable to believe just how quickly she was blossoming from a spoiled, nosy little brat into a smart, cute young lady – even if she was an unmitigated swot and head fucking prefect. "Even *she* knows this is all bullshit," he grumbled and cast a wry smile at Veronica.

"I told you to mind your *damned* language, Tommy." Mr. Johnson's voice raised a handful of decibels and he took a step forward, into what Tommy considered to be his personal space.

Things turned to shit pretty quickly at that point.

Tommy snatched the safety pin from his ear. A thick spurt of crimson sprayed down onto his carefully ripped, black King Kong t-shirt, and Tommy let out a blood-curdling shriek as he leapt at his advancing father, fists flailing towards Johnson Senior's face.

Mrs. Johnson let out a shrill, marrow-chilling scream and held her hands to her face in much the same pose as the terrified Fay Wray depicted on Tommy's blood stained shirt. Yet, she stood rooted to the spot by her horror as she watched her son land blow upon relentless blow into her husband's face.

Tommy felt a rush of exhilaration when his fist first connected with his father's nose, a satisfying crunch as the cartilage split asunder and blood spattered out from Mr. Johnson's nostrils. Tommy's father raised his own fists – although in defence rather than to return the flurry of blows – and Tommy knocked them away with ease. Then Tommy rained punch upon punch into his father's undefended face with a feeling deep down inside like he wouldn't be able to stop, even if he wanted to.

And he certainly didn't want to.

Mr. Johnson took a heavy blow to the cheek; Tommy's thick fist dislodging a cascade of shattered teeth and smashing the jaw bone clean out of its socket to leave his father with a bizarre, skewed grin that Tommy thought made him look like an escaped mental patient. Another blow to the cheek, yet another to what little remained of Mr. Johnson's nose and the poor man hit the polished oak wood floor like a sack of shit.

Tommy knelt astride his father's chest, raining fierce blows into the man's crumbling face and taking great delight in how the delicate bones beneath split, bloodied skin crunched and shifted under his fists.

Suddenly, there was a weight on his back and the banshee screeching of his mother's hysterical voice sharp and painful in his ear. Tommy almost toppled off his father's squirming, bloodied body as Mrs. Johnson clawed at his eyes from behind, her fat, wobbling breasts squashing into his spine. Tommy tried to shrug his mother off, but her expensively French manicured fingernails had found their way into his left eye and were digging at it with a strength he didn't know she had. Mrs. Johnson's other hand scratched at Tommy's face, the long, sharp nails raking down the greasy skin of his cheek, popping the tops off yellow-headed pimples as they went. Tommy quit pummelling at his father's face, his attention turning to his mother's vicious attack, the pain in his face almost making him regret his impulsive decision.

There came a dull, sickening *crunch,* and as quickly as she'd appeared, Tommy's mother was gone from his back, her lacquered nails gone from his eye. Tommy spun around just in time to see his mother slump sideways to the floor, her crumpled head connecting with the tiles with a wet smack and a thick pool of scarlet blood pouring from the deep, jagged split in her crown.

Tommy stared across at his little sister, who stood over him and his father's now lifeless body. She held in her delicate hands the poker from the iron fireside set Mrs. Johnson had bought a year or two ago – their living room fire was gas, but she'd thought it a quaint throwback to the good old days of having a coal fire – its heavy, pointed end dripping with their mother's blood and matted with gore-soaked clods of bleach-blonde hair.

"Can I come to the gig with you?" Veronica said with an impish smile, the one that never failed to win her brother over, even in his most surly teenage boy moments.

"Sure," Tommy mumbled beneath his breath. He clambered off Mr. Johnson's body and gave it a couple of hefty punts with his tan Doctor Martins for good measure. "It's a free country." One more kick for good luck and Tommy decided that the old man was pretty much dead – his body lay limp and oozing blood and snot onto the overpriced tiles he'd paid for with last year's Christmas bonus.

Tommy hauled his old Raleigh Chopper out of the garage and gave the tyres a good old squeeze to make sure they still had enough air in them. He'd had the bright orange bike since his twelfth birthday but had not ridden the thing in over a year now; somehow, the bike that had been the only thing in the world he'd *really* wanted five years ago didn't seem quite so cool now, especially since he'd almost taken his balls off on the unfortunately placed gear stick, whilst slamming to a sudden halt to impress some large breasted sixth former who lived on the next street over.

Still, needs must and all that. Tommy slammed the Chopper into second gear and had Veronica straddle the elongated seat behind him. She wrapped her skinny arms around his waist as he strained his arms high on the improbable handlebars and began to pedal for all he was worth. If they were lucky, all they'd have missed at the Old Barn would be the crappy support band.

All said, it had been a bad year to that point. Marc Bolan had died, wrapped around a tree by his pissed-up girlfriend – to many, Bolan had been more of a people's poet than a mere popstar, his unique voice a precursor to the rise of punk – his tragically premature death overshadowed by that of the bloated, preening monstrosity that was Elvis Aron Presley. In many ways, Presley had been the Johnny Rotten of *his* day; his music, raw and visceral, had been branded *nigger music* and banned from radio stations throughout the Bible-bashing states of the US – but that was long before he'd been railroaded into those asinine movies overstuffed with meaningless, saccharine songs and vacuous, cone-titted bikini babes. Tommy wished he'd known Elvis back then, to have witnessed the birth of something that special, something that had no doubt paved the way for what was happening in his life right now.

The Old Barn Dance Hall had, once upon a time been just that, an old barn. Well over a century old, the building had endured many incarnations – barn, blacksmith's workshop, whiskey warehouse, munitions factory during *both* world wars, chicken processing plant, brothel, pub and now a dance hall of somewhat dubious repute. Legend had it that back in the dark days of the Sixties, Gerry and the Pacemakers had played there, although that had never actually been substantiated. Mostly, it was gigged by local bands cutting their musical teeth – almost all of them rather badly.

Flakey and the gang were already there, half pissed up on the watered down John Smith's bitter the Old Barn served up to its underage patrons. You really had to drink a lot of that tepid, flat stuff to get to anywhere near decently inebriated, and thus many a sixteen year old in the town was quite adept at downing at least a gallon in one night's session.

Tommy was greeted by pretty much everyone as he walked through the sticky, beer-tang odor of the dance hall, the lads grinning, the birds checking him out – when you've got it, you've got it. Even Sweaty Betty gave Tommy the eye as he walked on by, although she was hardly the type of crumpet he went for – she was more than a tad overweight, had a tragic case of acne that marred her otherwise spectacular cleavage and, as rumor had it, had the tendency to perspire profusely when she was fucked, hence her rather unfortunate nickname. Tommy gave the tart a smile, maybe one day he'd test out that rumor for himself.

"You brought the swotty brat?" Flakey said with a cursory nod towards Veronica. He feigned disdain towards the girl, whilst at the same time quite blatantly checking out her breasts. Tommy knew full well his mate had a bit of a crush on his sister but was way too chicken to do anything about it. Maybe he was scared of what Tommy would say, but Tommy really couldn't think of a better person to relieve his brainbox little sister of her virginity.

"You're wearing *that*?" Tommy pointed at Flakey's t-shirt with disdain. Eddie the Head stared out at him from the middle of his friend's chest, his shit-eating, rictus grin beaming out over the words *Iron Maiden* and a reclining, scantily clad blonde with improbably sized tits. "Here?

Really, mate?"

The band started their set. No bullshit intro, just headfirst into the first number in their somewhat limited repertoire - *Your Grandmother Sucks Cocks in Hell*. The lead singer – some bloke who called himself Buboe, had three A-levels and was on his way to veterinary school in Edinburgh – screamed his angst-riddled lyrics out at the top of his lungs into the grubby old mic.

"I bought it down the market," Flakey said with a wry smile, as if the fact that his metal t-shirt was a cheap knock-off made it okay to wear at a punk gig – as if it was ironic or something.

"Yeah, but not at a *Sodomy* gig, mate." Tommy glanced at the handful of metalheads who stood around Flakey, all of whom seemed to have found something inherently more fascinating in their greasy pint glasses. "I thought you'd have grown out of all that metal shit by now, what happened to moving with the times, Flake'?" Tommy flashed his old friend a toothy smile.

The days were not that long gone when the two of them were ardent glam rock fans, complete with shoulder length hair, bell bottoms and platforms – they'd even fashioned their own shirts from Flakey's mom's Bacofoil in honor of their all time favorite, Gary Glitter, much to Mrs. Burke's chagrin. Then had come the time they'd discovered metal together, before Tommy had been hit by the venomous wave of punk that was thudding through the United Kingdom, and at the Old Barn, he would pogo until his knees throbbed like bastards and Flakey would merrily headbang alongside him, shedding snowflakes of his trademark desiccated skin in his wake.

"I think I'm destined to be a headbanger forever, mate," Flakey replied, with just a soupcon of regret in his voice.

"Join us?" Tommy said, his voice elevated above the band's screeching cacophony. He looked around at the assembled mass of punks, a pure vision of ripped t-shirts, splashes of tartan, safety pins and ill-advised piercings. Those closest to the stage were spitting their appreciation at Buboe's hate-filled lyrics, the lead singer and his inept bassist already glistening wet with shiny globs of audience sputum.

"I can't do that, mate," Flakey said, his eyes lowered. "Sorry."

Tommy flew at his friend, fists aimed squarely at Flakey's face. Blood spattered out in all directions, as Flakey's nose crumpled into a flat nothing in the center of his face. The lad staggered backwards a step or two, before his knees finally gave way and his legs collapsed beneath him.

It was as if some collective blue touch paper had been lit. The moment Flakey hit the deck, the air forced from him with a muted *woomph*, the crowd of punks that filled the Old Barn Dance Hall to well beyond Fire Department regulations turned on the metalheads, the discoites, the curious and each other in a frenzy of flailing fists, boots and vicious head butts.

And as the violence erupted around him, Tommy went about kicking his best friend to death – the kid he'd grown up with since before primary school, the one with whom he'd spent many happy hours over the long, hot summer holidays hunting for hedgerow porn and firing off stones at the gypsy caravan site with the metal catapults Flakey's dad had bought them – relishing the feel of the lad's ribs cracking beneath his boots like so much dry kindling, the sight of Flakey's scabby, round face smothered in wet, sticky blood and his bloodied teeth scattered around him like some obscene halo.

And the band played on, screaming out their filth and

odium-filled song until a bunch of blood-smeared, shirtless punks dragged them from the stage and stamped on their hypocritical heads one by wailing one, silencing their faux anti-establishmentism once and for all.

The dance hall quickly descended into a sea of fighting, the bar was smashed up in mere seconds, the surly fat guy behind it glassed in the throat by a broken bottle of his own watered down, cheap import vodka, his lifeless, bulky frame trampled afoot by the warring youths to lay ignominiously in a spreading pool of spilled blood.

And then, as quickly as it had begun, it was all over.

Tommy quit hoofing at his best mate's body, and stood over it, as if admiring his handiwork. Poor old Flakey was barely recognisable, his face a shattered, twisted mask of congealing blood, one eye swollen shut, the other dangling down his cheek like a solitary, bloodied Clacker – the toy they'd tried to ban because it broke kid's wrists. His arms and legs were broken, the bones snapped and poking through the lad's torn, dry skin, and blood had soaked through his Eddie t-shirt and made it glisten wetly in the dim light of the dance hall.

The crowd in the dance hall stood around Tommy. They stared with an unnerving intensity at him, as if wondering what the hell they were supposed to do next. At their feet, the losers, the dead, the dying, the age-worn wooden floor drenched and sticky with their blood. The metalheads who'd not torn off their shirts and joined the affray alongside the warring punks were dead, along with fifty or so of the punks – all punched, kicked, stamped and glassed to death by their compatriots, who'd turned on them for no other reason than they were simply caught up in the mindless violence of the moment.

"Sorted," Tommy growled through his teeth, his face showing no emotion at all.

"Can we go now?" Veronica said quietly. She'd appeared by her brother's side, her face splashed with fresh blood that was not her own, her left eye closing beneath a wicked purple bruise from where she'd caught someone's fist. She cocked her head to one side, catching the faraway sounds of police sirens; the noise echoed around the eerily silent dance hall like the wailing of lonely, yet diminutive ghosts.

"Sure thing," Tommy said with a grin. "Why the fuck not?"

Tommy Johnson led the punks out of the old Barn, their clomping boots trailing clots of coagulating blood, sticky clumps of mashed flesh, and matted hair out into the street. Veronica tagged along behind, and behind her trailed the punks – a hundred and fifty or so, their numbers thinned somewhat by the violent cull – and together they made their way towards the bright lights of the city.

The town was quiet, it was a Sunday night after all, and Tommy and his followers encountered very few people in the lonely, sodium-lit streets. Those they did come across – an old boy walking his fat, waddling basset hound, a young couple snogging in the lad's clapped out Hillman Minx, a couple of drunks slumped in the piss-soaked doorway of Woolworths – were duly set upon with the same gusto and bloodlust as the poor unfortunates in the dance hall. Not one of them stood a chance against a horde of punks who descended on them in a silent hail of fists and boots, and they were unceremoniously beaten to a bloodied pulp. All, that is, except for the girl in the Hillman – she'd turned on her boyfriend the second Tommy had yanked open the door of the pale blue car, and the poor boy hadn't even had the time to pull up his pants or tuck in his skinny, jutting erection before she'd pulled his hair out by the fistful and dragged him kicking and screaming from the car. She'd joined in the beating of her fella, smashing her bony fists into his face, tearing at his eyes and kicking his balls so hard that his scrotum had burst open like some exotic, overripe fruit.

As the crowd moved on, having tipped the car onto its side and smashed all of the windows, the girl blended in with the blood stained, sweat-streaked punks, her eyes glued to Tommy, a serene look of contentment upon her pretty young face.

Frustrated by the lack of people out and about on that balmy Sunday night, and just itching to satisfy his craving for death and destruction, Tommy made his way towards the motorway that skirted the edge of town. Beneath the mighty concrete arches, there lived a ragtag community of the homeless, the drunk and the addicted, and Tommy figured they would be just what the doctor ordered to slake his thirst for blood. Behind him, moving as one in silence – the only sound, that of heavy boots on paving slabs – the crowd followed on.

They arrived at the motorway underpass at around two in the morning, just as the police were doing their level best to piece together what the hell had happened at the Old Barn; arc lights had been set up, a cordon stretched around the perimeter to keep away the non-existent crowds and plain clothes police officers were pottering about inside, wearing little plastic bootees over their feet to keep the blood, brains and shit off of their cheap shoes.

Most of the inhabitants of the cardboard and tarp shantytown were either asleep, or in some sort of substance-induced unconsciousness, and as such were pretty much sitting ducks. Tommy led the charge, his fists raised high above his head in a silent call to arms, and the punks charged in, trampling the makeshift homes underfoot and pummelling the poor unfortunates within with angry fists and heavy feet. Veronica dragged a scruffy, stinking woman out from a half-crumpled Bendix washing machine box by her foot and set about kicking her face in; the woman in so much of a drunken stupor that she didn't even attempt to defend herself. A dozen or so punks joined in the fun, landing kick upon bone-shattering kick the length and breadth of the woman's body, her ragged clothing quickly stained scarlet as bones splintered and poked through her split skin. And once the woman stopped writhing and nothing more than wet gurgles bubbled from her mouth, Veronica delivered the *coup de grace* with an impish smile on her cute lips, jumping as high as she could manage to land with both feet on the woman's head; the loud, crackling, popping sound that it made as it shattered drove the punks into even more of a frenzy and they continued their kicking even as the crinkled slop of the homeless woman's brains oozed out onto the concrete.

The motorway above was quiet, little more than the rumble of heavy lorries going about their night time business, and so there was little to drown out the screams and weak cries for help, the sickening, wet sounds of snapping bones and rending flesh, as systematically, Tommy Johnson, his sweet kid sister, and their army of punks beat and kicked and murdered the inhabitants of that desperately sad, makeshift community.

Tommy stood in the center of the melee with a satisfied expression on his blood-spattered face, his once shiny Doctor Martins smeared with blood and gore, and he surveyed the delicious carnage that surrounded him. Most of the homeless were dead now, those who were still somehow managing to cling to what pitiful life they'd had were well on their way out, dutifully despatched by the stomping, crushing boots of the blood-soaked punks; many of whom had removed their shirts – girls as well as the boys

– and their gore streaked skin shone wetly in the orange light that streamed from the lamp posts that dotted the road above them.

Walking slowly, stepping over the shattered, twisted corpses that lay beneath his feet, Tommy made his way away from the thickening rivulets of blood that trickled slowly down the slope to drain away into the gutters. He glanced westward, towards where he knew London lay, and began walking in that direction, the bloodied gang of punks following his lead and surrounding him like obedient puppies at feeding time.

Walking through the sleeping streets through the night, pausing to rest for a few hours, when the night was at its darkest, picking up random waifs, strays and people of the night along the way, Tommy and the punks arrived at the Royal Methodist High School a little before nine in the morning, just as the first classes of the day were settling in to their rote learning and inherent boredom. Silently, Tommy pushed open the main gates to the school – they were closed but not locked, what reason would they have to lock them? – and he and his followers streamed in *en masse*, with just one purpose etched in their collective mind.

Phil Hodgson – *Mr.* Hodgson to his pupils – sighed out loud as he surveyed the twenty or so tired, disinterested faces before him. Music Theory class was never a favorite of theirs, but then again they approached the practical class with almost the same level of boredom; even playing the instruments failed to ignite much enthusiasm in his class these days. Not that he could really blame them, Hodgson was stuck teaching Mozart, Beethoven and the like – dinosaurs of the music world – when a music revolution was going on all around them. He'd much rather be teaching his students the less than subtle nuances of Stiff Little

Fingers, The Dammed and The Stranglers than the over-puffed symphonies of the ancient composers – now, *that* would illicit a modicum of interest in his class!

He became aware of the commotion going on outside his class five minutes or so after Tommy and his punks stormed the building, and at first assumed it to be yet another bomb scare – they'd had three already that year, each one having turned out to be a prankster phoning in with a fake Irish accent and pretending to be Provisional IRA. But, when he stuck his head out of his classroom door and saw the stomping herd of blood-smeared punks heading his way, Hodgson knew immediately that this was something altogether different.

"Everybody out!" the teacher yelled at the class, his uncharacteristically raised voice perking up most of the fuzzy heads in the room. *"Now!"* He pointed towards the fire door at the back of the class – the one with the old drum kit and viola cases piled in front of it.

"A fire drill! Brilliant!" one of the kids shouted out as he leapt from his seat, no doubt delighted at the thought of missing Music Theory for something altogether more exciting. His classmates followed suit, jumping to their feet and making their way in a disorderly fashion towards the back of the class.

The classroom door burst open and a dozen or so punks streamed in, their eyes wide, faces blank and streaked with blood – both dried and fresh.

"C-Can I help you?" Hodgson stammered, knowing in his heart that he was in no position to help them at all.

The punks ignored him and made their way towards the teenagers who were busy shifting the pile of instrument cases from the fire door. Some of the kids turned to see what the commotion was, the color draining from their faces as they saw what was approaching them.

"Is that you, Tommy Johnson?" Hodgson recognised

immediately the pupil he'd had the pleasure of teaching the previous year – a gifted and charismatic student, Johnson had devoured everything the curriculum had to throw at him, and more. He'd also mastered at least five instruments to an astounding level, even though all he'd been interested in playing were Bolan, Slade, The Sweet, Glitter and the rest. "What is the meaning of this?"

Tommy looked over at his old teacher from the midst of the invading punks, his eyes registering a flicker of recognition, the question sounding particularly absurd – there *was* no meaning; that was rather the point.

Then the punks fell upon the kids at the back of the class, boots kicking out, fists connecting with innocent faces with wet, crunching sounds. Some of the kids fought back but were beaten down by the sheer weight of numbers of their assailants, whilst some turned on their classmates, punching, kicking, stomping with a look of absolute bloodlust upon their acne-dotted faces.

"Stop this!" Hodgson cried out, a sinking feeling of helplessness setting in his gut. "Stop this at once!"

Of course, the punks ignored him, carrying on with their violent frenzy, silent amongst the screams and bloodied gurgles of his pupils, and the sounds of cracking bones and rending flesh.

"Help me, Sir!" a voice jolted Hodgson and a bloodied hand clutched at the hem of his hound's-tooth jacket. He glanced down, grateful for the distraction away from the bloody carnage in his classroom, and looked into the swollen eyes of Evelyn Watson, her face a mask of glistening, wet blood, most of her teeth broken or missing. Hodgson could also see that the girl had wet her school regulated uniform skirt. "*Pleeeeese!*" she wailed as three punks descended upon her, their teeth bared in a grimace of naked aggression.

There came a moment of stillness, and for Phil Hodgson it was as if time had stilled. Evelyn stared up at him with hope in her eyes, whilst the punks – two lads and a girl – glowered at the poor girl, as if wondering what indignities they were going to inflict upon her next. The punk girl raised her eyes towards Hodgson, and he imagined that there was still a grain of respect in there for an authority figure. In slow motion she wiped a hand across her crimson-streaked cheek, absently tugging on the safety pin that skewered her septum as she did so, and her eyes made contact with the teacher's.

Hodgson looked down at Evelyn, at the pleading look on her oh so young face, the bubbles of snot that popped and dribbled from her nose, the bloodied stumps of what remained of her front teeth. The teacher aimed his first kick at Evelyn's midriff, connecting heavy and hard with the girl's solar plexus and knocking the wind from her lungs with an audible *oomph!*

Evelyn Watson crumpled to the polished wooden floor of the music room like a felled deer, her blood-soaked hand slipped from the teacher's jacket, and a thick spray of blood and phlegm coughed up from her throat. The three punks then set about kicking her to death, their vicious blows shattering her prone body – helped along by Mr. Hodgson who booted at the girl's broken face even as she stared up at him with those imploring eyes. And, as his pupil died amidst the flurry of frenzied boots, Phil Hodgson felt – and thought – nothing, his body and mind working as if on some ferocious autopilot.

And when the girl was dead, Hodgson joined in with the despatch of what remained of his class, kicking, beating, head butting and stamping on those who had not turned on their fellow pupils, all the while, struggling to stay upright on the blood-slicked floor.

When Tommy and his punks finally exited the high

school, almost half of the students and staff lay dead or dying in the classrooms, the hallways and the schoolyard. Those who had turned on their fellows had been spared, and they left the school along with the punks, with Tommy in their midst, as if he were the beating heart of the monster that the gang had become. In all, just short of for hundred died that morning, and Tommy's followers had swelled in number to well over six hundred.

Tommy led them all out of the school gates, and around the outskirts of the town, single minded in their determination to reach the capital city. Because the punks had hit first at the headmaster's office, the alarm wasn't raised until long after the fact, and so the police had arrived at the school after the punks had left, once more a step behind, and yet again ill-prepared for the gruesome sights that greeted them.

***

They arrived in London somewhere around one that afternoon, the sheer number of booted, blood-stained punks creating widespread panic as they made their way through Wandsworth, Brixton and ever onwards towards the heart of that great and historic city, as Big Ben heralded their arrival with its mighty, resonant chimes.

The punks attacked everyone who had the misfortune to get in their way – city gents enjoying a quiet lunch in St. James' Park, young mothers strolling through Hyde Park with their squirming offspring in expensive prams, wealthy shoppers making their way to Harrods, the homeless and the unemployed alike; and those that were not beaten to death joined Tommy's ranks; although very few of them actually got to lay eyes on the leader himself, as Tommy was ensconced within the very center of the swelling crowd, from where he directed their purpose.

Of course, such a swarm of people – punks, suits, mothers, the displaced, young and old alike – of that magnitude did not go unnoticed, nor unreported, and by the time they reached Regent's Park, Tommy and his gang of twelve or so thousand were met by some show of force from the Metropolitan Police force.

*"Stop right where you are!"* Police Sergeant John Tiplady shouted from behind the barricade his officers had hastily erected in anticipation of the punks' arrival, his voice harsh and tinny as it boomed through the megaphone he held with both trembling hands. He'd been briefed on the size of the gang by the lads in the helicopter that hovered high above the central London streets, and although they'd given him an estimate of the numbers involved, he was entirely unprepared to find himself face to face with literally thousands upon thousands of people. "If you don't stop and disperse, we will open fire!" Tiplady ordered with as much authority as he could muster. His officers only had rubber bullets and tear gas, of course, because for real ammunition, they'd have to call out the Army – and who the hell would have thought they'd need bullets to stop what had initially been reported as a gang of scruffy teenagers? And besides which, just how in God's name were they supposed to discern the trouble makers from the innocent civilians caught up in their midst?

But, as Sgt Tiplady watched the punks and their eclectic band of comrades swarm towards the flimsy blockade with grim determination etched upon their otherwise eerily vacant faces, he began to wish he'd put in that call.

The police officer eyed the approaching throng, a prickling chill crawling around to the back of his skull and settling there. The last time he'd seen such an accumulation of people was during the Silver Jubilee celebrations on Pall Mall earlier on in the summer – and they'd been a jovial lot, all decked out in Union Jack shirts and hats, singing merrily amidst copious amounts of red, white and blue bunting, whilst waiting to catch a glimpse of Queen Elizabeth waving from her balcony.

But this lot – they were different by far.

Bloodied, advancing with menace glinting in their eyes, the bizarre mix of people from every walk of life, the swarm had but one commonality – a blank, emotionless expression upon each and every face.

"Why the zoo, Sir?" a young officer to Tiplady's right asked, the tremble of fear wobbling his voice.

"Your guess is as good as mine, constable," the Sergeant replied, honestly. He cast a cursory glance over his shoulder, at the majestic entrance to the Regent's Park Zoo – *The* London Zoo – and wondered the same. The place was crammed with school trips and mothers with their young offspring; it was a busy Monday indeed for the place, and Tiplady and his woefully thin blue line was all that stood between them and the swarm of uncontrolled citizens who were approaching with a murderous gleam in their collective eye. "It's our job to keep everyone safe," Tiplady said, "even those people." He pointed at the advancing horde. "Until we know what is going on here, or what they are protesting about, we must remember that everyone is a citizen."

It was at that point that the swarm quickened their pace, moving swiftly, silently towards the police barricade, oblivious to the weaponry that pointed in their direction.

"Hold your fire!" Tiplady barked his order at his officers, sensing their trigger-happy nervousness. "Stop where you are!" he shouted at the swarm through the megaphone at the top of his lungs, straining his voice as he did so, and knowing full well that he really was wasting his breath. And as the swarm reached the cordon with fists flailing, Police Sergeant John Tiplady made the all too late decision to call in the Army and commanded his officers to open fire.

The rubber bullets felled a few of the first punks to reach the police line, the force of the non-fatal ammunition knocking the wind from them. The tear gas that followed had the first wave of the swarm coughing and spluttering, eyes streaming, but still they came. The police were all too quickly overpowered, as the swarm split down its center to form a pincer movement that caught the cops by surprise, their numbers quickly beaten down and trampled underfoot from both flanks.

Tiplady gave the order to retreat as the barricades were breached and all around him, his officers were reduced to fist-fighting the punks, suits, destitute and kids, their guns torn from their hands and used as bludgeons against them. The young constable to Tiplady's right went down beneath a group of six or seven punks, his skull cracking with a sharp, sodden sound on the concrete, his final cries drowned out by the sound of his bones shattering beneath the relentless pounding of vicious, booted feet.

As Tiplady, and what remained of his officers, made their way towards the zoo's entrance, he happened to catch the eye of a youth in a blood stained King Kong t-shirt – the 1933 original, not the laughable DeLaurentis version Tiplady had taken his grandkids to see the previous summer – and a ragged earlobe crusted with old blood. The lad was in the center of the monstrous gang, surrounded by a dozen or so punks and was quite noticeably not participating in the violence that was so intently aimed at Tiplady's officers. There was just something about the youth that chilled the police officer right down to his marrow's marrow; a look in his eyes that sparked with something not quite natural, a controlled, malevolent intelligence of sorts, and raw, unadulterated *hate*.

And then he was gone, swallowed up by the swarm of beating fists and stomping boots, as Tiplady and his remaining handful of bloodied, defeated officers pushed their way through the tollgates and into the sanctuary of London Zoo.

"Call for back up!" Tiplady yelled into his walkie-talkie, protocol forgotten.

"Copy, sir. Over," came the crackling reply from the helicopter that hovered overhead, the thumping sound of its rotors providing an eerily appropriate soundtrack to the carnage that was going on unabated below it.

"I want SWAT, the Army – the Air Force – the bloody *Coast Guard* if they're available! Over," Tiplady screamed into the radio, the panic in his voice coming through loud and clear – the swarm had made its way through the zoo gates and was advancing with that same slow, deliberate pace that he'd seen outside.

"Roger that. Over," the chopper pilot replied, "hold on down there – over and out." And with that he was gone, the only sound, the *wump-wump-wump* of the helicopter as it maintained its vigil above the horrors below.

"What the bloody hell else does he think we're going to do?" Tiplady growled beneath his breath. Shielding his eyes against the glare of the afternoon sun, he studied the advancing swarm, watched as groups split away from the main body of the crowd as it pushed through the bottleneck the zoo's entrance created, each group fanning out along the walkways and setting upon anyone who wasn't sensible enough to flee their unrelenting approach. Tiplady had never felt so helpless in his life, and he'd been on the Normandy beaches during D-day, a kid of nineteen awaiting evacuation with his heart thumping so hard in his chest he feared it would burst, and the contents of his loosened bowels sagging his fatigues down at the back.

The swarm pushed on through the zoo gates in a seemingly never-ending stream of bloodied aggression, swallowing up those who didn't – or couldn't – run, the alarmed shrieks of the zoo's exhibits adding to the screams and cries of the poor unfortunates who were so viciously beaten and trampled underfoot.

Knowing all too well that to attempt to help any of the zoo's visitors would certainly result in his own brutal undoing, Sergeant Tiplady ushered his battered few remaining officers towards the imposing Victorian buildings that resided at the far end of the zoo, as far away from the marauding swarm and blood curdling screams of its victims as was possible; determined to hole up until the requested backup arrived – and most importantly of all, to *survive*.

Which is how Sergeant Tiplady and his battle weary bunch of police officers found themselves hunkered down within the cool confines of the insect house, their only defence, what remained of their rubber bullets. They found a spot at the rear of the building, through a thick wooden door marked 'STAFF ONLY' that was sandwiched between the display of oversized, hairy-assed spiders and hissing cockroaches the size of a grown man's fist.

The room beyond reeked of ammonia and was alive with the incessant chirruping of the myriad crickets that were there to serve as food for the more exotic inhabitants of the insect house, which gave it the creepy atmosphere of some particularly bad Hammer Horror film. As Tiplady led his officers to the back of the dingy room, he nervously eyed the row upon row of tiny doors that opened up into the cages beyond – this was how the creeping, crawling things the zoo's visitors gawked at were fed.

The door opened behind them. A thin, dishevelled man burst through, slamming the thing shut behind himself and leaning his lanky frame against it.

Sergeant Tiplady spun around, heart thumping wildly in his chest. In unison, the other officers turned on their heels, guns at the ready – and through sheer nervousness, one of the guys let off a round, its report deafening in the enclosed space.

"Oi!" a voice shouted from the gloom, "don't shoot!" The man was lucky that the rubber bullet had gone wide of its mark, although that didn't stop him checking his body for holes.

"Stand down!" Tiplady barked. Through the dim, dust riddled light, he could make out the London Zoo emblem on the man's jumper, and the pallid, sweaty look of sheer panic on his face. "Identify yourself, sir!"

"Jeffrey Richardson," came the breathless reply, "I'm curator of the insect house." Richardson locked the door and approached the police officers who had invaded his sanctuary. "It's good to see the police are here – but shouldn't you be out there?"

"We were," Tiplady told him, the gray, waxy look on his face telling the rest of the story. "We've called for backup, the Army should be here any minute."

"They're killing everybody." Richardson's voice was barely a whisper. "I only managed to get away because I pretended to be one of them." He lifted up his hands to show Tiplady his scraped, bloodied knuckles. "I ran as soon as I had the chance."

Tiplady decided against asking the obvious question, there'd be time for that later – when they got themselves out of this mess; the poor chap seemed ready to collapse as it was.

"It's like they're *swarming*," Richardson said, more

to himself than for the benefit of the policemen. "Thousands of individuals acting as one *macroorganism*," his tone was quite matter-of-fact, as if he were lecturing a bunch of disinterested students.

"You mean, like locusts?" Tiplady asked, his interest piqued – he was quite the fan of the BBC2 nature programme, *The World About Us*, not that he'd ever admit that to his colleagues down the station.

Richardson shook his head, a puzzled frown etching its deep lines across his forehead. "No, locusts are just a whole load of grasshoppers that get together and go in the same direction, this is far more coordinated – they're even sending out scouts to check out the place." Here he paused, his eyes darting madly about the room, twitching towards the door, as if it would crash open any second. "Ants," he declared with a wry smile playing along his thin, colorless lips. "They're acting like a colony of bloody ants."

"Ants?" Tiplady replied, noting the smirks from his officers.

"Yeah," Richardson said. "The crowd move as one, they have soldiers – mostly the punk rockers, from what I could see – and defense, and then there's the scouts. Did you know that there are some species of ants that raid other ant nests and take slaves, killing any ant that refuses to join them?"

"I did not," Tiplady replied honestly. It sounded a tad incredulous to him, but after what he'd witnessed that afternoon – and what was still going on in the bright, English summer sunshine beyond the insect house – he was prepared to believe almost anything.

"I'll bet you a thousand quid that there's a queen somewhere in the middle of it all," Richardson said as he mopped the sweat from his brow with a decidedly grubby handkerchief, "coordinating the whole thing – she'll be surrounded by a tight squad of defence and won't get her hands dirty in the melee for fear of getting killed; without her the colony will become an uncoordinated mess."

This caught Tiplady's attention. "Does the queen have to be a female?" he asked.

Richardson shook his head. "I don't suppose so," he replied, "although in all instances within social insects it is – but what's happening here can hardly be described as typical." He attempted a smile, failed miserably. "Why do you ask?"

"Because I saw him," Tiplady said. "I actually *saw* the bastard." He hit the button on his radio and it crackled to life. "This is Police Sergeant Tiplady, do you read me? Over," he growled.

"Loud and clear. Over," the helicopter pilot replied, his voice strangely alien in the confines of the back room.

"Is Dave with you? Over."

"Affirmative. Over."

"Does he have his rifle? Over," Tiplady asked, as mentally he crossed his fingers and toes. Dave Smalley was the force's sharpshooter – they'd been sending him up in the chopper since the London Hilton bombing back in "75, although not all that often armed.

"Affirmative. Over."

Tiplady let out a sigh of relief. "Young man, punk rocker, ripped shirt with King Kong on the front—"

"—what?"

*"King bloody Kong!"* Tiplady bellowed into the radio. "Over!

"Sorry, sir."

"Tall, black hair, should be in the middle of it all—surrounded by a dozen punks, none of them fighting. Over," Tiplady spoke as quickly as he could, doing his best not to trip over his rushed words.

"Located, sir. Over." The pilot replied following a painful moment of silence. "He's by the elephants. Over."

Tiplady couldn't help but snort at that, as absurd as the whole thing seemed to him.

"Awaiting further instructions. Over."

"Shoot him. Over," Tiplady ordered.

"Could you please repeat that? Over."

"Kill the bastard. Over."

"Affirmative. Over." The radio fell silent and all eyes settled on Tiplady, who felt as if the weight of the entire world had just fallen about his shoulders.

There came the sounds of angry fists pounding on the door, the smashing of glass in the exhibit beyond the dingy back room, and Tiplady offered up a silent prayer to a God he hoped was listening.

Outside, amidst the stink of spilled blood and fresh elephant dung, and the screams of the swarm's hopelessly overpowered victims, there came a sharp *crack* from above. And, before he had the time to look upwards, Tommy Johnson's head exploded like a popped light bulb. Fragments of shattered skull and pinky-gray brain matter showered the punks who surrounded him, their protective human shield no match for Dave Smalley and his sniper rifle.

Dead as the proverbial, Tommy slumped to the hot concrete with blood pouring from the ragged hole in his head, with what remained of his brain slopping out amongst the discarded ice cream wrappers and cigarette butts that lay upon the ground.

"It's stopped," Tiplady said. The pounding on the door had fallen silent, as did the clumping of uncountable footsteps outside. The only sounds now were the faint thrum of the chopper and the muted wails of the injured.

Taking the lead, the police sergeant pulled open the door and made his way through the exhibit, picking his way carefully past the people who stood all but motionless amidst the wrecked displays. Tarantulas, cockroaches, oversized centipedes and a whole host of other creeping things were enjoying their impromptu freedom and crawled with abandon over the stilled swarmers and their lifeless victims.

Tiplady held his breath and stepped out into the sunlight, astounded at the sight that greeted him. The zoo was crammed with people, bloodied, dishevelled, broken, their faces wrinkled with the expression of those who are awakening from some particularly vivid and disturbing dream. Around them lay the beaten, crushed and bleeding bodies of the innocent, people whose only mistake had been to be in the wrong place at very much the wrong time – and Tiplady knew in his heart that it was going to take a hell of a long time to sort through this whole damned mess.

And, somewhere in the background, a transistor radio blared out *Anarchy in the UK*, which Police Sergeant John Tiplady thought to be quite ironic.

Comforted by the music, Veronica Johnson cowered in the darkness of the bat exhibit, taking solace from the cool lightlessness and the close proximity of a dozen of Tommy's old friends. They all sat in the silence and contemplated Tommy's untimely death, their bond strengthening even as the tears flowed. And, beyond the double doors, the swarm began to stir once more, slipping back into their erstwhile catatonic state as Veronica's emergent influence seeped into their collective subconscious.

This turn of events was inevitable, really, as when a swarm's leader is removed; it simply adapts and creates a new one.

The Pistols played on, it was impossible to suppress the music now, and Lydon's grotesque snarl decried all that England held dear and heralded a whole new era of death and destruction.

# Ocean's Bounty
### Andrew J Lucas

> Though nightmares vaulted,
> dreamscapes ply,
> And with intent through ether fly.
> *The King in Yellow*

It was in October of 1940 that our ship, the *Ocean's Bounty* first answered the call. To the captain it was our duty; to the rest of us it was simply a pay cheque. We were late to the game and our small tramp was unable to meet the minimum speed required to join the Canadian escorted convoys, but that didn't stop us—no sir. Cpt. Whitaker insisted on taking to the North Atlantic without a military escort and a desperate War Department took us on. Of course they only allowed us to move cargo of a lesser strategic importance fully expecting we would probably never make port. We'd crossed the Atlantic three times by

February of 1941 without even spotting a friendly ship let alone a German. Each time the British had shaken their heads at our ramshackle converted fishing boat and dutifully unloaded our shipment of tinned meat, condensed milk, and various sundry goods. I suppose the brass expected we would fall prey to a Kraut U-boat, and I guess in a way we did.

Outside the night was clear and a full moon illuminated the dark swells of the North Atlantic. It was a perfect night for U boats to hunt, but in spite of the dangerous waters we were traversing, morale was high. We were doing our part for the war effort and the crew felt that a small ship like ours would be ignored by the Germans in favour of the plump pickings of a full convoy. The rest of the crew were below decks nursing our temperamental engines or enjoying each other's company in the ship's mess hall. The seas were high that night and Frankie Ramirez, the radio operator, was keeping me company on the bridge.

Frankie was a jumpy sort, obsessed with trying to keep in contact with whatever convoy the *Ocean's Bounty* was racing to keep up with. One passage during the summer we had been leapfrogged by three entire convoys, one after the other. Of course, two of those were attacked by German submarines and many of the faster ships were sent to the bottom of the Atlantic. Jean Paul, the engineer, who was always cursing the reliability of our engines, espoused that our slow crawl and the solitude of our travel made us almost invisible to the submariners, whereas a loud cruiser-escorted convoy practically screamed for attention. Personally I just hoped our luck held out until the war ended, but in 1941 that didn't seem likely to happen anytime soon, especially as our neighbours to the south were reluctant to join the fun.

This trip we were carrying pallets of tinned goods, salted meats, and a few barrels of fresh vegetables. We had all stocked up on the various contraband that would make us popular in port when we arrived. Halifax had a thriving underground industry providing Canadian whiskey, Hershey's chocolate, and packs of Lucky Strikes to industrious mariners. Frankie had gotten into my stock and was generously offering me a fag while he delicately searched the radio dial for a signal. I knew better than to complain or distract him from his task.

"Cheers, Frankie," I said as I graciously accepted one of my own cigarettes. "Anything?"

Frankie had one ear covered by the radio's headset and the other cupped by the hand, which held his own dangling cigarette. I watched the glowing end of his smoke as it slowly advanced up the bending tube of ash suspended between his fingers. It was a little aggravating watching him waste my cigarettes, when each one of them was worth a pint or a dance in an English pub.

"Maybe."

Frankie was a man of few words but he had a way with the radio, which was uncanny. The way he could coax a signal from out of thin air was unearthly. Tonight he was listening to something and I'd found it was always best not to break his concentration. Whatever the radio was picking up must have been a music program or something, because Frankie was singing along with whatever he was hearing.

"Ph'nglui mglw'nafh," he whispered.

He must have been picking up a French free radio channel, because what he was singing certainly wasn't English.

"Cthulhu R'lyeh."

He sure as hell couldn't hold a tune. He was so bad that the hairs on the back of my neck were standing on end.

"Wgah'nagl fhtagn."

Frankie was butchering the song so much that I couldn't recognize the song and the words didn't seem like anything a human voice could produce let alone a language we could understand.

"Frankie!" I'd had enough.

"Eh?" he seemed distracted.

"Shut up! You're driving me crazy."

Frankie seemed confused, I guess he didn't realize he'd been singing along to whatever tune he'd been so engrossed in.

"Adjust course," Frankie suddenly snarled.

"Huh?"

"Adjust the fucking course!" he screamed as he abandoned his seat where he had been perched over the radio for the last few hours and scrambled to the wheel.

The sudden burst of activity took me by surprise, as did Frankie's strength as he heaved me aside. He spun the wheel hand-over-hand pulling the ship into a tight turn that threw me hard to the deck plates. Frankie stood bracing himself against the pitching deck squinting to see into the dark beyond the bridge's glass windows. I dragged myself to my feet just in time to see a mammoth shadow slide along the left side of the ship, eclipsing the moon and stars as it passed. A moment later the boat rocked violently to port rising a good meter or so into the air before savagely crashing back into the water.

This time I managed to retain my footing and was at Frankie's side staring into the night. I was scared beyond measure and shaking from adrenaline.

"What the hell was that, Frankie?"

"Cthulhu R'lyeh," Frankie whispered under his breath.

"Frankie? Snap out of it!" I shouted, shaking him after a moment his eyes focused on me again.

"What the hell was that?" I shouted at him again.

"I don't know."

In apparent answer a grinding noise followed by a deep thud came from somewhere below deck. We looked at each other in terror, knowing full well that a torpedo hit was a death sentence for any ship alone on the Atlantic. Frankie frantically shut down the engines while I grabbed the bridge's set of binoculars and rushed out to the ship's foredeck, intent on finding out what was out there. I probably should have headed in the opposite direction down into the engine room, but I had to know what that shadow was.

It wasn't hard to find as right off the port bow of the *Ocean's Bounty* was my worst fear – a German U-boat. The German's conning tower was almost level with our bridge and I could imagine a Kraut submariner lining up a salvo. The sheer wall of metal heaved and shuddered in the ocean swell and I could see a broad swath of shiny metal where our keel had scraped across the superstructure of the submarine. The damage didn't look that severe, but here and there I could spot equipment mounts and railings, which had been bent or ripped off by our strike. The U-boat looked sound but I could only imagine what the effect of this close a strike had been on our own ship.

As if in answer to this thought a second resounding boom echoed through the ship, and a blast of heat and smoke billowed up from below ship. I headed off at a run realizing that there was nothing I could do about the Germans, they would sink the ship or not, but unless I got below decks right away the *Ocean's Bounty* was either going to sink or explode on its own.

I wasn't wrong, the ship was taking on water and the engines were aflame by the time I got below. Frankie had joined Jean Paul and together they were operating the ancient hand-pumped fire equipment.

They seemed to have the blaze under control and a third pair of hands would have only gotten in the way, so I sought out the captain and rest of the crew. The mess had taken the brunt of the damage as the collision had pushed a beam directly against the door and sealed the crew within. It was horrific, the crew had been enjoying their supper in the mess and as I looked through the porthole I could see my captain and crewmates suspended in the frigid seawater that had poured in. As I sealed the mess room entirely, securely entombing my captain and crewmates, I reminded myself that I still had two men fighting to keep the engines from exploding and a German sub on the verge of blowing us up.

A frantic hour or so later the three of us were standing on the foredeck considering our options and staring at the impassive expanse of dull grey metal that had killed 13 of our comrades and crippled our ship. It hadn't taken the opportunity to put a torpedo into our side or unlimber its deck gun, but it also hadn't taken any initiative to help us either. The U-boat sat a few meters off our bow as stoic and unmoving as a rocky Newfoundland shoal. I took note of the ship's designation U-587, hoping I wouldn't take those numbers to my grave.

"Jean Paul."

"Aye, sir."

I could tell the man was fatigued. Fighting the fire, breathing in god knows what, and watching his comrades drown had obviously taken a toll on the usually vivacious Acadian.

"How are the engines?"

Jean Paul considered the question a moment before responding.

"They'll get us to Liverpool if we're lucky."

"Okay," I responded, hoping to project a confidence I really didn't feel. "Frankie, get me that Chicago Typewriter you keep behind your bunk."

"Sir?"

Frankie had bartered a few cases of good Canadian Whiskey for a Thompson submachine gun on our last trip. Every now and then the crew would take turns burning rounds into the ocean swells on clear days. It could send a whole clip of ammo within a minute down range up to 50 meters. Where I was going, I didn't expect to need anywhere near that range.

"Look. That U-boat hasn't moved for almost two hours." I explained. "Either it was crippled when we hit it, or it's waiting for us to move away before plunking one in our side while we're unawares. Either way if it gets underway before we do we're dead."

"But ..." Jean Paul began.

"No buts. Someone has to check it out. You have to nurse those engines back to working order. Frankie you try to get someone on the radio."

"I'll try but all I'm getting is some foreign program."

Frankie looked rattled, and I couldn't blame him but we were desperate. If there was a British ship anywhere nearby I needed Frankie to get them on the horn. I put a hand on his shoulder and pulled him close. The contact seemed to steady him.

"Look, you did good seeing that German bastard at all ..."

"I didn't see it, the radio warned me," Frankie protested.

I paused at the interruption. "If we'd hit it dead on we wouldn't even be talking about it right now."

Jean Paul and I set about preparing the line and Frankie went to retrieve his submachine gun. He left still muttering about the radio, poor guy. He was so obviously shaken by the night's events; I just hoped he could hold it together while I boarded the German U-boat. I didn't want to have to worry about him losing it when I was about to board an enemy vessel.

Once the *Ocean's Bounty* had been secured alongside the U-boat I had no choice but to board it. I didn't know much about U-boats but I expected they had more than enough crew to repel a single Canadian merchant marine. My only real hope was to negotiate with the German submariners, the Thompson was meant to make my argument just that bit more persuasive.

I girded my loins as it were and threw open the upper lock and trained my weapon down into the conning tower.

I wasn't immediately greeted by submachine gun fire, which I took as a good sign. Throwing a cautious thumbs up to Frankie, who was watching anxiously from the *Ocean's Bounty*'s bridge, I proceeded into the tower. I tried to keep the Thompson pointed down as I climbed the rungs, but was forced to sling it before I slipped and broke my neck. My rational mind told me that the Germans hadn't emerged to exercise their superior firepower for a reason, perhaps they wanted to negotiate, perhaps they didn't want to attack us, and perhaps, just perhaps, the boat was adrift and deserted. It was unlikely that I was venturing down this dark, steel hole simply to be met with a volley of lead, but I was still heading into a dark, steel hole and my gut knew it.

I descended quickly, sliding down the iron ladder and coming up hard against the steel door sealing the U-boat. Taking a deep breath to steady myself, I cranked the wheel and unsealed the hatch. Pulling the hatch up and out with a god-awful screech that surely alerted every German seaman within that I was about to enter, I was assaulted by a stench of such foulness that it brought me to my knees. It was only with the utmost of self-control that I stopped myself from heaving my breakfast upon the Nazi deck. I'd heard from a British submariner I'd met in Plymouth that submarines were renowned for their ability to capture and magnify all the assorted odors associated with running a sealed canister filled with heavy equipment, fuel, chemicals, and sweating humanity – but this was beyond the pale.

Preparing myself as best I could, I wrapped my thick, woollen scarf about my mouth and nose, which was of scant help blocking the putrid all-pervasive stench, but the smell of the wool distracted such that I could enter that charnel house. And a charnel house it was, the conning tower was occupied with the corpses of three German seamen, each evidently having died of exposure or dehydration. They were huddled against the outer lock evidently attempting to escape the constraints of their vessel – unsuccessfully it seemed.

The conning tower was joined to the main hull by a second watertight hatch that someone, perhaps these three dead men, had jammed by inserting a pry bar into the opening mechanism. The hatch was securely sealed from within the conning tower, though it was simple to unjam the mechanism by removing the iron bar. I wondered why the three men hadn't done so, perhaps in their half-starved and weakened state their minds simply didn't register that they could unjam the hatch and escape, or they were too weak to do so. I hefted the heavy tool for a moment and discounted that theory for as heavy as the iron was, a child would have been able to push it out of the position it had been wedged into.

I could not fathom what would have driven men to such an act of insanity or what would have kept their crewmates from rushing to their aid.

It took me only a moment to dislodge the pry bar and enter the U-boat. In comparison to the conning tower, the boat's control centre was a breath of air. Stale and laden with the smells of a working vessel to be sure, but without the cloying reek of death and madness. The room was illuminated by a few dim gauges and a single bulb above one of the instrument panels. The boat rocked gently in the grip of the ocean's swells with an almost relaxing rhythm. I moved about the control room looking for signs of life or at least occupation, but there were none, aside from the single illuminated control panel.

The rest of the equipment within the control room was inactive, except for this one station. Now I was no military type, but like all seamen I recognized a radio when I saw one. This one was very similar to the equipment on the *Ocean's Bounty*, having all the requisite dials, switches, and levers that I vaguely recognized. Except for the Germanic labels on the dials it could have been taken from a British or Canadian ship. The major difference was a strange rotary typewriter and a reel-to-reel tape recorder next to the radio and plugged into the receiver. The tape deck's use was obvious and I supposed that this close to England the vessel had been spying on Commonwealth radio traffic. As to the use of the typewriter, I was baffled as it seemed incomplete: there was no paper feed and where a carriage return should be was a bizarre arrangement of moving rotors. Tapping a few keys produced lights under other keys, but never the same light when I pressed the same key multiple times.

It was beyond strange and I felt intuitively that this would be something that the Admiralty would be interested in seeing. I closed the typewriter into the sturdy case that housed it and sealed it shut. I was picking up the case and a stack of official looking documents and journals scattered about the station when I heard a sound behind me. Turning, I saw a dishevelled German dressed only in a shirt and heavily stained coveralls. Both of us looked surprised to see the other and stood silently for a moment wondering if the other was real or a trick of the imagination. It was the

German who broke the silence.

"Schwein! Lassen Sie mich!" he shouted, spittle spraying from his mouth as he moved towards me wild-eyed.

I looked about for my weapon and spied it directly behind the man lying upon an arrangement of nautical maps and navigation equipment. It might as well have been back on the *Ocean's Bounty* for all the good it did me. Luckily the German hadn't seen the gun and seemed to be entirely unarmed but was moving towards me with intent in his eyes and balled fists raised. The man was nearly brown with caked dirt and oil, and his overalls had huge brown stains down the front whose origin I could only guess at. I stepped back hesitant to engage him.

"Cthulhu wgah'nagl fhtagn," he growled as he lunged at me.

The words while strangely familiar were gibberish, but his eyes showed the madness within. On pure instinct I swung the heavy case at my side, striking the charging Kraut directly in the temple. He fell heavily, a dark purple bruise marring his terror-filled face. He fell to the deck and struggled to regain his footing, one hand clasping his damaged face. I was shocked at the damage I had inflicted, but the typewriter was sturdily built and the fear-fuelled blow had surely stunned the man. Yet he was trying to get to his feet and was even now on his knees. In a moment he would be coming at me again. I swung the German typewriter again, striking him in the same location, deepening the cavity I had created with my first hit. Blood and gore erupted from the wound and the man fell again.

I struck again and again until his skull collapsed inward and grey matter and crimson blood coated my weapon. Standing above him trying to regain my calm, not that being enclosed in an enemy vessel had allowed me any real sense of calm to begin with, I breathed deeply and grabbed Freddie's Tommy, vowing to keep it close at hand from then on. The weapon was cold and heavy, but allowed my confidence to return in spite of the gore-covered body at my feet.

"Cthulhu verzeihen. Ihre vassel winkt." The German wheezed at my feet and shuddered.

Jumping back I reflexively pulled the trigger on the machine gun but nothing happened – I had left the safety on during my climb into the U-boat and forgotten to take it off – stupid. At my feet the German chanted something through his ruined face, a supplication to our Lord perhaps. Fearfully I struggled to release the safety on the unfamiliar weapon, stepping back as I did so. Dropping the typewriter I used both hands to fiddle with the latch and just as I had the weapon primed, the German was on his feet, staring at me through the butchery I had made of his face, shouting again with a spray of bloody froth.

"Ihre vassel winkt!"

He lunged at me and I pulled frantically on the trigger of the Thompson. A dozen rounds or so peppered the man, ripping flesh away from his body from his chest to his face. Blood, gore, and viscera exploded from the man, coating the walls and instruments behind him. He fell again and I held the trigger down until the magazine emptied. There was little recognizable of him than a lump of vaguely misshaped gore when I was done. Panting, I shouldered the weapon and stepped back from my ghastly handiwork.

I had no idea if the man had been alone or not, but any element of stealth I may have had was now gone. I had surely alerted the entire crew with my fireworks and it was imperative that I get out of the vessel now while I still had the chance. I picked up the typewriter, journals, and a handful of maps and turned towards the conning tower, my mind on escape. Holding my captured booty close to my chest, I slung the Thompson and gripped the iron ladder, making to pull myself up and out to safety.

"Verzeihen R'Lyeh," came a moist whisper from behind me.

I looked back and the body of the German seaman was shuddering and convulsing. I stared in horrific disbelief as the corpse staggered to its feet. Its shredded muscles barely supported it, and here and there bright bone was plainly exposed; yet it stood. More than that, it began shuffling towards me in spite of the intestines and gore now pouring from its abdomen. I screamed and slammed the hatch shut, spinning the wheel to secure it. A moment later, an object of unearthly strength threw itself against the hatch, causing it to shudder against my back. I scrambled to pick up the pry bar and only just got it in place before the wheel spun with insane speed. The wheel caught the metal bar, bending it slightly but it held.

Safe for the moment, I rested my head against the cold metal, attempting to rally my mind against the horror I had just escaped. I shuddered and whimpered to myself, trying to make sense of what I had just escaped, but I couldn't. Nothing in our training or my life had prepared me to face a creature that could absorb that much punishment and still keep coming. I had never dreamt that such a creature existed, nor should it. It was the same song that Frankie had been humming on the bridge a few hours and a lifetime ago. Had the two been in contact or had they both been picking up on something different entirely. A broadcast not meant for human ears and minds, a dream song not meant for human voices to speak, syllables our tongue rebel to form.

It was with these thoughts dominating my mind that

I left the U-boat behind, sealing the conning tower's hatch one last time. Frankie and Jean Paul were waiting for me aboard the *Ocean's Bounty*, with a firm hand lifting me back to the ship, supporting my fear-weakened body. In the crisp North Atlantic air the horrors I had encountered below quickly receded from my tortured mind. Surely it had been only a trick of the light and my own fearful mind that had interpreted my fight with the Kraut in such a ghastly way. I was no soldier; perhaps my response was typical of a man seeing combat for the first time.

Back aboard the *Ocean's Bounty*, I ordered the ship to make for England at our best possible speed, barely a crawl but I wanted, no *needed*, to be away from that vessel and what it contained. We lacked the ability to scuttle the German submarine and it was far from a given that our own boat would not take on more water and sink on her own. Our only hope was to travel as far and as fast as we could manage and hope that we would be able to intercept a friendly convoy before our engines gave out. We'd try for England's shores but none of us really expected to make it.

As the *Ocean's Bounty* made way, I watched the bobbing tower of the U-boat recede beyond the horizon, taking with it the horrors it contained. I hoped the submarine would be sunk upon sighting by the Royal Navy, taking its inhuman crew to the depths where they belonged. Frankie and I manned the bridge while Jean Paul struggled below decks nursing the engines. I looked forward, searching for sight of land, while Frankie, now inseparable from his Tommy gun, searched the airwaves for a friendly signal. The dull throbbing of the labouring engines was soothing, but as ever Frankie's incessant crooning song got on my nerves.

"Ph'nglui mglw'nafh," Frankie whispered to himself, tuning the radio to an emergency frequency.

"Mayday, any ships within range, please respond."

He listened for a response for a minute or so, droning his foreign song all the while.

"Cthulhu R'lyeh, wgah'nagl fhtagn."

Then he moved to another channel. I noticed he kept his finger on the transmitter button while scanning the radio bands. I suppose this was to keep the channel active in case someone was out there listening on some arcane, obscure frequency.

I calmed myself, watching the German submarine recede into the dark, taking with it the horror I had so recently encountered. It was as if I was waking from a dream, a nightmare that couldn't possibly be real, a dream receding into the dark. Though I suspected that when I closed my eyes to sleep, the nightmare visage of the Kraut officer I'd killed would be there to greet me.

I shook my head to clear it and turned my thoughts to the prize I'd secured from the abandoned U-boat. Though I knew the boat still had occupants, I could not think of them as men and in doing so abdicated any responsibility for their rescue. My ship was sourly wounded and it was debatable whether the *Ocean's Bounty* would be able to make a friendly port in her condition. Most of the crew were dead and she was taking on water, though thankfully at a slow rate. Even if we put into Liverpool or Bristol, we were too far out to turn back to Halifax, the ship would need at least a month in dry dock for repairs before setting sail again. It would be a tough sell to make to the Admiralty to save her, but perhaps the German codebook and salvage would be just the bargaining chip the captain would need to convince them.

The captain! My mind rebelled against his fate and that of most of the crew, a watery death I had condemned then to with my own hand. There wasn't time for me to find a better alternative, one that would save the ship and the crew. Cpt. Whitaker might have been able to find a way to stop the ship from sinking but he was in the mess when the hull ruptured on the other wrong side of the bulkhead. If I could take back those fear-filled minutes of panic I would, but now I had a responsibility to the remaining crew and to the *Ocean's Bounty*, Whitaker's legacy.

I opened the German typewriter case and explored the contents. Baffled by the strange assortment of keys, rotors, and lights, I turned my attention to the more pedestrian objects within the wooden case. The codebook was surprisingly ordinary, simply containing lists of four-letter combinations referenced against dates and times. The Admiralty would go spare once I delivered this into their hands, might even change the course of the war, but at the moment it was simply gibberish. There was however the log book of Oberfunkmeister Arno Krause, the boat's senior radio operator. Perhaps in this I would find some clue to the fate of the U-boat receding in our wake.

I settled into the pilot's station, keenly aware of the salty breeze penetrating the bridge where the impact with the U-boat had cracked the row of windows at the front of the ship, allowing the ocean's breeze into the room along with the occasional blast of water as the ship crested the waves. Nestling the logbook in one arm to protect it, I turned the pages and delved into Arno Krause's life.

The book was written in German of course and the man's penmanship was impeccable, which made it significantly easier for my rusty colonial German to comprehend. For the most part the log was unremarkable, at least early on. Entries detailing weather reports, reference pages to use in the codebook, and the occasional gripe the man had against his fellow seaman. In retrospect, these journal entries seemed trite and inconsequential considering the man's final fate, for Krause's log book included a faded photograph of himself and a pretty girl who I assumed was Emma from the maudlin passages within the book praising her virtues. The young man in the picture was undoubtedly the same twisted, broken horror of a man I had encountered within the submarine, may his soul rest in peace.

As I read further into the book, the tone changed from the day-to-day operation of the U-boat's radio and sophisticated acoustic hydrophone to an obsession with the latter piece of equipment. I was at a loss to interpret the increasingly rambling entries of the man and his steadily deteriorating penmanship. What was significantly more concerning was the man's apparent descent into madness and paranoia. Sometime about a month ago, the dates were confusing and seemed to reference back to pages of the codebook, was when the madness seemed to have struck him.

As far as I could tell, Kaptian Riechman, the U-boat commander, had received orders to proceed to a certain latitude and longitude and await further orders. I recognized the location from my own navigational maps as a few miles south of the *Ocean's Bounty*'s present location. It had been an unlucky coincidence that our ship had even crossed the U-boat's drifting path, let alone struck it. Once the U-boat had reached its assigned location, it was to wait for a broadcast from the Kriegsmarine Wolf Pack command, identifying one of the plump convoys that plied the Atlantic. That broadcast had never arrived and Krause's log entries had devolved into incoherent ramblings and paranoid supplications to a god he apparently no longer believed in. It was difficult to understand what had triggered the man's malady of both the mind and soul. I kept at the book until late in the next night. Jean Paul brought me a selection of canned meats and an aluminum tumbler of rancid coffee. Obviously he'd scrounged up the meal from someone's bunk. With the mess flooded and filled with the dead crew, I wasn't surprised that Jean Paul wasn't eager to unseal that bulkhead, but I was thankful for the scant fare he brought me.

"What is it you have there, Captain?" he asked.

Captain. I suppose as the senior surviving officer that it was my due but I didn't want command, not upon the backs of the dead and certainly not with a crippled ship.

"A log book from the U-boat, Jean Paul. The voyage to England will be treacherous with just the three of us and we all must keep our wits about us. I hope this book will help me understand what happened back at that boat."

"Mon dieu Captain, some things are best left unexamined. That boat was cursed. Leave it be."

"There's a mystery here, Jean Paul."

"You should leave it be. I have boilers to tend if we're to make it to shore."

With that he left the bridge and I returned to the German radio officer's logbook. The deeper I got into the book, the more uneasy I felt, and Jean Paul's misgivings did not help my piece of mind. The log entries began to lose their coherence after the U-boat took up station to await a British convoy. The boat was submerged for long hours, surfacing only to recharge its batteries and to establish contact with the Kriegsmarine. The rest of the time the boat drifted with the Atlantic currents, the boat as idle as the crew. Krause occupied his time listening to the ocean's depths with the boat's hydrophones. I read them, enthralled at the changes in the man's tone as boredom took hold of his mind.

The man knew his equipment, log entries detailed his capture of whale song and shoals of tuna, each accompanied by sophisticated calculations guessing the size of each contact. It was amazing, the accuracy the man could elicit from microphones mounted on the U-boat. The equipment was designed to detect engine noises from passing ships above the submerged boat but could detect sounds from any direction from miles around. Deciphering these sounds was the radioman's job and Krause was apparently quite gifted at it – perhaps that was his downfall.

It may have been the endless hours straining to hear sounds that just weren't there, or some undiagnosed mental disorder, but Krause's log took a turn for the bizarre. The last few entries detailed his detection of sounds of singing, but not whale song, emanating from somewhere in the depths. Obviously the man was mistaken, but for many days he listened and documented the sounds in his book. I examined the passages intently but could discern no actual language, English, German, or otherwise contained within the random letters. In fact, some of the transcription was not even recognizable as Cyrillic letters, but I attributed this to the decaying sanity of the man.

The last entry in Krause's log stated simply that he would need to activate the sonar to fully determine the location, source, and size of the mysterious sounds. He theorized that it was perhaps an undiscovered underwater volcano and that the rhythmic 'chanting' was simply the boiling off of superheated water and nothing more, but he had to be sure and only the sonar would give him that surety. The entry then turned into a rambling account of the data the sonar returned and a mathematical analysis scratched into the margins of the logbook.

But the data made no sense. He attributed sonar returns to sweeping arches on one pulse, when on a return signal he identified broad walls of stone. The contact seemed to move and change as he swept the sonar across it and the geometric shapes his analysis produced made no sense. It was as if his mathematics were insufficient to the task of mapping the object the U-boat was drifting above. I was not a sonar man myself but the man's technique seemed sound –- at least initially. The last few calculation consisted of scrawled, bloody scratches that obscured whatever final thoughts the man had put to paper before madness took him.

What had happened on that boat was a mystery that Krause's logbook did little to solve. I put the book back with the German typewriter and codebook, and shut the case. Let the Admiralty puzzle out the man's diary; I had a ship to nurse back to port.

"Frankie, anything on the radio?"

Frankie turned to me from where he was hunched over his radio. I was surprised that it was now dawn and I had been reading throughout the night as we limped along. Frankie looked as fatigued as I felt.

"Nothing, Sir."

"Well, keep at it."

Frankie turned back to his radio and I looked out over the calm ocean and listened to the labouring engines. I hoped they would hold until we made port or until Frankie's radio picked up something other than that incessant music he was humming under his breath.

A few more days of listening to Frankie chatter and sing into his radio headset would drive me crazy.

# Raven's Curse
## Nick Stead

Death's shadow circled overhead on wings of black, that messenger between worlds, traveller beyond the veil, creature of both nature and spirit. Summoned by the clash of steel, he comes for the fallen, hungry for the flesh of once brave men turned to nothing more than carrion. That day was no different, the battlefield an irresistible banquet through the corvid's eyes. Thus the raven began his descent, his brethren not far behind.

Bran watched his namesake gliding towards him, teeth gritted against the agony within his veins. His foot throbbed where the dart had made its bloody well deep in his flesh; such a small wound rendering him useless as the fight raged on. The barb had appeared harmless when first he'd removed it from its newly formed sheath of red tissue and white bone, but once the pain had begun to creep beyond its initial passage and up the length of his leg, a terrible realisation had sunk in. He lay with his back resting against a large stone, helpless as the excruciating sensation spread across his torso and down his other limbs, its passage marked by the darkening of the blood vessels beneath his skin.

The poison had transformed his body from a mighty vessel of muscle and sinew to a prison of agony and discomfort for his tortured soul. A soul they called Bran the Blessed, but it seemed then his blessing had faded. Perhaps he was no more than a mortal man after all, his body soon to die and feed the raven regarding him with its beady eyes.

A figure lurked on the edge of Bran's vision, his gaze shifting from the corvid to the being who now stood over him. Anger seared through him when he recognised the man he'd made a deal with all those years ago, a deal which was no longer being upheld. For reasons unbeknownst to him, Gythraul had broken their pact, and Bran felt his battle rage returning to have been deceived so, especially when he had never once gone back on his end of the bargain. Yet his fury was useless whilst his body remained in no fit shape to act on it, and all he could do was voice his displeasure.

"You," he snarled through the pain. "We had a deal. You promised me immortality!"

"Yes, I promised immortality," Gythraul replied. "And I am a creature of my word. You shall live on, even with your body damaged beyond repair."

"You mean I will endure like this? How am I meant to live with this pain when it binds me so? I cannot move for the agony this poison has caused, let alone continue to fight and to rule."

Gythraul shrugged. "You asked for immortality and I gave it. The condition of your body was not part of our deal."

"Then let us make a new one."

The man laughed, the shape of him flickering for the

briefest of moments, betraying his true nature. "But you have nothing more I want."

"Please," Bran said, defeated. "There must be something you can do to save me from an eternity of this suffering."

"There is one thing you can do," Gythraul answered. "It won't reverse the effects of the poison but it will free you from the agony of your flesh, without sacrificing your soul to the Otherworld."

"Tell me," Bran commanded.

Gythraul smirked and knelt beside the stricken king, whispering in his ear. The creature's words carried promise of a different torment to the one Bran was currently trapped in, but the effects of the poison intensified and he resigned himself to the alternative he was being offered. Then the other man was back on his feet, leaving Bran to suffer in his ruined body. But the king knew what he had to do.

***

Centuries later, Rob advanced across the modern day battlefield known as the London Underground, careful to observe that unwritten rule that direct eye contact must be avoided at all costs. It was far from his favourite method of transport, the constant bustle at odds with the towns he'd grown up in. But nothing could sully his mood that day, not even the annoying kids continuously bumping into his legs while their teacher desperately tried to control them, or the idiot who ploughed into him on the way out with no apology whatsoever.

Never had he felt so alive, having reached an all-time high over the last few months ever since that lucky break he'd been hoping and wishing for while he'd struggled to make it alone in a world too cruel to indie authors. Even with his gifts of imagination and a way with words, he'd begun to despair his talent was fated to go undiscovered as the years passed and his royalties refused to grow fatter than double figures. Then had come that life changing moment and suddenly he was on the road to fame and fortune, his dreams beginning to come true at last. And Rob had never been happier.

A rock star of the literary world, he lived for those moments on stage, reading to a live audience and feeding off the adoration of his fans as they hung on to his every word. Interviews and signings and even question and answer sessions at conventions – he loved it all. And the limelight loved him, or so he liked to think. It was hard to believe he'd been a nervous wreck whenever it came to public speaking just a year or two ago, awkward in front of people and too self-conscious to ever be successful out in the real world. But as he came to realise people really enjoyed his work, he'd finally found his confidence. Now he revelled in the exposure, and he was truly looking forward to the next con that weekend.

His rise to fame wasn't the only reason for Rob's newfound swagger. Celebrity status and a confidence boost had done wonders for his sex life, his thoughts wandering from the girl he'd been with the night before to all the fun he intended to have in London. He no longer wanted for female company, his phone already filled with contacts for casual encounters. Life was good.

Rob emerged from the Underground to find one of those contacts had just sent him a text, feeling that usual pang of excitement deep in his belly at the sight of her message. Of all the women he'd met, Jenny was by far the one he'd grown closest to, though he couldn't quite explain what it was about her that set her apart from all the rest. There was just something about this girl that had his heart racing whenever they were in touch, and he found himself enjoying time with her outside the bedroom as much as in it. He'd even considered dropping the others and perhaps one day they would end up in a more conventional relationship, but that time had not yet come and so he continued to have fun elsewhere. Even though it was her he truly wanted.

It looked like the weekend was going to be even better than he'd thought, the message saying she was also in London for a few days and asking if he wanted to hang out. Rob didn't need asking twice. Moments later he was back on the tube, on his way to meet her.

***

The young author couldn't keep the stupid grin from his face once he'd spotted her by the ticket barrier. Such an expensive slip of card, the ticket almost escaped trembling fingers in his eagerness to reach the one woman who'd successfully placed him under her spell, but he snatched it back before it could flutter to the ground and shoved it in the machine. Jenny pretended not to notice his clumsiness, greeting him with a warm embrace.

"So what are you doing in London?" Rob asked, trying to act cool.

"Oh you know, just sightseeing. I had more left than I thought from this month's wage, thought maybe I'd check out the con this weekend and see what all the fuss is about with this up and coming author."

"And I thought you had standards; I hear he's a dick."

"He is," she laughed. "But his body makes up for it."

"Well if you're done sightseeing that body is available right now."

"Later. I want to visit the Tower of London first."

"Sure," Rob said. "You've never been before?"

"I have but the history fascinates me. I want to stop by again. And who knows, maybe it'll give you some inspiration for your next story."

"Maybe," he answered.

It didn't take long to reach the historic building, a solitary raven eyeballing them from the top of the outer wall. Grey clouds overhead gave the palace a sinister quality, and the writer couldn't help but feel there was something eerie about the presence of the corvid amidst the threat of a coming storm. A strong wind ruffled feathers as black as the Reaper's robe, the bird cawing in protest.

"Are you wanting to go inside?" Rob asked.

"No, this is close enough. Can't you feel that sense of the ages, echoes of the past?"

"What, like ghosts? There is something creepy about this place."

"No, not ghosts. Just stand with me a moment and open yourself to it; you might be surprised by what you feel."

Rob humoured her, though all he really wanted to do was take her back to his hotel room and kick off the weekend fun. He still had to check in yet and dump his overnight bag there, plus he was feeling ready for a beer or several and then there was that damn raven still glaring at him. Later he would feel foolish for being so unnerved by a dumb bird, yet in that moment its dark eyes seemed to be sucking him into the void where all mortals must one day go. He had that tickly feeling of his hairs standing to attention at fear's command, thinking there was no wonder these animals were so closely linked to death and the afterlife, if there even was anything beyond this world. In that moment anything seemed possible, and he had no trouble believing the raven was in fact Death's messenger.

"You feel it, don't you," Jenny said, watching him closely.

"I guess. Can we go now?"

"Do you know any of the stories surrounding the palace?"

Rob shrugged. "I might have heard one or two, why?"

"The one that's always fascinated me is the story of Bran the Blessed. Do you know who he is?"

"No, but I've a feeling I'm about to find out."

"The stories differ but all agree he was once a mighty Welsh king who ruled over Britain. Some claim he was a giant, others a god. Of course, modern thinkers would have us believe he was no more than a man, if he ever existed at all. Yet all the legends agree on one thing that sets him apart from other men – when he fell in battle, he ordered his seven surviving companions to cut off his head so that he might live on in this world, free of the agony of his wounded body.

"There are those that say Bran enjoyed seven years like that, happy despite the loss of his body and providing entertainment for his seven comrades, still capable of thought and speech. Eventually he fell silent and they buried him right here, under the White Tower. And they say the head was buried facing France so as to ward off invasion, where it remains still, if you ignore the Arthurian legends that he was later dug up and cast into the sea.

"But what most stories don't tell you is why the head stopped talking; why they buried him. You see, his comrades found entertainment elsewhere and they soon forgot the once great king, leaving his head alone and unattended. And alive or no, a severed head is still a calling card for all the scavengers of the land. The irony being that it was ravens that were to be his undoing – the very animal he was named for.

"The birds descended on him in a flurry of dark,

frenzied hunger. First they pecked at his flesh and he screamed for help that never came. Then they pecked out his eyes and still his pleas fell on deaf ears. Finally they pecked out his tongue and he was silent forevermore.”

“Oh, I can definitely do something with that story next time I have a short one to write. Is that why they keep ravens here then? Is that nosy bastard one of the Tower Ravens?”

“So they say but I doubt that’s one of them; they clip their wings so they can’t go too far. Just a weird coincidence it’s about right now, I guess.”

“Okay, I vote we get the hell out of here before it decides our heads would make a great meal an’ all. Come on, I need to go check in.”

She agreed to go back with him, much to his relief, and it wasn’t long before they were in the hotel. The raven was soon forgotten as their passions rose, and the fun truly began.

***

Excited chatter filled the darkened room as Rob made his way to the stage, a hush falling over the audience the moment he stepped into the spotlight. Their expectant faces were barely visible in the gloom beyond the stage lighting, but he could feel their eyes on him as he launched into his introduction. Yet much as he’d come to live for these moments, the writer’s mind was firmly on the night before. It was a wonder he’d made it to the con at all after so little sleep, the natural high alone helping him to power through the day.

He ran on autopilot throughout the performance, seeing only Jenny in his mind’s eye. It was impossible to pick her out in the rows of seats while the rest of the lights were dimmed, but he was confident she was down there somewhere, watching with the same lust she'd awoken in him. That confidence oozed into his reading, and the applause seemed louder than ever when he reached the end of the excerpt from his latest book.

After the reading he invited questions, happy to hear a few familiar voices of loyal fans returning to see him time and again. A square of light briefly appeared at the other end of the room as the door opened and closed, filtering through from the corridor beyond and illuminating the patch of floor in the aisle between the rows of chairs. Rob's eye was drawn away from the man whose question he was taking and towards that invasive brightness, cold dread sucking all the happiness and excitement from his heart and turning his blood to ice at the sight of it there. The raven. The same one from the day before, he was certain of it.

"No more questions," he said, not quite succeeding in keeping the fear from his voice. If he'd thought the presence of the bird had been unnerving outside the Tower of London, it was nothing compared to what he felt then. After all, this wasn't exactly its natural habitat and it seemed more than weird coincidence for it to turn up again inside the building. And then there was the grisly story Jenny had told him. Unwanted images of sharp beaks and deadly talons took shape inside his skull, pecking and clawing at his vulnerable flesh until he was left blind and mute just like Bran was said to have been. Some rational part of his mind tried to tell him it was only a bird, yet he wasn't convinced. Instead it was beginning to seem like a portent of doom, sent by the Reaper himself. That grim thought was too much, the last of his nerve failing him and driving his legs to action.

Rob hurried off the stage and rushed for the door, heart pounding ever faster as he drew nearer to the source of his terror. He was almost too afraid to pass the bird, yet it was the only way to exit the room so he forced himself onwards, determined to escape unscathed. Except when he reached the area by the door, it was to find the corvid was nowhere to be seen, not even when the lights went back up.

Gossip from the crowd filled his ears, riding on the wave of blood rushing to his head and making his face burn red with embarrassment. But the young man didn't slow. He just wanted out of that room as quickly as possible, his heart still beating terror's song even after he'd made it into the corridor with no further sight or sound of the animal. And somehow its sudden disappearance was even more terrifying. Had it even been there at all or was he hallucinating? He supposed it could just be the lack of sleep causing him to see things, though he couldn't shake the feeling there was more to it than that and he remained on edge for the rest of the day, even once he was back at his table for more signings. The end of that first day at the con couldn't come soon enough.

***

Rob had finally calmed by the evening, Jenny helping to take his mind off the raven once again. Dinner was pleasant enough to chase away any leftover sense of unease, and by the time they were out drinking he was back to his usual self.

"Bro, there you are!" a male voice called out.

"Tom?" he answered. "You didn't tell me you were coming down from Wales!"

"Yeah well, surprise," his friend replied with a hint of sarcasm. "Thought I'd come keep you out of trouble."

"But how did you find us?"

"I may have had a little help."

Jenny smirked and slinked off to buy them a drink, giving the two a chance to catch up. Rob soon lost sight of her in the mass of bodies all crowding round the bar and clamouring to be served. She was gone that long, he found himself chatting to a group of other women while Tom looked on with disapproval, scoring another number for his ever growing list.

Turning back to his best mate, he simply asked "What?"

Tom shook his head. "Look, bro, we're all really pleased for you that things are going so well and you're so happy. Just promise me you won't turn into a massive dick now you're a celebrity, okay? Don't be that guy."

"Please, this is me you're talking about. Fame isn't gonna change me."

"But it already has. Since when were you a player? You could at least have the decency to save chatting up other girls for when Jenny isn't around, instead of doing it right under her nose."

"And what's wrong with wanting a bit of fun? She knows the score."

Before his mate could say anything else, Jenny returned with a round of drinks. The subject was closed for debate, though Rob had a feeling he hadn't heard the last of it, not that it was anyone else's business. Who was Tom to lecture him on such things anyway? It was his life to do with as he pleased, and he wasn't out to intentionally hurt anyone. He saw no harm in enjoying himself while he still had his youth and his good looks, and he wasn't about to stop because of friends and family judging him.

The rest of the night passed in a drunken haze. Passions rose again once he and Jenny were back in his hotel room, but they were interrupted by a knock on the door. Next thing Rob knew, Tom was there, for reasons he couldn't quite fathom.

"Promise me, bro," his mate repeated.

"Not now man, for fuck's sake!"

"Promise me."

"Fuck off!"

"Promise me."

His friend just wasn't getting the message and with the testosterone coursing through his veins, fuelled by all the beer, Rob lost control, lashing out before he was even aware of what he'd done. Part of him was horrified at the realisation he'd just punched a mate who was closer to a brother than his real siblings, but part of him didn't care, simply wanting to pick up where he'd been forced to leave off with Jenny. It took a moment before he noticed something was very wrong.

A bruise formed where his fist had connected with Tom's face. Yet the discolouration didn't stop there, his friend's skin greying and puckering round wounds opening up all over his skin. Wounds that could have been caused by a bird's beak.

His best mate's eyes fell from their sockets, tasty morsels for the ravens to dine on. And still this ghoulish apparition insisted on saying the words, "Promise me."

Only when his tongue slipped out from between damaged lips did the ghastly spectre cease to speak. A wound appeared around his neck, his head sliding off the bloody stump and crashing to the floor, landing on Rob's feet and eliciting a horrified cry from the author. The decapitated body collapsed and lay lifeless, yet the head continued to mouth its now silent plea of, "Promise me."

A caw sounded from across the room, the raven returned. It flew directly at Rob, and he suddenly found himself paralysed and helpless as it reached out with its talons to inflict similar damage to him.

***

The writer awoke drenched in cold sweat, heart thudding in his chest and a scream in his throat. His mind felt like it had turned to mush with the effects of too much beer combined with grogginess, real memories and those from the dream merging into a confused mess until he wasn't sure where reality ended and his imagination began. They had definitely been out drinking after the meal, of that much he was sure. But had Tom really been in the club or was seeing his friend purely part of the dream?

He rolled over to see if Jenny was awake, but the other side of the bed was devoid of that comforting warmth of someone he was intimate with. That had his heart pounding all over again. Groping for his phone in the darkness, he finally located it on the table by the bed and checked the time on the display to find it was still way too early – four in the morning to be exact. Where would she have gone at that time of night?

Light flooded back into the room as Rob hit the switch, squinting against the sudden brightness. He climbed out of bed to check she definitely wasn't in the bathroom, when his eyes finally adjusted and fell on a package left by the door. Something about that filled him with new dread.

The last thing he wanted was to peer inside that ominous looking box, made sinister simply by its unexplained appearance, much like the raven from the day before. A horrible thought took hold, his mind convinced he'd just fallen into the pages of one of his own horror stories, and his fear for Jenny's whereabouts grew. And with no clear memory of coming to bed, he couldn't even be sure they'd both made it back to the room. What if something terrible had happened while he'd been too drunk to do anything about it?

He approached the package cautiously, as if he thought it contained a bomb that might explode. Except it wasn't a bomb he feared. That sense of foreboding only heightened when he drew close enough to read his name smeared on the cardboard in what he could only hope was red ink. A voice in his head told him to run, to leave the parcel for the police to investigate and to seek refuge where the sender couldn't find him. But morbid curiosity overrode it. He had to know what was inside, had to confirm his worst fears. So he lifted the top flaps.

It was the smell that hit him first, the stench of dead flesh already beginning to rot. The young man gagged and fought to keep down the beer sloshing round his stomach, succeeding long enough to lean back over the box and take a proper look inside. He immediately wished he hadn't, a raven flying out and directly at his face, just like in the nightmare. It dropped something at his feet as he raised his hands to ward it off, veering away and landing on the headboard where it perched, watching intently with its soul-sucking gaze. Yet that wasn't the worst of the package's contents.

Rob had just had chance to catch a glimpse of what else was inside before the raven had driven him back, and this time he couldn't keep down the raging torrent of bile it had given rise to. The gruesome surprise wasn't quite the one he'd feared, but that made it no less horrific. The image had seared itself into his brain, where he felt sure it would haunt him to the end of his days, creating a wound even time couldn't heal. He tried closing his eyes to calm himself once he'd finished heaving, but even then he could see it still. Not the severed head of the woman he was coming to care for deeply, but two balls plucked from their sockets in the skull that once housed them, green discs catching the light in a brief illusion of life. A tongue lay beside them, dull in contrast to those glittering emeralds decorating the grisly orbs. Emerald green. Like Jenny's.

And then there was the matter of the thing the raven had been carrying. With shaking hands, Rob reached out for the bloodstained scrap of paper, unfolding it to find a note, which simply read 'Come to the White Tower if you want to see her again.'

The author looked at the raven as if the animal understood what was going on, but his tongue seemed to have been ripped from him along with Jenny's, the horror of the situation rendering him mute. So he simply nodded to the bird to indicate he would do as instructed. He would go. What other choice did he have?

***

Rob was in a state of shock as he made his way over to the Tower of London, the very place where this nightmare had begun. He was starting to believe there was indeed something otherworldly about that raven he kept seeing, and he bitterly wished Jenny had never insisted on visiting the palace that first day together. Now her fascination with its gruesome past had cost her dearly, a life without sight or taste a fate worse than death as far as he was concerned. His one comfort was the note, which seemed to indicate she was alive. And yet that piece of knowledge was bittersweet, for the future he'd envisioned them having together could never be the same with the mutilations inflicted on her by the sick bastard behind all this. With no tongue, they would never be able to talk as they had in the months they'd known each other. She'd never again laugh at his jokes or look at him with those beautiful eyes filled with warmth and affection.

Anger stirred beneath the shock, a beast lurking in

the mist. Whoever had taken it upon themselves to utterly ruin two lives, Rob swore he would find a way to make them pay. And he decided he would start with the death of that raven next time he saw it, supernatural or no.

The young man made his way up to the entrance gate, but there was nobody there. No sinister looking figures waited in the darkness, nor was there a broken Jenny bound and sobbing bloody tears from empty sockets. Even the street was deserted, despite the fact there were still late nightclubs open and many were still out partying around the city. He found the lack of people more unnerving than if he'd been faced with the sight of someone waiting for him, and he hesitated by the entrance, unsure what to do.

As he stood rooted by indecision, the gate creaked open, making him jump. He eyed it warily; fully aware of the ancient rite that went on nightly, the one they called the Ceremony of the Keys. And that rite should have included locking that very gate hours ago while he'd probably still been out drinking. Security should have been much tighter; the palace protected not just by lock and key but also the Tower Guard and more CCTV cameras than he could count. So how was it possible for him to seemingly be offered a free pass into the grounds, when it should have been closed to the public at such an early hour?

Still there was no sign of anyone around and though some rational part of his mind insisted he should turn back and call the police, Rob made the decision to venture through the open gate. There he paused, the sound of his own heartbeat deafeningly loud in his ears as he scanned the shadows for any Tower Guards doing the rounds. He expected to be caught at any moment, yet the security he should have had to face seemed non-existent. The author had no explanation for the ease with which he was able to creep between the walls and through to the White Tower, his heart beating faster with every step he took. But no guards came running to apprehend him, nor did any alarms go up to alert them to the presence of an intruder.

At the foot of the iconic castle keep, finally he could see the figure of the man he was meant to meet. Fresh dread seized hold when he realised there was no sign of Jenny, and he began to fear he was already too late to save her, his treacherous mind seeing fit to show him a mental image of her mutilated corpse. Another wave of nausea passed through him, made worse when the stranger called out to him by name.

"Fear not, Rob. We will not be disturbed."

"Who are you?" he asked, forcing himself to walk over to the sinister figure.

"I've gone by many names but originally I was Gythraul, though that probably doesn't answer your question so shall we simply say I am someone who is here to help?"

"Here to help? You tortured Jenny, you sick bastard!"

"No, Rob, he didn't," a female voice called out.

The writer stared incredulously as a second figure stepped out from the shadows, her outline utterly feminine and as desirable as ever in the darkness.

"Jenny? But I don't understand, whose eyes and tongue were in that package if they weren't yours?"

"Whose indeed? Do you even remember her name, I wonder?"

"What?" he said, confused.

The man who'd identified himself as Gythraul clicked his fingers and a second woman appeared in a trembling heap on the floor, pitiful noises rising from her throat but failing to become words without a tongue to form them. Rob could do little more than gawp at her, unable to explain how she was just suddenly there, when a moment ago it had only been the three of them. A second shock stabbed through him when a beam of moonlight revealed more of her features and recognition began to creep in. Her face was distinctive enough for him to match it to his confused memories from earlier in the night, even with the macabre alteration, which had robbed her of her sight. The empty sockets were still red raw; bloody tunnels of torn skin and ripped tissue leading into a world of agony and despair. Rob couldn't hold that empty gaze for long.

"Why?" he managed.

"Oh this was your doing as much as mine," she answered. "You should have listened to your friend Tom. Now the cost for her number will be her life."

"Don't do this. Just let me take her to a hospital and no one has to know what happened, I swear. You'll never hear from me again."

"I think not."

Rob turned back to Gythraul in desperation. "You said you were here to help. Help us, please."

"And so I am," he answered the author. But his eyes were on Jenny as he asked, "Shall we begin, Branwen?"

"Yes. My brother has suffered long enough."

Rob was struggling to make sense of the conversation. It was becoming clear he'd never really known Jenny at all but part of him was still having trouble connecting the woman he'd thought he'd known with the two psychopaths stood in front of him. Yet there was one terrible realisation worming its way through the confusion, a thought he simply couldn't ignore once it had planted itself in the forefront of his brain. Gythraul and Jenny, or Branwen or whoever she truly was, had wanted him here when they killed the girl they'd already tortured. It was possible they just wanted to make him watch, but there was a good chance they meant to kill him too or why else risk bringing him to the White Tower?

Gythraul extended an arm as if reaching for something, a black sacrificial dagger appearing in his outstretched hand, seemingly plucked from the darkness itself. He knelt beside his victim, smirking when she flinched from his touch. Jenny's attention was also on the other woman, and Rob seized his chance.

He knew abandoning the girl to her grim fate would forever haunt him, but he consoled himself with the thought there was nothing he could do. The odds were against him and even if he could somehow overpower the two psychos, without eyes the girl would likely slow them down and probably only get them caught again. So he took the coward's way out, turning to run from the real life horror story he'd found himself trapped in. But with the supernatural at work, it was never going to be that easy.

Rob had barely broken into a sprint before he felt something wrap around his legs, sending him crashing to the ground. That same force pulled him backwards so that he lay beside the girl he'd inadvertently condemned with his insatiable lust, her throat still whole and unmarred but not for long, judging from the way Gythraul was pressing his blade against her skin. If her eyes hadn't been taken she might have been giving him a pleading look, but there were only those two pits of grisly emptiness. The young man was glad she couldn't see his revulsion as he fought to regain his feet and make another run for it, yet something was keeping him pinned down, and no matter how he wanted to look away from the scene of horror unfolding around him, his eyes remained fixed on the girl and their captors. And worse than that eyeless stare was Gythraul himself.

Something was happening to the strange man, a change no more impossible than any of the other night's events, but still no less unbelievable. Wisps of darkness seemed to be peeling away from him as if he'd been wearing the very shadows as a disguise, his human face shedding to reveal something monstrous beneath. Those new features almost resembled a skull, his brow becoming much more pronounced with bony ridges replacing eyebrows, and the flesh sank inwards to resemble sockets, which appeared as empty as those of his victim. The nasal cavity was most definitely empty and his lips were gone, exposing fangs. Horns grew either side of his head and bat-like wings formed on the back of that skeletal frame, while a thin tail sprouted from the base of the spine. Rob had only one word for the image his eyes now presented him with, even though the rational part of his mind tried to tell him it couldn't possibly be. Such beings just didn't exist.

That bony brow gave the demon a fierce look as if his features were twisted into a permanent snarl. But would it have made it any less horrific if he'd still appeared human when he ran his dagger across the girl's delicate neck? Her skin split around the blade's edge, a crimson spring gushing forth. Gythraul held the girl over a patch of earth so that the bloody fountain bathed the dirt in its red waters, feeding the soil with the power of the stolen life until the ground began to shake.

Rob watched as something rose up from beneath the soil, feeling another bout of revulsion when the earth parted to reveal what was unmistakeably human flesh. A face soon became visible, one which might have looked like it was merely sleeping if it hadn't been for the damage inflicted upon it. Yet the skin appeared to be healthy and very much alive where it remained intact, and the torn tissue glistened in the moonlight as if the wounds were fresh, showing neither signs of healing nor decay.

The demon tossed the girl's corpse aside once she'd served her purpose and grabbed at the face with a clawed hand, pulling it free of the soil by its hair to reveal it was no more than a severed head. Rob was in for another shock when he realised it was male and bore the injuries described in the story of Bran the Blessed. And though discovering the legend was real was no less crazy than being in the presence of a demon and whatever Jenny was, it made it no easier to come to terms with.

"So we meet again, Bran," Gythraul addressed the head. "You're lucky your sister cares more about you than your old comrades."

"Get on with it," Branwen said. "Have I not honoured our deal?"

If the demon had still been wearing his human face, Rob had the sense he would have been smirking again as he answered, "Yes, I suppose you have. Though I for one am disappointed our arrangement is about to come to an end."

"We have each endured immortality long enough, my brother and I. Time for you to deliver on your end of the bargain and set us free, so we might finally find peace in the Otherworld. It is what Bran would want if he could still speak for himself, I know it. He would never have made the original deal if he'd known the suffering it would entail for us both."

"Very well. You shall both know peace before the night is through."

There came another pang in Rob's belly when they turned their attention back to him, but this was far from the explosive excitement the woman he'd grown so close to usually inflicted upon him. He knew only cold fear as she looked at him with eyes that had somehow become inhuman. All warmth and affection had apparently drained out with the girl's blood they'd spilled, leaving icy hatred and a cruelty born of past injustices. And that was worse still than Gythraul's true nature.

He renewed his efforts to break free of his invisible bonds but the demon's power over him was absolute. There was no escape when the blade pressed against his throat just as it had to the girl's, and the writer couldn't hold back the pitiful pleas rising unbidden from his throat, even though he knew there was nothing he could say to convince them to spare him. Then he felt the dagger slide in to his flesh and his pleas turned to gurgles, the world losing focus and his vision dimming.

Yet the sharp metal edge didn't stop at that initial gash. Rob's world descended into a deep ache as Gythraul worked at the wound, slicing through muscle and sinew and even bone. The demon chanted something all the while, the words in a language the author didn't recognise, but they rang in his ears and implanted themselves in his brain, echoing round his skull in those final moments.

The end drew nearer, consciousness slipping away with the blood loss. He could no longer feel his body from the neck down, the warmth of it simply gone, the sensation of his limbs and torso resting on the hard ground cut away with the severing of his spinal column. His head came away from the bloody stump of his neck in the demon's hand, but still death did not take him.

Rob opened his eyes to find his vision had cleared, his hold on reality horrifyingly firm and growing stronger by the minute. He could see his body laid lifeless on the floor below, limbs unresponsive to his brain's desperate commands. Yet his voice was uncompromised despite the lack of organs that should have been needed to work it, proven by the screams escaping his mouth, even with the larynx itself now split into two pieces.

Gythraul laughed and set him back down beside his body. "And so a guardian remains at the White Tower and France will not invade. I release Bran from his oath."

"Wait," Branwen commanded. "We are not quite done

yet."

A flap of wings heralded the return of the cursed raven that had started the entire nightmare, Rob's screams doubling in volume as it came into view, landing just in front of his prone head. Its beak darted forward and with no arms to fight it off or legs to carry him from the attack, he remained utterly helpless while it pecked at his vulnerable flesh. That vicious beak was the last thing he ever saw, first stealing his left eye, and then filling what remained of his field of vision as it took his right, casting the writer's world into eternal darkness. Finally it lunged at the tongue just asking to be plucked from between the open jaws, bringing his screams to an abrupt end.

"Now you may bury him."

What was left of Rob might have been condemned to an eternity of blackness, robbed of his ability to speak and communicate, but his head was still very much alive. He felt the soil shifting beneath what flesh remained undamaged, slowly swallowing him up in what was to be his post as the new guard of the White Tower. But mostly what he felt was pain. And as his head sank into the dirt, he could hear the voices of his tormentors as clearly as ever.

"I do wonder why you waited so long for this. It must be a century or more since our deal ended."

"And I thought you prided yourself on knowing the affairs of those who interest you. Do you not recognise Bran's replacement?"

"Should I?"

"He is a descendant of one of the seven."

Understanding seemed to dawn on the demon. "This wasn't just about setting Bran free. You wanted revenge."

"Yes. Not only is he of the same blood of one of those

who betrayed my brother, but he indulges in the same sins they did. They neglected Bran for women and now I find an heir every bit as unscrupulous as his ancestor. Perhaps it is wrong to hold him accountable for wrongs of the past, but he has hurt plenty of others in the here and now, whether he meant to or no, and now he will pay the price. And Bran and I can finally rest in peace."

"Then let me free you from this life, if that is your wish."

"It is."

Rob could hear more chanting in the strange language but it was slowly growing more distant, his head sinking deep into the ground until all sounds of the mortal world were lost to him. The soil was an uncomfortable weight pressing against his skull and adding to the discomfort of his wounds, the throbbing made worse for the dirt clinging to the damaged nerves as finally he came to a stop. There he would remain in his silent blackness, trapped in his agony and despair with only his own thoughts for company. Forever.

# Down Where the Hogweed Grows Tall

## David Turnbull

### *Sunday Night*

"You should see the size of the hogweed," said Jan Elsby.

"Hogweed?" asked Matt, looking up from his copy of Gardener's News.

"Down in the *dip*," replied Jan. "Must be about four or five feet high. I noticed it this afternoon."

The *dip* traced the back gardens of the seven detached houses that made up the horseshoe curve of Holmedean Crescent. It was the remains of a drainage trench that hadn't been filled in properly once the formerly heavily forested area had been cleared during the construction phase of the estate. Matt laid the magazine on the armrest of his chair. "You're sure it's hogweed."

"I know what hogweed looks like," said Jan. "I walked

right into a hogweed plant when I was thirteen. Came out in red blisters all over my arm."

Matt stood up.

"Where are you going?" asked Jan.

"To take a look," he replied. "That stuff is invasive. I don't need hogweed spores blowing in over the back wall. Once that stuff takes root it colonises and leaves no room for anything else."

"If you see Marcus or Liz while you're out there tell them we're coming to their barbeque on Saturday," Jan called after him.

"The trouble he's caused," muttered Matt. "I don't know why you even accepted the invite.

"Be nice," Jan warned him. "Things have calmed down."

The sun was just on the brink of setting, blushing the clouds with a pinkish hue. Pollen heavy bees buzzed around the parade of colourful blooms that stood in the well-tended soil of Matt's flowerbeds. He stepped up to the back wall and rested his arms there as he peered down into the *dip.*

His first reaction was that Jan had underestimated the height of the hogweed, closer to six or seven-foot tall in some parts he reckoned. It had populated the entire ditch, some of it rooted down in the belly, some of it climbing the slope that rose gently toward the back wall.

The fat and phallic purple stems looked as thick as sapling trees, each one sprouting countless red-spotted branches. The huddles of incised green leaves on these branches gave way to huge clusters of white flowers, forming cauliflower helmets at the head. *Creepy looking stuff,* thought Matt, and shivered a little in spite of the balmy evening temperature.

A pungent smell was rising up from the *dip* – an odd and unsettling mixture of celery and parsley, with something far more fetid at its core. There seemed to be a raw potency about the smell that flirted tantalisingly with his libido. He didn't recall ever hearing anything about the scent of hogweed being an aphrodisiac, but it was fairly making his blood race.

The way the weeds swayed in the gathering night breeze, leaves rustling, eerie white heads bobbing, had more than a touch of malevolent intent about it. Matt looked back at his bedding plants and wondered what precautions he might take to protect them against an orgy of incursion if hogweed managed to take root in the fertile soil he had so lovingly cultivated.

The sun had almost completely set and the light was fading fast but he caught a hint of something moving down in the *dip*. He was about to dismiss this as a cat or an urban fox out on its nocturnal prowl. But then the shadowy figure appeared to stand upright.

Matt gasped and stepped back a little as the figure moved with an almost seductive liquidity through the stems of the hogweed. "You don't want to go tramping around in that stuff," he called, regaining himself a bit. "You could get badly stung."

The figure turned its head toward the sound of his voice and the disquieting face that gazed back at him appeared somehow woven into a latticework of green stems and ragged leaves. Matt wasn't entirely sure whether the face was male or female, or whether it was in fact someone wearing a mask. But for a brief moment he was filled with such an overwhelming sense of sexual covetousness that his knees almost buckled under him.

Then the image was gone. With it came the rapid dissipation of his inexplicable lust. He was left not at all sure whether it was simply the gloom of the gathering dusk that had played a trick on his eyes.

### *Monday Night*

"Turn around you cowardly bastard."

Sheila Spinnetti was watching Matt Elsby from her bedroom window. He was down by his back wall, just as he had been at sunset the previous night, staring intently at the weed infested *dip*.

Last night he hadn't known that she was watching him. Tonight though, as he'd walked along his garden path, he'd turned around. Their eyes met. She'd tried to hold the stare, as if she could somehow trap him into finally acknowledging her, but he broke away and hurried on down to the wall.

Now she just wanted him to turn around once more so she could show him how hurt she was by his spineless attitude. It wasn't as if she had any intention of blurting everything out to his wife. It wasn't even that what had passed between them back in February really meant that much to her. She just needed him to acknowledge that it had happened so that they could both move on.

It had been three weeks to the day after Carlos had passed away that Matt had knocked on her door. She had finally convinced her daughter to resume her studies at university and persuaded Sophia, her overbearing sister-in-law, to return home to Italy.

Matt was standing there, hood of his anorak up against a squally shower of rain, a familiar looking casserole dish in his hand. "Jan asked me to bring this round," he said. "She borrowed it and – what with everything, she forgot to return it."

Sheila smiled. She knew that Jan was away in Bristol visiting her elderly mother. "She told you to use this as an excuse to come and check on me, didn't she?"

Matt blushed a little.

"So, how *are* you?" he asked.

"I'm fine," she replied. "I just wish people would stop fussing. I'm not the first woman ever to be widowed her forties."

Matt stepped awkwardly from one foot to the other.

"I wasn't having a go at you," she assured him. "My sister-in-law has only just got home and already I've had her on the phone for forty-five minutes."

She stepped to one side.

"Got time for a coffee? We can catch up on what the kids are doing. Magda is in her final year now. Where is it that Stephen is working?"

Pulling down his hood Matt stepped into the hallway. "Dundee," he said. "I took him back up there after Christmas. What a bloody drive that was."

Sheila laughed.

"Remember when they were both little and we all used to joke about how we'd be in-laws one day?"

"You never know," Matt said. "There's still time."

In the end it had been a bottle of red wine that they'd shared instead of a coffee. No matter how many times she'd tried to replay it in her mind since then she still couldn't remember how they'd ended up in bed together. Their lovemaking had been urgent and without any real passion on either side, both of them made somewhat clumsy and inconsiderate by the alcohol.

Her next clear memory was Matt tiptoeing out of her bedroom. The hands on her bedside clock told her it was four thirty. A little lump had risen in her throat. She'd wanted to call after him. "It's fine. It didn't mean anything." But she'd found herself choked by her tears, grief for her bereavement and guiltiness for her infidelity overwhelming her.

Since then Matt had diligently avoided her, bowing his head if she was out taking some rubbish to the bin when he got into his car in the morning, making his excuses if Jan invited her around to their house for a chat. She watched him now, pacing up and down by the wall, head jutting forward every now and then, as if he was seeing something amongst those big, ugly looking weeds.

"Just turn around and look at me," she whispered under her breath. "Or else I swear I'm going to corner you at the barbeque on Saturday – and you won't like what I've go to say."

She looked now to where those hideously erect hogweed stems swayed uncannily under the light from the summer moon, bobbing their white, clustered heads back and forth. It seemed as if they might be steadily advancing up the slope of the *dip* in a ponderous procession of thrusting masculinity.

She could hear the creepy rustling of their leaves through the crack where the window was slightly ajar. It seemed that within the incessantly hissing murmur she could almost catch the hint of an enticing voice whispering an invite to come and join it the *dip*.

It felt as if she was being inappropriately propositioned and it stirred an unwelcomingly sensual memory of that illicit night when she had sought carnal solace in the arms of her neighbour. She wondered if Matt could hear it too. She wondered if he too was suddenly experiencing an inexplicable urge to revisit their lustful liaison.

### *Tuesday Night*

"Heracleum Mantegazzianum," said Anil. "That's its scientific name."

He and his sister were down by the back wall, looking over at the hogweed down in the *dip*. "You're such a geek, baby brother," said Anjali, reading the content of a text message received on her phone.

"According to the *Wildlife and Countryside Act of 1981*

it's an offence to cause Giant Hogweed to grow in the wild," continued Anil. "Hogweed can live for seven years. Each plant can produce up to a hundred thousand seeds. And less of the baby brother, by the way."

"Two minutes is a big deal when you're a twin," said Anjali, repeating the same old worn out phrase he felt he'd been hearing for the last seventeen years of his existence.

"Let me take a few photos on your phone," he asked.

Anjali raised an eyebrow, plucked pencil thin.

"What do you want to take photos of that ugly looking stuff for?"

"I'm going to write about it on my blog and I want some pictures to go with it."

Anjali laughed. "Nobody reads your nerdy little blog."

"They do," insisted Anil.

"I bet you can't name a single person," she challenged.

"Dhilip," said Anil.

"Dhilip is our cousin," she said. "And he's only ten years old."

"You said I couldn't name a single person," Anil pointed out.

Anjali pushed him away. "Just stop pawing at me and I'll take some pictures for you." She held up her phone and pointed it down into the *dip,* clicking rapidly as she took snapshots of the ugly looking weeds from various different angles. "It reminds me of that drawing that used to give you nightmares when you were little," she said.

"What drawing?"

"The one in that book of Fairy Tales I had. It showed the knight trying to hack his way through the ring of prickly briars that surrounded Sleeping Beauty's castle.

You used to wake up screaming because you thought all the thorny stems were crawling over your bed."

"Rubbish!"

"You did too!"

"Can you see him down there?" came a voice to their left.

They both turned and looked over the garden fences to where Mr Elsby was leaning with over his own back wall three doors away. "There's someone down there in the *dip*," he called to them. "I swear they've been down there every night. I can't tell if it's a man or a woman."

"Hogweed is *phototoxic*," Anil called back. "If anyone is down there they're at risk of *phytophotodermatitis* – which means severe skin inflammations brought by sensitivity to sunlight."

*"Geek"* mouthed Anjali and rolled her eyes.

"I bet it's that creep *Chav*, trying to get a look into my bedroom window," she said. "You should see some of the texts he's sent me. If Mum ever read them…"

*"Chiv,"* corrected Anil. "He's *tagged* his name all over the bus shelter in black marker pen. And you encourage him. Flirting all the time."

"In your dreams," snapped Anjali.

A sudden inexplicable and wholly unexpected image that flashed in her head. She saw herself and Chiv in a shockingly pornographic tryst. Heat flushed in her cheeks. She shook her head and blinked to clear the image away.

Down in the *dip* something shadowy seemed to be weaving in and out of the chunky stems of the hogweed. They could see the white bunches of flowers juddering and rustling. Amongst the dense foliage of green leaves Anjali thought that whoever it was might be wearing some sort of facemask. It wasn't *Chiv* she was sure of that. A horrible knot started to tighten in the pit of her stomach.

"I don't like it," she said.

"There's no-one there," Anil reasoned. "It's just the way the light is falling on the leaves."

Mr Elsby leaned forward and peered into the *dip*. His breathing sounded heavy. Anjali felt her own inhalation of breath rise and fall to match the rhythm of his. The almost instinctive synchronicity of this backwards and forwards volley made it feel as if something intimate was passing between them. She felt herself blush again.

"There's no one there," insisted Anil. "It just looks as if there is."

### *Wednesday Night*

Justine awoke to find Geraldine's side of the bed empty. She reached across to touch the slight indentation where her partner lain on the mattress. There was still a residue of body warmth on the sheets.

Not long gone then.

Fumbling for her watch she saw that it was two twenty in the morning. She listened for the tell-tale sound of laboured breathing. If Geraldine was still in the room she could guide her gently back to bed without the risk of waking her up.

Recently Geraldine's nocturnal sojourns had been happening at least a couple of times a week. She couldn't help herself. It was a medical condition. The prognosis didn't really help as far as Geraldine was concerned. She was embarrassed and increasingly unsettled every time she had an episode.

So, whenever possible, Justine tried to get her back into bed, tuck her in, stroke her hair to sooth her back into a normal sleep pattern. Then in the morning she could simply offer a re-assuring white lie. *"Another good night, Hun. Slept right through."*

She didn't see this as being in any way deceptive.

Their doctor had said that episodes were cumulative. Anxiety was one of the key factors that caused people to sleepwalk. If they became anxious about having just experienced an episode, another was almost sure to follow shortly behind.

Positive now that Geraldine was no longer in the room Justine switched on the light. The door was slightly open. She put on her slippers, wrapped herself in her towelling gown and went out into the hall. The bathroom was the first place she checked. Once she had found Geraldine actually seated in the dry bathtub, trying to rub conditioner into her hair, wide eyed but still clearly fast asleep.

No sign of her in the bathroom, or in the spare bedroom.

Justine went slowly down the stairs, listening for the clatter of tins in the kitchen. On another occasion she had found Geraldine earnestly re-arranging the entire contents of their cupboards. She passed through the living room, hoping that Geraldine might simply be seated on the couch, staring intently at the blank television screen, as she did every so often.

No sign of her there - or in the kitchen.

But the kitchen door was wide open – the odd and somewhat sexual scent of that hogweed stuff wafting in on the night breeze. This was a first. She'd heard of the partners of sleepwalkers hiding keys and suchlike to prevent their loved ones leaving the house. But, till now, Geraldine's somnambulism had been thankfully domesticated.

*At least she didn't go out the front door into the street,* thought Justine, stepping into the garden. The moon was full in the sky above, casting a bright glow onto the sloping asphalt covered roof of the garden shed. *That would be a new one,* she thought. *Pottering around in the shed.*

But, as she made her way up the path, it became clear that the brass padlock on the shed door was still firmly clicked shut. Justine turned around in a little circle, wondering if Geraldine had somehow managed to climb over the fence into the neighbouring garden. She felt something twisting softly around her ankle and bent down to pick it up. Hanging limply in her hand was Geraldine's light blue nightdress.

*Christ!*

Instinct propelled her towards the back wall.

Immediately she saw Geraldine down in the *dip*, stark naked, hips swaying as she danced grotesquely amongst the looming forms of those dreadful weeds, legs slightly parted, grinding like a cheap whore turning a trick in a seedy lap dancing club. For the briefest moment she could have sworn that someone else was there with her, hidden like some Peeping Tom, almost camouflaged within the forest of fat purple stems and sultry green leaves.

Then the moment was gone and there was only poor Geraldine, dancing erotically to whatever music she was hearing in her dreams. Justine didn't want to call out. She was just as afraid of alerting the neighbours as she was of waking Geraldine up. She tried to climb over the wall. All she did was scrape her knees when her slippers failed to gain proper purchase on the brickwork. She turned around and saw that there was a light on in Fergal Meaney's kitchen next door.

Fergal would have been out in his cab picking up fares from the pubs and clubs in the town centre. Geraldine wasn't going to be too happy if someone else found out about her condition, but Justine didn't feel she had much choice. She couldn't just leave her down there until she woke of her own accord. She might hurt herself.

Fergal came to the kitchen window when she knocked on his back door. As she stood there, huge rip in her dressing gown from where it had been caught when she climbed over the adjoining fence, he did an almost comical double take. The back door swung open almost immediately,

"Justine?" he asked. "What's going on? It's after two in the morning, so it is."

Justine had never experienced any attraction whatsoever to men - but now as Fergal stood before her she found herself gripped with an irresistible urge to drop her dressing gown and rip off her nightdress and press his hands firmly against her breasts. She felt her nipples harden. Worried that she might actually be about to translate the urge into action she shook the feeling away.

"It's Geraldine," she said. "She's – well – you see she sleepwalks. And – you need to help me, Fergal. She's down in the *dip*."

"The *dip*? What the feck is she doing down there?"

"She sleepwalks," said Justine, choking back her tears. "She won't even know where she is. I couldn't get over the wall."

Fergal began to stride along his path, heading for the back wall. Justine ran alongside of him. "Thank you," she said. "Just help her back up and try not to wake her."

Fergal looked over the wall to where Geraldine continued to gyrate nakedly amongst the hogweed. "Bloody Hell!" he cried, vaulting up onto the wall. Justine took off her torn dressing gown and again felt those awful alien urges rise within her.

"Take this to cover her up," she said hurriedly. "She would die of embarrassment if she knew."

Taking the gown Fergal dropped over onto the other side of the wall.

"Be careful - down there," called a voice.

Both Justine and Fergal turned to see Matt Elsby stood by his back wall, dressed in a set of blue pyjamas. "I saw you - from my - bedroom window," he said, chest heaving as he breathed as heavily as someone who had just run a marathon. He spoke like an asthmatic; drawing gulps of air between his words. "I swear - there's been someone - prowling about down there the past - couple of nights. Maybe - they're checking whether they can burgle our houses - through the back doors."

"Well they'll be long gone by now, so they will," said Fergal, starting down the *dip's* shallow incline.

"I meant - be careful of the hogweed," said Matt. "It's toxic - stuff. If it touches - your skin it can cause - blisters or burns. The Puriwal kid said there - was a name for it. *Photoderma* - something."

Fergal rolled down the sleeves on his sweatshirt and pulled up the hood. Then he retrieved his leather driving gloves from the pockets of his jeans and edged his way down the slope.

### *Thursday Night*

Chiv lay on his bed, his week's pilfered trawl scattered around him on the duvet – three cell phones, an iPad, a Netbook and a pink purse. He picked up the pink purse, opened it and removed the loose change inside. He counted four pounds and forty-five pence in coins. Hardly worth the fucking effort.

He picked up the purse and turned it over in his hands. It looked new. He wondered if he could use it as a present to get into Anjali Puriwal's good books. He thought about her silky black hair and the tantalising habit she had of looking sideways at you from the corner of her smoky brown eyes and felt that old familiar knot twist in his stomach.

She'd be eighteen soon - almost a year older than

him. But that didn't make a difference. Stuck up bitches like her always went for bad boys and Chiv liked to think he was as bad as they came. Making a mental note to squeeze the date of her birthday out of her wimp of a twin brother he put the purse and the rest of his haul back under his mattress and retrieved the tightly rolled joint that was also hidden away under there.

Holding the joint between his thumb and forefinger he glanced at his watch. One in the morning. His parents would both be fast asleep. But *skunk* had a shitty stink about it that matched the suggestion implied by its name and if he lit up inside the house the smell was bound to still be hanging around in the morning.

Slowly he snuck downstairs and out into the back garden. Despite the early hour it was still warm. He could see a window left open in his parents' bedroom. If he struck a match the chances were that one of them might hear it and catch him red handed.

He walked to the back wall and looked down into the dip. When he'd first started thieving he'd stashed stuff down there. But since his mother had *put her foot down* and insisted he was old enough to make his own bed and change the sheets when necessary, he'd been provided with an excellent opportunity to hide his ill-gotten gains much closer to home.

There were a lot more weeds down there than he remembered. Tall, almost menacing looking things, all huddled densely together like the crowd at a football match. They stank too. The smell stung his eyes and made his nose drip. That might be a good thing though. It would mask the smell of the *skunk*. And if he got right down into the belly of the *dip,* where the weeds seemed thickest, no one would even be able to make out he was there.

With a last glance over his shoulder he hauled himself over the wall and edged his way down the embankment.

Some of the weeds were a good foot taller than he was. He could feel their bristly leaves brushing against his hands and his cheeks. They began to itch like crazy. But he had a bad craving for the buzz of the *skunk* now, so he pushed on, doggedly shouldering his way past the purple stems.

When he thought he was far enough into the forest of weeds he hunkered down and lit the joint. Sucking the first draw of the sickly smoke down into his lungs he closed his eyes and imagined Anjali in his room. He imagined her glancing cheekily sideways at him as she undressed. He imagined her lying down naked on his bed – ready for him.

Something made him open his eyes. He blinked when he saw what appeared to be one of the weeds leaning down towards him, its fat head apparently coming straight at him. It looked like Anjali. Then it looked like a face that was woven out of interlaced stems and twigs.

It touched his forehead and the touch felt like a kiss. Then the kiss started to burn as if it was eating into his skull like acid. He squeezed his eyes shut and took another long drag from the joint in the hope that it would ease the pain. The intensity dulled to a pulsing throb. When he opened his eyes the weed, or the person, or whatever it had been was gone.

He looked at the red poker end of the joint.

"Strong shit," he whispered.

Closing his eyes, he rocked back and forth. The soles of his sneakers seemed to sink deep into the fudge of the loam. It felt like root tubers were actually sprouting from his feet, snaking through the rubber on the soles and penetrating the warm, welcoming moistness of the soil. The night wind caressed his hair and breathed promises into his ears. Erotic hallucinations of Anjali

Puriwal filled his mind.

"Strong shit," he whispered again and slipped his trembling hand into his jeans.

### *Friday Night*

Fergal sat in his kitchen with the back door wide open. His chair was facing the garden so that he could look at the back wall. He had on a pair of battered earphones and on his lap sat an old and scratched, but perfectly functional CD Walkman that he'd retrieved from a cardboard box in the cupboard under the stairs. The album endlessly spinning inside the Walkman was Nursery Cryme by the 70's rock band Genesis.

Fergal had grown up listening to Genesis. They were his older brother's favourite band. Fergal had never been that into them - but a couple of years ago when he'd seen a copy of Nursery Cryme in the sale bin in HMV the sight of the distinctive cover art with the little girl, playing croquette on her striped yellow lawn, had been enough for him to buy it in the reckless surge of a nostalgic whim.

As far as he recalled the only time he had actually listened to it was in the car on the way home. Since then it had sat unloved and neglected in his CD rack. But the other night when he'd been down in the *dip* helping his poor bewildered neighbour back up to her garden wall a fragment of a song he was sure came from the album popped into his head.

It been stuck there all of the following night when he'd been out picking up fares and soon as he'd returned home he'd sought out the CD - as much to confirm that he wasn't imagining things as anything else.

And, sure enough, there it was, track three, *The Return of the Giant Hogweed.*

He'd shivered when he read the title and felt his heart

skip a beat when he listened to the lyrics. Now he'd lost count of how many times he'd listened to it as he sat there breathing in the trenchant scent of the wanton colony that grew in the dip. The song told of hogweed brought back from Russia by a Victorian botanist to Kew Gardens and how it diligently and malevolently planned a cruel revenge on the human race.

Fergal looked down at the blisters that were raised on the backs of his wrists from where the leaves had brushed against exposed flesh when he was helping Geraldine on with the dressing gown. *Too fecking close for comfort,* he thought, resetting the track to the start and listening again in stunned fascination to the portentous tone of the words.

Sweat beaded on his brow as he recalled passing amongst the huge intimidating forms of the hogweed. Geraldine had been out of it. Eyes staring blankly ahead, plump, slightly overweight body heaving and gyrating in a manner he found uncomfortably suggestive. So much so that when he'd placed the dressing gown over her shoulder he'd found himself getting an erection.

Then there was the sense of being watched from somewhere deep in the tangle of stems. Not some opportunist burglar as Matt Elsby would have had it – but something else entirely. It had the feel of something raw and almost animalistic. Something with a predatory and lustful intent that stalked and circled just out of view as he coaxed and cajoled poor Geraldine up the slope to where Justine waited, ashen faced, eyes brimming with tears.

His thoughts turned to the prolific fecundity of the hogweed. He couldn't help but compare this to his own demoralising sterility. He thought of his ex-wife and how his inability to give her the child she wanted had led to the break up of their marriage. He thought of her now, pregnant to another man – happy at last.

In his ears Peter Gabriel sang of a botanical creature stirring to wreak its long-awaited vengeance. Matt didn't truly think that this was what was happening down in the *dip*. But he was becoming increasingly convinced that the invasive nature of hogweed had drawn something else to it.

Something that had dwelled the old forest that was once as dense and formidable around these parts as the colony of hogweed in the *dip* was becoming. Something that had lain dormant as constructs of concrete and clay were erected all around it. Something darkly aroused by the wanton promiscuity of the hogweed.

*If this was a movie,* he thought, *I'd have a fecking shotgun on my lap, so I would. Ready to blow the bastard to Kingdom come when he finally scaled the wall with his rampant hogweed horde at his back.*

The night breeze picked up and the smell of the hogweed intensified, filling the kitchen with the acrid aroma of its odious stench. It smelled to him like the aftermath of an ejaculation. The rustle of the leaves sounded like the laboured breath of lovemaking. He felt himself becoming unnervingly aroused again. He cried for his loneliness and yearned for some inexplicable reason to go back down into the *dip*, to lie naked in the fertile soil and spend his worthless seed.

The Genesis song came to an end.

He reset it to the beginning.


### *Saturday Night*


Marcus Bowman watched his neighbours through the haze of smoke rising up from the barbeque briquettes. From what he could see everyone on the Crescent had actually turned up. That was far more than he'd hoped for. He might have been quietly pleased with the response had it not been apparent that most of them clearly had an ulterior motive for accepting his invite.

His little garden party was being hijacked and turned into some sort of spontaneous neighbourhood watch meeting. The number one item on the agenda was the issue of the hogweed infestation down in the dip. That very minute Puriwal from number five was pontificating about how his son had uncovered some sort of bylaw placing certain obligations on local authorities and how they should get up a petition to hand into the next local councillors' surgery.

He could see Geraldine from number seven pointing at the painful red blotching on her face and neck as she animatedly nodded her head in the direction of the dip. "The blistering has gone down a bit," said her partner, Justine. "But the hospital can't rule out permanent scarring."

Sheila Spinnetti from number three kept scowling at Matt Elsby from number one. Marcus wasn't clear what had passed between the two of them but whatever it was she seemed pretty damned pissed off. Meanwhile Fergal Meaney looked scared, hovering on the fringe of the crowd, casting edgy little glances back at the *dip* as he necked huge gulps from a bottle of cold beer.

Marcus flipped over a couple of burgers and pushed a half-browned bratwurst to the side of the griddle. He peered through the smoke to the back wall. He could see the swaying white flowered multitude of the hogweed, surrounding the back wall like an army besieging some medieval castle. He felt like Macbeth behind his lonely ramparts. Any minute now a messenger would arrive to swear that he'd looked toward Birnam and witnessed a forest on the move.

He saw Liz cast an anxious glance at the glass that sat beside the tongs and spatulas on the little table beside him. He could tell that she was wondering whether there was anything other than lemonade in there. Probably dreading the possibility that he'd been tempted to down something stronger before he plucked up the courage to do what he'd set out to do.

A twinge of guilt spurred him into action.

He picked up the glass and tapped the side loudly with a fork.

"I have something I need to say."

Everyone turned to face him.

Marcus cleared his throat.

"My name is Marcus Bowman - and I'm an alcoholic. It's been three months since my last drink."

An embarrassed silence fell over his guests. There was a shuffling of feet and a bowing of heads. Liz came and stood beside him, hair tousled around her eyes from the gentle summer breeze. She took his hand and squeezed his fingers. It gave him the spur he needed.

"I want to apologise to each and every one of you," he said. "I've literally been the neighbour from hell. My drinking has caused all sorts of upsets on the Crescent. I've come home roaring drunk and disturbed your sleep. I've urinated in your front gardens. I've knocked over your dustbins. I've been obnoxious and arrogant to anyone who's dared to challenge my behaviour. But I've turned a corner."

Marcus could feel all their eyes on him now. Liz squeezed his fingers again. He took a sip of lemonade and wished it was a tot of whisky.

"I blew my career as an English teacher," he confessed. "I could barely hold down the job I was forced to take as an insurance salesman. I damned near destroyed my marriage. I almost got myself thrown out of my own home."

Liz blushed and tried to disguise this with an

embarrassed smile.

"But I'm facing my demons," he continued. "I'm in an addiction programme and this public apology is all part of the healing process. I want you all to know that I am genuinely…"

The sight of a figure clambering awkwardly over the back wall stopped him in full flow. Everyone turned around to see what he was looking at. The figure stumbled onto the lawn. They all gasped and took a step back. Anjali Puriwal screamed. Fergal Meany let out an exclamation entirely befitting his Catholic upbringing – "Jesus, Mary and Joseph!"

The teenage boy who was standing before them looked both dreadful and yet full of Puckish mischievousness. He was naked as sin and partially aroused. His skin had a sickly green tinge about it. He looked almost reptilian; severe, angry blisters raised on almost every inch of flesh, bits of hogweed leaf tangled into his hair. The spaced out look in his eyes and the slackness of his jaw suggested he was high on something.

Marcus felt a pang of jealousy.

"Are you the little shit who's been prowling around down there?" challenged Matt Elsby.

"It's Chiv!" exclaimed Anil Puriwal.

She began snapping photos of the poor dishevelled boy on her mobile phone.

"Stop that at once," yelled Mr Puriwal.

"Chester?" Someone's voice started firing questions. "Is that you? What have you done to yourself? Where are your clothes? What were you doing down in the *dip*? Is that where you keep disappearing to?"

The boy's mother stepped forward.

"Chester? Do you hear me?"

A dreadful grin curved on the boy's face.

"He's drunk," said Jan Elsby.

"On drugs more like," said Matt.

The boy's father pushed his way forward.

"I told you," he railed at his wife. "But you wouldn't listen."

"The *Green* invites you down into its domain to indulge in the fecundity of the soil," said the boy in a voice that sounded almost surreal in its apparent disembodiment.

Marcus felt a snaking trail of sweat trace the length of his spine.

The messenger had arrived.

"Who's the *Green*?" asked the boy's mother.

"Is he your partner in crime?" challenged Matt Elsby and cast another quick glance at the back wall.

Marcus watched Fergal raise his half-consumed bottle of beer. "Jack in the fecking Green," he said and pressed the neck of the bottle to his lip with his trembling hand. "I knew it, so I did."

"The Green Man," said Anil Puriwal, as if faithfully reciting something he'd read. "A pagan fertility symbol - perversely featured in woodcarvings in quite a few Christian churches."

"Geek," sneered his sister and snapped another picture of the naked boy, much to her parents" obvious annoyance.

Geraldine turned to Justine. "I told you there was something down there. You said I dreamt it."

Sheila Spinnetti started pounding her temples with her tightly clenched fists. "His voice is in my head. It won't stop. He wants us to go down into the *dip*. He wants us to go down naked as the day we were born."

Marcus felt something enter his own head. The words of an obscure piece of poetry he'd learned when he was studying for his English Literature Degree and long since forgotten. He found himself speaking the words out loud.

*Men gaped at the hue of him*

*Ingrained in garb and mien*
*A fellow fiercely grim*
*And all a glittering green*
Chiv turned back to the wall.

For a moment no one else moved.

The breeze tumbled warmly into the garden. The musky stench of the hogweed became overwhelming. When Marcus inhaled deeply it was like the old familiar burn of whiskey on the back of his throat. He felt his nose turn numb as a sensual shudder ran through him. Something stirred in his groin, something that had long ago been numbed by the deadening effect of his reckless alcohol abuse.

A vision somehow materialised before him.

A landscape thousands of years old. A swamp, hung with creepers and vines, where the *Green* held undisputed sway, omnipresent amongst the fertile abundance of the rushes and the stems and the leaves and the lilies.

Then all was devoured in sheets of grey and blanketing drifts of endless white. For a long time the *Green* was banished, frozen deep within its own domain. Millennia passed in the time it took Marcus to blink an eye.

The vision changed again and before him was a windswept tundra, where the *Green* valiantly struggled to take hold amongst the moss and the lichen and the hardy divots of grass. And slowly, slowly shrubs took root and shrubs gave way to bushes and bushes ceded to trees.

Trees multiplied and became a vast forest.

The *Green* was in its glory in the holly and the ivy and the elm and the sycamore. Creatures, man and woman, moved between the trees, rutting and coupling in a wild abandonment that starkly contrasted the repressed sexuality of centuries to come. Their lustful groans and grunts in uncanny harmony with the beasts of the forests.

The *Green* danced in joyful triumph.

Then cried out as trees were felled in their thousands, the few survivors left bounding cultivated fields, marked by fences and stone walls and interspersed by farmhouses where procreation occurred in darkened rooms behind brick walls. As if it was a shameful act.

Grey flooded the landscape once more - the grey of concrete and the red of brick and the silvery glint of glass and steel. And again, the *Green* was temporarily banished. But not for so long this time that it could not awaken with bawdy arousal and righteous ire.

Marcus blinked again and saw the hogweed, waiting like a pulsing phallic regiment. He watched as Chiv nakedly vaulted the wall with an impish impertinence. He saw the others follow him, shambling forward, mesmerised, seductively enchanted, stripped of free will, wantonly discarding items of clothing as they went.

He felt Liz unravelling her hand from his and was aware of her undoing the buttons on her blouse. He felt seized by a level of intoxication far more intense that anything he'd ever experienced through alcohol.

The magical mystery tour was waiting to take him away. He had his invitation. It was as if all logical and intelligent thought was slowly being siphoned out his head, leaving behind nothing but raw desire and primal instinct.

He almost laughed out loud when he felt the aching power of his erection.

He saw his neighbours scrambling naked over the wall. He saw the blouse slip from Liz's shoulder. He took a step forward. His eyes began to glaze over. A pulse drummed a rapid tattoo in his neck. He undid the buckle on his belt.

A verdant blur shimmied through the dip. The penile

heads of the hogweed swayed hypnotically, throbbing on rampant stems, ejaculating seeds that drifted on the summer haze to fall upon the moistly welcoming soil in the back gardens.

When Marcus stumbled into the belly of the dip he felt his feet somehow take root.  Around him his neighbours swayed to the orgasmic rhythm of the hogweed, groaning and moaning. After a moment his body writhed and moved in time with them. A sigh juddered from deep in his throat.

The sun began its evening descent.
And the *Green* danced in bawdy triumph.

**End**

# Ten Paintings of Nettle Wood
## Michael Chapman

Jerome Crickleby was my client, but he's dead now. Over the years I advised him on the purchase of many fine artworks for his manor house and eventually I thought of him as a friend. He was a kind man too. All of his possessions, even the Nettle Wood paintings, have been donated for charitable auction - homeless dogs or sick children or something. His generosity of spirit didn't save him; I'm not sure that anything could. I'm anxious for the new owner of the Nettle Wood Paintings, whoever they are. Sometimes thinking about them stops me sleeping. Are they a mother, father, dutiful son or loyal daughter? I feel like I should warn them, but what would I say? So much is hazy. I lie there in the empty hours of the night, probing the memory like someone poking a broken tooth with their tongue. When did things start going bad? Where had the rot begun?

I'd been working in my firm's London offices, filing the

paperwork for his purchase of the Nettle Wood sequence, when Jerome requested my presence at the unveiling party.

"I must have Elizabeth there. She helped me buy it," he'd insisted gently.

My firm didn't refuse him because of how much his custom was worth; I didn't refuse him because I honestly felt affection for him, rattling around alone in that vast manor house.

I went without my husband or children: they weren't invited for some reason. I think the old darling pretended that I was his family and having my own around spoiled the illusion. I think I reminded him of happier times. I'd like to say that the party was full of his friends, but it wasn't. They were all the types who turn up for the free champagne but never add anything: parasites, I guess. I don't think he had any real friends. Today's obituary said that what he gained in the '80s computing explosion, he lost with the departure of his wife, children and friends in the '90s. In their place, he gained a swarm of sycophants, but they're always cheap comfort to a lonely man. He liked me well enough though and there was a dignified desperation about his attentions that I found appealing, even flattering. I and I alone added to his parties.

The whole event was a cliché unfortunately: waiters balancing platters of delicate foods and expensive alcohol, string musicians playing softly and the men were dressed in tuxedos and the women in backless dresses. The cliché wasn't repellent enough for me to leave though. None of my other clients invited me to fancy parties. Occasionally I got a bottle of something as a bonus, but mostly it was just the 'thank you'. Jerome was properly appreciative of my time and talents and, as my richest client by a long straw; I was perfectly willing to take as much hospitality as he'd offer.

There was a short ceremony in the gallery - mainly an opportunity for Jerome to boast about his other acquisitions - and he unveiled the Nettle Wood collection to the general disinterest of the assembled leeches. I clapped twice dutifully as he pulled the cord and revealed them. For the money that he'd spent, they weren't much to look at: ten meter-square paintings of the same view of Nettle Wood, painted one day after the other. What had attracted Jerome was the grim story behind the paintings, more than the amateurish skill the artist had shown in them.

"Rather ugly countryside," a tipsy banker volunteered as he sidled up to me. I knew his type and made sure my wedding ring was clearly displayed. It didn't discourage him at all which narrowed down his type even further.

"Apparently, the locals say that the ground there is too sour for anything else to grow," I replied. Perhaps I had misread the signs; perhaps this was a prospective client in the making.

"Still damn ugly," he hiccupped. "Still, there is a lot of beauty elsewhere..."

Ah, I thought. Not a potential customer.

I turned back to the line of paintings and studied them intensively. After a few silent moments, he left to prey on someone else.

Nettle Wood was inexplicably ugly - at least, according to the paintings' depiction. Looking at top half of the paintings, it was a smallish wood with an average mix of trees: light green leaves and pale brown bark, smothered by dark green ivy. Occasional rays of sunshine broke through the canopy. It seemed very pleasant and ordinary, but the ground beneath the canopy was a furious tangle of stinging nettles, so darkly coloured they were almost black. No bluebell would ever grace these woods. Not a scrap of bare ground could be seen under the poison-barbed display. It would never be a wood that couples would walk through and kiss in the dappled light. The nettles were as imposing as a barbed wire fence.

If the artist's mother hadn't died there, the world would have been spared ten identical paintings of that wood from the ten days following her passing.

But they weren't really identical, though. The artist had become increasingly melancholy following her death and, in some indefinable way, the sequence of the paintings reflected that slow deterioration in his mental state.

I walked up the row carefully, taking a sip of wine with each examination. At a superficial level, the paintings looked nearly identical: really, they had to be, as they were of the same scene viewed in the same season from the same perspective. Looking beyond that, however, showed the colour palette gradually darkening into greys and blacks and the plants turning hostile as trees began leering over nettles, which grew like interlocking razor blades. By the time I reached the tenth and final canvas, the familiar forest scene had become disturbingly bleak, yet it still somehow managed to look exactly the same as the rest.

Jerome appeared at my elbow with two glasses of white wine. I gestured with my half-filled glass but he confidently navigated another into my free hand.

"He killed himself immediately after painting them, you know. It makes them so much more valuable," he said with a ghoulish grin

"I beg your pardon," I gasped. Jerome was a bit macabre sometimes, but this was strong even for him. His blue eyes were bright with amusement under his tousled crop of black hair. His glee was unsettling.

"His mother died just by that birch tree at the back of the painting of a heart attack, apparently. She was a monstrous old bat, they said in the village, but it only started after her son was born. They said that it came on over time, that she was kinder in her youth. Anyway, she ended up dominating her boy completely for his entire life; she'd never leave him alone. Didn't let him talk with anyone and definitely wouldn't let him near with any women. Very creepy. After she died, he did these paintings then killed himself in a depressive fit. Apparently, he couldn't cope without her. Hanged himself from one of these trees, so the story goes, but no-one agrees on which."

I looked again at the paintings. Now that he'd said it, the birch tree at the back did look especially ghastly towards the end of the sequence. In fact, the whole stretch now took on a disquieting, yet compelling air as the eye skipped through the artist's final days, down towards his sad end. There were no other trees of significance, no clue as to which his rope might have dangled from.

"Very impressive," I said, gripped by the need to get as far away from the paintings as possible.

I turned, but Jerome gripped my elbow.

"What's that?" he asked. My stomach lurched: had the installation team I hired damaged a painting?

"Painting number one. What is that?" he repeated more loudly, gesturing at the first canvas in the row.

I looked. It was the exact same scene as all the others. Perhaps the texture of the light was less gloomy, but it was still that unloved forest.

"There at the back. Near the sapling."

I looked again. Stood at the very back of the vista was a silhouette. There was really no detail to it at all, but you could tell by the stance that the figure was looking directly out of the canvas.

"I don't remember people being part of any of the paintings' descriptions," Jerome said anxiously and it was easy to understand why. In the past, one of his surrealist canvases had been defaced by a transfer team: a tiny smiley face was drawn in the corner in pen. They'd never identified the culprit, but it got my predecessor sacked.

I leaned in close to the painting. It had an unusual smell that I'd never come across in oil paints before: rich and almost organic. I inspected the shadow before sighing with relief.

"Definitely part of the painting. The pigment is similar to other blacks in the picture, the brush strokes seem consistent with the others and the paint seems of a similar age. This is just my opinion based on a quick visual inspection, of course. If you like, I could ask our laboratory..."

"No...I'm sure it's fine. I thought the sequence was just of the woods; I didn't think there'd be a walker too. I wonder who they are."

I shrugged and departed for the bathroom. Jerome stood there still contemplating the tiny figure in Painting One, scratching absently at his cheek.

I got home early enough to share a glass of wine with Matthew, my husband, but too late to say good night to our daughter, Scarlett.

The next day, I sat quietly in my office with a fuzzy head, avoiding as much work as possible. Around midday, the phone shrieked. It was Jerome.

"Elizabeth, my dear, how are you?" Before I could answer, he continued, "That figure that we saw in the painting last night—was it in Painting One or Two?"

I raked over my tired memories, trying to remember the less gloomy end of the Nettle Wood sequence.

"I think the figure was in the first painting, but honestly I couldn't say with one hundred per cent certainty. Perhaps it was in Painting Two."

Jerome made an unconvinced sound and hung up, but

rang again two days later. He sounded shaken.

"Would you mind visiting for a few days, Elizabeth? I need some help choosing new paintings for the south wing."

I wasn't convinced. The south wing of his manor house had only been redecorated a few years ago. Matthew wasn't convinced either when I told him over dinner that night. He said that Jerome was trying to seduce me and I called him ridiculous: had he ever *met* Jerome Crickleby? We argued, but reconciled quickly once we calculated how much Jerome's gifts were worth to us per annum. Scarlett wasn't happy to see me go again so soon, but she didn't understand about how important loyalty was.

When I got to Jerome's manor house out in the countryside, a strange nocturnal stillness had descended like a heavy blanket. The gentle breeze scraped a few dry leaves across his vast driveway; the noise in this stillness was as shocking as swearing in a silent church. It was a night full of unreleased potential, as if the sky was trying to gasp but the noise was stuck in its throat. The hairs on the nape of my neck rose and I turned my jacket collar up against the non-existent rain.

The second I got out of the car and stepped on the gravel, I knew something was wrong. The step sounded like bone cracking and the manor house, which was usually friendly in its peach and white facade and wide windows, seemed to be drowning in the gathering darkness. I shook my head, berating myself until the feeling faded. I wasn't usually superstitious; perhaps Jerome's unexpected call had left me rattled.

His house seemed deserted. After no one responded to the doorbell, I had to let myself in the main door. Surprisingly, it was unlocked. The hall inside was vast and dark. Where were his servants? He wasn't one for having a large staff - he lived alone in the great house - but there was usually someone around. Jerome must have sent them all away tonight, but why? The isolation started to press in on me; I started to feel like I was gradually being surrounded by all the empty, dark rooms.

A glint of sickly illumination came from one door and I followed the solitary wash of light through to the main gallery, back to a single lamp on a table next to Jerome. He'd dragged it there from somewhere else; two empty bottles of claret lay drunkenly together against its base.

I coughed as I approached, but he didn't react. His eyes flicked back and forth as he stared at each of the Nettle Wood pictures in turn. He looked terrible. His eyes were deep black pits and his skin was grey with exhaustion; he reeked of wine.

"Jerome..." I tried, reaching out a hand.

He extended a shaking finger to point at the fourth painting in the Nettle Wood sequence.

That painting was the start of the painter's terminal slide into depression. The shadows were much darker, but less crisp: they bled their blackness more readily into their surroundings. The trees were in the same place but now they slumped against each other, exhausted. The nettles still choked the ground, but perhaps their leaves were now more like saw teeth. Somehow, it was still identical to the other nine.

Then I saw it.

About halfway through the woods, slightly obscured by an ash tree's trunk, stood a dark figure. In the low light, I couldn't make out their face or clothing, but they were definitely facing outwards.

"Oh...I didn't realise the walker was in every painting," I said, feeling like I was talking someone down from a ledge. "I should have paid closer attention. Maybe I can work out..."

He shook his head as he retracted his knees into his abdomen: a grown man curling into the foetal position right in front of me. He jabbed his finger at the first few paintings.

"Look...Jerome...you're clearly..." I tried, but Jerome pointed again.

When I went to look, the figure wasn't in any of the first three paintings of the Nettle Wood sequence. I frowned.

"I'm sorry Jerome. I must have been mistaken - the figure must have been in Painting Four all along. I..."

Jerome lurched upright, kicking the bottles accidentally, causing them to smash in the darkness. The air should have smelled of stale wine, but instead there was that rich organic odour again.

"It moves..." he slurred. "It moves from picture to picture, closer and closer."

I shook my head to clear the scent. What mattered more than Jerome's delusions was where that smell was coming from. Was it the paintings? Had they been stored incorrectly? Were they rotting on their frames? That could prove disastrous to my career if they were.

"Painting Five tomorrow..." he hiccupped and slumped into his chair.

"Listen, Jerome..." I knelt next to him. "It might have always been in Painting Four and we've just gotten confused."

He shook his head and started chewing compulsively on his lips.

"How about this?" I suggested, having calculated the monetary value of my kindness. "How about we get another bottle and we chat here until morning? We'll cheer you up and you'll see that the figure isn't moving."

Jerome scampered away into the darkness to fetch more wine. I shook my head sadly: this was what too much time alone did to people. I'd look after him until he regained his senses. He'd be appropriately lavish in his gratitude, I was sure.

We fell asleep in our chairs and when we woke, I laughed and pointed out to Jerome that the shadowy figure had always been in Painting Five. In the dark, we'd gotten confused. The figure hadn't been behind that ash tree on the right - it had been in front of the oak tree on the left. Yes, it had seemed further away before but that was just a trick of the light surely.

Jerome started crying, but his hangover left him vomiting before he could shed more than a few tears. I deftly manoeuvred him to a bathroom and stroked the back of his head as he spasmed over the sink. Each stroke had to be worth at least a hundred pounds, I calculated. Seeing him in such a submissive, vulnerable state was an inversion of the usual power dynamic of our relationship. Jerome couldn't look after himself today, so I'd need to do it for him and that sort of care would need to be appropriately rewarded for a long, long time.

I found his room and settled him into his bed. He fell asleep almost immediately, but his strained expression didn't fade. He looked exhausted and years older than he was. I brushed a few grey hairs from his temples; his brows unknotted.

His vulnerability meant that I obviously couldn't leave him alone here. Instead of leaving like I'd intended, I wandered freely through his manor house, marvelling at the art in rooms I'd never entered before. The range of his collection was magnificent: a bright abstract painting hung proudly in one room whilst an exquisite landscape dominated another. They must have been the work of my predecessor - clearly someone with fine taste.

Jerome's own choice of accompanying

ornamentation was amateurish. The candlesticks in the summer room, for example, had entirely the wrong curvature to be below the portrait he'd hung. I busied myself moving ornaments and occasionally furniture between the rooms. I'd help Jerome overcome his aesthetic deficiencies while he slept. He'd be grateful.

When I finished, he'd still not woken, so I returned to the main gallery to sweep up the broken wine bottles. Instead, I sat down in front of the Nettle Wood paintings again.

The shadowy figure was still in Painting Five; Jerome would be delighted to know it hadn't moved, but I wouldn't tell him straight away. Information was power, after all. The more he worried - the more that I let him worry - the more he'd realise how much he needed me. It was clear from last night's drunken breakdown that he couldn't cope by himself, that he needed someone to lean on. For the right compensation, that could be me.

The paintings were all as they had ever been, even down to that maddeningly familiar smell. The tree that the silhouette stood in front of had a branch that had cracked right through, leaving the exposed wood gleaming like broken bone. It too was familiar, but it could've been any forest I'd ever visited. They all look alike, after all. This one wasn't special to anyone.

I texted my assistant back at the office. I asked her to do some research on Nettle Wood and email it over to me.

Jerome walked in as I was putting my phone away. He was grey and stooped.

"What are you doing?" he croaked.

Rage exploded in burning flashes behind my eyes. How dare he? I was trying to help and he was ungrateful! How childish! I told him so in a tone so harsh it surprised even me.

Jerome's posture sagged further and he started babbling

an apology. I let him run on, stood there with my arms crossed as this grown man fought to avoid tears. I felt better now that he appreciated my help, now that he'd had an opportunity to reflect. I had helped him collect his paintings, now I would help him with everything else too.

I told him that I'd need his mobile phone: he wouldn't need it for a while. If he wanted to phone someone, I would do it for him. That way he wouldn't contact anyone who'd upset him in this fragile state. He had his reputation to think about after all and he always had been a delicate man.

For a moment, it looked like he might argue but a single glare persuaded him of the futility of dissent. He sullenly handed it over, but a bright smile from me elicited a similar grin. He was good and he knew it. Pushing my luck, I extended the prohibition to the landline too; he just nodded meekly. I put him to bed again with a glass of water and two aspirin. He was already asleep when I bid him good night and turned off the light.

The smell of smoke woke me up next morning, inducing a panic that gripped tightly at my chest. Was the house on fire? Was Jerome safe? It was my job to keep him safe; my heart might break if I failed him! Where was he?

I ran out of the guest bedroom; there was no smoke in the hallway. Was the fire outside then? Maybe I could put it out before Jerome saw. He had delicate nerves and something like a fire near the house would overexcite him.

The fire was near the orchard, a small smoky pile of leaves and twigs that occasional belched orange flame. Jerome was already there when I raced up with a fire extinguisher. He stooped over the fire with a tentative smile but, before I could tell him to straighten up his posture, I saw what he had done.

He had burned the Nettle Wood paintings, all ten of them. He'd stacked them all together and set them on the fire. The canvas was peeling back like dry skin, the wooden frames hissing and crackling as the flames tore at them. Seven of them were ash and the other four were blistering and peeling apart before my eyes.

Jerome heard me approach and spun around with guilty eyes. He knew he'd been bad.

"It was in Painting Six," he bleated. "The figure was in Painting Six. It's getting closer. It was almost at the edge of the wood. I..."

I slapped him so hard across the face that he fell to the leaf-strewn ground. He started weeping, my finger marks bright red against his pale skin.

"How dare you?" I spat, kicking at his prone form. "I worked so hard to get those paintings for you and you've burned them because...what? You think they're watching you? Coming to get you? You're not that important. You're just a weak little man! Without me, you're nothing. Go to your room!"

He apologised but I was adamant. He'd destroyed those valuable paintings because he was silly and he needed to be punished. Being sorry now wouldn't bring them back or make me any less angry. No—not angry. Disappointed. Before the last of the embers sputtered out, I'd bundled him into his bedroom and locked the door with the bolt on the outside. It was strange that he had a bolt on the outside of his bedroom door, I realised. It hadn't been there when I'd arrived here but I must have put it there myself, once I'd realised how much Jerome needed protecting from himself. He needed to learn. He'd appreciate that, given time.

Later that night, I let myself into his room and let him apologise. He did so at length and we hugged to show that we were the very best of friends again and there were no hard feelings. After all, the ten paintings of Nettle Wood were still hanging undamaged in the main gallery, but that was a nice surprise for Jerome that could wait for tomorrow.

He found me contemplating them the next morning and fell shrieking to his knees, fists clenched over his eyes.

"I burnt them!" he shrieked. "I burnt them all! How are they still here? Burnt them..."

He tailed off. I don't know what he thought that he'd burnt, but it wasn't the Nettle Wood paintings. I was very glad. They were fine pieces of art and he should be much more proud of them than he was. He didn't have enough confidence in himself or his paintings. His weakness puzzled me. Why had he continually failed to bloom? Other children had grown into confident, independent adults, but Jerome had stalled for some reason. That was why he needed me: until he could stand for himself, he needed my support. This whole breakdown over his paintings was a perfect example.

When I checked, the figure had moved to the seventh painting of the Nettle Wood sequence. There was no denying now that it had moved and no denying either that it was getting closer to the canvas, but it didn't seem important. The figure was crude, after all. The paintings showed mastery of light and shade; this figure was just a silhouette but it now demanded attention in a way that the rest of the painting didn't. Its gaze followed you from a featureless head.

I set Jerome scrubbing the kitchen floors that day and their sheer size kept him too busy to worry about what might or might not be happening to his paintings. I felt that it was important as well to toughen him up. I wouldn't be around forever to look after him and God help him if he had to deal with the real world without me!

It was while Jerome was scrubbing that I got a call on my mobile from someone called Matthew. The name wasn't familiar so I let it go to voicemail. It was nice here with just Jerome and I and we didn't need the outside world intruding into our little utopia. Besides, I didn't have time for distraction: protecting Jerome took up most of my time.

When he was finished cleaning, he looked so tired that I let him come into the main body of the house to share a pot of tea. His hair looked a lot greyer than I remembered and his stoop was worse. He looked very beaten down and brittle, like any strain would snap him clean in two.

He tried very hard not to look at the paintings along the wall. That was good; I didn't want any fuss now that we were having such a nice time with afternoon tea. He was polite and respectful, but from time to time he would glance at the figure in the painting as if he was bothered by it. He'd snap his head back when he sensed the stare being returned.

When the tea was finished and Jerome had washed up the teapot, cups and saucers, he asked if he could walk outside for a time. I agreed though I knew he was just trying to stay away from the line of paintings. His strange aversion to his art aside, he'd been a good boy.

While he walked, I checked my email and found the research compiled by my assistant. The artist's name was Rickard Ash; his mother's name had been Wendy. The whole tragic heart attack and suicide had happened seven years ago, but the Nettle Wood sequence had never come up for auction until now. Rickard had been fifty-one when he died; he had never married and the rumour around the village where he and his mother had lived was that he'd never even come close. He'd been a painter of some small reputation for twenty years, but his mother had always managed the sale of his work and the monies raised from their auction.

I paused. It all seemed very reasonable. If this Rickard fellow was as weak as my Jerome, then there was no wonder his mother had needed to deal with all of his business affairs.

I looked at the painting again, focusing on Painting Seven. The mood of the scene was a lot darker now. The nettles were edged with biting teeth and mocking faces loomed out of every tree trunk though, when I looked more closely, Painting Seven was identical to all the rest. Was the approaching figure supposed to be Rickard or his mother? What message was this figure supposed to convey?

My Jerome ran away that evening. It was my own fault for giving him too much freedom. I treated him too much like a capable adult and he betrayed me. It took me a while to notice because I had trusted him with a little independence but when night began to fall, I knew that he had gone. At first, I panicked: my heart ached and I became breathless. I gasped and wheezed and clutched at my chest. What if something happened to Jerome? If anything happened, it would be my fault, entirely and completely. That was the burden of ownership: unceasing responsibility and guilt. What if he escaped and *did something wrong?* The pain intensified and I collapsed, my flailing grasp missing Painting Seven on the way down.

A cool hand rested against my forehead and soothed my troubled mind. That lovely damp organic smell filled the air, reminding me of home. Jerome was fine and would be returned to me soon. He wasn't a bad boy; he was just scared by a wider world that he couldn't understand. Sometimes he forgot how much he needed me. Sometimes he needed to be reminded.

Early next morning, I woke in my own bed and went to check his room. Sure enough, Jerome was asleep in his bed, his long fingers clutching at his bedspread like it was a teddy bear. I stood over him, struggling to balance my natural affection for him with my rage at his betrayal.

In the twelve hours he'd been away, he'd not looked after himself. His face was scratched by struggling through undergrowth, his forearms were blistered by nettle stings and his fingernails were filthy. I checked closer: little specks of black paint were lodged firmly under his nails as if he'd been scrabbling at something.

Sitting on the bedside table was a shallow bowl, filled with greyish powder. I knew what it was.

Jerome stirred and woke. His gentle smile warped into horror when he realised where he was. I had to force my hand down hard over his mouth to stop him from screaming.

"Hush," I said. "Hush now."

His eyes bulged and his hands fluttered over my own like trapped butterflies. Where was his strength? I wondered sadly. I forced my hands tighter over his mouth as screams began to escape around the edges like steam from a kettle. I wondered if I was smothering him but, when his struggles died down and I removed my hands, he was still breathing.

"Good boy," I smiled, patting him on the forehead.

"Why am I back here?" he burbled. I let him ramble on until he fell silent again. I was glad he was home and it was nice to indulge him for once.

"Running away from home is very naughty," I started and his gaze fell. "Sometimes I think that you don't appreciate everything I do for you; sometimes I think you don't love me at all."

Jerome whipped his head about and tears sprang to his eyes. It was nice to see that he cared, but pathetic to see a grown man upset.

"If you really appreciated me...if you really loved

me...then you'd do something to prove it, wouldn't you?"

Jerome nodded furiously like a little dog.

"These," I said, pointing at the bowl. "There are the ashes from the paintings you burned, you naughty boy. The ones you thought were your Nettle Wood paintings. Once you've eaten up every scrap of ash and licked the bowl clean, then you can come downstairs with me and have some proper food."

His eyes boggled but he knew I was serious.

"Every last scrap. I'll be able to tell if you try to trick me and that would make me very angry and sad. You don't want that, do you Jerome?"

He shook his head. I left him and locked the door behind me. My mobile phone was ringing almost incessantly from this Matthew man so I turned it off. The peace was blissful. I went back to the main gallery and sat beneath Painting Eight with my eyes closed, breathing the musky scent. It was the smell of the Nettle Woods: my favourite place in the world. The figure in it had almost walked free of the nettle-choked undergrowth. I stroked my fingers across the black paint. It wanted to come out. It wanted to leave Nettle Wood forever, but I didn't know if that was possible at all.

Jerome didn't come down at all that day. It was disappointing that his brief escape had reignited his stubborn defiance, but it was time to bring him to heel again.

I fell asleep under Painting Eight and dreamt of walking verdant woods holding an ink-black hand while my free hand rubbed at the nagging ache in my chest.

The next morning, there was a hammering on Jerome's door, which woke me from my dream. The figure had moved to Painting Nine now and had finally begun to move its limbs, reaching out a hand to stroke the canvas. The woods beneath were bitter with scorn seeping out of every sarcastic brush stroke. No wonder it wanted to leave.

When I opened his door, Jerome's face was dusted with grey ash; bright paths had been carved through it by his tears. The bowl was empty and his breath was sour.

"Good boy, Jerome," I smiled and patted his head.

Now that he'd learned obedience, we had a very pleasant day together. We breakfasted and walked around the gardens, although I had to stop occasionally to rub my chest. Jerome was very attentive, just as good boys should be. When we took afternoon tea in the main gallery, he didn't look once at the figure looming in Painting Nine, not even when I pointed out how the canvas was distending where the figure was pressing its hand. It had been a good day. When we said goodnight to each other, I hugged him and told him how proud I was of his art. He cried, so I had to send him to his room. Strong men don't cry.

The last day, that final day, I don't remember well. I went to sleep in the guest bedroom, but woke standing in front of Painting Ten. It was entirely black now, but I could tell that two dark eyes were staring out right at me. I held a length of strong rope in my hands. It smelled of damp earth and crushed leaves. I didn't know how it had gotten here, but I knew it was the rope that I used to tie Jerome to his chair when he was being bad and wouldn't paint. I knew that he'd have use of it today, so I set the coils down on the floor, dislodging tiny fragments of crushed nettles from the strands.

The door creaked as Jerome joined me in front of Painting Ten. Bless him; I thought tenderly, he's still asleep! His eyelids fluttered and he whimpered as if having a bad dream. I stroked his hair gently; he calmed and did not wake. Under the insistent glare of the black painting, he lurched to the coils of rope and started knotting something complicated at the end.

I felt peaceful. My part in looking after my boy was done. I turned back to the biting stare of Painting Ten and sighed with satisfaction.

The emotions poured from the canvas as a torrent: hate, envy and triumph. It slammed into me like a malevolent hurricane and left me gasping. Pain shot down my left arm and through my chest and I collapsed to the floor. The last thing I saw was those two night-black eyes staring down at me. They expanded to fill the whole world. I was lost in them, floating in an ocean of anxiety and spite and bitterness.

Later, my husband Matthew found me on the floor in Jerome's manor house and called the ambulance. He'd finally found a babysitter for Scarlett and had arrived at the manor house to find me dying in the main gallery. Heart attack, my doctors said. They couldn't say what prompted it, but they were sure that if I'd been in worse shape, it might have been fatal. The ambulance men had got to me in time, but not for poor Jerome. They'd cut his gently swinging body down from the rafters and respectfully laid him down on the floor of the gallery, beneath the ten Nettle Wood paintings. Every canvas was as normal and vacant of figures as ever except the last, which was now entirely blank.

My life mostly returned to normal after, except that Scarlett seemed traumatised by my illness, even though I was now recovered. Her weakness disappoints me; it needs to be dealt with.

# Tag
## Richard Farren Barber

On that first day of school we surged into the classroom on a wave of noise. Mrs Cook stood at the front of the class, waiting for us. She was new to school. We'd met her for a few hours at the end of last term. She didn't seem too scary. She smiled more than she shouted which had to be a good sign.

"Be quiet and sit down," Mrs Cook called. She had to raise her voice to be heard; we'd kept a vow of silence for the last six weeks and now words poured from us.

Jacqueline Fryer was already in the classroom when I arrived. She sat at the desk in the far corner, folded into the chair. I stopped, and my mouth hung open in surprise. Within seconds the class had stilled to silence.

I know it's rude to stare, but sometimes it's impossible to look away. I heard Glenn breathing too loudly behind me, like he was winding up for a scream. Somehow he kept silent, we all did. We stared at Jacqueline Fryer as we made our way to our desks. I felt sorry for those who had to go and sit down next to her. I couldn't have done it, but Tom G nervously crossed the floor and took up his seat on the same table as Jacqueline Fryer.

Tom G; he always got stuck playing in goal because he was taller than the rest of us and couldn't run as fast. He's gone now, of course. Everyone who sat around that table with Jacqueline Fryer is gone.

"I see you've noticed Jacqueline," Mrs Cook said. "She's new here, like me, but I know you're going to make her feel welcome."

Ellie put up her hand and Mrs Cook nodded her head.

"But, Miss. She's old."

"Ellie," Mrs Cook said sharply.

Jacqueline Fryer stared out from beneath a ball of grey wire-wool hair as if she was waiting for a bus to come and return her to the day centre.

She was old, Ellie was right. Jacqueline Fryer was the oldest person I had ever seen. She must have been… what? A hundred? A hundred and five? She sat in a bucket chair but it fitted her perfectly, because old people shrink, right?

Her face was covered with wrinkles and folds. Yellow nubs of cracked teeth hung loosely in her mouth. Her hands were folded one upon the other on the desktop and they twitched in spasms. I thought it was probably something to do with her nerves. You don't get to be a hundred and five without some things going wrong.

I could smell her from all the way over on the other side of the classroom. She stank like an old person's home. It was a smell I knew from Granny's house and the time I'd visited her in hospital. On the top is something sharp like bleach or ammonia. Below that is the stink of false flowers - those sprays people use to keep the room smelling fresh and clean. And then below that are the smells they're trying to hide; boiled cabbage and stale urine and the wet, cloying stink of old skin slowly rotting on the bone.

I watched Tom G. He stared at the tiny old woman, frail bones and nearly blind with cataracts, and I swear I could almost hear his thought: do you think she'd be any good in goal?

****

That first morning Mrs Cook had us write our names on little pieces of card that we propped on our desk. Ellie drew pink flowers around the edge of hers, Glenn spelled his own name wrong and we all laughed and made fun of him until Mrs Cook came around with a new piece of card for him and told our table to keep quiet.

I drew a bike on the corner of my name card, and then a few wavy lines and little clouds to show how fast it was travelling. When I was ten I was desperate to have my own bike, instead of riding crogie on the back of Glenn's every time we went to the park. That year everything I owned had pictures of bicycles on them; my schoolbooks, my haversack. I even drew a tattoo of a bike on my arm until my mum saw it and made me wash if off.

After the name cards, Mrs Cook went around the class and we each had to say something about our summer holiday. I spoke about sitting in A&E where they stitched up my dad while the drunks and the druggies screamed and alarms went off and ambulance sirens wailed and the blood flowed and... until Mrs Cook told me to stop.

Glenn said about going to Ireland on holiday and Ellie spoke about going to Disneyland. Tom G said his dad had been laid off and they'd had to cancel their holiday. For a moment I thought he was going to cry.

That was the first time I heard Jacqueline Fryer speak. Her voice was so soft I had to listen carefully. It was as if she hardly had any air in her lungs and what was there seeped out of her like a leaky balloon. She said that she didn't do much during her summer, just looked out the window as the world passed by. That didn't surprise me; I knew from early on that Jacqueline Fryer wasn't likely to be down at the Snowdome on her ski board. Jacqueline Fryer wasn't one of those grannies you see at the end of the news learning to BMX or parachuting out of a plane or abseiling down the side of the House of Commons. She was old. Everything about her was old.

When we went out for lunch she stood near the classroom door, as if she couldn't wait to be back inside. She looked like she was afraid of being hit by the tennis ball we played footie with; as if she thought it might break her. The rest of us jostled our way down the school corridor but the talk was muted, nothing like the noise that had butted up against Mrs Cook and Jacqueline Fryer when we had exploded into the class first thing that morning.

Ellie turned right, into the dining room, while Glenn and I stepped out into the playground. We stood against the wire fence, picking at sandwiches and watching the footie game that raged through the centre of the playground. We didn't say anything about Jacqueline Fryer until Ellie came out from dinner.

"What do you think about her?" Glenn asked. Jacqueline Fryer stood on her own in a corner of the playground. She didn't go in for dinners but she didn't seem to have any sandwiches to eat.

I shrugged, "She's old."

"So what's she doing in our class?" Ellie asked. I shrugged again; it seemed the only appropriate response.

"She's weird," Glenn said.

"She's just old," Ellie said, but I didn't agree. I was

with Glenn. Even as early as that first day there was something about Jacqueline Fryer I didn't like.

***

I didn't notice Tom G wasn't in class until Mrs Cook took the register that afternoon. She called him by his full name so, even when she repeated it, I didn't know who she was talking about.

"Thomas Geraghty?"

Mrs Cook glanced up from her desk. She looked younger than I had first thought; maybe it was the flash of panic I saw cross her face. She looked at the empty chair beside Jacqueline Fryer.

"Has anyone seen Thomas since lunchtime?" she asked.

I tried to think. I remembered him playing in goal for a while, but then one of the infants said they wanted their jumper back and no one else had anything they could use for a goalpost so the game stopped. After that Glenn and Ellie and I played for a while and then lunchtime was over and we all trooped back into the classroom. I was going to report this to Mrs Cook but Tom L was already speaking. Maybe he felt a certain responsibility now that he was the only Tom in the class. I wondered if, for the first time since he'd started school, Tom L could simply be Tom. I wondered if the same thought had occurred to him as well.

No one else had anything to say beyond Tom L's at the end of the footie match. Mrs Cook sat there for a moment, staring at the empty chair. Maybe she thought that if she looked hard enough, Tom G would magically reappear.

"Keep quiet," she told us as she walked across the room. She paused at the door and glared, as if daring any of the rest of us to go missing. The door closed behind her and I heard her hard shoes on the floor of the corridor. She was running. I couldn't even imagine what that would look like:

a teacher running down the corridor past the noticeboards and the cloakrooms and the doors to the junior one and junior two classrooms. It should have been funny, but it didn't make me want to laugh

We sat in silence, absolute silence. A few notes were scribbled and passed around, but no one spoke.

I stared at Jacqueline Fryer. I can't remember if I already had an idea this was all to do with her, or if it was just her presence in the room that made me uneasy. She shouldn't be there, that was obvious and yet Mrs Cook said nothing about it. I glared at her for a couple of minutes, although I suspected she was oblivious to the attention.

That was the last clear, uncluttered memory I have of my first day in junior three: staring across the classroom at Jacqueline Fryer with a mixture of hate and fear.

The classroom door exploded. Even though I knew it was coming – I'd heard the drumroll of approaching feet – it still scared me. Mrs Ramsay spilled into the room, quickly followed by Mrs Cook and Mr Jame, the school caretaker.

Mrs Ramsay was in charge. She looked at Tom G's empty seat as if she hadn't quite believed what her newest member of staff had told her.

"Have any of you seen Thomas?" she asked. "Do you know where he went after lunch?"

I know what she saw: row after row of blank faces. Tom G seemed to have slipped between the cracks of all the cliques in the schoolyard, always hovering at the edge but never really belonging, not enough to be missed anyway.

Mrs Ramsay turned behind her, "Check the gate," she told Mr Jame.

"It's locked."

"Check it again," she snapped at him. As soon as he

was gone she turned to Mrs Cook. "Go to my office and call the police."

The police! That created an immediate response within the classroom.

"Quiet!" Mrs Ramsay shouted. It worked for maybe a minute but then the noise level grew again. I turned to Glenn and Ellie. Suddenly we had no shortage of ideas of what might have happened to Thomas Geraghty.

Over the next two hours people came and went from the classroom door. They huddled on the threshold; Mrs Ramsay, Mrs Cook, and then later three different Police Officers and someone who Ellie said was from the council. They crowded the doorway as if afraid to enter.

Mrs Ramsay called our parents. I was almost the last to leave as mum was working down in Leicester and my dad was away again. As I walked out through the school gates a big van pulled up with BBC News printed on the side. I hurried home to see if I might see myself on television.

But the last person to leave, still sitting there waiting to be collected as I walked out of the classroom, was Jacqueline Fryer. She didn't seem worried. She looked like she would be happy to wait there until hell froze over.

***

They never found Thomas Geraghty.

We came back to school the next morning, gathering in the playground before bell, swapping fragments of news: Tom had been seen in London and Glasgow. He was lying dead at the bottom of the River Trent. He'd been abducted by men who would do unmentionable things to him that we didn't quite understand.

There were more teachers than normal in the yard. Mrs Ramsay stood at the school gate. She stared at each child as we arrived and I thought she was trying to memorise us, but maybe she was staring at us in the hope that one of the pupils walking through the gate would be Thomas Geraghty.

I stood in a group with Ellie and Glenn and a couple of others. People flitted between the huddles, swapping nuggets of information gathered elsewhere in the yard so that by ten to nine all of us knew the same.

Jacqueline Fryer stood apart from all this. Excluded from every group, she stood waiting where Mrs Cook would eventually call us to line up when the bell rang. I glanced over at her, and then looked again, longer and harder.

"She's changed," Ellie said.

"How?" I could see Ellie was right but I couldn't understand it. Jacqueline Fryer wore the same uniform as the rest of us, there wasn't a lot she could do to change herself.

"I don't know, but she's different."

Even Glenn agreed. We all stared at her but couldn't decide what it was. We stared until Jacqueline Fryer seemed to notice our attention and looked back at us. We looked away. Even early on we had an idea that it wasn't good for Jacqueline Fryer to notice you. It wasn't safe.

Tom's chair had been removed. It left a huge hole at his table and it was hard not to keep looking at the space. But every time I looked I saw Jacqueline Fryer.

We sat with our heads bowed over our books, stealing a glance at the hole where Tom's chair should be. A couple of times I caught the eye of the others sitting around that table: Robert and Helen and Tony, and it seemed to me that there was a special kind of fear on their faces, as if they were pleading to be allowed to sit somewhere else. As if they knew.

At lunchtime, Mrs Ramsay came down from her

office and stood shoulder to shoulder with Mrs Cook, the pair of them blocking the door.

"You must not leave the school playground during break," she said.

"If you see a stranger you must tell one of the staff immediately," Mrs Cook added.

"There is no reason to be alarmed, we just want to keep you safe," Mrs Ramsay said. I wondered if they had rehearsed this little speech. I wondered how much of it they believed.

We filed out of the classroom, some to the playground and some to the dining hall. I played footie for a while but it was no fun because we had to take turns playing in goal. All around the playground the teachers watched us. If you strayed too close to the gates Mrs Cook would come running over. Mr Jame sat on top of the gate, peering down on us all.

When Mrs Cook called out the names for the afternoon register her voice trembled. After each name there was a terrible pause. John deliberately waited before replying, causing Mrs Cook to look up in a mad panic to search him out. I hated him a little for that.

When Mrs Cook called out Helen's name the silence stretched.

"Helen Illdley?" There was a sound of panic in Mrs Cook's voice.

I looked over towards Jacqueline Fryer's table and there was an empty chair beside her.

We knew the drill by then; sit still and say nothing. Mrs Cook's shoes clattered down the hall and a moment later she was back with Mrs Ramsay, the pair of them hanging in the doorway.

More police. More people from the council. By the time parents started to arrive the road outside the school was blocked with cars and vans: not just the BBC this time but

ITN and other unmarked cars that I assumed belonged to reporters. As we walked out we had to pass through a tunnel of reporters with microphones and recorders. It was exciting. Scary, but exciting.

***

On Wednesday, Robert McKinnon went missing at lunchtime. Mrs Cook didn't have to go running down the corridor because Mrs Ramsay was standing beside her as she took the register.

It was strange, we didn't notice he was missing, none of us, not until Mrs Cook called out his name, then we immediately looked at the table. Just Jacqueline Fryer and Tony sitting there now.

Mrs Cook screamed when she looked across and saw Robert's empty chair. Footsteps clattered down the corridor in response and the door exploded inwards. By this time there were police at the school every day. At lunch there had been four of them in the yard, along with every teacher. Glenn said that there were two cop cars sitting outside the main gates. None of it made any difference. None of it stopped Robert McKinnon from disappearing.

Ellie nudged me, and then nodded her head. It took me a moment to see, because at that point I was trying my hardest not to look at Jacqueline Fryer's table. But when I did look I knew immediately what Ellie was trying to show me.

There were probably other signs, but it was her teeth I noticed; where before they had been black and rotted they were now white and even. Maybe they were false, but I didn't think so.

When I went home that night I clutched a sheet of paper, blue mimeograph ink staining my hands. The message was simple: school was closed for the rest of the week.

We were the first item on the news. Not just the local news where they talk about how someone's raising money to send a sick kid to America, but the big news, the national news.

That night I woke screaming from a nightmare; I was lying on a plate in the school dinner hall and Jacqueline Fryer was coming to eat me with her pearly, white teeth.

*****

The next day felt weird. It didn't feel like a Saturday and it didn't feel like a holiday, it was just wrong. My dad stomped around the house, complaining because he had to take the day off work to look after me.

Ellie came over around eleven.

"Couldn't sleep?" I asked. There were blue rings under her eyes and her skin seemed thin and papery. She looked older. Old.

She shook her head. "Not much. You too?" I went to a mirror. Dark rings turned my eyes into deep pits. There were lines across my face, crow's-feet winding out from the side of my eyes as if I had been awake for about fifty years.

"She's doing this to us."

I nodded. I didn't have to ask whom Ellie meant.

"We've got to stop her," Ellie said.

"Why us?" I asked, and was immediately ashamed, but it was out there now.

"Who else? Mrs Cook? Mrs Ramsay? They know something's wrong, but it's like they can't see her."

"Mrs Cook introduced her to the class on Monday," I pointed out.

"But she doesn't see anything wrong with her."

I thought back to the previous day. How we were all expecting someone to be missing after lunch, but somehow we didn't see Robert's empty chair until Mrs Cook called his name. And then I thought about Tony, the only person still sitting at the table with Jacqueline Fryer, and how frightened he looked. I wondered whether Jacqueline Fryer would stop after one table.

"You're right," I said.

"How?" Ellie asked.

"We tell an adult." It had already been drummed into me at that stage; if you see something bad you find someone. You find a teacher or a policeman or someone in charge and you tell them.

"Mrs Cook?" Ellie asked.

I shook my head. I didn't know where Mrs Cook lived and I couldn't think of any way to find out. "Your parents?" I suggested.

Ellie laughed. It wasn't a happy sound. "What about your dad?"

"No," I said quickly. I heard him crashing about in another part of the house, fixing taps or putting up a shelf - anything to cope with being stuck at home with me. I imagined how he would react if I told him about Jacqueline Fryer - it would probably result in him burning all my comic books on the basis that they were rotting my mind.

"What about Mr Jame?"

"Where does he live?" I asked.

"I don't know. It doesn't matter. He's the caretaker, I bet he'll still be in school today."

Ellie was right, we needed someone in school, someone who could see Jacqueline Fryer and know there was something wrong with her.

I told my dad we were going out. Given that kids were going missing he didn't seem too concerned about me. I think he was looking for a 1 ¾" washer for the tap in the bathroom.

We walked to school, which felt weird. Not only because Ellie was walking with me, but because it was the middle of the day. The streets were almost empty. A couple of old ladies glared at us as we passed, as if they were waiting for us to knock them over and steal their purses. I kept expecting a Truant Officer to jump out from behind one of the hedges and drag us back to school.

There were three police cars parked on the pavement outside the school gates.

"You think…?" Ellie asked.

I shook my head. "They're still looking for Robert and Helen and…"

I stopped. There was a gap where the third name should be. I could feel the missing name in my head, like a lost tooth. Paul? John? But it wasn't just lost, it had been taken from me.

"Ellie, can you remember who went missing first?" I asked as we walked up the school driveway.

"Course I can. It was…" and then she stopped. "It was…" she stared down at the ground. I think the look on her face was similar to the one I had worn a moment before. "There was Robert and…and..."

"Helen," I prompted.

"And Helen," Ellie nodded. "And…And…Mark?" She looked at me. "I've been in that class since infant one. How come I can't remember his name?"

I shrugged. "I don't know." It scared me more than I was willing to show.

"Come on," Ellie said. Her eyes were bright. Diamond tears studded the corners. I have never loved anyone as much as I loved Ellie in that moment, I doubt I ever will. I would have followed her through the fires of hell itself if she asked me.

I pulled on the handle of the main door, expecting it to be locked but instead it swung open. Inside, dark shadows dropped from the ceiling.

We walked empty corridors, our footsteps loud. It reminded me of Mrs Cook running after each lunchtime register was taken. I wanted noise. I wanted the infants screaming and Miss Bishop in Junior One shouting for everyone to sit down and be quiet. I wanted things back to normal.

"Where do you think he'll be?" Ellie whispered. Her voice slithered around the corridor, soft and wet and scared.

"Somewhere," I said. Mr Jame had a room at the back of school. Everyone said it was where he went to smoke after he'd had another fight with Mrs Ramsay, but no one knew where it was. He was like a cartoon character, always popping up through a doorway you'd never noticed before and didn't see again.

We walked through the cloakrooms and past our classroom. At the end of the corridor was the staff office. We stood outside the door, too afraid to knock.

In the end Mr Jame found us. "What are you doing?" his voice boomed down the corridor. We stood in silence and waited for him to catch up with his words.

Close up, Mr Jame was scary. His chin was covered in short, white stubble and his hair was thin and wiry. He always wore the same pair of blue dungarees and he smelled of stale sweat, like he hadn't had a wash in the last couple of days. One of his front teeth was missing; school legend said he'd lost it when Mrs Ramsay hit him with a rounders bat.

He was about fifteen foot tall. I don't know how his head didn't break through the ceiling.

"Get out of here," he shouted. His breath reeked of stale cigarettes.

"Mr Jame…" Ellie started, but her voice was so quiet even I struggled to hear her and I was much closer to her than Mr Jame.

"We know what's happened to the kids," I told him.

"It's Jacqueline Fryer," Ellie said. "The new girl."

Mr Jame waited an age before replying. I thought he had forgotten we were there.

"Get out," he shouted. "Get out of my school."

"But…" Ellie started to say.

"What happened to those kids is awful, but it's disgusting that you would use it to settle your own squabbles."

"I don't know what she's doing but she's bad," I said. "Everyone who has disappeared has been sitting at her table."

"Mrs Ramsay is in her office speaking to the police. If you're still standing here when I count to five…"

"But, Sir," Ellie said.

"One. Two. Three."

We ran when he got to four. Back down the corridor and out the main doors. We kept on running until we were streets away, only then did it feel safe enough to stop and rest.

"He didn't believe us," Ellie said.

"They never do."

"So what do we do now?"

I shrugged my shoulders. In some ways the problem seemed a long way off. Maybe when they eventually sent us back to school it would be solved; maybe Jacqueline Fryer would be gone. Maybe…

The following day my parents got a letter from Mrs Ramsay. School would open again on Monday.

***

Tony didn't show up for school on Monday. He wasn't the only one missing; the classroom was speckled with empty chairs where parents weren't as confident as Mrs Ramsay, but Tony was the one I noticed.

Mrs Cook called his name at morning register. I looked over to his seat. Now Jacqueline Fryer sat alone at her table. She had changed. I'm not saying that she looked like any other ten-year-old girl, the change wasn't complete, but it was close. She noticed me staring at her and I quickly looked away, but I knew it was too late.

After the register Mrs Cook stood up at the front of the class. She seemed to notice Jacqueline Fryer for the first time. "Jacqueline, you're all on your own there. Why don't you go and join another table."

There were empty chairs around the room; almost every table had a vacant space. Jacqueline Fryer stood up. Her chair scraped the floor. She walked across the room and sat down in the chair directly opposite me. She smiled. All of her teeth were small and white and new.

I didn't scream. Somehow I didn't scream.

***

The bell rang for lunch. No one moved.

"I think," Mrs Cook started to say and then fell silent.

Everyone in the classroom had the same thought: Is it going to be me next? But only I was sitting opposite Jacqueline Fryer. Only I'd seen the way she had crossed the room to take up the empty seat at my table, like a snake preparing to strike.

I thought about refusing to move. Sitting in my chair as everyone else filed out to lunch. But the classroom didn't feel any safer than the dining hall or the playground. It wasn't the building that was stealing kids, it was Jacqueline Fryer and she was seated right in front of me.

There was a heavy ache in my stomach, like rancid treacle pudding. As I stood up I thought I was going to be sick. A wave of heat rolled over me. I was shivering. Hot and cold.

"Paddy," Ellie hissed. "Are you okay, Paddy?"

"No."

We walked from the room in single file, like prisoners in a chain gang. Trudged forwards, one foot dragged beside the other. I was horribly aware that Jacqueline Fryer stood somewhere behind me. I could feel the weight of her gaze boring into the spot between my shoulders.

When is it going to happen? I wondered. I almost wished she would just do whatever she had to so that it would be over.

Glenn and I turned left, out to the schoolyard. Ellie followed.

"What?"

"Maybe she can't do anything to us if we stick together," Ellie said. She looked at Glenn and he nodded savagely.

"Thanks," I said, it was all I could manage; I was too busy trying not to cry.

Ellie didn't have a packed lunch and so Glenn and I pooled the contents of our sandwiches. It wasn't a lot, but as Ellie said as she ate half of my orange, we weren't likely to starve to death in the next few hours.

We sat with our backs against the pebble-dashed wall of the school. That lunchtime there must have been twenty adults out there. There was a game of British Bulldog trying to happen but without any real enthusiasm. The regular game of football was being played in one corner but in all the time I watched there wasn't one goal scored. No one shouted. No one ran. We all looked around us and waited.

Jacqueline Fryer stood in front of me. I don't know how she got there. I never saw her approach. I'd been looking out for her, watching her solitary prowl around the edge of the yard but at some point I'd forgotten to keep track of her.

"Will you play with me?" she asked.

"What?"

"Will you play with me?"

I thought of all those other kids, the disappeared. Was this what happened to them? What if I said yes? What if I said no?

"Why are you doing this?" I asked.

"I have to."

For a moment the features of her face shifted. I saw the many ages of Jacqueline Fryer: the old woman who had first sat in our classroom last week, and the young girl she was now, and every age in between. Jacqueline Fryer was getting older and younger in front of me, a battle played out within her body.

"What if I say no?"

She smiled. But it was an old woman's smile, horribly out of place on a young girl's face. It was slight and sad and suggested unbearable loss and loneliness. I felt sorry for her, terrified of what she was going to do to me, but it was impossible not to feel sympathy.

"What did you do with the others? Robert and…" I stretched for the rest of the names but they were taken from me. "How do you do that?" I whispered. "How do you steal them so completely?"

"They're still here," Jacqueline Fryer said. "They'll always be here."

I felt Ellie's arm slip inside mine. "You're not taking him, we won't let you."

"Yeah," Glenn said. He put a nervous hand on my shoulder, as if he was afraid I would float away.

Jacqueline Fryer smiled.

Is that it? Is that all it takes? I wondered. All around the playground the cordon of adults stared at the children as they played. I couldn't see any of them watching us.

"I don't need you," she said. "There are plenty of others."

She started to back away.

"No," I said.

"We'll catch up later," Jacqueline Fryer promised.

I scrambled to my feet, almost throwing off Ellie and Glenn. Jacqueline Fryer was already halfway across the playground, she moved like a shark slipping through water.

I ran across the tarmac. Sets of adult eyes watched the sudden burst of movement but they probably thought it was a game. When I caught up with Jacqueline Fryer I put my hand on her shoulder.

"Tag," I whispered.

She whirled around and in that moment I was sure I was lost. Her eyes were white and wet with large cataracts, like looking through fogged windows. Her skin was almost transparent, blue veins curled along her temples. She was old. Not just granny old, or even great-granny old. She was older than history. I felt the breath sucked from my lungs, tasted ash in my mouth. She reached out a hand to claim me.

"Hiya," Ellie said. I felt her hand on my arm, young and alive. And then Glenn too, on the other side of me, holding me up. I smiled.

Jacqueline Fryer looked like a ten-year-old girl again.

"It's not going to be that easy," I said to her. "We're going to stay with you."

She tried to pull free from my grip but I held on. The harder she pulled the tighter I squeezed her arm. We spent the rest of the lunch hour like that; a strange game of stick-in-the-mud.

When the bell rang I knew we'd won. Jacqueline Fryer thrummed with hunger but we'd managed to keep her from feeding. We bustled back into school, passing through the narrow doors. I felt my grip loosen as we jostled in the crowd. My arm stretched over the head of some Infant Two kid. Jacqueline Fryer turned to look at me, white eyes staring blindly in my direction, and then I felt the connection break. Some idiot kid barged into me and I put my hands out to stop myself falling over. When I looked up Jacqueline Fryer was gone.

***

We filed back into the classroom. Mrs Cook and Mrs Ramsay both stood in the doorway, watching us. Their faces were grey as ash. Their lips moved silently, I couldn't decide if they were counting us or praying. Maybe it was both.

Mrs Cook sat at her desk for the register. Mrs Ramsay stood at her side like a soldier. Her voice cracked with each name she announced, and it seemed that however quickly we replied, it was never quick enough; there was always that hungry pause, that deep silence.

She skipped the names of all the children who had been kept at home. It didn't take long to call the register.

When she reached the end of the list she looked up to Mrs Ramsay. Her voice was near silence, hardly more than a breath. "All here," she said. "They're all here." Her smile was as brittle as ice, but it was there.

I looked at the empty chair directly opposite me. She hadn't called Jacqueline Fryer's name. I wanted to go up to Mrs Cook's desk and see if Jacqueline Fryer was on the register, if she had ever been there.

***

That's it… that's the end of my story. Or it was until today. I put down the journal – chicken-scratch notes from a ten year old boy I don't remember being.

I've kept in contact with Ellie. She lives up north now, Newcastle. We exchange emails and Christmas cards and swear to meet up but I haven't seen her for five years, not since we both left university. I don't think her husband likes me, and in truth, I know that I despise him. I try to tell myself it has nothing to do with my feelings for Ellie, that whatever feelings I once had for her are long dead, but I'm not that good at lying.

I sit in my cramped, rented flat. Unpacked boxes are stacked in a corner after the move and I promise myself I'll sort them, but the start of the school year is always hectic and part of me knows even now that those boxes will be untouched until half-term. I've got everything I need to survive; my cups and plates, my clothes, my lesson plans.

The first day is always the worst. I walk through the school gates, scared as a first year, looking lost and out of place. Stanethorpe seems a nice enough place. The kids all look smart in their "start of year" uniforms, before the blazers have become tattered and ripped and the ties have been converted into thin strands of cotton. The year sixes have a wary sort of confidence; they're top of the pile, for this year at least, and although the realisation sits uncomfortably on some of their shoulders, it's still there. I watch them in the playground and although the faces are strange to me, I can spot them even before they file into my classroom for register.

"My name is Mr Willesley," I tell them when they are settled. Rows and rows of clean faces. Bright, young faces.

"But you can call me sir."

Some of them laugh, a little nervous, as if they're not sure if they should. From the corner of my eye I see one boy pick up his pen and write in his schoolbook.

I spend the morning getting to know their names. They write cards that they prop up in front of their desk and then I get them to introduce the person sitting beside them to the rest of the class.

I take lunch in the staffroom. Another first day ordeal; meeting the other teachers. Even now, when I walk into the staff room, I'm still ten years old and the fog of cigarette smoke stings my eyes as I wait to have Mrs Ramsay ask, "what are you doing in here, boy?" I don't think that fear will ever go away.

After lunch the children file back into my classroom. The blazers are already a little ragged, the ties crooked. Some of the boys carry their jumpers rolled up beneath their arms: goalposts. I smile, some things never change.

When I take the afternoon register one of my children is missing. As I run towards the Head Teacher's office I hear, way back in my mind, buried beneath years of memories, Mrs Cook's shoes clack-clack on the floor of St Francis's corridor. I taste the flavour of panic.

And so tonight I sit in my flat with Ellie's phone number in front of me. I've got the register open on my lap and I look at the names. I've read through them, fifty, a hundred times. There is no Jacqueline Fryer but I know she's there. I just can't see her.

END

# An Occurrence at Harmony Bridge
Trevor Kennedy

*The following is inspired, in part, by Ambrose Bierce's 'An Occurrence at Owl Creek Bridge' and the 1961 French film version of it,* La Rivière du hibou, *directed by Robert Enrico, and which was later featured as an episode of* The Twilight Zone, *originally broadcast in 1964.*

*For Jessica*

*July, 1876*

THE NOOSE WAS tightening its grip around Crazy Sam's neck. The pressure on his throat and lungs was immense as he struggled for breath, gasping and wheezing, whilst pulling on the thick rope which was grinding on his Adam's apple, burning the flesh as it moved along it. He could feel his bowels about to give in.

The silk stream below Harmony Bridge continued to flicker past just as it always did, splashing delicately off the rocks and weeds in its path as fish leapt playfully from it and birds in nearby trees chirped gaily, the natural world oblivious to the main spectacle on the bridge on this beautiful summer's morn on the outskirts of the God-fearing town of Jericho, Tennessee. The domineering mountains and valleys which surrounded the town in some ways appeared to be cutting it off from the rest of civilisation, enclosing it for its own protection. Or perhaps they were shielding the rest of the world from Crazy Sam and the cynical darkness that ran within him, and, it must be said, from the rest of the town and its hypocrisy and secrets.

Sheriff Joshua, with his impressive frame, bushy dark hair and nicotine-stained moustache, and his deputies were in charge of the hanging, with the Reverend Thomas and many of the other townsfolk – those who had formed the lynch mob which had snatched Crazy Sam from his bed as he lay with a notorious lady of ill-repute – also in attendance. Old Doc Minnis was there, too, rotund, balding, as serious-looking as always, holding his trusty leather satchel of medical instruments in his right hand while puffing on his clay pipe held in the other. The Reverend had said a prayer as the baying crowd of onlookers waited excitedly with a frenzied blood-lust for the main event. One couldn't really blame them, to be fair.

Sam had been a bad man. He'd killed and robbed many of their kith and kin over the years, the brains behind the robbing of several banks and small businesses with his gang of undesirables, a rancid cancer on the reputation of Jericho, one which was about to be cut out permanently. Always drunk, always involved in some fight or another, the residents were finally about to say farewell to the scum of the earth that was Crazy Sam once and for all.

After his prayer, Reverend Thomas asked Sam if he had any last words. "I'll see every last one of you dirty, stinkin' bastards in Hell!" came the reply.

The game was almost up for Samuel Ichabod

Clemence, a man of Ulster-Scots stock, his people (good, decent hard-working folk, unlike the rotten apple he had become) heralding from County Antrim, his life spanning just twenty-five years, two and a half decades of malevolence and mayhem.

A song sparrow perched itself on Harmony Bridge and whistled a pleasant melody on this radiant, hot day, as the noose tightened around Crazy Sam's neck for the final time and his mind slipped into darkness.

*October, 2044*

Michael awoke from a bad dream. He had been asleep on a double bed but his surroundings were unfamiliar, his memory fuzzy. As he looked around the room he found himself in, he realised it was a hotel room and a rather decadent one at that, quite possibly 5-star. He was dressed in a sharp black suit and tie which he had apparently fallen asleep in, although he couldn't recall ever owning one like it, or – much more importantly – how he had come to be in this place and situation. Had he been to a funeral (which would account for the suit), gotten drunk and blacked out, he mused, but had no recollection of anything of the sort. In fact, he had very little recollection of *anything* at all, including his own name.

Michael stared around the room for several minutes, trying to make sense of what was going on around him. It was night time, he knew that at least, as a sliver of moonlight slipped through the curtains of the hotel room. Thirsty, he stumbled out of the silk-sheeted bed to the room's adjoining bathroom and drank from the cold water tap until he was satisfied. He staggered back into the bedroom area and sat on the edge of the bed, pondering what to do next.

As he sat in a confused trance attempting to work out what exactly was going on – or who exactly he was – a couple of memories suddenly struck him: He had a daughter, a two-year-old named Lachelle! He wanted to see her again so badly. He also remembered the year: 2023. *Wasn't it?*

Michael went to the bathroom again and this time ran the tap and threw water around his face. He was feeling a little fresher and decided he had to exit the hotel and get some help from somewhere – anywhere really.

When Michael left the hotel room, he found himself in a poorly lit corridor, the décor of which contrasted profoundly with the bedroom. It felt old, decrepit, damp and fusty, the brown and cream striped wallpaper adding to the feeling that the place hadn't been decorated since the 1960s.

A foul smell hung in the air like a diseased, soiled blanket, stale and death-like. As Michael walked cautiously forward, past the doors of rooms with odd, runic symbols scraped recklessly onto them instead of numbers, he began to hear some commotion at the furthest end of the passageway. Faint at first, gradually becoming more audible, he realised it was a form of chanting by both male and female voices. Michael could not understand the words they were speaking, though, as they were in no language he had ever heard before – or could remember hearing. What language did he speak anyway? *English, wasn't it?* The repeated chants were guttural, unnatural-sounding, almost hypnotising but becoming more and more clear, as Michael pressed on towards them.

*Nūllus est deus. Nūllus est deus. Nūllus est deus. Nūllus est deus. Nūllus est deus. Nūllus est deus. Nūllus est deus. Nūllus est deus. Nūllus est deus. Nūllus est deus . . .*

A semi-mesmerized Michael reached the door of the

room where this drumming cacophony of sinister words was coming from. It was lying wide open, broken off from its hinges in part and covered in the runic scrapings.

*Nūllus est deus. Nūllus est deus. Nūllus est—*

The chanting from the room's occupants broke off as Michael looked inside, to be greeted by a sight of utter depravity and insanity, the stink from before only increasing tenfold. The walls were stained with what appeared to be fresh blood. The only object in the room, which lay in its centre, was a large king-sized bed with only a mattress on it, and on this was around two dozen naked bodies, lying randomly upon it and on top of each other. On closer inspection, as his eyes adjusted to the macabre horror in front of them and noticed several sudden movements, Michael realised that only about half of the bodies were dead and the rest – those that were squirming and slithering around the others – were alive and feasting on the body parts of the deceased, tearing at their flesh and bones in a frenzy, gorging on them, slurping their blood, like desperate addicts who had just stumbled upon a new fix after many months of sobriety.

When Michael screamed and winced in disgust, these horrible *non*-humans momentarily stopped what they were doing and looked up at him – but they had no eyes, just empty, black, bottomless sockets from most hellish of nightmares. They seemed to be pleased that he had walked in on them and stared at him *(through him?)* blankly, but also with a menacing, gleeful delight at the same time. Michael turned on his heels and ran without direction back down the corridor where he had just come from. He knew he had to get outside, despite not knowing where exactly outside was – or even who *he* was himself. As he ran and ran, the corridor in the hotel soon became another one just like it, and as he rounded that one it became another one almost exactly the same, and again and again and again.

The hotel was a maze and Michael was its prisoner –
corridors upon corridors upon corridors, scratched doors
upon scratched doors upon seemingly never-ending
scratched doors, the vile chantings of the wicked beings
echoing and echoing all around:

*Nūllus est deus. Nūllus est deus. Nūllus est deus.
Nūllus est deus. Nūllus est deus. Nūllus est deus. Nūllus est
deus. Nūllus est deus. Nūllus est deus. Nūllus est deus.
Nūllus est deus. Nūllus est deus. Nūllus est deus. Nūllus est
deus. Nūllus est deus. Nūllus est deus. Nūllus est deus.
Nūllus est deus. Nūllus est deus. Nūllus est deus . . .*

Eventually, the chanting suddenly ceased and Michael
could hear a knocking sound instead. The sound of rapping
on glass, it appeared. As the banging noises grew louder,
Michael rounded yet another corner of one of the corridors
to now find himself in a lobby of sorts and the apparent
entrance of this cursed hotel.

The lobby was bleak and desolate, a brown-carpeted
reception area with an unpopulated check-in desk *(who the
fuck would want to check into this hell-hole anyway?!)* and
several worn-out sofas that looked like they had been
transported directly from the mid-twentieth-century. Light
was bleeding in from somewhere – *daylight?* – as Michael
realised where the knocking was coming from. There was
a young woman – blonde-haired, slim, wearing a torn blue
jacket and jeans, aged in her early-to-mid-twenties perhaps
– banging incessantly from the outside of the entrance to
the hotel in a panicked state of disarray.

"Come quickly, you have to come *right* now!" she
hollered at him through the glass.

Michael had no option but to trust the girl and bolted
over to the double doors and attempted to pull them open.
But they weren't for budging, despite how much he pulled
and struggled with them.

"They're locked! They're fucking locked! What the

fuck is going on here?!"

The young woman calmed somewhat. "Step back a bit, get out of the way, old man!"

Michael did as he was told.

To Michael's surprise, she removed a small revolver from inside of her jacket and fired three rapid shots at the door, splintering the glass everywhere before kicking it with all her might, resulting in the shards smashing and flying all around the ground before grabbing a stunned Michael by the arm and pulling him outside into the world that awaited him. "We have very little time left. You've been trapped in that place for much longer than you think. We have to move, and fast. I'll explain everything once we get out of the city."

*The city?*

As Michael exited the front area of the hotel, the heat and light from the sun above almost blinded him. And then it all came flooding back to him – his name, who he was, where he was from . . .

He instantly recognised his surroundings but there was something very *off* about them, too.

Belfast City Centre was a mess.

As Michael and his female companion walked through the debris of Royal Avenue – the crashed and long-abandoned cars and buses, the smashed-up, looted shops, the corpses in varying states of decay strewn everywhere, the plucky rats nibbling on what remained of the human body parts – he looked ahead at the remains of what was once the City Hall, now a collapsed-in, half burnt-out skeleton of a ruin, the once decadent statue of Queen Victoria toppled over, disregarded and forgotten about.

"What on earth has happened?" a dejected, forlorn Michael enquired.

"I'll explain later. Everything's fucked up. Everything," replied his rescuer.

"No, wait." Michael pulled the girl back. "Tell me now. I *need* to know," he pleaded.

"Later, I promise you. It's not safe here." The girl freed herself from Michael's grip and began to walk away.

"Wait a minute, who are you? Why did you pull me out of there? What's your name?"

The girl turned around and smiled at Michael.

"Don't you recognise these eyes?"

"Why should I?"

A pause.

"Because they're your eyes . . . *Dad*!"

Another pause. Another smile from the girl. A moment of shock and then confused realisation for Michael.

The girl broke Michael's stunned silence.

"Welcome to Hell, Daddy-o. Your granddaughter Margot is just dying to meet you!"

As a jet-black crow swooped down from the burning sky above and landed on Queen Victoria's head, Lachelle took her father by the hand and together they walked by what was left of Belfast City Hall and through the barren wasteland towards their future.

*July, 1876*

Sheriff Joshua and his deputies cut Crazy Sam down from the noose. The dead body dropped onto the wooden beams of the bridge with a heavy thud that startled the song sparrow and rudely interrupted its song.

Old Doc Minnis examined Sam's remains and declared him dead.

A solemn Reverend Thomas asked God to have mercy on the soul of Samuel Ichabod Clemence and then invited the townsfolk who had attended the hanging back to the church for refreshments which his wife had prepared.

As the sombre residents of Jericho made their way back into town, below their feet on Harmony Bridge, the silk stream continued to flicker and the fish continued to leap playfully.

The song sparrow, having now seen enough, took to the skies contentedly, sweeping up into those domineering mountains and valleys of Tennessee for a new adventure.

It was a beautiful summer's morn.

# Face of an Angel
### James H. Longmore

John Johnson blinked the rain from his eyes and eased out a melancholy sigh. He was walking along the cheerless sea front arm in arm with his wife, Crystal who struggled to keep up as he strode along at his usual brisk pace; resting her chin low to her chest to keep the clinging rain out of her face. As he walked, John's mind serenaded him with an old Morrissey song he thought he'd forgotten after thirty years; something about trudging over wet sand and having your clothes stolen – a perfectly depressing song that seemed to fit his day to a tee.

Squinting out to sea, John studied the foam topped waves that jostled their way inland to flop on the sodden sand, and tried to recall the happy childhood memories that their soothing sound usually conjured. He looked up at the gray, bloated clouds that rolled in from the chilled Atlantic to discharge a fine rain that found its way beneath even the most waterproofed clothing to leave a body icy and shivering. Mirrored beneath the swollen bellies of the low clouds, the sea rolled muddied and listless against the litter-strewn beach.

Truth was, John had forgotten just how miserable

Blackpool was at this time of the year; how the west coast of Northern England was miserable pretty much *any* time of the year, let alone mid-October. John surprised himself that in just forty-six years his mind had rose-tinted that minor fact.

Even the famous tower – the poor man's Eiffel – had not been spared harassment from the nebulous mist that clung to its upper structures like myriad slumbering ghosts. But, despite its grim surroundings, John was uplifted a little to see that the Tower remained proud and erect against the cold, damp air; it reminded him of an elderly war veteran at a cenotaph.

Down on the beach, deck chairs were piled up and hunkered down for the winter beneath flapping, green tarpaulin, and the optimistic purveyors of donkey rides sought shelter next to their shivering, sad-faced charges. Most of the beach front amenities were closed against the promised onslaught of winter, although many of the pubs and arcades remained open; there remained a workable clientele for those particular amusements all year round.

John mused to himself that Addison would love all of this. His daughter was just entering her *Goth* phase, which John thought a little premature, but which Crystal had assured him it was all part of the girl's blossoming and her own way of dealing with her brother's death. As such, Addison loved the dark and disconsolate and that made John sad inside; his baby girl was metamorphosing from all things pink and Disney Princess to black bedroom walls with finger nails to match, and music that sounded like the sound track to a 1970's Dennis Wheatley movie.

The last of Blackpool's *bona fide* holiday makers had retreated once school resumed and the cooler weather took a hold in September; smiling, wholesome families with two-point-four children and blue-collar careers who crowded the beach with SF50, noise and sand castles and frolicked in the sea no matter how frigid and murky it was. Those same carefree-for-two-weeks families filled the bed and breakfast establishments that were the backbone of the Blackpool economy; queued to see the end of pier variety shows, and merrily frittered away their hard-earned into the slot machines come evening time.

Sadly, this late in the year, the town was almost exclusively the realm of drunken, raucous bachelor and bachelorette parties. As testimony to the nocturnal debauchery such soirees elicited, the gutters along the sea front road were awash with discarded novelty 'L' plates, lackluster plastic tiaras, tattered sashes – *'bride'*, *'official bridesmaid'*, *'mother of the bride'* – and used condoms that clung to the curb stones like sickly, stranded jellyfish.

This was John's first trip back to his native England since he'd moved to the States a dozen years ago; his wife's first trip *anywhere* out of her native Maryland – ever. Never ones to stray far from their homeland, the Americans.

It was also their first vacation since Declan, who would have turned six come Christmas Day.

It had been the thing of every parent's nightmares, the kind of occurrence that you don't believe that you could ever live through. One minute, little Declan Johnson had been happily playing upstairs with his big sister, the next, the heart-chilling *thump-thump-thump* as his small body bounced down the stairs.

As quickly as that, John and Crystal's son was gone.

Within the precious few seconds, it had taken John and Crystal to get to him, Declan was already dead at the foot of the staircase and had looked for all the world like a crumpled, broken toy. His neck had twisted almost all the way around to face his back and there was a surprised look on the beautiful face that had always reminded John so much of Crystal. There had been very little blood – just the tiniest trickle from one nostril – nor any snapped limb bones. It had appeared to John as if he could have simply turned his boy's head back the right way around, patted him on the behind and sent him on his way to watch SpongeBob and the gang.

Only, life isn't quite like that.

Addison Johnson was a smart kid (as well as having the extra advantage of being a doe-eyed blonde and cute as a button) who knew full well that the safety gate at the top of the Johnson's precipitous stairs was supposed to be kept closed at *all* times for the safety of her sibling. Just that once, she'd forgotten to shut it behind her; a simple – but ultimately devastating – mistake. As distraught as they had been, it had been impossible for John and Crystal to lay the blame for such a tragic accident on a seven-year-old. So, the Johnsons had taken the easier route and blamed themselves.

And each other.

Most days, John managed to convince himself that he'd gotten over what had happened that fateful morning, and he figured Crystal was well on her way there too. But then there were the days that he knew that no, no he hadn't; there were some things in life you were never supposed to get over.

He'd booked the trip to England without telling Crystal and had presented it to her in a way that made it impossible to say no. He'd paid for the tickets, organized the itinerary and enthused that she simply *had* to take the trip, especially when it included the wonderful place of his childhood vacations. Cold, miserable seaside resort holidays were, after all, as great a British tradition as the Queen and being polite.

Crystal had agreed with some reluctance. They had been

forced to leave Addison with Crystal's Mother as a last resort since their regular sitter had let them down at the last minute. That had been an inconvenience, for sure, but a freak gas explosion that levelled the poor girl's entire apartment complex and killed six people could hardly be considered Stacey the Sitter's fault. John and Crystal had decided not to tell Addison about the accident until they returned home, as their daughter had grown quite fond of Stacey. They'd briefed Crystal's Mom to keep her Granddaughter away from any news reports about the explosion, and about how Stacey's head still hadn't been found.

The tragedy had brought back a whole slew of unhappy memories for the Johnsons but Crystal had conceded that yes, they probably *were* long overdue for some alone time. So, after a frantic last-minute scrabble to organize Crystal's passport – she'd never had/needed one – John had introduced his wife to the inimitable delights of Great Britain.

Once they had visited with John's small family and handful of friends (the *obligated* part of their trip, as John referred to it), he'd driven her northwards to Blackpool, away from the cynical tourist trap that is the *London Town* that Americans love to visit and think they've seen all of England.

Now, though, plodding through the litter-strewn streets and drizzling precipitation with his visibly fed-up wife, John had to admit that Blackpool had fared far better in his memory than it had in real life. Perhaps he'd have been better off leaving it there?

"I'm sorry, babe," John said. He slipped an arm around Crystal's slim waist. "Not quite Disney World, is it?" He made with a light laugh.

"It's okay, Hun," His wife's voice was muffled against her chest. "I wasn't expecting ninety-eight and hundred percent humidity." She returned John's laugh to let him know that all was well with Mrs. Johnson, despite outward appearances. "It's actually quite fascinating to see what you Brits consider a good vacation."

"It doesn't rain *all* of the time," John protested, although he had to admit to himself that it pretty much did. "When the sun comes out, Blackpool is the best place in the world." He wasn't even convincing himself by this stage.

"It's fine, sweetheart, honestly." Crystal turned her head to face him, intense blue eyes sparkling behind her rain-speckled spectacles, and a beautiful half-smile played on her lips. "This is part of what made the man I love." She kissed his nose. "And looking at those donkeys, it makes sense how come you wound up with that ex-wife of yours."

They giggled together, and John was forced to admit that yes, at least one of the threadbare beasts huddled down on the beach did bear more than a passing resemblance to the first Mrs. Johnson.

And John remembered all over again why he had fallen so helplessly in love with Crystal the very first time he'd laid eyes on her.

John Johnson – hated that name, a product of unimaginative parents – had been on solo vacation in the US following a spectacularly messy divorce from the erstwhile, donkey-faced Mrs. Johnson. He was finishing up his trip with the East Coast, and it was on a chilled and drizzly day not a million miles away from this one that he'd bumped into his future second wife on the Chesapeake Bay.

He'd made an emphatic vow never to remarry – *ever* – and meeting someone other than for a casual one- or two-night stand was the furthest from his agenda than one could have imagined when the fair-skinned, flame-haired Crystal Whitsell had blazed into his life.

John had been on the guided tour around the

Chesapeake Bay Decoy Museum, more to be indoors until the rain eased off than with an interest in how the locals lured ducks to their untimely death. John had cracked a joke about how the real museum was probably hiding in the reeds across the way which was sadly met with confused looks throughout the group; this, he chalked up to the whole Americans/lack of irony thing. There was, however, one exception to the stony-faced quiet, that being the aforementioned Ms. Whitsell.

She'd laughed at his joke with such gusto that at first John had thought she *was* being ironic; but then she'd flashed him a smile that melted his heart and made his knees go weak. Cliché or no, it was love at first sight for John and, as it worked out, for Crystal too.

John didn't return to the UK. He'd spent the remaining days of his vacation horizontal with Crystal in her ranch house bedroom, and when his two weeks were up, he'd simply married the gal and stayed Stateside.

Hard to believe those twelve years had flown by so quickly since then. John had acclimatized nicely to life in America; enough to have formed a circle of good friends who all '*love the accent*', to write cheque as '*check*' and not get annoyed when the spellcheckers on his laptop and cell phone chastised him for stubbornly putting the *u* back where it belonged in *color*.

"So." Crystal's loud sniffle broke John from his reverie. He could see that the end of his wife's pretty, button nose was beginning to run and glow red in the chilled air. "Are you going to feed me, or not?"

"Seaside air making you hungry, my love?" He smiled.

More like I'm freezing my balls off." Crystal returned the smile.

"But you don't have–"

"Exactly." Crystal gave her husband a playful elbow in the ribs.

They giggled together like a couple of love-struck teens; the familiar pattern of an old joke shared lifting their spirits.

John then realized that he was hungry too. Most likely the power of suggestion, married to the fact that they had missed breakfast at the bed and breakfast. The landlady, Mrs. Staniforth – a sharp-faced, humorless widow – was quite the stickler for punctuality and they'd stayed in bed an extra five minutes for a morning quickie. There was also the heavenly smell of hot cooking oil that wafted along the street and tugged on both his nostalgia and his taste buds.

"Remember I promised you traditional British food?" John asked. "Well, it doesn't come any better than Blackpool fish and chips." He grinned at his wife.

"Sounds good to me." Crystal sniffed the air and the scent of frying food made her mouth water. "As long as we can sit down, my feet are killing me." She'd seen people walking around eating from what appeared to be old newspapers and she really didn't fancy that much.

John promised her that they could sit down, and led her towards the door of a fish and chip restaurant which stood invitingly open a few short steps away. The restaurant was imaginatively named *The Fish Plaice*, which was a common, supposedly witty play on the latter word. As Crystal would point out later, a plaice is a fish so the name boiled down to *The Fish Fish* and she failed to understand how that was supposed to work. Again with the American/irony thing.

Once seated, Crystal took off her glasses and dried them off them with a rough paper napkin. "You really weren't joking when you said these places were no frills." Crystal eyed their table with its plastic tablecloth and old, tarnished *Sheffield Steel* flatware. She glanced at the take-out counter where a steady stream of damp, bedraggled people were buying steaming piles of fish and chips – *French fries* to her and her countrymen – that were bundled up in *real* newspaper. She shuddered to think of the countless health and safety implications of consuming newsprint.

"I'm sorry, sweetheart; would you like to go someplace else?" there was disappointment in John's voice. "I think I saw a sushi place near the B and B."

Crystal smiled that smile of hers that could light up the darkest of any situation. "Just teasing, babe, this is absolutely perfect." She reached out across the table and placed her freezing hand on top of his.

"What can I get you?" a gruff voice broke their moment.

John and Crystal looked up and were greeted by the unsmiling, lined face that belonged to their waitress, the *only* waitress in the place (*Plaice?*). John found himself eye level with her unfeasibly large, sagging breasts and name badge that read '**oris**'.

"The D wore off," the woman pre-empted John's question. "And Mr. Patel won't replace it until next season." She offered a half smile and tapped her order pad with a stubby pencil to signal the end of their chit-chat.

"I'd like the fish and chips and a cup of tea, please," Crystal spoke up and her accent and ever-sunny disposition brightened even Doris's dour countenance some. Was that the trace of a smile on the old girl's lips?

"And for me, too," John added.

"Peas?" Doris growled.

"Yes please." Crystal replied.

Doris snorted and looked down her nose at the American. John allowed himself a smile, it was kind of fun to see his wife on the receiving end of what he put up with on her home turf. It had been the longest time before he'd quit saying *alumin-i-um* and asking for chips with his food and getting a packet of Lays.

"Boiled or mushy?" Doris asked and glanced at John. Was that a raised eyebrow?

"Mushy," John chimed in, not accustomed to ordering food for his wife. "You'll love them, my dear," he added upon seeing Crystal's grimace.

Doris nodded and stomped off, as if customers ordering food just about ruined her day, every day.

Crystal had learned the hard way to mistrust her husband over weird British delicacies after the black pudding incident two nights previous. John had not disclosed that the main ingredient was *pig's blood* until after she'd eaten a belly full and declared it delicious.

"Ooh, look!" Crystal exclaimed, peering through the greasy, rain spattered window. "They have a palmists."

John was careful not to show his exasperation. One roll of the eyes or a wistful sigh was all it would take to break the amicable mood they were enjoying.

Crystal's obsession with all things otherworldly had begun with a psychic reading when Addison had been running around in diapers, and had reached fever pitch after their son's death. More recently, Crystal had either calmed down with the whole thing, or had gotten better at hiding it from her husband who she knew to be – at the very least – sceptical.

Crystal had always been a believer, the more *spiritual* of the two of them. She'd never embraced conventional religion like those Bible-thumping, praise-be-to-Jesus types she'd grown up with, but she was in tune with the new age spiritualism movement and firmly believed in *'there must be* something *after we die'*. So much so that Crystal habitually paid visits to palm readers, psychics, tarot readers and the rest, as if searching for answers to questions she didn't yet know how to ask.

She'd kept the recording of her first reading. So old now

that it was on a cassette tape and John had had to scour the local thrift stores for one of those old-style player/recorders just so she could listen – and re-listen *ad infinitum* – to it. She'd even insisted that John hear it at least the once.

To be fair to the psychic guy on the cassette, he was quite obviously very good at what he did. He'd nailed most of Crystal's particulars without giving away the fact that he was doing what all mentalists did well – reading her body language whilst feeding her the usual loaded questions. He'd managed a spot-on guess about the Johnson kids, although it was probably not too difficult to guess that a married woman of a certain age would most likely have children, but to get the gender and ages exactly right? John had been forced to admit that appeared to be more that just a stroke of good luck on the psychic's part. After hitting that nail on the head though, the guy on the tape went down in John's estimation.

*You have a daughter.*

A fifty percent chance of getting that one right.

*She has the face of an angel.*

What parent doesn't think their little Princess is just the cutest thing on God's green Earth?

*And the mind of a devil.*

Wait, What!?

Who the hell says *that* to a parent? Sure, Addison had all the makings of being a handful; she was already ruling the roost with her manipulative, at times petulant behavior. But then again, what little girl didn't?

The reading had ended abruptly after that, and Crystal had never made her husband listen to the recording again, never even mentioned it, although John knew that she still played it from time to time.

After that reading, John thought that Crystal had

seemed different around her daughter. It was a subtle change that John had hoped only he – and not Addison – could pick up on, and on occasion he would catch the feeling that in some way, his wife was wary of the girl.

"Two fish and chips." Doris plonked the utilitarian, white plates in front of the Johnsons. "If you want a bap instead of bread, it's a pound extra," She grumbled. "Each."

John assured the dour waitress that no, they wouldn't be requiring baps, whilst suppressing a smirk at the word for bread bun that his childish generation had hijacked as a euphemism for breasts.

"Can we go?" Crystal asked her husband. "After we've finished eating – this." She peered down at the thickly battered fish and mountain of fries before her as if it had just beamed down from some alien mother ship. She poked her fork at the spreading puddle of mushy peas that soaked into her fish and looked like lumpy snot or something Linda Blair threw up. "I'd love for us both to have a reading."

"I can't see why not," John was truthful here. With all the best will in the world, he genuinely couldn't think of an excuse *not* to visit the palmist across the street, as much as he detested the idea. Crystal had him cornered.

"Awesome." She smiled, and John was pleased to have made his wife happy, even if it was only because he had no other choice.

John peered with some trepidation across the road at the palmist's gaudy shop front, hoping against hope that it would be closed for off-season. But no, the garish, red and yellow neon sign that declared *Palm's Read, tarot, fortune's told* shone bright and illiterate through the drizzle. Above the flickering neon, a fading, hand painted sign declared; *Gypsy Rose.*

Really?

There was a small, grubby window adjacent to the narrow doorway. It was adorned with frayed, crocheted silk curtains which thus completed the cliché that had been a seaside town staple since the mid eighteen-hundreds. Yet one more way of extracting money from gullible holiday makers on their way to the pubs, slot machines and bingo.

John dug into his food like a workhouse kid. As he shovelled the greasy fare into his mouth, he tried to conceal the initial disappointment that the fish was a flat, bland fillet of haddock and not the thick, flaky cod of his childhood – hadn't he read that cod were on the endangered species list now? Even so, it did taste good sprinkled with salt, swimming in malt vinegar and nostalgia, accompanied by soft, doughy bread and mushy peas.

"This reminds me of that dip at Charlotte's wedding," Crystal ventured. "I thought *that* was guacamole, too." She held a small sample of the green mush to her mouth and gave it a tentative prod with her tongue.

God only knew what the stuff at her sister's wedding reception had been, but it was neither peas nor guacamole; although John was surprised that his wife had remembered a small detail such as the dip over the embarrassment of the ceremony itself.

It had been an ostentatious church wedding, despite the fact that it was Charlotte Whitsell's second marriage. Daddy, it turned out, was good friends with Reverend Hopkins and had pledged the equivalent of a hospital wing to the Church's Restoration Fund.

John had not wanted to take the children in the first place – Addison had just turned four, Declan one – because he had plans to get hopelessly drunk at the free bar during the lavish country club reception. Sadly, he'd been overruled by Crystal who had informed him that Charlotte had absolutely *insisted* the kids attend.

The ceremony had begun by the time they'd taken their pew – last minute diaper change in the car – behind Crystal's Mom and her ginormous hat (John remembered pondering over just how many birds had died to decorate that hideous millinery – and had even started to count the feathers in order to make the calculation) when Addison had begun to grizzle. Crystal had tried everything in her power to placate the girl, even the dreaded, last resort pacifier she'd not had since she turned three, but the low growl of her daughter's grizzling had quickly degenerated into a full-blown wail.

John would remember vividly to his dying day the marrow-chilling looks from *everyone* in the church as his daughter's loud screams echoed around the high, vaulted ceilings. It had felt to him like two hundred people – the normally serene and mild-mannered Reverend Hopkins included – were willing him and his family to just curl up and die.

Then Addison had thrown up.

Not only on Crystal, but down the back of the mother of the bride and all over the poor unfortunates who sat either side of the woman.

Of course, Crystal and John had been mortified beyond comprehension at Addison's display; by the sound of the unworldly, guttural screams that came out of their daughter, one would have expected her to have projectile vomited pea green soup. But no, it was half-digested, rancid milk that stank like death and the Denny's pancakes Addison had wolfed down for breakfast.

The Reverend Hopkins, who was on his way over to ask – no doubt most politely – that the Johnsons take their screaming child outside so he could continue with the wedding vows, caught some thick, gray vomit globs on his cassock and John had thought at the time that it looked as if Addison was *aiming* the stuff at him.

Declan, thankfully, had been far too young to be embarrassed by the episode, or even to remember it.

John and Crystal had had no choice but to remove Addison from the church, and the ceremony itself was delayed an hour whilst Crystal's Mom changed outfits and the Reverend Hopkins slipped into non-vomit-stained vestments.

Addison had stopped crying almost as soon as they stepped out of the church and into the spring sunshine, much to the relief of John's frayed nerves. He'd driven Crystal and the kids back to the hotel where they'd washed up, changed clothes and decided to sit the ceremony out and plan their apologies for the evening reception.

As it turned out, John and Crystal's shame amongst the Whitsell family had been fairly short lived as Charlotte's marriage hadn't actually lasted all that long; what with New Hubby doing jail time for beating the crap out of his bride on their honeymoon.

Charlotte had been left severely brain damaged and with matching detached retinas by her husband's uncharacteristic and – as far as the police could tell – unprovoked attack. To this day, the poor woman wiled away her days in a private clinic muttering quietly to herself about the dark, sinister things that skulked in the periphery of what remained of her vision.

With hindsight, and a not immeasurable amount of cynical superstition, Addison's outburst in the church had seemed to John to have been a portent of sorts, almost like a black cat crossing one's path, or the unfortunate sighting of a solitary magpie. So much so, in fact that when – due to an unfortunate oversight by the photographer – he and Crystal had received their copy of the wedding album, John had half expected to see unpleasant, otherworldly things lurking in the background of the pictures.

But no, just happy, smiling faces oblivious to the impending fate of the happy couple. And Addison's angry, screaming face in the cool gloom of the church.

"Yeah, what was that stuff?" John asked. "It tasted worse that Addison's throw-up." He grinned at Crystal and saw the familiar – and much loved – wrinkles at the corners of his wife's infinitely kissable mouth.

"You know I don't like to think about Charlotte's wedding," she replied. "I've never been so embarrassed in my entire life." That smile again. "Although it did stop my parents talking to me for three years, the pretentious asses."

John reached over the table and held his wife's hand.

Crystal had only recommenced communications with her family after Declan had died.

They ate in silence awhile, each lost in their own private thoughts. John studied his wife's reaction to the congealing pool of bright green peas that lurked upon her plate and it looked to him as if she was actually enjoying them. That or she was at least putting on the pretense of enjoying them.

"We should check in with home," Crystal broke the quiet. "Make sure everything's okay."

"It's six in the morning over there," John reminded her. "Addison won't even be awake yet, and you know what your Mother's like if she doesn't get her full eight hours." John shivered as he pictured his Mother-in-Law asleep in his and Crystal's bed, having refused the guest bed because she said it was too lumpy. John had had to bite his tongue on that one, no matter how much it rankled; theirs was the bed in which he made love to Crystal, in which they had created two children together.

Crystal's Mom – Janice – with some cajoling had agreed to housesit. Crystal's proviso at not cancelling their trip had been that the house was not left empty and Addison got to stay home to be in familiar surroundings, especially since their regular sitter had so resolutely let them down.

Crystal's mother had seemed reluctant at first; of late she seemed to have caught some of her daughter's wariness around Addison, especially since the colored pencil incident at school.

John wasn't sure exactly why that particular incident above all others had disturbed Janice as much as it did. It wasn't as if it had been entirely Addison's fault and the school had said that the other kid would be okay; the doctors had saved his left eye and there'd been some great advances in prosthetic eyes in recent years. In the end, John put his mother-in-law's odd behaviour down to Janice's advancing years and lingering upset following her husband's untimely death at just sixty-two.

John glanced at the fob on his bunch of keys that he'd rested on the table, an old habit as his growing clutter of keys tended to dig into his leg if he kept them in his pocket.

The fob had a picture of Addison on it. She was all broad, beaming smile, flaxen hair the color of morning sunshine, perfectly round cheeks, a tiny snub nose, and those deep, dark, browner-than-brown eyes that sometimes and in a certain light would appear black. John often found himself contemplating his daughter's photograph, more so since Declan's passing, and reflecting upon how little she looked like him, or his wife; so much so, that he and Crystal would sometimes joke that perhaps there had been a mix-up of babies at the hospital.

There were occasions, though, where John thought that Addison looked a little like her Mom, and times that Crystal would make such comments as; *she has your pout, John,* or *she's just like her damned father,* although he thought they were more wishful thinking than anything else.

Declan had quickly grown out of his mother's features and had been the absolute spit of John, there had been times that John had thought that looking into his son's beautiful face was like looking in a mirror.

At that moment John realized that he missed his daughter terribly.

"Well, I think it's beaten me," John declared and pushed his plate an inch or two towards the middle of the table for emphasis.

"Me too," Crystal said through a mouthful of fries. "That was really good."

"Despite appearances to the contrary?" John laughed.

"I even ate some of that fake guacamole stuff," Crystal sounded rather proud of herself, like a kid who's forced spinach down for the very first time.

"I knew you'd like it," John said. "We should buy a few cans to take home."

"Don't push it, buster." Crystal flashed her husband that smile again.

John slurped down the tepid brown liquid in his teacup.

"Ready to go see the tower?" he asked.

"After we go see Gypsy Rose," Crystal reminded.

As if he'd *really* forgotten.

The rain had eased up some by the time they stepped back outside, although the sky remained ominously swollen, as if the clouds were conspiring to birth something vast and monstrous. John had settled up with Doris, argued a little with Crystal about her making him leave a five pounds tip – *that was almost eight bucks*, he'd protested – and ushered his wife out of the restaurant.

They had to wait for a sparsely patronized tram to rumble by and then they were across the road, through the palmist's narrow door and into the eerie – if somewhat hopelessly clichéd – realm of one astonishingly ancient, gnarled Gypsy Rose.

"Welcome!" she cried in a theatrical, non-specific eastern European accent. "I was expecting you."

Of course she was, John chuckled to himself, how could she not be? He recalled a favorite cartoon from long, long ago in which there was a sign outside a clairvoyant's premises – not entirely dissimilar to this one, it had to be said, despite being an ocean away – that declared *'Closed due to unforeseen circumstances.'*

John smiled at his thoughts and stepped forward, wrinkling his nose against the heady stink of incense and naphthalene.

"Come in, come in, sit down." Gypsy Rose beckoned them both into her cramped, ill-lit parlour. She pulled up a chair at the side of the room and motioned for John to plant his ass on it. As he did so, the palmist led Crystal by the hand to a rickety wooden chair opposite her own.

Gypsy Rose – and John seriously doubted that she was a true gypsy, or that she was actually named Rose (more likely she was from some inner-city council estate in Manchester and was really called Edna) settled herself down and caressed the crystal ball that sat in the center of the small, square table.

"It's ten pounds for a reading, ball, palm or tarot," Gypsy Rose told them. Her phoney accent slipped a little and John thought that he'd caught the undercurrent of a twang that could actually have come from Yorkshire, on the opposite side of the Pennines. "In advance."

Crystal fished through her wallet and handed over what she hoped was a ten-pound note and nothing larger. It was difficult to tell in the poor light, but then again that was most likely the whole point of the half a watt bulb that swung gently over the table. John was about to crack a smart one about how it was supposed to be *cross the lady's hand with silver* and not bank notes but thought better of it.

Gypsy Rose cast a withering glance towards John, as if daring him to say *anything* that would spoil the ambience. John felt almost as if she *were* reading his mind; that she'd made a connection with his psyche and knew what his cynical old brain was thinking. That thought creeped John out, the idea of Gypsy Rose skulking around inside his brain made him feel queasy.

John met Rose's eyes with his and he sank back in his chair, suitably chastised and annoyed with himself for succumbing to the psychic mumbo-jumbo; anymore, and he'd be begging her to read his palm too.

"Palm please."

Crystal held out her hand, palm up, across the table.

"You have had a troubled life thus far," Gypsy Rose began her shtick. "I see both tragedy and loss." She stroked Crystal's palm and traced the lines with a crooked finger. "But I see a true, lasting love. You are a lucky lady." She looked up into Crystal's trusting face. "The man you are with now is the love of your life," she continued. "But not your first love."

Wait, what?

John sat forward in his chair.

"Your first is a love that runs far beyond our plane of reality and nestles deep within your soul. It is a love that has always been within you, and one which grows stronger as each day passes."

John made ready to be offended but checked himself. The old charlatan had seen the scepticism in his face and this was her giving him a metaphorical – or should that be *metaphysical?* – slap down.

"Can you tell me what my future holds?" Crystal slipped

all too comfortably into the occasion.

"Of course, I can, my dear," the psychic said with the lightest of chuckles. "Your lifeline is a long and healthy one." She traced what John assumed had to be his wife's lifeline with the gnarled finger. "And where it crosses here, and here, shows that you have two children." She must have heard Crystal's sharp intake of breath. "No, not two. It's one child. You *had* two."

John leaned forward and placed a comforting hand on Crystal's shoulder, she leaned her head against it.

"We *did*," his wife told the woman.

"Ahh, there is your tragedy," the old woman declared as if she'd known all along. "I am *so* sorry for your pain." She pulled Crystal's hand closer still and squinted at it with screwed up eyes. "I see a shortened line for the pain, my dear."

*You're full of it, lady*, John thought to himself, and then hoped again that Gypsy Rose wasn't reading his mind.

"I can see your child in this one." Gypsy Rose studied a crooked line that traversed Crystal's palm. "This one is a strong, steady line. It –" She paused, stared at Crystal's upturned palm, and the color drained from her wizened face.

"What is it? What do you see?" Crystal sounded a little shaky.

"Your daughter," there was a tremor in the old woman's voice that hadn't been there a second before, her phoney accent all but forgotten. "God have mercy on us all," she sounded terrified.

"Addison? What is it?" Crystal insisted.

"She has the face of an angel –"

The words hung heavy in the cloying air like an early morning fog. Gypsy Rose reached beneath her little table and calmly pulled out a small, snub-nosed revolver.

She raised the gun to her temple and pulled the trigger.

The blunt *crack!* was dulled by the heavy, musky cloths that draped the room and the bright flash from the muzzle startled John's eyes and they clamped shut.

*In that instant, John saw Addison in his mind's eye; felt her presence seep into his brain to create black, shadowy corners. He saw his daughter's cold, dark eyes and in them the unholy commotion in the church, Charlotte beaten to a pulp and rotting in an asylum, the gas explosion and decapitated sitter, Crystal's father laying prematurely stiff and pale in his casket, a kid blinded in one eye by a yellow pencil and other, myriad seemingly inconsequential things that compounded to make perfect, terrifying sense. He saw Declan at the bottom of the stairs, eyes glassy and unmoving, that ugly knot in his neck where knobbed bones had snapped out of place and John felt – knew – that far from being the harbinger of evil, his daughter – his beautiful Addison with her wispy, summer-sun hair and darker-than-dark brown eyes – was the reason.*

Gypsy Rose's lifeless body slumped without ceremony from her chair and hit the floor with a dull, wet thud. The gray slop of her brains oozed from the ragged quarter–sized hole above her left ear and a scarlet torrent of blood flowed from her nose.

Crystal Johnson turned to her husband with a sad look in her eyes. "Oh no," she said quietly, "not again."

## THE END

## <u>Other HellBound Books Titles</u>
## <u>Available at: www.hellboundbookspublishing.com</u>

### Of Mice and Wolfmen
Joe Pasquale

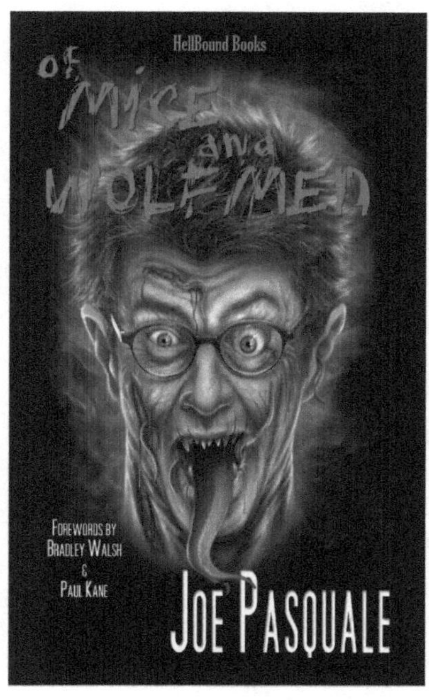


From the thought-provoking whimsical, the horrifying "what if," the wonderfully macabre, to the downright terrifying - Joe Pasquale delivers a dozen tales guaranteed to have the reader glancing over their shoulder as nighttime approaches, and those long, dark shadows begin to creep in.

Skulking within these pages, we have, for your ghoulish delectation, the blood-sucking undead, lycanthropes, the world's greatest escapologist, a restaurant most vile, a creature spawned in the very pit of Hell itself, and a warped version of The King of Rock 'n' Roll to chill the very blood in your veins.

Mr. Pasquale never fails to surprise - nor to shock, and every single one of his stories hits home, and hits hard. He writes as a lifelong fan of horror, of a childhood spent reading the greats - and it certainly shows here.

## VHS Nasty: The Video Nasties
### Tony Newton & David Bond

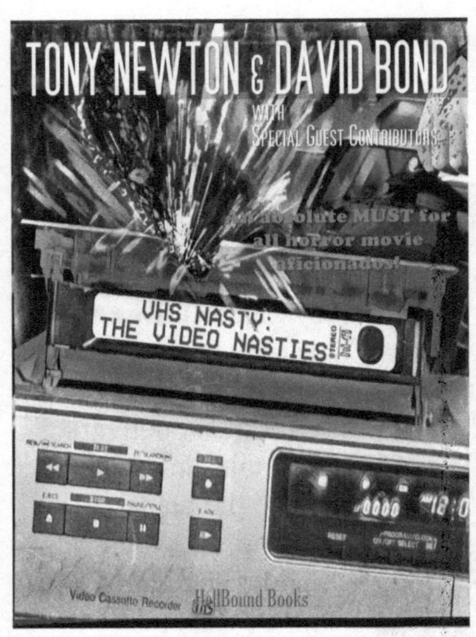


HellBound Books are proud to present our very first non-fiction "coffee-table" book! A fascinating expose of the 1980's video nasty phenomenon that gripped Britain and led to some of the most draconian censorship the country had seen for decades.

*VHS Nasty: The Video Nasties* is the definitive, full-colour guide to the halcyon days of the 1980s, when the British government and its nanny state, headed by the self-proclaimed and totally unelected "Protector of Public Morals," Mary Whitehouse, decided it would dictate what the viewing public could-and, more specifically, couldn't-watch in the privacy of their own homes.

The fight to control the voracious, countrywide spread of video players brought about the much-maligned Video Recordings Act 1984, which came complete with a list of "video nasties," horror movies deemed much too disturbing for the delicate sensitivities of the British public, and which were not to be viewed on home VCRs. And, not only were those films banned, producers and directors were prosecuted, video stores were raided by the police, and video cassettes were burned (Fahrenheit 451 anyone?).

Naturally, the act not only blighted the whole video/home entertainment revolution but it also inadvertently created the cult underground movement and a huge collector's market for the iconic films, many of which still change hands for phenomenal sums of money!

*I Spit on Your Grave, The Driller Killer, Cannibal Holocaust, Xtro, The Texas Chainsaw Massacre,* and *The Evil Dead* were just a handful of the initial 72 titles that made the "must-see" list of the 1980's horror aficionados, all of whom moved heaven and hell to get their hands on a copy!
Tony Newton and David Bond lead us through the history of those dark, draconian days with an engaging, conversational style that makes for simply terrific reading. They also provide a comprehensive, title-by-title list of each and every one of the banned and prosecuted films, along with comments and memories of some of the producers, directors, writers, and actors responsible for creating the whole video nasty phenomenon.

With insightful contributions from: Lloyd Kaufman, Taylor Sprow, Ramsey Campbell, Graham Masterton, Barbie Wilde, Nicholas Vince, John Thomson, Ruggero Deodato (Cannibal Holocaust), Steve Wright, Terry M. West, Richard Stanley, James Cullen Bressack (Blood Lake), Mark Miller (Seraphim Films), Colin McCracken, Eric Weston (Evilspeak), Glenn Criddle, Max Weinstein, John Penney (The Return of the Living Dead 3, Hellgate), and many, many more.

## Dracula: Annotated for the 125th Anniversary
### Bram Stoker, Dacre Stoker, Robert Eighteen-Bisang

Annotated, edited, and in the author's full, original form, Dracula: Annotated is the very first edition of Bram Stoker's timeless classic horror novel to be written by a member of Bram Stoker's family, Dacre Stoker, his great grandnephew, with the assistance of award-winning vampire expert, Robert Eighteen-Bisang.

This book includes the entire version of Dracula—not only Constable's text of 1897 and Dracula's Guest, but outlines of Bram's original first, second, and third chapters.

Within these pages are all of the pre-publication deletions from the original typescript, as well as Bram's hand-written changes and the entire abridged edition of 1901—read for the first time the changes Bram made to create his dramatic adaptation of Dracula in 1897 and note the differences in the Doubleday & McClure and William Rider texts.

This exceptional, incredibly unique slice of literary history represents a rare insight into the remarkable creative process of Bram Stoker, the grand master of horror himself.

## Pede
James H Longmore

*A brutally affectionate homage to the creature feature!*

The once luxurious Mountainview Spa Hotel in the heart of California's Coachella valley lies decaying, abandoned and heavily boarded up - the site of a radioactive, "dirty" bomb explosion five years' before. Zoology Professor, Jane Lucas, harbors a lifelong phobia of *Scolopendra gigantea,* the Giant Centipede, despite being the world's leading authority on the creature.

Following the savage deaths of two teenagers who broke into the hotel to cavort in the natural underground spa and the discovery of centipede remains almost three times natural size, the professor teams up with four of her students to investigate.

Their expedition soon becomes a fight for survival when they're trapped inside the hotel with a gang of violent thugs and a voracious swarm of oversized centipedes that infest the place - and then discover another creature even more terrifying is hunting in the Mountainview's deserted hallways: a centipede of impossibly monstrous proportions... ravenous and desperate to feed.

Made In Britain

**A HellBound Books LLC
Publication**

https://www.hellboundbookspublishing.com

**Printed in the United States of America**